Last Chance Harbor

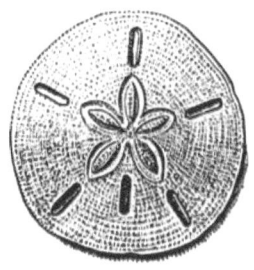

by
VICKIE McKEEHAN

beachdevils
PRESS

Last Chance Harbor
A Pelican Pointe Novel

Published by Beachdevils Press
Copyright © 2014 Vickie McKeehan
All rights reserved.

Last Chance Harbor
A Pelican Pointe Novel
Copyright © 2014 Vickie McKeehan

ISBN-10: 0692260781
ISBN-13: 978-0692260784

beachdevils
PRESS
Published by
Beachdevils Press
All Titles Available at Amazon

Cover design by Vanessa Mendozzi
Pelican Pointe map by artist, Jess Johnson

You can visit the author at:
www.vickiemckeehan.com
www.facebook.com/VickieMcKeehan
http://vickiemckeehan.wordpress.com/
www.twitter.com/VickieMcKeehan

Don't miss these other exciting titles by bestselling
author

Vickie McKeehan

The Pelican Pointe Series
PROMISE COVE
HIDDEN MOON BAY
DANCING TIDES
LIGHTHOUSE REEF
STARLIGHT DUNES
LAST CHANCE HARBOR
SEA GLASS COTTAGE
LAVENDER BEACH
SANDCASTLES UNDER THE CHRISTMAS
MOON
BENEATH WINTER SAND
KEEPING CAPE SUMMER (2018)

The Evil Secrets Trilogy
JUST EVIL Book One
DEEPER EVIL Book Two
ENDING EVIL Book Three
EVIL SECRETS TRILOGY BOXED SET

The Skye Cree Novels
THE BONES OF OTHERS
THE BONES WILL TELL
THE BOX OF BONES
HIS GARDEN OF BONES
TRUTH IN THE BONES
SEA OF BONES (2018)

For the wanderers who aren't afraid of new beginnings.

Acknowledgements
To my team, Jess, Dana, and Kristi.
You help me look good and I love you for it.

As always, any mistakes belong to me.

Life is short.
It can come and go like a feather in the wind.
~ **Shania Twain**

Last Chance Harbor

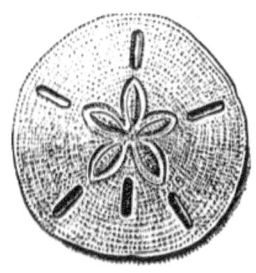

by
VICKIE McKEEHAN

Welcome to Pelican Pointe

To see the complete Cast of Characters list go to my website:
www.vickiemckeehan.com
under the Pelican Pointe Series tab.

Prologue

Twenty years earlier
Pelican Pointe, California

He'd known for years that his journey would come to a bitter end. Somehow he knew. Happy endings were for somebody else. Not him. These days, it seemed everything about his life spiraled out of his control—his days tough to get through. Lately, it took everything he could muster to put one foot in front of the other.

Sitting here perched on the rocks under the Smuggler's Bay pier, he felt better than he had that morning when he'd started out.

He stared out across the harbor, watched as the clouds overhead drifted in front of a full moon. The shadows briefly put an end to the shimmering glow off the water. When it did pop back out again, glistening like a pearl, he turned to the woman he loved.

Tonight, the lovers had the beach to themselves. In the middle of the night they bunched together, snuggled against the stiff February wind as it slapped around the boats moored in the bay. Watching the tide surge and ebb, Layne and Brooke could have built up a fire for warmth. But that would have drawn attention to themselves which was the last thing either one wanted to do. Grabbing a little alone time was difficult enough without advertising that they'd stolen a few precious hours to be together. Lately, whenever they got within five feet of the other, they had a hard time keeping their hands to themselves. It was the main reason neither one felt the nip in the air.

With moonlight shining its beam like a beacon across the bay, the couple talked about their future together. Sometimes it was a sore subject.

Glancing up at the towering lighthouse above them on the cliff, Layne made a promise. "Soon we'll be able to leave here. Take the kids and just go, start over. Pelican Pointe will be nothing more than a dot in our rearview mirror. You'll see."

"When? You keep saying that but it never happens," Brooke said in challenge.

"I know you're anxious to leave, get on with our life together, but... I have commitments, obligations," a weary Layne reminded her. "I thought you understood that when we started this thing."

Annoyed, Brooke slapped his roving hands away from her chest. "*This thing* you so casually call it is supposed to be *our* life. And I'm sick and tired of hearing about your responsibilities. I want a firm date. I want in on your plan. Tonight. You seem to think about everyone else all the time but me. I'm sick and tired of it."

"It isn't that simple and you know it," Layne tossed back, beginning to get miffed at her attitude.

"Sure it is. All you have to do is pack up your stuff, put it in the car, and back out of the driveway. What's so hard about that? Especially when you keep telling me how much you love me. How many times have you told me that you can't even stand to look at her anymore after everything she's done, after the horrible way she's treated you and the kids?"

He puffed out a breath and could see the vapor hang in the air. "I'm doing the best I can."

"Look at yourself, Layne. The stress is making you sick. Your wife's ruined you financially, bad-mouths you in front of your own children or anyone else who's standing close enough to hear. She's reduced us to meeting like this on a cold stretch of dark beach."

A pained look crossed his face knowing every word was true. But he didn't like it when Brooke couldn't understand, when she got a little too pushy, like now. Her attitude had his temper doing a slow slide toward irritation. "It's much more complicated than that. My kids aren't doing well." Layne sent her a pleading look and added, "But you knew that already. What you don't know is that my middle one sometimes cries at night."

"And I've told you this before. If there's anything wrong with the kids it's due to your wife's erratic behavior, her anger, her mood swings, and less about anything you've done. You're a good father, Layne," Brooke said, warming as she always did to the way he looked at her with his soft gray eyes.

"But that's the point. I can't leave them in that environment—with her. I worry about them all the time when I'm not there."

"There's always something happening with your kids. Why do you always let her use them the way she does? She's a drama queen about every little thing. She's been that way all her life and we both know it. She isn't going to up and change now, Layne. There's not enough medication in the world that will make her into a decent human being. She's too manipulative. And the fact that you fall for her act all the time does nothing to help the kids. You've become her enabler. I've never seen anyone get more mileage out of her kids than your wife gets. What kind of a mother uses her own children at every opportunity to hurt those that want to spend time with them? Your father just wants to spend a little quality time with the kids but she refuses to let him anywhere near them. I've never understood why unless it's to wield leverage over you?"

Layne ran both hands through his mop of brown hair. "You know her pretty well."

"I ought to. We went to school together. I've seen her in action for years, seen the devious way she cons people. There's always been something off about her."

"She threatens to hurt the kids, or threatens to stop taking care of them, feeding them, if I so much as mention leaving. I can't risk it or them with her acting that way."

"That's what I'm saying. She's always threatening to do something bad to them and you fall for it every single time. You're making this a lot more difficult than it has to be."

"There's no denying that divorce is tough on kids, Brooke. She's made me out to be the bad guy to her family and friends, told them what an awful person I am."

"What do you care what her friends or her family thinks? See, that's exactly what I'm talking about. You consider everyone else before you think about me. What about me? If it's the kids you're worried about then we'll fight for custody *after* you get a divorce."

"No judge in his right mind will award me custody and you know it."

"You give up too easily. Your wife's had mental problems since she was in her teens. We both know that. If they tell the truth, her family knows it as well. Her father even had her locked up in a mental ward when she was sixteen. From there she went to a rehab program. Nothing anyone did for her over the years managed to change her into a feeling, caring individual. Not sure anything can at this point. Sometimes I don't think she even has a heart."

"I should never have married her. But I had no idea how unstable she was, how volatile, how crazy."

"Yeah, well, now you do. And you still refuse to do anything about it."

"I feel trapped."

"Let me ask you this. Is there something she's holding over your head? Did you inadvertently become a party to her schemes to bilk people out of money? Is that why you won't leave?"

"Of course not."

"It's like you've given up. When's the last time you slept in a bed? You've been sleeping on the couch for the last three years. What kind of wife tells anyone within earshot she can't stand the sight of her own husband? What kind of wife tells people she has to steal because her husband doesn't earn enough money? She could get a job, you know, help out with some of the bills, take some money out of that precious bank account she keeps hidden away. But she won't do that either. You've spent how much of your own cash hiring lawyers to get her out of the messes she's created?"

"I know. I know. But if I try to take the kids she's promised a long, dirty battle."

"That's because dirty battles are the only thing she knows. It makes me wonder what kind of marriage you had before I entered the picture. Our being together didn't create her mood swings, didn't make her mean, or didn't put the kids in a war zone. What kind of a homelife is that for you and the kids? Sometimes I wonder what they think of their daddy. Do they ever ask why Daddy hasn't slept in Mommy's bed in three years? Or why she's angry all the time? Or why she's so cruel? Don't deny it. Mental illness aside, she's mean. There's no getting around that. It's time you face that fact."

He drew in the heavy night air, thought about how three hours earlier he'd tucked his kids under soft blankets in their beds and left them sleeping. "It isn't their fault I'm stuck in a loveless marriage."

This time, she took his hand and rubbed it along her cheek. "I worry about the kids, too. Since she tried to set the house on fire last Christmas, living with that woman has to be downright scary. It's all over town how she screams and yells at them while you're at work. The neighbors know it, they hear the kids crying, but they never do anything about it. The kids have no friends because she doesn't want the hassle. She won't allow them a normal living environment."

"I promise you that I'll get a divorce."

"When? That's what I'm asking. Don't you love me? You said you did, that you'd do anything for me. You've made an awful lot of promises. But so far, you haven't kept any of them. You keep backing down to her."

"Of course, I love you. But..."

"No buts. I'm the one who's been putting up with all this for almost a year now, listening to all your problems, putting up with your wife's drama. Not many girlfriends would do it. I'm tired of all this negativity in my life, all the sneaking around that we have to do. I'm ready to get out of Pelican Pointe and start over somewhere else—anywhere else—with you, with your kids. I love you, Layne, but you have to show me that you're serious. Give me something to hope for."

About that time, they heard the rocks crunch behind them. It sounded as if someone was having trouble navigating over the stony shoreline. But then it also sounded as if someone had discovered their meeting place.

"Who's there?" Brooke called out into the darkness.

When no one answered, they both turned to look behind them to make out the noise.

They never saw the .38 until the end of the barrel flashed.

By that time, it was too late.

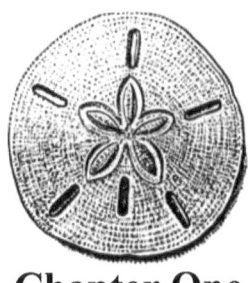

Chapter One

Present Day
Pelican Pointe, California

Ryder McLachlan stood in the middle of the demolition zone watching the crew of fifteen men gut the inside of the old Pelican Pointe Elementary School.

He considered himself fortunate to be a part of the team chosen for the work. Knowing he'd be creating something from nothing—making over an old abandoned building left unused for decades—gave him a sense of satisfaction he couldn't shake. Not since getting here had he felt like his life was finally starting to click into place. Right now, this minute, he thought it might be okay.

Even though he didn't have kids, bringing back a school felt like the right kind of renovation he could sink his teeth into. Good thing he could do more than swing a hammer.

For the next five months the goal was to put up new interior walls, build out new classrooms, administration offices, renovate the cafeteria and the gymnasium. All from the plans Logan Donnelly had designed himself. They had six months to finish before the doors opened in the fall.

Which meant the project was more than ambitious. It was herculean in scope and size. They couldn't afford to fall behind not even for a day.

Ryder intended to make the most of the experience. So far, the other men on the crew had shown they were proficient and knowledgeable. He figured if he could take with him more than he already knew, it'd be a huge plus that would benefit him on other jobs in the area once they did the final walk-through on this one.

But that was months away. Even now River Amandez, the archeologist, planned on turning one of the older buildings on Ocean Street into a Chumash museum. He wanted in on that project, too.

Even though his days were long and exhausting—he spent his early morning-hours from five a.m. to seven doing odd jobs around Taggert Farms—construction was what he loved the most. Maybe because he was good at it. That's why he didn't mind putting in sixteen-hour days, six days a week. God knows, he needed the cash.

Right now, he had a roof over his head, thanks to his buddy from the army, Cord Bennett. The little cottage on the farm allowed him to save money on rent. These days, he didn't see Cord much. Since the guy was in the process of going to med classes for veterinarian school, they barely had time to exchange hellos.

Wearing a mask over his nose to keep from breathing in flying paint chips, dust from wood and masonry, or any pesky insulation particles hanging in the air, he dropped the cloth down around his chin long enough so he could guzzle a full bottle of water.

When Logan Donnelly and Troy Dayton sauntered up, Ryder sent them a nod in greeting. "How's it going?"

"Not bad for six weeks in," Logan said, looking around at the organized chaos. Ryder knew Logan usually made his living as an artist, a sculptor. But since moving to Pelican Pointe and redoing the lighthouse on the bluffs, it was common knowledge Logan had turned into the town's go-to contractor.

Since Ryder first met him, the boss had cut his hair back. It still draped down to his shoulders, no longer curled around his ass as it had in the past.

"We're almost down to the brick and mortar and in some places the two-by-fours," Ryder reported as he watched two of his team knock down ceiling tiles from the foyer.

"Great progress," Logan echoed again. "Like I said, I'm very pleased we've gutted this much."

"Hard not to make a dent in the crappy insides when there's so much here that's useless—rotting wood, peeling paint, a crumbling foundation," Ryder said, pointing to the decades-old mortar. "Can't believe this sat vacant for such a long time. Despite that though, it has a good shell, a good framework to work with."

"First thing to go was the asbestos around the old pipes," Troy threw out. "Right after we got the permits, Logan hired a team to get that job out of the way." Logan's right-hand man scratched the back of his neck where his curly, white-blond hair had grown longer, enough to tie back into a stubby ponytail. The guy didn't look much older than legal drinking age, but Ryder had to concede the young man was a go-getter. Troy would take on any job and not bitch about it.

"The whole town would have chipped in to get it done 'cause they're excited to see this place get a complete makeover," Troy went on. "The kids get a new school and the parents don't have to stick them on a bus every morning for a long trip out of town."

"You wait and see, as soon as we get around to hanging the drywall and the playground equipment comes in, we'll have to fight off volunteers who want to be a part of it all," Logan threw in. "Nick's adamant he wants this place opened on time and ready to go by the last week in August."

Nick was the financial wizard. The man had a stake in the school opening on time since his oldest daughter started kindergarten in the fall. With men like Nick and Logan at the helm, with a town committed to seeing the project to the end, Ryder had no doubt they would pull it off.

"It's doable," Ryder said when the group was joined by Zach Dennison. Zach lived right down the street with his sister, Bree. The two had grown up here in what he considered an idyllic little town. There had been a time he'd have given anything to have roots someplace else other than the Philadelphia row house where he'd grown up. But his childhood was a testament to what a person could do with a strong single mother steering the helm.

"The wiring's got to go. It's outdated," Zach informed them.

"Which translates to fire hazard," Ryder added.

"Everything is scheduled to come out," Logan reminded the team. "We don't cut corners on things like wiring or plumbing. That's nonnegotiable. The only things slated for recycling are materials we know will hold up over time."

Something about that had Ryder grinning. "Like those glass blocks in the entryway."

Logan grinned back. "Exactly. Those should work great in the bathrooms across the top, don't you think?"

"The blocks let in plenty of light while keeping the rooms aesthetic."

"Plus it adds a stylish, nostalgic flair. That's what I'm thinking, too," Logan said in agreement. "I like knowing we're on the same page."

Down the hallway, Drake Boedecker and Paul Bonner were going at it over whether or not a wall in question was loadbearing. Hearing the argument heat up, the boss turned without preamble and headed that way.

Ryder took one look at the amused faces on Zach and Troy and shook his head. "It's Logan's turn to walk into the middle of that. I've tried."

Troy guffawed with laughter. "We all have, depending on what day it is."

"Might as well get used to the fact that those two will argue about anything," Zach grumbled.

Troy bobbed his head in agreement. "Which beer is better? Which hockey player will score first in the next game? Pepsi or Coke? For the last week they've even been taking bets as to when Brent Cody and River are gonna have a kid together."

"Sounds like Drake and Paul just like to hear each other talk," Ryder noted.

"There you go. By the way, we should probably call around and get a gaggin' wagon out of San Sebastian to put us on their stop for breakfast and lunch," Zach suggested. "The men need a quick source of food."

Ryder cocked his head. "Not a bad idea. But until that happens they'll either have to pack a sandwich from home or walk down to the Hilltop Diner."

"To hell with that, I'm close enough to walk home and heat up some of Bree's leftover lasagna," Zach said.

At the mention of Zach's sister, Bree, Troy's head jerked up. "How is she? I've been meaning to stop in at McCready's and say hi."

"Yeah, well, I don't like it that she has to work at a bar, slinging drinks. But since it's only part-time and jobs are hard to come by and we need the money—"

"It takes every penny to scrape by these days. I get it," Troy said bobbing his head. "Quite a few of us are in the same boat."

Ryder watched as the younger man hemmed and hawed as he always seemed to do around Zach until finally Troy found the courage to speak up.

"I'd like to take Bree out sometime."

That explained a lot, thought Ryder as he watched a frown break out across Zach's forehead.

"Are you asking me for my permission to date my kid sister?"

"I guess I am."

"I don't like that business with Gina Purvis," Zach admitted.

That statement kicked up Troy's anger.

"I didn't do a damn thing to Gina," Troy reminded Zach, nose to nose. "It's common knowledge that Carl Knudsen killed her. Even if it did happen while you were out of town, you don't have the right to throw that up to me. You should know that by now."

A measure of respect for Troy moved over Ryder. While he listened to the byplay between the two men he decided construction sites were often like little soap operas and mini-dramas. This was just one of them. During the few months he'd been here, he'd come to terms with small-town dynamics. They weren't all that much different from what happened in the old neighborhood back home— particularly when the summer heat brought out temperamental moods.

Zach grudgingly came to terms with Troy wanting to ask out his sister just as Ryder's stomach told him it was time to break for lunch.

Walking out to his copper-colored Ford F-150 pickup, he snatched up a small cooler off the bench seat that held the egg sandwich he'd packed himself, and started down the block.

Crossing Ocean Street, he left behind the undercurrents at the site for the peaceful allure of Smuggler's Bay.

He waved to River. The archaeologist was still overseeing the workers at the active dig site that had grown wider in scope and depth since bringing a Chumash canoe out of the ground intact. The hundreds-of-years-old planked tomol would be the focal point to the museum she planned.

Bypassing the pier, he made his way down to the sandy beach where he found a place to sit on a mound of boulders to watch the surf roll in.

At thirty-three, he'd spent his share of time seeing the world on the government's dime. There had been all those years spent overseas in lonely places, scattered bases, he'd seen for the first time when he'd left home at eighteen, right out of high school.

Like many a young kid had done, he'd craved adventure, longed to see somewhere else other than the East Falls section of Philly where he'd grown up. He'd found it. Just not the fun kind he'd expected. Instead of fulfillment, he'd mostly found a dose of desolation and solitude that he'd carry the rest of his life. Not exactly something the Army recruiters mentioned when he'd signed up as a teen.

He'd fought in countries like Iraq and Afghanistan and he'd come back with his body intact. He supposed he couldn't ask for more than that.

But life outside war had a way of bringing humility to the forefront without taking a limb. He'd planned a life with Bethany. That had evaporated along with everything he owned. The woman he'd trusted with his home, his bank account, didn't exist. She never had. The scam artist he'd fallen for had stolen his money, had taken every dime out of his checking and savings accounts and cleaned him out, left him broke and feeling like a fool. Zero balances had incurred charges, charges that had racked up over months. By the time he'd gotten back stateside, she'd even thrown away all his clothes.

Bethany Davis or whoever the hell she really was had disappeared to parts unknown. He still wasn't sure where the bitch had ended up. All he knew for certain, he'd had to start over with nothing.

So when he'd received the invitation to Cord Bennett's wedding taking place out west in some hole-in-the-wall called Pelican Pointe, California, he'd packed up his few clothes. Without too much thought or worry, all he'd known for certain was that it put distance between the last place he'd spent with Bethany and his bad luck. Three-thousand miles away from the City of Brotherly Love, he'd rolled the dice and made the decision to stay here. There hadn't been a lot to lose—except for leaving his mom behind—he'd been ready to make a fresh start.

Peeling back the cellophane on his egg and cheese sandwich, he took a bite as the waves crashed up against the rocks with a roar. The sun was out, the temperature in the high seventies, the February wind off the water, cool and crisp.

Three months ago Ryder had chosen to make the best of his brand-new situation—because it sure as hell beat spending his winter back in Philadelphia.

Julianne Dickinson drummed her fingers on the steering wheel. Keeping time to the beat, she hit the Pelican Pointe city limits about the same time Tom Petty's *Runnin' Down a Dream* blasted through the car speakers. The song fit the situation.

Since Nick Harris and Murphy had given her the opportunity of a lifetime, Julianne had been running down her own dream. Come September, at the age of twenty-nine, she'd become principal of her own school.

It was a big responsibility for someone who'd spent the last seven years teaching first graders to sound out their letters, grasp symbols and concepts, and pen their own names without getting a letter backwards.

The job might've seemed daunting to anyone else, but not to Julianne. Somehow Nick and Murphy thought she was up to the task and she didn't intend to let them down. She'd always been willing to take a risk. Even though others saw her as nothing more than the dependable, boring schoolteacher, Julianne Dickinson knew better. That's what made it a dream come true for her.

When she came to the intersection at Main Street and Cape May, she took a left toward the ocean. Her eyes drifted to the rows of houses along the street. She noticed the tricycles in the driveways, the toys littering the yards, indications there were plenty of young families sprouting up. In her mind it made for the perfect place to start a new school. Maybe one day the town would flourish enough so they could build a middle school for these same eager students.

Looking at the Craftsman bungalows on either side of the street, she couldn't wait to find her place and move here. Her lease on the house she rented in Santa Cruz was up at the end of May. Perfect timing translated to good karma. She wanted to be settled here by the end of the school year. That's why she'd already given the landlord her notice. She'd already started cleaning out closets, tossing away old clothes she hadn't had on since college, and boxing up things she didn't use every day.

The things she couldn't part with though were what she considered her thrift store finds. The pieces she called her trash to treasures. The ones she recycled for cash that provided her with a much-needed second income—like the dining chairs she'd found sitting outside a dumpster. All they'd needed was a little TLC. She'd cleaned them up, brushed on a new coat of stain, added new fabric to the seats—a cute apple-red material she'd had on hand—and sold them for a tidy sum. Whatever profit she made went into her "house fund." After all, a teacher had to make ends meet in creative, sometimes very distinctive ways.

Growing up the way she had with her dad, a carpenter, she'd picked up a few skills over the years. Enough that she could spot a quality piece worth fixing up. In fact, she'd managed to save enough to buy a house. And now, with a better paying job in her future, she'd take the time to find the right house, plunk down her hard-earned savings on one where she could let her imagination and sense of style run wild.

No more rentals for Julianne Dickinson. She was more than ready to become a property owner.

Yes, she was making plans—big ones—starting over in this little town with new people, she looked forward to beginning her thirtieth year with a change of scenery.

She pulled her lime-green Volkswagen van to the curb behind a row of pickup trucks and heard the sounds of a construction crew. Jackhammers blasted concrete. Drills whirled while sledge hammers met up with drywall and wood.

Music to her ears, she thought now, as she closed the door on the car and stood at the curb staring at the renovation—the sooner the ugly duckling phase was behind them, the sooner the gorgeous swan could emerge. Julianne understood that, understood transformations.

Stepping through the main entrance, ever mindful of the school's long history, she took the time to consider how many students had walked through these same doors. Her breath hitched at the realization of the huge job she'd taken on.

Bawdy language sailed down the hallway and mingled with eardrum-busting grunge rock. Conversations flew back and forth about how to get rid of a block of concrete. The men were in the process of knocking down walls and destroying the floors. To her, they seemed to be having the time of their lives. Much like her students did at recess.

She went in search of Logan and found him in the auditorium along with several of his crewmembers. But as she stood there looking around at the powder of dust coating what had once been a large stage, she couldn't help but marvel at what a tremendous space it was. She pictured the amphitheater crammed to capacity. Parents and teachers would come to watch the cast of *A Christmas Carol* recite their lines. Going over a list of all the plays and programs in her head that they could put on here, she saw potential, even among the mess. It would be a perfect place for years to come where they could hold band concerts and talent shows and savor the community spirit she yearned to foster.

Daydreaming, Julianne had no idea she'd drawn the attention of every male on site. When she finally realized she was the center of attention and that every eye had landed on her, she suddenly felt self-conscious. She had the presence of mind to stick out a hand in greeting.

Every one of them grinned and waved back, but it was Logan who joined her below what used to be the orchestra pit.

"This is a surprise. What are you doing here?"

Julianne beamed at him. "I stayed away until now. But I just had to see what you'd done so far. I know it seems

I'm anxious but I couldn't come to Pelican Pointe without checking it out."

Logan threw his arms out wide. "What did I tell you guys? Expect visitors to drop by on a daily basis just to check up on our progress. Unannounced."

"Oops," Julianne said in embarrassment. "Sorry."

"No need to apologize. Before you got here I was just explaining to the guys how we'd likely have to beat off volunteers with a stick once we get down to refinishing this place. I'm glad you're here. You can provide your input now or whenever you want to drop by. Let us know how best to recycle what was here."

"You mean like desks? That sounds perfect."

"Desks and other things like light fixtures, tables and chairs. I tracked down the man who salvaged most of the inner furnishings, still lives on the outskirts of town. Cleef Atkins is his name, has to be in his eighties. Anyway, the man has most of the original stuff in his barn collecting cobwebs."

"Oh Logan, you're a wonder. Leave it to you to find out what happened to what was here. I would love to be a part of that. Count me in."

"Hey, it's all about upcycling what we can to keep costs down."

"I also wanted to see if there's any word yet on the accreditation while I'm here."

"Nick obtained a temporary accreditation from the state board of education. They'll audit us throughout the school year to see how we adhere to the curriculum and standards they set." Logan glanced around. "Sorry about all the dust. But you'd better get used to it or grab one of those masks we keep by the main door to prevent breathing in so much of it. We need to get you a hardhat."

"Oh. Well."

All at once she felt a plastic helmet shoved into her belly. Her head turned to see one of the men, tall and lean, standing next to her.

"It's heavier than it looks," Julianne commented after gripping the bump cap in her hand and awkwardly plunking the thing on top of her head.

"Heavy, but necessary," Ryder stressed to their visitor as he adjusted the hat down over her mahogany-colored hair. "Especially since you're standing where the plaster may come down on your head at any moment," he added.

"This is Ryder McLachlan, one of the talented guys who'll be turning this place into your state-of-the-art school. Ryder this is Julianne Dickinson, the soon-to-be principal," Logan explained.

"The principal?" Ryder's eyebrows raised a good inch or two.

Logan grinned at his reaction. "Yeah, not really like any principal I ever had either."

"There's a compliment in there somewhere," Julianne reasoned as she held out her hand to Ryder. She met the man's ocean-blue eyes with a wide smile and did her best not to stare at his strong jawline and his coal-black hair that curled up at the ends.

"Thanks for taking on this disaster area. I'm hoping your skill will help turn it from the relic of the fifties into the ultramodern vision I have for it."

She was the vision, thought Ryder. Wide chocolate eyes with little vanilla flecks floating around the edges stared back at him, giving off a doe-eyed innocence. His eyes darted to the little brunette's left hand. Her ring finger was bare. Of course, that didn't mean anything he reminded himself—and thought of Bethany. That put the kibosh on his attraction. When he noticed Logan was talking to him, he pulled out of his daze, feeling like an idiot. When would he ever learn?

"But hey, why don't you give Julianne the tour of the areas we've gutted so far, show her the blueprints. Maybe get her take on the layout we're planning."

"Me? Why me?"

"Because you have better manners than Drake or Paul in mixed company. And Zach and Troy are in the back unloading a shipment of dry wall and flooring," Logan returned easily.

"Ah, okay." Ryder steered her away from the auditorium slash cafeteria to the front of the building where the administrative offices would get a revamp. He figured the woman should at least get a good look at where she planned to spend most of her day.

His principal certainly hadn't resembled Julianne Dickinson. Not even close. As Ryder recalled Mr. Pointer had possessed a big nose to go with his pot belly and a mean streak toward boys who broke the rules. Even in fourth grade, Ryder had a tendency to break the rules. Which meant he had done all he could to avoid landing on Mr. Pointer's radar.

He looked over at the pretty brunette walking beside him. "I was just thinking about my own days spent in the principal's office. You look nothing like beak-nosed Mr. Pointer."

She stifled a chuckle. "Ah, and what did Mr. Pointer look like?"

"Mean, with beady eyes. I'm sure he was into something seedy and sinister. Of course, that's the take of a ten-year-old who was usually in trouble for something or other. I've matured since then."

This time she burst into a laugh. "Oh, I can see you've moved on."

"You're much too young to be a principal," Ryder observed. "You must be coming from another school." Okay, that might've been one of the dumbest things he'd said to a female since sixth grade. Why all of a sudden did he feel like the biggest half-wit within seventy-five miles?

"I'm from Santa Cruz. And right now I teach first grade." Inexplicably nervous, she went on, "I think they gave me the job because my experience is with young children. And let's face it. Pelican Pointe is brimming with a good many kids enrolled in kindergarten and first grade for the fall classes. But that's a good thing because they'll get to progress together year after year for the duration they're here. It's the upper grades, fifth and sixth, that we're having trouble filling out and which may prevent us from becoming the public facility we want. And you probably don't want to know any of this," Julianne huffed out.

"On the contrary, anything that pertains to the school is our priority-one for the next six months."

"Then I'll need a place to do interviews. I'd like to take the potential candidates on a walk-through of the place, have them get a feel for how wonderful it's going to be."

He took out the schematics, went over the design. "How about setting you up right about here, near the side door for now, so you can have easy access during business hours?"

"That'll work."

"Will you be disappointed if it turns out the school becomes a private institution?"

"Not at all."

About that time, someone shouted, "Hey, Ryder, over here. Look what I found."

Ryder wheeled around and stared at Troy who held out a rectangular, wooden box about fifteen-inches long and eight-inches wide.

"What is it? Where'd you get that?"

"I found it under a pile of bricks near an interior wall we knocked down. See how beat up the top is. According to the old drawings it was in the area that used to be a classroom, third-grade, I think."

"Julianne, this is Troy."

"Hi," she said with a tilt of her head, studying the man toting the mini trunk. But it was the ornate carvings on the rounded lid that held her attention. "Could it have been hidden in a wall all this time? Is that even possible?"

Ryder tapped the layout of the master plan they'd been poring over. "Could be, or it was tucked away in one of the lockers that lined the front hallway, right about here. This building sat vacant for so long, anyone could've walked in at any time and stuffed it there for safekeeping."

"What do you suppose is in it?" Julianne wanted to know. "Looks like a miniature treasure chest, doesn't it?" She reached to touch, ran her hand across the top. "And check out the tiny ceramic inlay along the sides, beautiful work."

Troy grinned. "A treasure chest was my first thought, too. It was the decorative insets that caught my eye underneath all the rubble."

"Maybe it contains gold doubloons," Julianne cracked, eyeing the intricate turquoise design around the sides. "This woodwork took some time to create."

Troy had thought the same thing.

"Wouldn't that be something if it had treasure in it? Did you open it up yet?" Ryder asked.

"Nah, I didn't look, but Logan went through it already. There are some old papers, a few photographs. Some of them are class pictures. You know, like the ones you take as a group with your classmates and teacher."

Julianne smiled again. "Lined up by height with the tall kids either sitting in chairs in front or standing in the back, lording their height over all the short kids."

Her sense of humor made Ryder laugh. "Let me guess, you represented the short stack down in front."

"You got it. And you probably led the pack in the back." She turned to Troy. "Both of you did. What are you going to do with the box?"

"Logan said since you're the principal I should give it to you."

"Me?"

"Yep. He said you might want to use it to display in the trophy case for later. You know, like those time capsules they dig up. Some of those pictures are really old. Here," Troy said, pushing the mementoes toward the teacher.

"What a cool idea," Julianne agreed, latching onto the dusty box. "I'll plan on doing just that whenever the school opens. I'll make sure to put the relic of a box where everyone will see it, too."

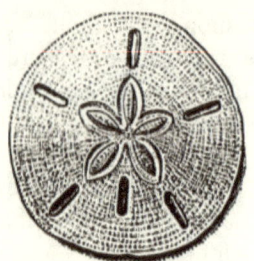

Chapter Two

Once Julianne left the construction site, she made a right on Ocean Street so she could check out the cottages and bungalows in the neighborhood. Creeping along at a crawl, she took out her phone to make notes. Whether or not the property was for sale didn't matter. She had a habit of pulling over to admire the lawns or the front porches or the architecture of anything that caught her eye. She could always find something interesting to appreciate in other people's tastes or eclectic styles. Besides, she knew what she liked.

She didn't often get to splurge on her decorating ideas though, at least not on her meager teacher's salary—even if she did have a knack for finding discarded things and fixing them up for resale. In fact, it was one of the ways she managed to stretch her paycheck from month to month with a second income. It's one of the reasons she drove the van, a 1967 refurbished minibus, she used to haul around her finds.

Not many people appreciated old things that could be upcycled. Julianne did. Thank goodness, Danny Panguino, a mechanic and her longtime boyfriend had, too. She remembered the day Danny had found the Volkswagen in the middle of a salvage yard, rusted out and needing a second chance, or maybe a third.

The couple had spent hours and hours together restoring it to its former glory—Danny concentrating on what was under the hood while she focused on its interior.

Remembering Danny always brought her tremendous pain and sadness. She supposed the despair would always be there. If Danny hadn't crossed paths with a drunk driver at the age of twenty-three, she wondered how many kids they might have had by now.

What good did it do to get bogged down in old memories though? Even if they were the best part of her, she made herself shake off the glum mood. She patted the dashboard of the van they'd nicknamed the Turtle because it wasn't exactly a speedy mode of getting from one place to another. "Just remember, you're a part of everything I do, Danny. You always will be. I loved you for so long I feel like you're so much a part of me."

Danny was one of the reasons she'd started her side business back in college. They'd called it, *Reclaimed Treasures*. It wasn't much. It didn't even have a location outside the garage in her rented house. In spite of that though, over the years she'd picked up a following, a string of loyal repeat customers.

Every week she used Craigslist and a website she'd started to post photos of what she had for sale—like those dining room chairs she'd refinished and sold to a couple of newlyweds looking for a bargain. She'd have to remember to ask the mayor, or maybe Nick, if she had to give it up. She hoped not. *Reclaimed Treasures* was more than a part-time interest to her. Since working her way through UC Santa Cruz with an assortment of odd jobs, she'd been able to turn a hobby she adored into extra cash. And she'd never have done it without Danny's help.

She passed the Pueblo-style adobe house belonging to Brent Cody, who was now Pelican Pointe's police chief. The two had gone out a few times but in spite of Brent's mother's best efforts to hook them up, nothing ever came of it. No spark, she grumbled as she thought of the forty-year-old cop. Sometimes a pairing just wasn't meant to be. And now, they guy had found the archaeologist,

River Amandez, who had a little three-year-old boy named Luke. The child would no doubt, in a couple years, be a student walking through the doors of her school.

Funny the way life circled around to the right finish. That thought made her lips curve up.

She'd almost driven the length of Ocean Street when she fixed her gaze on the hideous pink Cape Cod cottage with the purple trim sitting at the very end of the block. The yard was overgrown—the house practically wrapped in a jungle of wild honeysuckle vines. The poor thing looked as though at one time it had been an ugly Christmas decoration or had just popped out of a Hansel and Gretel nightmare. Either way, it obviously had seen neglect over the years. But despite its shabby exterior, a Martha's Vineyard charm oozed out of the two-story gingerbread framework. But it was the overall architecture—the long porch, the columns, the lattice trim that dripped from the roof, along with its potential—that made her stomp on the brake so hard it almost caused the van to fishtail even at twenty-five miles an hour.

Pulling the van into the driveway, she realized there was no for sale sign anywhere. In fact, it looked as though the town had done its best to forget the house existed.

But to Julianne, the long-abandoned place needed her.

She got out, ignored the sagging porch and rickety steps, walked up to the arched front doorway and took hold of the handle. It was almost as if she heard someone whispering in her ear to go on in, explore the place to its full advantage. But she wasn't quite ready to add B&E to her resume.

Instead, she stepped to the windows, peered inside, or tried to. The pane of glass was so dirty she had to use her fingertips to wipe a clear spot so she could see beyond the shadows. When she realized it was empty, she all but did a happy dance.

After inspecting the foundation and deemed it solid enough, she frowned in the direction of a man walking around the corner of the house, his hands stuffed down in the pockets of a pair of khaki shorts. When she saw his friendly grin and the hand he lifted in her direction, it went a long way to putting her more at ease. She hadn't heard a car drive up or footsteps. Startled at his presence because it seemed as if he'd appeared out of nowhere, it took her a few seconds to recover and wave back.

As soon as she did, she introduced herself. "Hi, I'm Julianne Dickinson. Are you the owner?"

"Not me," the man responded.

"Would you happen to know who is then?" She went on, a bit bothered that he hadn't introduced himself.

"The Jennings family owns the property, a man by the name of Landon Jennings. It backs up to The Plant Habitat, the garden center, over on Landings Bay. You can't miss it. The place takes up the entire block around the corner. The house hasn't had anyone living here for some time, not since the 90s when Eleanor died. Before that, she and her three kids called this place home."

The idea of a single mom raising her children here alone made it even more appealing to Julianne. It reminded her she probably needed to call her dad. "It doesn't look like they've been using it for anything other than storage lately."

"That's probably true."

"Do you think this Mr. Jennings would part with it?"

"What about living so close to McCready's? Have you thought about that?"

For the first time, Julianne considered the pub down the street near the wharf, noted its proximity. "The house is at the end of the block. It's not that close."

"Close enough. Although come to think of it, the joint only gets really loud one night a week on Saturday evenings when Flynn allows live music."

"Well then see that won't be much of a problem."

The man stared up at the house. "It's in pretty sad

shape, the worst house on the block."

She ran her hand across the peeling paint on the porch and assessed the wood. "I can fix it up, get it from ugly duckling stage to its beautiful swan phase. By the time I get done with it, it'll be a showplace, best on the block. You'll see."

"Like you did the Turtle?"

She blinked in surprise but blurted out, "I had help with the van. This time around I'm on my own."

"Not for long," the man muttered.

Because his comment hit home, she started to ask him to clarify what he meant, to ask how he knew about her minibus, but she found herself staring at empty air. The man had vanished as if he'd never been there at all. In his place, a gust of wind kicked up causing a chill to move over her.

"Hey," she shouted after him. No response equaled a wall of silence. Her eyes darted around the yard. There was no movement, no stranger.

As the sun dipped over the harbor, she forced herself to shrug off the incident. What choice did she have? But the nippy breeze from the water had her taking the eerie feeling back to the car to grab her sweater.

Once she'd stretched it on, she headed around the house to search out the garden center. As the neighbor had directed, she found a ten-acre plot of land that took up most of the block along Landings Bay. The Plant Habitat consisted of a greenhouse and several outdoor growing areas with rows and rows of fragrant flowers and ornamentals. After wandering through the grounds for almost half an hour, a customer finally pointed out Landon Jennings to her.

The man, in his late fifties, was in the middle of hosing down the concrete walkway when she introduced herself and explained why she was there. He looked reasonable enough, maybe that's why he surprised her with his obstinate reaction.

"You want to buy the house on Ocean Street? Are you

nuts? No one's lived there for years, not since my sister died."

"Eleanor, right? That's what one of your neighbors told me. Anyway, I'm getting a job here." She went into the specifics and then added, "If I find the property I want, I could start fixing it up right away. I've already been approved by the bank here in Pelican Pointe for the loan. And I have my down payment. I'm a viable buyer, Mr. Jennings. I'd have three months to work on it before the school year's finished at the end of May. I have it all planned out. I'd spend my weekends putting in the sweat equity and then I'd have the additional summer months before the fall semester starts to complete the work. See how important it is for me to do this now, in February, and not wait until I get here?"

"Look, I encourage you to make your home here. It's a great little town. Bringing back the school is a worthwhile way to grow the community, which I'm all for, but I'm telling you that house is not right for you. It isn't livable. I ought to know. Before we started using it to store tools we didn't want to get wet and rusted out, we used it for a break area. Inside it's a mess. The floors are dirty and—"

"If I could just see the inside for myself I'd be able to determine how much work it needs, I'd be able to go on to another property if it isn't what I want. We'd have to come to a fair price, of course," Julianne reminded him before he could do too much more objecting.

"Listen to me. I wouldn't feel right selling you a house that needs that kind of major renovations."

"But would you consider it?" Julianne insisted, just as stubborn.

Landon ran his hands through his hair. "I'd have to ask my wife and get her take. But I really don't think it's a good idea. The place would need an expensive remodel."

"That's okay. I'm used to refurbishing stuff so I'm up to the task."

"There are other houses in the area. Why this one?"

How could she make him understand? "I don't know exactly. I guess because it just called to me."

Back at the site, Ryder packed up his borrowed tools for the day. But unlike the other crewmembers who headed home for a relaxing evening, his job wasn't finished yet.

Working at both the construction site *and* Taggert Farms allowed him to stay busy, the busier he stayed, the least amount of time he had to spend thinking about Bethany. Thinking about her only got him pissed off. It wasn't every day a man allowed a woman to play him for such a fool.

He'd almost let her ruin his life. How many times would he have to vow to never make that same mistake again?

After loading his truck, Ryder switched gears. In the time it took him to make his way to Main Street, he went from Logan's employee to being part of another, different kind of team.

The place where he worked covered twenty-five fertile acres of rotating pasture land. Set back on majestic cliffs overlooking the Pacific Ocean and its rocky shoreline, the farm was home to thirty-six Holstein and Jersey cross-bred cows that produced enough milk to supply grocery store chains all over the state of California.

Since Nick and Jordan Harris had taken over the operation, it boasted ten full-time workers, including Silas and Sammy Medina. Having been a part of the business for decades, the two men were the backbone of the outfit. No one knew the ins and outs of the organic venture like Silas and Sammy. They made sure the vast vegetable garden kept up a steady prolific pace in a growing season that never seemed to end. The men made sure to meet state certifications and followed through with crop rotation so the soil would never burn out from overuse.

Their cousins, Ben and Marty, maintained the packing, shipping, and delivery duties. Everyone chipped in when it came to harvesting the long list of seasonal crops that grew in abundance. Kale, spinach, carrots, broccoli, sweet corn, and five different varieties of lettuce, left the farm daily headed to health food stores all over the West Coast.

With Cord Bennett busy at school, Ryder had taken up the slack. His handy list of chores included the morning and evening milking, the bookkeeping and payroll, along with all the administrative duties Cord didn't have time to do.

It fell to Ryder to make sure nothing slipped through the cracks. From tinkering with the solar-powered watering system on the weekends, to researching the best fertilizer methods into the late-hours of the night, Ryder had resolved to return the favor for the buddy who'd saved him from wallowing in a vat of self-pity. Cord Bennett had thrown him a lifeline and he didn't intend to let him down.

He'd almost reached the outskirts of town before he realized he'd forgotten to pick up the vegetable seedlings at the nursery he'd promised Silas.

Shooting a U, he backtracked, pulling into the parking lot of The Plant Habitat before they closed their doors for the day.

"How's it going?" Ryder asked the woman behind the counter he knew as Shelby Jennings. He could count on Shelby to always offer up a hundred-watt smile for her customers.

"It's going good, honey. You barely made it before we turned out the lights. Long day?"

"It's always a long day. Did Silas phone in an order this morning?"

"He did indeed and you're here to pick it up. Got seventy-five asparagus starter plants, one-hundred drought-resistant broccoli plants, another hundred hardy tomato plants..." Shelby spent the next few minutes ticking off the entire list.

After confirming each item, Ryder remembered something he'd forgotten. "Cord wants to add red pears to our line of fruit. Could you order fifty seedlings for starters and then let me know when they come in?"

"You got it. Caleb can help you load if you want. He's still around...somewhere," Shelby said, picking up the microphone to direct her son to the front of the store.

But Ryder shook his head. "That's okay. I can manage."

Later, Ryder was shoving trays of bedding plants into the back of his pickup when he looked up and gaped at the pretty brunette he'd met just that afternoon at the school.

"Hey, Julianne, what are you doing here?"

"I came by to try to talk Landon Jennings into selling me that old gingerbread house around the corner."

Ryder stared at her. "The one at the very end of the block before it takes that dog-leg turn up to the lighthouse? That gingerbread house?"

"One and the same."

"What would you do with it?"

"After I fix it up? Live in it, silly."

He whistled through his teeth. "That's a major overhaul, almost as ambitious as the one at the school."

"Oh please, not even close. The yard's a little overgrown which makes it look worse than it actually is. After re-planking that front porch, putting new shingles on the roof, sprucing up the paint, I'd have a real find. Besides, what most people see as an eyesore, I see as a treasure."

"If you say so. I'd go see for myself but I have cows to milk."

"Cows? Are you a farmer in your spare time?"

"How'd you guess? I work two jobs. I live in a house that comes on the property I help maintain a farm."

"Welcome to my world."

"You too?"

"You bet. You ever tried to live on a teacher's salary? It's not far off poverty level."

"Ah, I see what you mean. What's your second job?"

She told him about *Reclaimed Treasures*.

"Have you ever remodeled a home before? It's a little different than shining up old things and reselling them."

Because that statement wasn't what she expected, one hand flew out and she drilled a finger into his chest. "If that's a challenge, I'd like to point out that I don't need your help. In fact, I don't remember asking for it. I'm not asking for anyone's to pitch in. But the next time I reupholster a chair and sell it for a huge profit, I'll be sure to think of Ryder McLachlan who knows positively everything about what I do after meeting me…twice."

He held up his hands in defense. "Whoa, whoa, slow down. I didn't mean to piss you off by suggesting you were asking for my help or that you even needed it. All I meant was that I've done plenty of remodeling jobs and it's a ton of work."

Her irritation faded as fast as it had ignited. But she wanted to set him straight. "Geez, I had no idea. And here I thought it would be a walk in the park." She rolled her eyes and went on, "So you don't think a woman is capable of renovating a house all by her little ol' self? Wow, what century did you time-travel from, Ryder? Let me know so I can avoid setting the time machine for that particular period. In case you haven't noticed, women do all sorts of jobs that men do these days. Or didn't you get the memo?"

He felt his annoyance close to overdrive. "My mother could do any job a man could do, like shovel her own driveway out from under eight inches of snowfall. I watched her do it as a kid."

"She must be so proud of her son then," Julianne said with a snarl.

"To tell you the truth, she is. I was raised by a single

mom, a nurse, a wonder woman in my eyes. My dad was a great guy, too. They were just two opposites who had the misfortune to marry and discover they made each other miserable afterward. It happens."

Her disdain ebbed, replaced by the soft spot she had for guys who felt that way about their moms and dads. "So, you were from a one-parent household too?"

"Didn't have much choice in the matter. My parents divorced when I was five. Then when I was about ten my father dropped dead of a heart attack in the middle of a pickup basketball game with a group of friends from work."

"I'm sorry, Ryder."

At the sentiment, he narrowed his eyes. "So you came from a one-parent, single-mom outfit, too?"

"No mother, a single father though. My mother made it clear early on she didn't want the hassle of taking care of a kid. So she took off. Having a kid always seemed to get in the way of her social life. Anyway, when I was three or four she bolted out of Santa Cruz so fast she never looked back. I don't even remember much about her. My poor dad kept thinking she'd come back. But after years and years of not hearing from her, he finally wised up and divorced her when I was around eight or so. My dad didn't have to keep me either. He could just as easily have packed me off for my grandparents to bring up. But he didn't do that. Even though he worked a lot, he'd take me along on jobs with him. We managed just fine."

"Ah yes, all the busybodies who love to preach about how us kids from divorce are destined for failure should shut the hell up."

"Why Ryder McLachlan, do you realize what just happened here?"

"What?"

"I think we may have stumbled on something we actually agree on. Imagine that."

"We aren't failures because we didn't grow up having

both parents in the home."

"Exactly. Life isn't perfect. Divorce happens. Kids adapt. Some adults are better at parenting than others."

Realization dawned on him. "That's how you learned to use a drill. Your father taught you."

She grinned. "Among other tools. He often took me to work with him. I mostly got in the way until I was around six. That's when he started letting me use a hammer. John Dickinson is a highly skilled carpenter, always in demand, one of the best in Santa Cruz. Despite the so-called studies, I had a normal upbringing in a loving, nurturing home. It just so happened to be with a single father instead of a mother. The statistics should focus on the fact some women aren't meant to be mothers."

Ryder agreed. "I really hate all that bogus crap that claims children from one-parent, broken homes, are doomed to failure. It's bullshit. Oh, sorry for my language. Sometimes the Philly side of me surfaces along with my Army background."

"No, it's okay. I'm beginning to connect with the Philly side. Those studies defy logic. In my case, my mother wasn't someone I'd have wanted raising me or influencing my upbringing in the first place. I'm lucky she ditched me when she did."

"Why do you suppose they do it?"

"Do what? Take off?

"No, why do you suppose all those ill-informed, so-called experts peddle that garbage, telling ordinary folks to stick it out in an unhappy situation? A marriage that breeds a lot of infighting every day doesn't set a good example for how kids should treat each other down the road."

"You want my opinion? I think in some cases those so-called experts scare people into sticking it out. They leave parents too nervous and aware of those 'statistics' to start over. It takes courage to begin again. One parent invariably ends up using the kids to justify staying which makes for a miserable home life. Who knows? Maybe some people enjoy the martyr role. Whatever the reason, it's unfair to the kids though, don't you think?"

"That's the truth. Aren't people like us the experts—the kids who've been through divorce and turned out something other than the wretched serial killers they thought we would be? Both my parents were definitely not a good match. Once they divorced, I didn't miss the nightly yelling and screaming matches. I was happy things had calmed down. Once they worked out visitation, I got to see both of them in a more serene setting. For the first time in my life I saw them happy, not with each other, but in their own way. It made a huge difference to me."

"There you go. Who in their right mind would miss the daily drama of an unhappy parent who just doesn't want to be there? You know, some of my brightest students are from one-parent homes. I have this one little boy who does math so well he could teach the other kids in his sleep. He and his sisters live with their father. I had his sisters earlier when I first started teaching and all three kids are fairly brilliant."

Ryder rocked back on his heels. "So, are we okay here?"

She smiled. "Sure. Now go milk your cows, Ryder. I need to head back home anyway so I can work on my next pitch to Landon Jennings. And besides, I have to figure out my lesson plan for March."

After grabbing a burger at the Hilltop Diner, Troy headed to McCready's for a beer. Since turning legal, drinking wasn't exactly something he did often. And tonight it wasn't a brew he had on his mind but rather a certain gorgeous redhead.

He hadn't taken two steps inside the pub when he spotted Bree Dennison. She'd always made his heart do a little flip-flop. It might've been her pale blue eyes.

Clutching the jewelry box he'd made her, he hoped like hell she liked it. He'd taken the time to personalize the top more than he ever had before. He'd carved flowers into the design this time, poppies he'd painted a bright red-orange.

Troy wasn't sure why he felt so uncomfortable. After all, the two had gone to school together, known each other since first grade. Why should he be nervous about bringing a stupid homemade gift to a friend?

Because he wanted to be a lot more than Bree's friend, he thought as he took a seat at one of the little tables. He sat there waiting for her to make her way over, knew the moment she looked over and spotted him.

"Well, hello, stranger," Bree said in her cheery way. Her eyes immediately went to the jewelry box. "Oh, is that for me? Why, Troy, it's beautiful."

"You like it?" He watched as she ran her hand over the intricate petals and knew her reaction was genuine, particularly now that she'd thrown her arms around his neck.

Troy noticed her eyeing McCready standing behind the bar. As soon as Bree got her chance, she waited for the bartender to pour a drink for a customer and then neatly dropped into a chair beside him.

"You said you'd make one for me. But this is more detailed than the one you made Abby Bonner. Now I have something to hold my earrings. Thank you."

"My pleasure. I'm glad you like it." Why did he feel so clumsy all of a sudden? Despite his inept mindset, he couldn't take his eyes off her. When she caught him staring he cleared his throat. "Not too busy tonight?"

"No, but it's early yet. Are you still renting the little studio apartment over the Harris's garage at Promise Cove?"

"You bet. It's fixed up real nice, too."

"I'd love to see your place."

"You would? Then why don't you come out Saturday

night? I'll make you dinner."

"Get out! You cook?"

"Sure. Everyone has to eat."

"I'd love to but not Saturday night. I'm working. How about Sunday instead?"

"Sounds like I'm making Sunday dinner," Troy said with a grin.

"I don't think I've ever had a man cook for me before other than my dad."

"What about Zach?"

Bree tittered with laughter which brought a "get back to work" glare from McCready.

"My brother? Cook? No way. He barely knows how to work the microwave. And I don't consider that cooking unless I'm starving."

She leaned in closer and whispered, "Don't tell McCready this but that's what they serve here when our regulars want something to eat other than pretzels. We zap pizza in a microwave. It tastes like rubber and reminds me of cardboard. But folks gobble that stuff up in a pinch."

"Then it's a date and I guarantee it won't come out of a microwave or taste like rubber."

Chapter Three

By the time Julianne pulled up in the driveway of her little rental back in Santa Cruz it was almost eight. She left the van parked where it was because she could no longer fit it into the garage. With all her "projects" in various stages of fixing up, she'd run out of room there a year earlier. She definitely needed to start liquidating some of her inventory and do something about her "hoarder" side before she booked a moving truck.

Her mind on the cute little gingerbread house she'd checked out in Pelican Pointe, she snatched the wooden box off the backseat and headed to the door.

Even at night her eyes drifted to the flower beds where purple and yellow petunias dazzled in the moonlight, spilling over onto the walkway. She imagined her own yard, her own lawn and knew exactly what she'd plant if given the chance—bold purple pansies and celosia with a pop of golden tulips and prairie sun.

Stepping up to the deck, she had to admit she'd miss the little postage-sized bungalow she'd called home for the last five years. She'd rented the little studio from a friend of her father's after Danny died. It didn't have much of a front lawn, but with a nice view of the ocean, she'd never complained about living here.

As soon as she reached the glass-paneled front door and stuck the key in the lock, she realized she'd forgotten to leave a light on. Flipping the switch, she looked around the four walls. The one-bedroom, seven-hundred square-foot space was barely bigger than an apartment. But it suited her just fine. She'd furnished it with cast-offs, upcycled flea market finds and those creative trash to treasures she devoted her weekends to making over.

She stuffed the keepsake box into one of the cubby holes under the seat bench and spotted the blinking light signaling four messages on her answering machine. Each turned out to be four fellow teachers inviting her to the same book club event next week.

But one voice was especially biting. Julianne rolled her eyes as she listened to Nicole Cannon remind her again what a mistake it was to take the job in Pelican Pointe.

Pent-up frustration had Julianne letting out a huff. Why did it seem like certain friends could never be happy about another's success? Tonight she didn't need one more ding in her self-confidence. She was already wondering, asking herself almost daily, if she was really up to the task of becoming principal of her own school.

With that weighing on her mind, she trekked into the tiny kitchen, grabbed a carton of yogurt out of the fridge and sat down at the breakfast table she'd revamped—still stewing over Nicole's comment.

Nicole always could make her furious—even as a child. The two girls had grown up living across the street from each other. Competition through school seemed to get in the way of their friendship, building a huge divide between them—pettiness over grades, boys, and friends had caused the two from ever getting truly close. They should've been like sisters, Julianne thought now. But Nicole never seemed to be able to share in her happiness over anything. The woman certainly hadn't been pleased when Danny had entered the picture.

At the knock on the door, Julianne made her way back into the living room, spotted her petite neighbor, Lindeen Cody, through the glass. Lindeen held a large Tupperware container between both hands. Julianne smiled at the kindhearted woman she'd gotten to know over the years. Lindeen often brought over food.

"I saw your van pull up."

"Come on in."

"I can only stay for a minute. I baked a chicken enchilada casserole tonight. As usual made way too much for two people, thought you might like some."

"You're an angel, Mrs. Cody. How did you know I'm starving?"

"Thought so. You didn't take the time to eat supper again, did you? I worry about you. And you're always so late getting home."

"I drove over to Pelican Pointe after school to check out the progress. You should see what they've done so far, gutted the front half of the rooms already."

"Girl, you'll make many trips over there before that place is ready. The renovation couldn't be in better hands. And just wait until they ask for volunteers to paint, do touch-up work. The whole town will turn out."

"Logan said the same thing."

"Do you like the town?"

"Oh, I love it."

"Then what's wrong?"

"I'm just wondering if I'm really ready for this. It's such a big step."

"Nonsense. Has that Nicole Cannon been chipping away at your confidence again? Filling your head with doubt? Don't you dare let that small-minded woman zap your excitement about this, she isn't worth it."

"Thanks, Mrs. Cody. You never fail to say the right thing to pick up my spirits. I'll miss living down the street from you."

"That's the truth of it. I'll miss you, too. But you have to do what's best for you. Moving to Pelican Pointe is the right thing for your career. By the way, you know that ugly buffet you found on Craigslist and fixed up. I've reconsidered. I love the oak color stain you used. I'm thinking it'll be the perfect addition to my guest room."

"Are you sure? I'm asking two-hundred dollars."

"Since it's solid wood and since they don't make that kind of buffet anymore, the piece is a steal at that price and we both know it. Besides, I talked Marcus into a spring painting project. Give me three weeks and I'll be ready to take it off your hands."

"Perfect."

About that time another knock sounded at the door. Julianne looked through the glass, recognized her father's well-worn, steel-toed, work boots before anything else.

John Dickinson was a gentle giant of a man with a crop of dark brown hair turning gray at the temples. He had wide eyes that matched his daughter's with a spread of crow's feet at the corners. He possessed an easy laugh and sweet disposition that made him an asset to any job he started. He rarely got upset with his customers no matter how many times they changed their minds about the design of a kitchen or the color of paint or which wood stain might look better. The only time he showed a temper was if it concerned Julianne.

"Well, hello," his daughter said, greeting him with a hug. "What brings you here?"

"Just finished a job three streets over. Was in your neck of the woods so I decided to stop in, check on my little girl," John explained kissing his daughter on the cheek. "Hi there, Lindeen. How's Marcus?"

"Doing fine, John. He fell asleep on the couch after dinner," Lindeen returned. "I brought over a Mexican casserole. There's plenty for both of you. Now you two sit right down and eat the supper I brought. I'll get out of your way so you can enjoy it. Your girl here needs a little cheering up. Nicole's been chinking away at her armor again."

"I'm okay," Julianne said as Lindeen started to leave.

"I know you are," Lindeen remarked, patting her hand. "But a girl needs her dad to talk to now and then anyway."

When Lindeen had gone, John took the time to study his daughter. "What's this about a chink in your armor?

Nicole's jealous, is all. She's always been ever since you bested her in the spelling bee. You know better than to pay any attention to her pettiness. That girl's never going to be happy for you no matter what you do."

"I know. Look, sit down while I heat up the casserole and I'll tell you about the house I found in Pelican Pointe."

While the dish reheated, Julianne got down glasses for iced tea. For the first time all day, she dumped everything on the man who had always taken the time to listen to her problems. That included what she hoped to accomplish in her new home. When she was done, she sucked in a breath waiting for him to say something.

"I'm gonna miss you," John said, placing an arm around her shoulder.

"Pop, it's just fifty miles north. You'll see me on weekends."

"I know, but I won't be able to stop by on my way home from work to check up on my only child like I do now or have supper with her whenever I want. But you know what? I want you reaching for the stars because this is a fantastic opportunity for you. And this house sounds perfect for a first-time home. You were looking for a fixer-upper you could make your own. Why don't I come by Saturday and we take a look at it together?"

"Pop, Mr. Jennings hasn't even agreed to sell it to me yet."

"I've no doubt he will. If I know you, and I do, you'll see to it you wear him down until he says yes."

Alone, she tossed in a load of laundry then started working on her lesson plans for March and April. Halfway done, she allowed herself one glass of cabernet from the bottle it had taken her several days to drink. Sipping the vino, she decided she had to get out of the rut she'd been living in for the past couple years. Since Danny's death she'd needed a change of scenery. She hoped starting over in Pelican Pointe would allow her to do something different, get to know new people.

Making notes along the way, she thought of the three kids in her class who were still struggling to read. Not exactly a glowing reflection of her teaching skills. She needed to work on getting them to sound out their words in class more often. Maybe give a little more one-on-one time with each student.

Distracted, her mind drifted to the man who'd shown up at the house in Pelican Pointe. Why had he appeared at the exact moment that he had? And where had he gone? If not for him, she would never have known about the owner. Eventually she could have used the address to look up the info in public tax records. But it would've taken her several days to come up with the name. Knowing Jennings owned the property had saved her a good deal of time.

Who was the guy and why had he been dressed in khaki shorts in February? Whoever he was he hadn't exactly gone out of his way to introduce himself.

It wasn't until she was getting ready for bed that she remembered she hadn't gone through the box Troy had given her. In bare feet, she padded out to the tiny vestibule, retrieved it to take back to the bedroom.

Sitting cross-legged on the blankets, she got comfortable, flipped up the latch. Selecting one of the photos on top, she held it up to the light and stared at the color photo of a young boy about seven with a gap-toothed grin on his face.

Troy had been right. She sifted through group photographs labeled with the teachers' names. Starting with Miss Anderson's first-grade class right through Mrs. Paul's third. She skimmed the collection of old school pictures someone had exchanged with classmates twenty years in the past. Shuffling through the various images, she scrutinized the faces, lined them up on the bed until she counted fifteen in all. These kids were probably her age by now, she decided.

A few old baseball cards—Roy Campanella, Ted Williams, Mike Schmitt, and Ken Griffey—were tucked inside. She recognized the legendary names. Even though old, each one looked in mint condition. Who wouldn't know those superstars from another era? She read a few lines of statistics on back before picking up a small cloth bag, gray in color, complete with drawstrings. Pulling apart the opening, she looked inside, dumped an assortment of seashells and pretty stones, agates and quartz, into her palm.

She spied three well-used matchbox cars, one red, one blue, and one white. It told her the owner of the box had more than likely been a boy.

But that theory evaporated when she spotted the class ring, obviously belonging to someone much older. The silver, square-cut, dark-blue stone said male—and it belonged to someone who'd graduated college at the University of California Santa Barbara in 1984. There were no initials or other markings on either side panel and no engraving on the underside to indicate the owner.

Sorting through the papers she discovered an old deed to a property on Main Street, dated October 29, 1957. The name on the paperwork read Andrew Richmond.

Once she'd emptied out the contents, she sunk back in the pillows, considered the mystery. There was something logical about it when she'd thought the box belonged to a child. After all, a student could easily have brought it to school for show-and-tell, left it there and forgotten it. But how had it gone overlooked for years? That made no sense.

The college ring and the deed—two things a child normally wouldn't have as part of their belongings— added to the puzzle. Under what circumstances had someone hidden the box inside the school in the first place? Why hide a bunch of trinkets for two decades?

One glance at the clock told her she needed to call it a

night. She was about to dump everything back in and snap the lid shut when she took a closer look at the satiny, turquoise lining glued to the bottom and sides. How had she missed the huge reddish streak marring the colorful blue liner at the bottom?

Inspecting it closer, she noticed a slice of shiny fabric that didn't quite meet the wood. The gap created a pocket opening. Curious, she poked a finger into the hole, ran it around the sides loosening the old lining even more. Feeling as though she was invading someone's personal effects, she gingerly explored the fissure-like space with two fingers, then three.

There, halfway around the edge, she felt another piece of…something hiding beneath the lining. Whatever it was felt thick and rigid to the touch. The discovery had her gently tugging at the liner until she'd removed what looked like a stained piece of cloth measuring an eight-inch, ragged-cut square. It had been folded over so that it could fit. Whoever put it there had glued the lining back in place so that it would hide what was underneath. Whatever caused the discoloration to the cotton, the years had long since made the material stick together and impossible to pull apart.

Understanding hit her about the same time she realized what she held between her fingers—a bloodstained part of what had once been a blue and white striped shirt. She knew it had to be a shirt because on closer inspection she could make out the buttonhole and placket with topstitching.

Dropping it back into the box, Julianne didn't want to panic. But the longer she stared at it the more her mind raced toward dark and devious. Could this box somehow be connected to the serial killer, Carl Knudsen? After all, Pelican Pointe had been his old stomping ground for years. Carl's capture had been all over the news. Even now the man was locked up for his crimes. But could Carl have kept souvenirs from his victims? With that in mind, she reached for the phone to call the only person who might know—Chief of Police Brent Cody.

"You're sure of what you think it is," Brent asked over the phone. "It could be some kind of juice stain, maybe grape or cherry."

"I don't think so. You have to see it for yourself." She told him about her theory and how it might relate to the serial killer.

But Brent did his best to keep her from getting worked up and jumping to conclusions. "Maybe it came from a nosebleed."

"There's too much blood for that. But if it was that simple, then why would someone hide a piece of clothing from a nosebleed under the lining in a box? Why would anyone do that?"

"Ah. Good question. And you said Troy found this box at the school?"

"Yes. I stopped by there this afternoon. But no one actually bothered going through it until I opened it just now. I was told Logan had perused the contents but he wouldn't have seen anything out of the ordinary. When I first looked through it there was nothing that jumped out at me, certainly nothing like this. But that was before I saw the stain on the lining and then dug into the sides." And now she wished she hadn't brought it home at all.

"Okay, do you mind if I come pick it up tonight?"

"There's no need to make a trip over here, Brent. I'll bring it to you after school tomorrow. It isn't like it's going anywhere."

"Ordinarily I'd say that's a plan but I think it best to get it under lock and key as soon as possible so I can get it to the lab tomorrow. If it does test positive for human blood that means someone hid it for a reason. Maybe hid evidence, to what I don't know. You can bet there's a reason it was concealed for so long."

After what had turned out to be a very long day, she waited for Brent to make the jaunt from Pelican Pointe to Santa Cruz. When the knock on the door came just after eleven, she spotted the hulk of a guy and let him in.

"Julianne."

"Brent." Tilting her head, she grinned at the former sheriff. "How's married life treating you? Not to mention immediate fatherhood?"

A smile spread across his face. "Like fifty things coming at me all at once. But I wouldn't change a thing. How've you been? Bet you can't wait for next fall."

She drew in a deep breath. "There's a lot to do before next fall. It's a big change for me. I'm starting to look for houses there. I just might end up as one of your neighbors." She told him about the Jennings' house.

He frowned. "Did Landon Jennings agree to sell it to you?"

"Not yet, but I figure I could work on him until he does."

Brent pulled on his ear. "I should tell you it has a bit of a history."

"Any home that old that sits along that particular row of houses has to have a colorful past, right? Please don't tell me it's haunted or something equally disturbing."

"Eleanor Jennings lived there with her kids. It wasn't a happy home."

"What do you mean? I just assumed she died of old age after living a long and full life where she raised her brood of three kids there by herself." She noted the deliberate long look Brent sent her. "What?"

"Did someone in town lead you to believe that? Because it was a little more than that."

"No, I just... I imagined a happy ending, that's all."

"What's the first rule of assuming? Eleanor took her own life."

"In the house?"

She watched as Brent took a seat on the sofa. "No, no, it wasn't in the house."

"That's something, I guess. If not in the house, then where?"

"From what I remember about the woman from my grandmother, Eleanor was always acting out, doing things over the top."

"You mean she was a drama queen?"

"Big time."

"I'd say taking your own life counts as drama times three."

"And then some. Soon after her husband left her, Eleanor began to act even more erratic than she had before. One night she woke her kids up after they'd gone to bed, took them across the street, loaded them into a boat and then rowed all four of them out to the middle of the harbor. The kids sat there and watched as she jumped overboard into the water."

Julianne realized her mouth had fallen open. "That's horrific! What happened to the children?"

"It was Cooper, her oldest, who told the authorities what happened. He was able to attract the attention of a fisherman about four o'clock the next morning to get them back to shore."

"Eleanor was obviously a sick woman."

"I'd say that's the prevailing theory. Her body was never found."

"How terrifying for the kids to see her jump into the water like that and then disappear and not be able to do anything. Can you imagine what that must've been like for them? What awful memories they must remember about their mother?"

"When it happened the whole town knew Eleanor wasn't right in the head. But this was back during a time when few people ever got involved in domestic issues at all let alone wading into the world of mental illness."

"What became of the three children?"

"Cooper, Drea, and Caleb went to live with their aunt and uncle, Shelby and Landon Jennings, who adopted the kids the next year. They own the Plant Habitat."

"Ah. Well, that's kind of weird. I found Mr. Jennings there among his lilies and tulips this evening. That's probably why the man was so reluctant to talk about selling the house. Maybe he's afraid the kids will object to putting it up for sale."

"I don't think that's it. Give Landon some time and I think he'll gladly unload it at a price you'll be able to afford."

She groaned in realization. "Unload it on some unsuspecting out-of-town buyer? Brent, that's me. And I thought I'd found the perfect property."

"You shouldn't let what happened to Eleanor or the kids affect your decision about the place. Whether or not you choose to move forward is up to you though. Look, I hate to close this subject down but I need to pick up this box Troy found and get back home. See for myself what's inside."

She retrieved the box from the side table and handed it off, immediately pointing to the material. "See why I thought you should take a look. The placket, the buttonhole, this was once someone's shirt. "

"I agree with you." Brent inspected the cutout swath and said, "I came over here tonight intending to downplay this whole thing for you. But now that I've seen it…"

She shook her head. "There's no point in doing that for my benefit. I can see for myself that if anyone lost that amount of blood, they wouldn't be around for long. Am I right?"

He chewed his bottom lip, not wanting to answer. "Why would anyone bother to keep it or hide it in such a way by putting it with a bunch of keepsakes like this?"

She took him through the contents of the box. "All these things are the reason I decided it belonged to a child, the toys, the photos, the baseball cards, the pretty rocks and shells. That is, until I found the deed and the ring. Then I pulled the lining apart and found that icky, stiff piece of cloth. Who did it belong to? Because…

Serial killers often take mementoes." When she saw Brent's sidelong glance, she grinned. "I watch my share of crime shows."

"You and everyone else," he said, rifling through the stuff. "These baseball cards are worth a small fortune. Makes me wonder why these would just be sitting around and not in someone's collection."

"I figured as much. But factor everything in and the question is why would something so…bloody…be hidden away inside an elementary school with little toys and a bunch of rocks?"

She noted the expression on his face looked as though he was already trying to puzzle out the solution. "I guess Brent Cody has a mystery to solve."

"Indeed I do." When he stood up to go, he stopped like he'd just thought of something. "By the way, I need to warn you that Nick and Jordan are planning a welcome dinner for you. The entire town will probably turn out for it."

"The entire town? Why?"

He lifted a shoulder. "It's what Nick and Jordan do, what the town does. We all want you to feel at home there."

The sentiment meant she'd made the right decision to relocate. "Thanks for the heads-up. Do you have any idea when? Because I really need to do something with my hair."

Once again, he stared at the pretty brunette. "Your hair looks fine to me. I don't think I'm spoiling the surprise if all I tell you is…soon…very soon and leave it at that."

Ryder didn't sit down to grab any downtime until after eleven o'clock that night. Dropping into the well-worn leather recliner in a living room that brought to mind the'70s, he turned on Sports Center to catch him up on the evening's basketball scores.

Staring at the 55-inch flat-screen TV he considered how good he had it. No snow to shovel. No working on construction sites in sub-freezing temperatures. And since Bethany had cleaned him out, how many friends could he count on? Many had turned their backs on him, people he'd known since high school. Since Cord had him crashing in a place rent-free, Ryder considered himself lucky to count the man as a friend.

The work wasn't even that hard. All he had to do was put in a little extra effort around the farm and he had a roof over his head.

It didn't matter that someone had tacked up outdated paneling or furnished the place with ugly furniture. Ryder had no complaints. He knew he was fortunate to be right where he was right this minute. After several months here, he'd found he fit in with the rhythm of the farm and the little town without much effort. He could hunker down here for an evening of solitude with the supper he'd fixed himself or head into Pelican Pointe to catch the daily special at the Hilltop Diner if he chose to do so. These days, he wasn't looking for any more than that.

He didn't mind working around the cattle. Although the animals had given him some anxious moments until he discovered they were social creatures of habit. They were docile if handled with a firm, gentle hand and not the scary things he'd imagined them to be. For a city boy, it had taken him a few jittery first weeks before he gained a confidence around them. But once he had, everything had clicked into place. It was ridiculous now to think he'd ever been afraid of a bunch of cows.

If he had to pinpoint a fear, it would have to be all the times since settling in that he thought someone kept creeping around the house—watching him, especially when he was in the barn during the evening milking— like tonight.

The first time it had happened he thought he'd imagined things, conjured up some distant war memory. After all, the farm was remote, secluded, and he was used to the sights and sounds of a busy urban area. He couldn't deny the quiet had gotten to him. But he'd been here three months now and still the feeling remained. It hadn't gone away.

The second time had occurred in the middle of the night when he had awakened from a deep sleep to the sound of footsteps out in the hallway. He could've sworn someone had been stalking around on the hardwood floor. But when he'd gotten up to check, there'd been nothing to see, no one lurking in the rooms. Creaks and groans in an old house didn't add up to much. So he'd chalked it up to that and let it be.

But lately, he wasn't so sure.

Tonight during the milking, he hadn't been able to shake another presence. Call it a second sense from having been in a war zone but it felt like someone else had been standing next to him while he'd hooked each cow up to the machine.

A week ago, he'd caught a glimpse of a man coming out of the barn heading to the administrative offices. He'd even broken into a run in pursuit—and then watched as the figure had dissolved into mist right ahead of him.

Monday he'd started seeing that same guy hanging around the construction site. Maybe he had a stalker. But that made no sense. That's why he'd already decided to say something to Cord about it, get his take on whether someone was hanging around the farm that shouldn't be. But hell, these days Cord had enough to deal with.

"You afraid Cord will think you're nuts?"

Ryder flinched at the voice, kicked the recliner causing the chair to bolt upright. "What the hell? Who are you? How'd you get in here? You're trespassing not to mention breaking and entering."

"You know who I am. Everyone in town knows. I'm

pretty sure the guys on the job mentioned me before now. They talk while they work."

"Oh come on, that's just guys bullshitting one another about some ghost rumored to haunt the town. No way is Scott Phillips standing in my house. No way is he a fucking ghost!"

"Sure about that, are you? Go out to Eternal Gardens sometime, check the name on my headstone. I'd suggest going over to Promise Cove and asking my widow to show you the family photo album but that's incredibly insensitive to Jordan, not to mention my daughter, Hutton."

For some crazy reason he didn't doubt that reasoning. "What the hell do you want from me?"

"It's not a question of what I want, but rather what you want to get back from Bethany. What she took from you belonged to your grandfather, your family. It's an heirloom you need to get back."

"Damn straight I do," Ryder tossed out. But then it hit him. "How the hell do you know that? No one does."

"Yeah, I know. Not even your mother."

"If you know where Bethany is, tell me."

"Her name isn't Bethany. But you knew that already."

"Where is she? What is her real name? Tell me," Ryder demanded. But his words hung in the air unanswered and echoed off the walls as he watched the man fade right in front of him.

Mouth gaped open, he finally thought of something else to say, "Son of a bitch. How in the hell can I be talking to a freakin' ghost?"

Chapter Four

Ryder had never been one to procrastinate. He prided himself on meeting a problem head on, something he'd learned from both his mom and dad, not to mention his time spent in the military.

That was only one reason after finishing the morning milking that he decided to hunt down Cord.

It took him on a trip through the outbuildings, up and down the rows of growing vegetation looking for Cord's silver birch-metallic truck. But his friend was not at the farm.

He didn't find him at the veterinary clinic either.

One thing about a small town though, a person couldn't go very far. When Ryder reached the corner of Ocean Street and Cape May, he spotted a GMC Sierra pickup parked outside the Fanning Marine Rescue Center. He recognized Cord's ride.

The big iron gate was closed so Ryder took out his cell phone to text him.

Waiting for you outside. Do you have time to talk?

A minute later he got a response. *Sure. Be out in a sec.*

A few minutes later Ryder watched as the gate slid back and Cord came walking out wearing scrubs.

"You really do look the part."

Cord grinned. "Keegan and I were removing a plastic ring caught in a sea otter's mouth. We've been up since four-thirty. You seem to be adjusting to life in our little hamlet. Being away from Philly isn't driving you nuts yet?"

"The town's actually a nice place. No complaints. Besides, I'm beginning to hit my stride at both jobs."

"Good to hear it. So what's up?"

"I have to be at work in a few minutes so I'll just get to the point. I had a visitor last night."

Cord's smile evaporated. "Who?"

"I'm not crazy," Ryder stated when he saw Cord's concerned face. "But this guy keeps showing up. In fact, for the last three months I've felt as though someone keeps watching me. One night last January I almost grabbed my service pistol. Last night I saw him again, came right into the living room without so much as a knock on the door."

Cord's brow eased, a smile tipped the corners of his mouth. "You saw Scott? Scott Phillips?"

"I know he's some kind of local hero around here. But I don't know the man."

"I did. We served in Iraq together when I was there with the Guard. It was messy and deadly, a time I'd rather forget. I was there the day an IED blew Scott out of a Humvee."

"That's the problem, Cord. I don't believe in ghosts."

"You will," Cord said as he paced off several steps in front of the gate and back again. "I haven't seen him in months, not since my wedding day. He's all over town though."

"I've heard the rumors since I got here. For the last week, the guys have been running their mouths. I thought since I was the newcomer, they were just doing it for my benefit."

"I wish I could say that explained it. The thing is if you see him once, you're likely on his list for whatever reason."

"What kind of list? Why me? I'm not bothering anyone. I live a quiet life here, the way I want it."

"He goes after troubled people. Scott must think you're in need of help."

"You're kidding? But I don't need help. And I'm hardly in the troubled category."

Cord narrowed his eyes, stared long and hard at Ryder. "You're sure of that, are you?"

"Positive."

"Yeah? What about Bethany? What about the fact she took off with everything you ever owned."

"What about her? She's long gone. Sure, I'm pissed off about what she did. I think of it every single day. Who wouldn't? I'm working my ass off to stash some money aside like I had before she came into my life. You think I don't know that if it hadn't been for you loaning me the tools, I wouldn't even be able to take this job."

"That's ridiculous. Logan wouldn't let that stand in the way of giving you the job."

"Still, I appreciate it. It'll take me years to catch up to what I had before Bethany. But I'm game."

"I know you are. But if you want to find this woman, stick with Scott."

"Come on, Cord. Talk about ridiculous… That's the craziest thing I've ever heard of. We were in the same unit together." Ryder pushed up the sleeves of the hoodie he wore, held out his bare arm decorated with the black-and-red Army Ranger band capped off with a skull and crossbones. He tapped it with his other hand. "We got these together after training in Fort Benning. This says we're a band of brothers. I've trusted you with my life in combat."

"And you think I'd lie to you about this now? Lead you down the wrong path, give you erroneous info now? Is that it? Look, if it weren't for Scott I wouldn't be standing here today. That's a fact. I'd be dead by now or in prison."

"What are you talking about?"

"If Scott hadn't intervened it might be me who ended up a ghost haunting this town. But I changed my life into what makes me happy. After Nick and Ben dragged me here from a jail cell in Houston, I was messed up." Noticing the confused expression on Ryder's face, he added, "I tried to commit suicide, Ryder. Twice. I was so screwed up back then over what happened with Cassie I couldn't think straight. I couldn't see anything straight, feel anything but the guilt I was carrying around. Scott was the first one who clued into my depression and saved me. Then I met Keegan. She rescued me from my second attempt." Cord nodded toward Smuggler's Bay and the water beyond. "I got drunk one night, waded out too far into the water. I didn't want to live, Ryder. But Keegan saved me," he repeated.

"You're serious about this?"

"I am. There's a reason you're on Scott's radar. If I were you, I'd take the time to find out what it is."

Landon Jennings had spent his whole life in Pelican Pointe. Up to the day he'd finished high school, he hadn't been anywhere much at all. The son of rancher, Euell Jennings, Landon and his older sister, Eleanor, were well-known around town. There'd been a time when the Jennings family wielded plenty of power using cattle and timber and money as their bargaining chip. Owning the largest spread in and around Santa Cruz County along with the best stock went a long way to fattening their bank accounts. Their businesses during the fifties—a grocery store, a feed store, the bank—all thrived. Profits went hand in hand with their position and standing in the community.

But by the early seventies bad investments had forced Euell to begin selling off the land to pay off his debts. It didn't take long till there was nothing left to liquidate except the house and outbuildings. In a matter of years, the family went from a respected place of honor to barely scraping by to finally losing everything.

Spoiled by her father since her mother's death a decade earlier, Eleanor was used to getting what she wanted. Maybe it was for that reason she considered herself above everyone else—a combination between an heiress who'd come from old money and a celebrity who expected superstar treatment.

Whatever it was, Eleanor took the news about the family's reversal of fortune exceptionally hard. With the delusion shattered and the bank days away from foreclosing, the rancher decided to do the only thing he thought would put everything right. He went out to the barn one warm summer evening—the barn that was about to belong to someone else—removed his rifle from its case and aimed the gun barrel at his head.

The next morning Eleanor was the one who found her father like that with half his face blown away, leaving him almost unrecognizable.

After that day, his sister had never been quite the same. She never seemed to recover from their father's suicide or the knowledge that he had squandered away what she thought rightfully belonged to her. There was no old money anywhere and no new money on the horizon coming in.

Eleanor's classic attitude had always consisted of one common trait. Rules were for other people to follow and not meant for her.

The embarrassment of no longer being part of Pelican Pointe's "first family" was too much for her to bear. The humiliation of it all caused her to drink heavily. Before long she turned to drugs. Always a high-strung woman to begin with, after her father's death, she slipped across the line until she was finally picked up for theft at a grocery store in San Sebastian.

The first time the police caught her stealing, Landon had hocked everything he owned to bail her out of jail—a television, his stereo, jewelry belonging to their late mother—it didn't matter as long as he got Eleanor out of that awful place.

By the second time it happened though, Landon had wised up. He'd seen Eleanor for what she was. He'd been a hundred miles to the north away at college knowing full well Eleanor was never going to change. He'd gone to UC Davis to experience a little breathing room. There, he'd been able to escape his sister's continuous drama by finding a job working at a landscape company to pay his tuition and make ends meet. He realized he liked the solitude of gardening and growing things.

While Eleanor had continued to spiral downward back in Pelican Pointe, Landon ended up with a degree in horticulture and a new woman in his life who loved plants and growing things almost as much as he did.

Shelby had caught his eye as they'd sat next to each other in floriculture class. After the two decided to get married, Landon had brought his new wife back to the only town he knew, the town where he wanted to prove himself.

Landon looked over the rim of his first morning cup of coffee at the woman he still considered his bride.

"I don't think it's a good idea," he stated with some emphasis. "I'm willing to help the new principal out anyway I can, but I draw the line at selling her Eleanor's house."

"I'm not sure why this is upsetting you so much. It's a house, Landon, not a memorial to your sister. I'm sure Cooper, Caleb, and Drea will understand selling it is a way to finally put the past behind them and move on. Why can't you see that? In fact, if you need a push why don't you talk to them, get their thoughts. Caleb and Drea are right here so it won't take much effort there. You won't have to go far to have a sit down with them face to face. Since Cooper is off traipsing the globe and won't get back from wherever he is until summer, you'll have to settle for Skype or sending him a long email."

"You really don't see the problem here?"

"I really don't. I'm not sure why you do. The house deserves to have someone take care of it instead of sitting there the biggest eyesore on the block."

Landon grimaced. "I mow the lawn a couple of times a month May through October. I've never once pushed that chore off on the kids."

"You know that isn't enough. This young woman is making a new start here. I think the house could use a new start, too. It's time, don't you think?"

"Okay, if the kids don't have any objections I'll pitch in and help with the makeover myself. It's the least I can do."

"There you go. Don't you feel better at the idea of paying something forward, goodwill to be sure?"

"I suppose. But the kids haven't weighed in yet."

"Don't worry. They will."

The day started with a wintery marine layer keeping the sun out and the chill in. Jacket weather, Landon decided as he caught up with Caleb, his legally adopted, twenty-three-year-old son, who was busy loading one of their delivery trucks.

"Got quite a few stops to make this morning?" Landon asked, taking in the hardworking man he thought of as his own and had since the boy had celebrated his fourth birthday.

"The usual. Taking the rest of Ryder's order out to Taggert Farms this morning then stopping at Promise Cove to drop off Jordan's supply of seedlings. She always orders herbs this time of year. Why? What's up?"

Landon told him about Julianne Dickinson's interest in the house.

"Someone wants to actually buy it? Why?"

"That's what I said. Nick Harris and Patrick Murphy cautioned us all to do what we could to make sure the school principal feels welcome whenever she starts work here. It never occurred to me that she'd want Eleanor's house. There isn't even a 'for sale' sign in the yard. I guess that's why I'm surprised she approached me like she did."

"I never saw it coming either," Caleb admitted.

Landon rubbed the back of his neck. "I've been stewing about it since last night. Let's face it. If she doesn't buy it, with the school opening in the fall, there'll be others interested in moving into town and looking for real estate. If I don't sell it to her, there'll be other people asking."

"Makes sense. Now that locals have the prospect of sending their kids to a neighborhood school they'd be looking to settle here again," Caleb reasoned in agreement, understanding the town was growing and changing. "Still, the woman's biting off an awful chunk of work."

Wiping the sweat from his brow despite the cool temperatures, Caleb added, "But if you think I'll be upset to see it go, think again. I haven't been back inside that place since I was fifteen and swiped a bottle of beer out of the fridge, snuck in there to finish it off without you knowing about it."

"Yeah, you took two that night. Don't forget the one you gave to your friend at the time, Steven Hedeby."

Caleb grinned. "Yeah, I was trying to impress the jock football player. Why does it not surprise me that you even know about the beers? Never could sneak anything past you or Mom." He closed the rear door to the van and went around to the side, faced the man he considered his father. "Look, Drea and Cooper feel the same way about that house as I do. If someone wanted to tear it down, start from scratch, I wouldn't stand in their way."

"You mean that?"

"Sure I do. You can ask Drea, get Cooper's take all you want, but I'm telling you they won't care anymore than I do who ends up with the place or what they ultimately do with it. You might want to mention the history there. How unhappy we all were. Although I'm certain there are plenty of people who'll be willing to line up and share all the scurrilous details about Eleanor." After making sure he hadn't forgotten any part of the order, Caleb reached to slide the side door closed. "Could you put in a condition for me though, to the new owner?"

"A condition? What's that?"

"See if you can get them to agree to repaint the outside."

Curious, Landon lowered his gaze. "Any particular color?"

"Anything will do except that awful pink and purple."

Landon smiled. "Sure. I'll see what I can do."

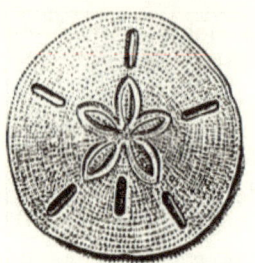

Chapter Five

Oblivious to the Jennings family dynamics playing out, Julianne learned on Thursday afternoon about Nick and Jordan's plans. They'd offered her a weekend stay at their Promise Cove B&B, beginning Friday night through Sunday.

"It's our off-season and we're practically empty. This weekend is our chance to pamper the new principal," Jordan explained. "We'd love to have you as our guest."

"How could I possibly say no to that?" she told the innkeeper over the phone.

"Why would you even want to?" Jordan said with a laugh.

"I'm blown away by your hospitality."

"It's our way of showing you how excited we are to have you make your home here. Ryder tells us you've already started house hunting. We're delighted to hear that."

Julianne told her about the little gingerbread house and how she was having second thoughts. "Am I being silly?"

"That's entirely a personal choice, however consider this. There are lots of older homes here. Each one has its own story. Take the one Brent and River are living in for example. It's where his grandmother passed away. One day Autumn was there, reading her books, canning, making her homemade candles, watching television, going about her business as usual and the next day she'd left us. Then there's the one Hayden uses for her bookstore. That house is where Ethan's grandfather died in the back bedroom. Then there's the place Ethan and Hayden recently fixed up on Landings Bay. They live in the house where Sissy Carr once lived. Who knows what she and that crook, Kent Springer, cooked up inside those very walls? But Ethan and Hayden bought it because they wanted to stay here, make a life here and that was the best possible house to do it."

"Ah, I see what you mean."

"Good because it'll be hard to find a house without a history, particularly in Pelican Pointe. I suppose that applies to anywhere really, unless you get a brand-new home. Whichever property you choose though, we want you to be happy here. So take your time and make sure you get the house that calls to you, whatever the reason. And don't listen to anyone else influence you. What do you know about the town? Have you researched it at all?"

"Not much, other than it seems like an amazing little town. I mean, there's a rescue center for marine life there and a Chumash museum in the planning stages. I think it'll be a great place to put down roots."

"Then pack your bag and come for a couple days. We'll do our best to make you feel right at home here."

After she hung up, Julianne decided she'd take a second look at the Jennings house. She couldn't explain her attraction to it other than the gorgeous view of the bay from the front porch. After talking it over with her dad, she felt certain this was the house she wanted. Finding the right property would go a long way to making her feel at home there.

Getting the owner onboard with the idea of selling it to her was simply a combination of persuasion and perseverance. Giving up wasn't an option. She'd discovered that for herself—first from her father—then later from Danny. Both men had given her a window into stubborn along with a dab of give and take. She'd learned mediation—which helped her every day in the classroom dealing with temperamental children—and the art of haggling. She discovered negotiating came as natural to her as teaching did. But even with skills in that arena, she'd get her dad's take before she hammered out a deal. It didn't matter with whom. Julianne trusted his judgment.

By the time she started tossing her stuff into a suitcase in anticipation of the weekend, she'd talked herself into giving the gingerbread house another chance. Maybe because she knew firsthand that sometimes a person had to let go of the past in a big way to get anywhere at all. Zipping the bag up, she thought of Danny. Memories flooded her.

It was definitely time to let go and begin again in a brand-new place.

Come Friday afternoon after school, Julianne followed Jordan's directions. She flew along the Pacific Coast Highway past the outskirts of Pelican Pointe on the way to Promise Cove. With the music cranked up and Rufus Wainwright blasting from the car speakers, she glanced out the window to see the water churn with foamy whitecaps.

Reducing her speed she veered off onto the narrow turnoff leading to the B&B. Heading west toward the ocean, it didn't take long before she saw the apple-green and white sign that read, "Promise Cove Bed and Breakfast, established 2009 by Scott Phillips. Jordan and Nick Harris, Proprietors."

Her van bounced along the paved driveway while she craned her neck to get a look at the surrounding woods on both sides of the lane. For a brief time she wondered if she'd somehow missed the property entirely. But then the thicket of cypress and willow gave up a glimpse of house, if you could call it that. She fixed her gaze on the massive Victorian. It reminded her of a Southern mansion or maybe a chateau in the south of France. Not that she would know what either looked like firsthand.

She stared up at the gabled roof, the deep angles that formed a contrast of lacy edges and bold triangles. Inching her minibus beside the long wraparound porch, she parked behind a Ford Explorer and hopped out. For a moment she thought she saw the guy she'd seen at the gingerbread house. If it were him he hadn't done laundry for two days because he wore the same shirt and khaki pants he'd had on Wednesday afternoon. Which was ridiculous, she decided.

Even as she reached to get her bag, Nick was right there to offer a hand.

"Have any trouble finding us?"

"Not a bit. Your directions were perfect." She looked around at the view, could hear the waves slap the shore from where she stood. "This place is amazing."

"We like it. I hope you don't mind but we took the liberty of making your visit a sort of 'welcome to Pelican Pointe' dinner. We've invited a few friends over for Saturday night."

She grinned. "I suspected as much. Besides, Brent Cody already let the cat out of the bag. It's okay. Good thing he warned me, otherwise I wouldn't have packed my little black dress."

She trailed after Nick as they made their way into the house where Jordan was dealing with two argumentative toddlers of different mindsets.

"No, Hutton, you cannot force your brother to play dress up if he doesn't want to." Spotting their guest, Jordan sighed. "There you are. Did Nick tell you about the little get-together we've planned for tomorrow night?"

"He did."

"Good. Then you'll settle in tonight with us, rest up from your workweek with a good eight hours sleep to go house hunting tomorrow."

"Actually I've decided to give the Jennings house another look, get my dad's take on whether or not fixing it up is even worth the effort." While she talked, Julianne glanced around the spacious parlor. Her eyes landed on a photograph sitting atop the mantel. The face of the man she'd seen Wednesday at the cottage stared back at her. She went over, examined the face, the uniform he wore. Snatching the picture off the shelf, she asked, "Who is this man?" She raised her head long enough to see the couple exchange furtive glances. "What?"

It was Nick who cleared his throat to speak. "That's the man who grew up here, in this house. Scott Phillips. He was married to Jordan. He's her first husband."

Julianne wondered if that explained why her hosts both looked so uncomfortable. She didn't think it was. The next words out of Jordan's mouth cut into her own muddled thoughts.

"Scott didn't come back from Iraq," Jordan explained.

"But… What do you mean he didn't come back? I saw him in town mid-week, had a conversation with him at the little bungalow. He's the one who told me where to find the owner."

Julianne saw the look of doubt form in the couple's eyes and realized neither one believed her. Even though it did sound preposterous, she knew what she'd seen with her own eyes. "He's the one who told me how much work it needed, pointed out how close it was to the pub."

"Since he grew up here, Scott would know all about its history from the beginning," Nick pointed out.

Astonished at his statement, Julianne appealed to them. "You believe me then? You don't think I'm delusional?"

"It's a long story. Why don't you go upstairs first and get settled. You're in the Coral Room this weekend. Take a shower or go for a walk around the grounds until dinner's ready. Nick will take your bags up."

"Okay, but… How is it you believe I had a conversation with a dead guy? Sorry," she added quickly for Jordan's benefit. "But you see my confusion."

"Unpack first," Jordan suggested again. "A walk will clear your head. We'll talk over dinner."

Upstairs, Nick let her inside the room. Once she got a look inside, she realized they'd given her one of the best suites in the house. Her eyes drifted to the focal point—the old antique four-poster bed with its soft, downy comforter. She took in the pale, sea-green walls, the stencils in the shape of white coral reef hand-painted as decorative trim. She stepped to study the beach-themed photographs depicting lighthouses and sandbars and said, "Oh, Nick, this is too much. You and Jordan have to let me pay you for my stay."

"I tell you what, you offer to babysit our kids sometime so that Jordan and I can take a break for an evening out and I'll be indebted to you for life."

Julianne chuckled. "That seems like a small price to pay for spending two nights in such a gorgeous setting."

"No, it isn't. Believe it when I say, it's a fair trade. I don't know how you manage twenty-five six-year-olds in a classroom without losing your sanity when some days we struggle to deal with two."

She smiled at him. "The secret is I deal with them and then they go home—to spend quality time with mom or dad."

Once he set her bag down on the settee, before he turned to go, Julianne stopped him. "Nick, by any chance would you be willing to tell me if you believe in ghosts?"

"As a matter of fact, I do."

"You didn't hesitate, not for a minute," she pointed out. "There has to be a reason for that."

"There is, and we'll discuss it later. Dinner won't be ready until around six-thirty. We got a little sidetracked this afternoon when Hutton thought Quake, that's our family dog, ran off. Turns out, he'd found a quiet place to take a nap under the back staircase without two little kids driving him nuts. Look, take a nap or whatever you want and enjoy your time here. Don't let Scott upset you."

Julianne drew in a quiet breath as she spun around in the luxurious room. She considered whether or not Scott had upset her. So far she couldn't say that he had. Sure, she'd been annoyed because he hadn't told her who he was that day at the house. But under the circumstances she probably wouldn't have believed him anyway.

"I mean, what could you do? Tell me you were a ghost right off the bat?" she muttered aloud as she set out her makeup and toiletries on the bathroom counter. Was that why he hadn't bothered with sticking around?

After unpacking her things, she threw open the French doors and walked out to the back deck, craned her neck to get a better look at the courtyard below. Even in winter the pathways burst with color. Orange lilies, yellow daisies, and lavender flounced in the breeze like models showing off on a Paris runway.

Was it silly to hope she could eat her bagel and jam out there tomorrow morning in the outdoor eating area among all the blossoms and fragrant petals?

The winding pathways led through forty-foot cypress, magnolias, and maples. Tall pines gave way to the majestic cliff. But it was the ocean in the distance that made her want to explore through the trails to reach the edge.

She slid out of her pumps, got rid of the blouse and skirt she'd worn to school. Changing into a pair of jeans and a sweater, she laced up her sneakers, threw on a jacket so she could take that walk around the grounds.

Making her way down the back staircase, she slipped out the door of the laundry room onto the travertine-paved terrace. There, she filled her lungs with the crisp air of late afternoon. She stopped to brush her hand over the tops of the slender red tulips before deciding which path to take to get to the bluffs. The grove of coniferous larch drew her toward the sea.

But first she had to navigate a narrow sliver of trail that led to underbrush and wild tangled vines full of ripe blackberries. She was by no means an expert at hiking through woods, but she knew enough to follow the ridgeline. As she passed through a field of Indian paintbrush that exploded with swatches of scarlet, on impulse, she dug out her camera phone to capture the vibrant wildflowers and started clicking.

When she took off walking again, she found herself among rows and rows of apple and cherry trees. The fields and rolling hills sprang to life with new blossoms and budding shrubs. She got a strong whiff of floral scent mingled with the smell of manure right before she actually spotted the fat black-and-white cows. The animals plodded along behind a solitary man who seemed so content with the chore he actually had a swagger about him.

Even as she watched Ryder McLachlan herd them into the barn, there was an aura of mystery about him. The man she'd met two days ago was an enigma, hoarding his past like a miser. He gave off vibes that said he had a stubborn streak a mile wide and twice as deep. But then what man didn't. He'd made it clear he didn't want to be attracted to her, or anyone for that matter.

She should leave it at that. With everything on her plate—the move, getting a house, a new job on the horizon—the last thing she needed was to add a stubborn persona into the mix of her chaotic life. But there was something about this particular guy she found intriguing. The way his eyes flared whenever they disagreed, like Wednesday night. The way he'd looked at her during their spat—as if with one deft stroke of a lean finger he could pluck out every secret she'd held since fourth grade.

Although Julianne didn't have much mystery about her, or many secrets to reveal, she liked to think loyalty came first. Therefore even Ryder's hotness couldn't get her to so easily crack under his touch.

Before yanking the barn door open, she took a deep breath. For the first time in a long time, Julianne decided she wanted to dig deeper into what troubled the farmer. After all, they were both starting over in a new place. It seemed like the neighborly thing to do.

As soon as she threw back the door the unexpected sound of soft rock hit her. She realized the building wasn't a barn at all but a milking station. While Starship's Grace Slick and Mickey Thomas promised that nothing was gonna stop them now, across the sea of cows, Julianne caught the annoyed look on Ryder's face at the interruption.

"Well, look at this ladies we have us a visitor."

"Interesting taste in music."

"The cows like it."

"Really? I had no idea. Sorry to bother you, but I was out and about walking and saw your farm, thought I'd stop in to check the place out."

"You have a way of popping up out of the blue. And it's not my farm. As it was explained to me, it's more of a co-op effort. That's the way Nick and Jordan do things. But technically they own the place."

"Ah, that makes sense being next door and all."

"So let me get this straight, you were out walking around my turf all the way from Santa Cruz?"

"Of course not." She gritted her teeth and wondered silently why the man always seemed to leap to such ridiculous assumptions.

"Then what on earth is a gorgeous female like you doing lurking around my cows on a Friday night? Shouldn't you be somewhere else kicking up your heels? Or is that something schoolteachers aren't allowed to do?"

"I've been known to kick up my heels a time or two."

"Good to know. So you like to party?"

"Did I say that?" she snapped, irritation building with every tick of the clock.

"You look like a woman tied to a rigid job keeping people in line."

"I keep six-year-olds in line. If that translates to rigid to you, then I make no apologies for it. I love teaching."

"I can tell. I seem to always say the wrong thing around you."

"What you do is push all the wrong buttons and frustrate me. You come across as someone as prickly as an old woman determined to keep the neighborhood kids off her lawn."

Ryder let out a roar of laughter. "You aren't that far off the mark. I like my solitude."

"So I've noticed. Nothing wrong with that, so I'll leave you to it. Thanks to the hospitality of Nick and Jordan, I'm staying at Promise Cove this weekend. For two whole days I'll be your neighbor. I just wanted to—"

"Stop in and be sociable." His lips curved up. "I got that. It's always a good idea to spend time checking out the area around the B&B. It's pretty country. Nick and Jordan offer first-rate amenities. In fact, I'm invited over there tomorrow night for your 'welcome to town' dinner. Oops, I hope I didn't let the cat out of the bag with that."

"Nope, I know all about it. Someone else warned me and this afternoon when I checked in, Nick confirmed it."

"Hard to keep a secret in a little town like Pelican Pointe. You'll realize it's a bit different than Santa Cruz."

"Oh, I don't know. Is it really all that different from any other place, say Philadelphia? Besides, people usually have a tough time keeping things hidden for long. Secrets have a way of turning up when you least expect them." She thought about the keepsake box Troy had found and the puzzle from the past it held. "After all, someone kept a big one for about two decades." She told him about what she'd found underneath the lining of the chest and watched as his mouth dropped open.

"You found a what?"

"A piece of shirt saturated in what looked to me like blood. I gave it to Brent Cody. It's obvious the person wearing it came to a violent end or was so gravely wounded they had to seek medical help."

"The obvious question is why the box was hidden away at the school in the first place? The bloody article of clothing has to factor in. You wouldn't think murder could ever touch a place like this."

"You're kidding? In Pelican Pointe you mean? They had a serial killer here for years."

For a second time, his mouth gaped open. "Wow, I had no idea. No one mentioned that part to me."

"The story made headlines for quite some time in Santa Cruz. I don't know how they dealt with it here but I'm sure it's something they'd like to put behind them."

"The blood on the shirt could mean nothing at all. Maybe someone killed a deer or something."

"I thought of that. It's possible there's a logical explanation. People around here go hunting all the time. But why hide a piece of fabric that has blood on it if it's from an animal or from a hunting trip? There would be no need to conceal it like that."

"True."

"In the event it's something more, like a cold case, if anyone's up to the task of solving it, I'd say it's Brent Cody."

"What does Brent think?"

"I haven't heard a thing from him. But I intend to ask him about it while I'm in town. Mind if I ask you a question. Think of it as more like a survey." She saw him bristle at the notion of an inquisition.

"Sure."

"Do you believe in ghosts?"

Their eyes lingered on each other for a split second before she saw him swallow hard, the color drain from his face. At that very moment, it seemed as if the former soldier had located the apparition in question hovering in the corner right along with the cows.

"Why would you ask me such a thing? Have you been talking to Cord?"

"Who's Cord?"

Ryder dropped his guard. "A friend of mine who believes Scott Phillips haunts this town. Ridiculous notion, huh?"

She gnawed the inside of her jaw, thinking, considering the possibilities. "Interesting."

"You're kidding? Why? Tell me why you asked the question."

"Because I talked to him. Scott, not your friend Cord. The day I stopped at the Jennings' house. There was this guy. He looked real enough to me. Anyway, while I busied myself checking out the exterior, the foundation, the porch, all of a sudden I look up and see this guy standing at the corner of the house staring back at me. I just assumed that he was a neighbor. And before you ask, yes, I'm certain it was Scott Phillips. I saw his picture tonight when I checked into the B&B. Nick and Jordan verified it."

Even before joining the military he'd always been a man prone to keeping his personal feelings closed off. Now was no different. He waged a mini-battle within. Should he risk disclosing details he'd told no one else but Cord? While he stood there conflicted, staring into her deep, dark chocolate eyes brimming with questions, those orbs tugged him into a decision. He told her about his own encounters with Scott. All of them.

"What do you think it means?"

"That we should probably stop drinking the water around here."

Julianne snorted with laughter. "Besides that."

He scratched his jaw. "Cord's theory is that Scott hangs around to guide troubled people away from their problems."

Julianne's brows knit. "But I don't have any problems that I know of and I'm not troubled about anything."

"That's what I said."

She suddenly realized the waning light meant she'd stayed too long. "The sun's going down."

"Please don't tell me you're a fairy princess who turns into an ogre at dusk?"

"How'd you guess? But you have to promise not to tell anyone. It would ruin my rep as the rigid, spinster schoolteacher."

"I never said you were a spinster."

"No? I thought that was implied." She glanced at her watch, realized she'd forgot to put it back on. "What time is it?"

"Almost six-thirty."

"Oh crap, I *do* have to head back. I don't want to be a no-show for dinner my first night at the inn."

When she started to walk off in the opposite direction, he grabbed her hand. "Let me drive you back. If you're worried about being late, it's the fastest way."

"That'll work. Why don't I drag you over there for supper, stay for the discussion about Scott. They promised me one."

"No way."

"So the former soldier is afraid to have a conversation about an imaginary ghost?"

"Calling me chicken won't work."

"Then come back with me and be there when we all sit down for a heart-to-heart. I'd say there's no better time for us to ask the local experts all the questions we have spinning around in our minds. Get some answers. It's the least they can do."

Chapter Six

"Look who I found on my walk," Julianne said as she sailed through the back door at the B&B. "I know Ryder wasn't invited for dinner but... Turns out, he's seen Scott, too."

That's as far as Julianne got when Jordan waved her off. "We're used to having people drop in all the time. Come on in, Ryder. You'll stay for dinner."

"It happens to be standard operating procedure to make room at the table for extra guests at the last minute," Nick added before giving Ryder a slap on the back. "How's it going at the construction site? I've been meaning to stop by but it's been hard to find the time."

Ryder brought him up to speed on their progress. It gave them a topic as the four adults settled around the huge mahogany dining table. Though the kids, Hutton and Scott, had already eaten supper, the toddlers busied themselves by playing with the toys scattered around the room.

They sat down to roasted salmon and steamed asparagus. The first bite of fish had Julianne letting out a loud sigh. "This is delicious. The creamy sauce makes it pop."

"It's simple to make using white wine and lemon," Jordan said. "I'll give you the recipe before you check out Sunday."

"I have several excellent prospects in the teaching department. Although my own principal keeps telling me hands off whenever I try to recruit the cream of the crop."

"Don't let up. We still have several positions to fill."

"I'm hoping to interview two next week. I'll do it in Santa Cruz although I do want them to see the school." Julianne bided her time, waited for a lag in banter to finally steer the conversation to Scott. "Truth is I dragged Ryder here tonight because he's had way more Scott encounters than I have. Don't look at me like that," she warned Ryder when he sent her a roll of his eyes. With a wave of her fork at him, she added, "They don't think you're crazy or hallucinating." She looked at Jordan. "Go ahead, tell him."

"No, you're not crazy," Jordan echoed. "I wish I could explain it better. But Scott's presence here is because he loves this place, the town, his family, his friends. He watches over us. And because he has no malice in his heart, none of us want to see him leave."

Noting the still-skeptical look on Ryder's face, Nick folded his napkin and stood up. He retrieved a photo from the sideboard, the one of his former Guard buddy dressed in a wetsuit. "This was taken during Scott's surfing days." He held the picture out to Ryder. "If this is the guy you've seen around town, he died in Iraq. I know because I was there the day it happened. You're not the first who thought they were paranoid or delusional after seeing him and I can guarantee you won't be the last."

"That's him," Ryder confirmed. "That's the guy who's been bugging me."

"Here, let me see that," Julianne said. "I saw the one in the living room on the mantel, the one where he's dressed in his uniform. This is the Scott I saw, relaxed, smiling and enjoying himself."

"I had a long talk with Cord," Ryder admitted. "The entire ghost thing is a little hard for me to swallow. But I know what I saw. Or rather who I saw. If someone offered me the chance to pick him out of a lineup, that's the guy I'd pick."

"When he talked to me, he tossed out one line that indicated he knew I'd had help from Danny, the man I loved at the time, fixing up our old relic of a van. It's something no one could've possibly known unless they were my neighbors back in Santa Cruz. But here in Pelican Pointe? That info would be of no particular interest to anyone. That's why it shocked me that he knew."

"And with me, Scott mentioned a detail about a former girlfriend no one knew about. Not even my mother knows, but I will eventually have to come clean about. Bethany lifted a family heirloom. That's only one reason she's a sore subject for me. Scott didn't have a problem bringing her up right off the bat. He knew that I'm hoping to locate her and get back what she stole."

Nick nodded. "Then Scott must feel he can help, help both of you."

"That's the same explanation Cord gave me. Not about Julianne, of course. Until tonight I had no idea she'd seen Scott, too. The thing is I don't feel as though I need help finding Bethany. She'll eventually turn up."

"And I don't feel I have any burgeoning problems that I need help solving," Julianne added.

"The amazing thing is you guys seem to think this is a normal occurrence," Ryder noted. "I feel like I'm smack in the middle of a *Twilight Zone* rerun minus Rod Serling's narration."

Jordan's lips bowed. "For us it's all so normal now. There was a time it wasn't. I understand that the idea of a ghost helping you solve an important aspect of your life might be ludicrous. But sometimes things happen that aren't explainable."

"Like crop circles or the Bermuda Triangle," Julianne piped up, earning a smile from her hostess.

"Look, I've experienced Scott firsthand," Nick pointed out. "Believe, don't believe, it's up to you. Jordan and I just want to assure you that no one thinks either of you are…nuts. And if you're afraid of him, I assure you Scott is never sinister. That's never part of his character."

Jordan decided a change of subject was in order. "We're fast approaching March and soliciting vendors for the street fair. If either of you are interested in a booth, now's the time to sign up."

"There's a street fair here in March?" Julianne asked, clearly taken with the idea.

Ryder could see her wheels turning as he dug into his fish. Picking up the beer Nick had provided, he told them about *Reclaimed Treasures*. "If they'll let anyone be a vendor, Julianne's a great candidate."

It was Nick who bobbed his head in agreement. "Sure. We encourage everyone here to buy local if they can. Last year, Jordan recruited the Crawford sisters to sell their quilts and Troy to hawk his jewelry boxes. Ask them about their experience before signing up. Last year's fair was a huge success, blew all the other years away combined."

Julianne picked up her wine glass. "I don't have to think about it. Go ahead and add me to the vendor list. Unless the fact I'm principal is considered a conflict of interest. Will that be a problem?"

"Why would it be? What our principal does on her own time—as long as it's a legal enterprise—is of no concern to the town council," Nick assured her.

"How do you find stuff to repurpose and refinish?" Jordan wondered.

"And when do you find the time?" Nick added.

"I'm good at utilizing the stuff people want to toss out. Whenever my neighbors do spring cleaning or move stuff out of their garage, I'm there, willing to take it off their hands. I keep my eye out for certain containers located in high traffic areas on my way to and from school. If I see something promising, I stop, inspect it, and then load it into the van. But I draw the line at actually dumpster diving. I'll cruise around it. I'll grab anything I see that looks like it has potential for resale. But my diving into one is a different story."

"Unless it's a Van Gogh," Ryder teased. "Then you're like, 'let me at that thing.'"

When Julianne hooted with laughter, he let himself enjoy the sound. That cheerful nature of hers reminded him of exotic marigolds reaching toward the sun. That beaming smile, the sparkle in her eyes, made his pulse ramp up.

After taking a sip of her merlot, she let out a huge sigh. "I'm gonna love living here."

"So does that mean whichever house you decide on, you'll need space for a workshop?" Ryder prodded.

Her face lit up. "Oh that would be perfect. Although I wouldn't know what to do with so much space."

"You'll find a use for it. The Jennings' house has a wide, detached, double-car garage." When she stared at him, Ryder lifted a shoulder in a shrug. "I went by there this afternoon after work to check the place out. Landon and his son, Caleb, were busy cutting the grass. But they let me take a tour around the property."

"Really? That's a good sign."

"How so?"

"Because it means they're open to a buyer."

Later, Julianne walked Ryder to his truck under a bright crescent moon. With a starlit sky that glistened like diamonds overhead, she breathed in the February chill and studied the man beside her. His toned shoulders and trim waist had her wondering what it would be like to see him naked. If he wrapped her up with those long arms...

The sound of his voice broke into her thoughts.

"Will you be okay staying here tonight?"

"Because of Scott?" Her laugh echoed out deep and rich. "More than okay. I trust Nick and Jordan when they say he isn't malevolent. Mostly because at the house that day Scott took the neighborly approach. The look in his eyes said friendly to me, not crazy. What about you?"

"I'm okay with it. Him. I guess."

"You on the other hand have a hard time trusting a female. You'd rather trust a ghost before a woman." She lifted one shoulder. "That's my take. What kind of number did Bethany do on you anyway? What did she steal?"

She saw him look away, waited several long seconds for him to speak.

"My grandfather on my dad's side of the family made his living as a cartoonist. His comic strips were syndicated in newspapers up and down the East Coast. When he died he left all of his sketches to my father. But after Dad died, they came to me."

At the emotion she saw in his eyes, the way he fought back tears, she reached out to him, ran her hand along his cheek.

"You have to understand, his drawings were my most prized possessions. Those cartoons were precious to me. I let that viper into my home, my bed and she betrayed every bit of trust I placed in her."

"You loved her."

Ryder filled his lungs with the heavy air, blew out an angry breath. "I was getting there in between tours. But you can rest assured I have no feelings now for the woman I knew as Bethany, except maybe contempt and disgust. Some days it's tough to forgive myself, how much faith and trust I put in her. I left for overseas, left my home and what was important to me with her. How did she repay me?"

"You had no way of knowing she would rip you off like that," Julianne pointed out.

"There were a few signs. But I look back and realize I spent a lot of time making up excuses for her."

"Like what?"

"Like the fact that she didn't really mean to insult my mother when she called her narcissistic. She didn't mean to pitch a fit every time I tried to return calls from my friends, friends I'd had since grade school. You get the picture. Anyway, that last time I got back stateside from Afghanistan I was bent on making a life together with her. Instead, when I got home I put my house key in the lock. It didn't work. I looked through the windows, only to that the place had all new furniture I didn't recognize."

"Oh Ryder. How long had it been since you'd received letters from her?"

"That was the kicker. The entire time she kept up this façade that everything was fine back home. I don't know how she managed that. Another example of how she outsmarted me."

"Criminals excel at deception. She didn't want you suspecting anything. Okay, go on."

"When I see the unfamiliar furniture, I figure Bethany bought new stuff. But at this point, I'm beginning to get a sick feeling in my gut. That's when I decided to go knock on my neighbor's door to see if he knew what was going on. He tells me Bethany put the house on the market six days after I landed at Bagram and it sold within the month. She got rid of my furniture or gave it away. Bottom line, she moved out, took everything I owned."

"Someone else was living in your house?"

"Sure was. A family of four bought it."

"But if the sale was done with phony paperwork—"

"I was gone fourteen months. It was obvious she'd been planning this long *before* my deployment. She ran a con and it worked." He ran a hand through his hair. He might as well tell her the rest. "One night I had too much to drink. She'd dragged me to a party for one of her friends. When we got back home, I might've signed some papers she shoved in front of me."

"What? Oh Ryder, I'm sorry."

"Yeah. I was an idiot. Believe me, I know it too."

"What happened after you found out?"

"I sat on the stoop that used to belong to me and waited for the new owners to come home from work. That evening they let me inside to take a tour—one last time and all that. Nothing of mine was left, not a single thing. The walls were a different color. I mean everything that belonged to me was gone. Not just my clothes, but every personal item that was important to me, photographs of my grandparents, my parents, relatives, cousins, friends. Things I'll never be able to replace."

"Your mother doesn't know any of this?"

"She knows Bethany and I broke up. That's all. She doesn't know I was sharing my life with a common, scum-sucking con artist. I know I'll have to tell her at some point. But it's difficult to admit to such blatant stupidity."

"You'll need to find the right time and tell her face-to-face, go back to Philly to do it. But then you already know what you have to do."

"Yeah."

"And up to now you've been unable to find any trace of her?"

"That's right. Even the name she used was phony. Why didn't I check up on that before I left? Why didn't I do a background check on her?"

"Stop it. That was certainly an option but not a normal routine occurrence between lovers. Perhaps in this day and time it's becoming more so, but you can't beat yourself up because you crossed paths with a scammer. You'll find her. I'll help you. You'll get her to give you back your grandfather's—"

"Don't you understand? What I had the sketches stored in is probably long gone by now. She more than likely sold it off right along with everything else."

"What were they stored in?"

"A brown leather blueprint tube that belonged to my grandfather on my mother's side. He was an architect. What difference does it make though? I doubt she knew or didn't care what was inside or how much I valued the drawings. They're gone and I won't be able to get them back."

"You don't know that for certain. Did you try looking in the immediate area for some of your stuff?"

"I wasted six weeks tracking down every pawn shop or thrift store within a fifty-mile radius of Philly. I didn't find a single item."

"Then the first step is finding her."

"You aren't listening to me, Julianne. Don't you see? I don't even know the woman's real name. I still don't."

"But you said you didn't need Scott's help, that she would likely surface on her own. You were bluffing back there."

He gave her a sheepish look. "I can explain. When it came time to re-enlist, I put in for discharge and went to work in construction, took every job that came along to try to make enough dough so I could put it aside. I moved in with my mom, saved my cash to hire a private investigator. I wasted the money because when it came to Bethany, the guy came up empty."

"I admit that is unusual. Did you turn her into the military police? NCIS?"

"You mean army CID?"

She lifted a shoulder. "Whatever it's called."

"No. Why would I? I wasn't living on base when it happened. I did call Philly PD. They took a report."

"But you were in the army when she did this to you. Because of that, the army investigators might want to know about it for their records. How long has it been since this happened?"

"Two years. But what good would it do to report her to the army now?"

"For one, it would ensure that what happened to you is on record. They get it on file and it means something. Second, it puts her alias on their radar so if she does this type of thing to another unsuspecting member of the military, it pops up. Not to mention her method of operation. Maybe she targets service personnel."

"That's not a bad idea. You aren't just beautiful but smart, too."

"Aww, thanks, I try."

"How do you know all this?"

"Brent Cody and I ate a few meals together."

"Is that code for dating? If so, then who is this Danny?"

"Brent and I never dated. Well, we went out once but nothing happened. We're just friends. We're more like cousins. As for Danny, he was the man I loved, grew up with. I think it's fair to say we were soul mates."

"See? Soul mates and yet you use the past tense. No relationship ever works out. It's pointless to think it does."

"Maybe you're right. But we didn't break up. Danny died in a car accident six weeks before our wedding day. This June, it'll be five years."

"I'm sorry."

"It's okay."

He needed to take that sad look off her face. After all, he'd been the one to put it there.

She wasn't prepared when he moved in, took her chin in his hands. At the tilt of his head to meet her mouth, she knew what he wanted, what she needed.

The smell of jasmine and the sea hung on the rush of the breeze that lifted her hair. But it was the kiss that had her body lifting to his. They floated together in the moment. Or she did. Her feet left the ground as their bodies fused. She wrapped her arms around his waist, returned the kiss, heat for heat.

His hands trailed up her back. His touch sent shockwaves from head to toe. Warmth untangled knots inside. A tidal wave of need spiked and stretched, waking primitive lust. Sweet and soft soon yielded to wild and hard.

They devoured. They ravaged.

They finally relinquished their hold on one another. Even then, their steamy breath still hung in the cool night air.

Ryder spoke first. "That was…"

"Hot," Julianne finished for him.

"And then some. I guess I'll see you here tomorrow night."

"Huh?"

"The party. For you."

"Oh. Right. Yeah. See you then."

She watched him hop into his truck, watched as it disappeared into the darkness before heading inside. Climbing the stairs to her room, it wasn't until she closed the door and leaned on the wood that she allowed herself to react. She let her hand fly to her heart, replaying the smoldering kiss. Feeling sixteen again, she felt her knees go weak.

"Damn it, Ryder McLachlan, you're gonna be hard to resist."

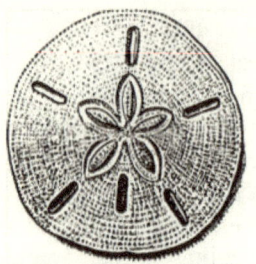

Chapter Seven

Before Julianne even opened her eyes the smell of cinnamon and bacon—two of her favorite things in the world—wafted into the room. Thinking someone must have come into the house and made French toast for her, she burrowed further into what felt like a soft cloud.

She wasn't nearly ready to get up yet. Then she remembered where she was. Promise Cove. What a romantic-sounding name to go with the smoldering kiss Ryder had laid on her last night. Which had kept her up till the wee hours. No wonder she was still groggy.

Flopping over on her side, she focused one eye on the clock. Seven-forty-five.

Intent on lounging, taking advantage of every second at the B&B, she groaned when her cell phone dinged with a text message. She snatched it off the nightstand to read the display. It was from her father.

Are we still on to look at the house today?

Yep. But I don't have a formal appointment to see the house.

Drop by then?

Why not? Play it by ear. She keyed in the address.

What time?

Ten okay with you?

See you there.

It wasn't so much the plan that got her moving but rather the continuous whiff of bacon. Because she needed to wake up, a shower sounded like the best option followed by a dose of caffeine.

She forced herself to sit up, to throw back the covers and crawl out of the warm cocoon. She'd almost reached the bathroom when she heard a plank creak coming from the deck outside. She wheeled around, saw a shadow cross in front of the French doors.

Broad daylight aside, she didn't hesitate. She crossed the floor, threw open the door. Scott stood a few feet away.

"How do you do that?"

"What?"

"Make the boards creak like that?"

"Trade secret."

"Oh for Pete's sake. You're enough of an enigma without talking in code. What can you tell me about the Jennings' house? Nick said you were the go-to guy on its history."

"I'd say the people who lived there know it best. I can't top firsthand information."

"But how do I get Landon Jennings to sell it to me? I'm not even sure he should, what with its past and all. What do you think?"

"I think it needs a new owner and some TLC."

"So it's worth buying? No horrible repairs lurking in the pipes or the walls?"

"That's what an inspector is for. Make your own assessment. Have your father check it out. After all, he's the expert."

"But can't you just give me a little insight here?"

"Like I said, give it some love. It's past time, Julianne."

It wasn't until the water from her shower sluiced over her body that she decided Scott hadn't been talking about the house, at least not entirely. It was past time she moved on from Danny. Ryder might prove the distraction she needed to do that. Based on the lip-lock they'd shared last night, if the man was half as good at sex as he was at kissing, it would be an "affair to remember." Smiling at her own joke, she grabbed a towel from the rack. Good thing she'd brought the sexiest dress she owned for tonight.

At ten o'clock she pulled up to the Ocean Street address about the same time her dad did. Before the two approached the house, they stood at the curb comparing strategies.

"I need your opinion on the foundation. Is it structurally sound? Does it have any cracks from past earthquake damage? That sort of thing. If you say it's a go then we'll hunt down Mr. Jennings at his nursery, bug him again about selling it."

John Dickinson took out a clipboard from his truck. "Got my list right here. If we get to look inside I'll check for signs of termites, mold and water damage, too."

"Check, check and recheck."

It wasn't until she looked up that she spotted Landon at the side of the house holding a tray of bedding plants while a woman knelt on the ground next to him spading the dirt.

"That's the owner," Julianne whispered to her dad.

"Looks like you're about to get your answer then," John stated. "Why would they be putting in plants now though?"

"I have a feeling it's what they do."

Julianne watched as the couple approached her van. "Mr. Jennings."

"Call me, Landon. And this is my wife, Shelby."

Shelby offered her hand. "Good to meet you. I understand from Landon you want to see inside. Come on, follow me. We'll show you what you're up against."

As she followed the couple up the path, she introduced them to her dad. "I've got the best carpenter in Santa Cruz right here."

"You'll need it," Landon muttered as he led the way up to the rickety porch. "Needs work but there's no termite damage. What you see is due to age."

The four walked into the living room.

The dust and grime made Julianne sneeze. But the bare, arched windows let in a wash of natural light and that meant only one thing. She wouldn't be living in a dungeon. It caused her to overlook the layer of grime on the hardwood floors.

As they stepped into the living room, John told his daughter, "If you're worried about the floors, we can sand and refinish the living room and bedrooms. The staircase needs some upgrading, new wood in places. Won't take all that much to get them back to the original wood."

Working their way into the kitchen, she sized up the room, walked off the square footage. "These pine cabinets would have to go. They date the place."

"We could replace this tile covering with the slate flooring I picked up on sale before Christmas at that salvage place. It'd work in here as an inexpensive alternative. You know the one. It has a nice copper look to it."

"But Pop, you were saving that for your vacation house."

"Like I'll ever have time to loiter around a vacation house," John pointed out. "It's yours if you want it. I'm happy to donate it to my daughter's first home," he said with a grin. "And I have boxes of travertine that will give that patio a nice European feel."

She threw her arms around her dad's neck. "Oh Pop, have I told you lately how much I love you?"

John grinned. "Not lately. You're overdue, baby girl."

"You really do want this house then?" Landon asked.

"Pop? What do you say? Is it in relatively good shape? Enough that we could renovate it."

"Why don't you talk to Mr. Jennings here while I go nose around the foundation. I'll let you know in a few."

Left alone with the owners, Julianne said the only thing she could think to say. "I'm sorry about your sister, Landon."

"That's nice of you to say. Eleanor was a very troubled woman for a good portion of her life going back all the way to her teen years."

"I'm sorry," she said again.

"We took the kids in...after it happened," Shelby offered. "Cooper, Drea and Caleb were naturally devastated. Caleb less so because he was so young at the time. You work with young children so you understand we had to get them counseling."

"Good call. Some relatives would resist that necessary step. I'm sure the children benefited from the wisdom of your decision. Are they upset at the thought of selling it?"

Shelby glanced at Landon. It was Landon who quietly said it all with one word. "No."

About that time her father came back in through the back door and announced, "The foundation is solid, no cracks except the usual for a house this old in earthquake country. I'd say if Mr. Jennings agrees this would make a fine house for a first-time buyer."

"What do you say, Mr. Jennings? Shall we talk price?"

"For years now I think this house has been a source of embarrassment to my children. That's right, Shelby and I consider these kids ours. As I see it, we have two choices. Tear the place down and leave the lot vacant or sell it to someone who wants to fix it up."

Julianne found herself holding her breath until Landon finally tossed out a price. She could tell it was low by the way her dad's eyes got bigger as he stood behind Landon. Countering his already ridiculous low price would only embarrass them all. Looking straight into her father's dark brown eyes, she understood his expression meant it was a go. She stuck her hand out to Landon. "Fantastic. You have a buyer."

"There's just one condition."

Her heart sank. There always had to be a condition. "What's that?"

"You have to paint the exterior some color other than the sickening pink."

"Really? That's your condition? Um, okay. Sure. I'd planned to repaint the outside eventually anyway. So that's not a problem. Does that mean we have a deal?"

"How about we sign the papers next week?"

Julianne couldn't help it. In her excitement she jumped into Landon's arms. She then turned to her father, hugged him wildly back and forth. Shelby was next.

"Pop, do you believe it? I'm about to become a homeowner."

"I know, baby. That's my girl."

For Ryder the Saturday work at the school consisted of helping to haul out the week's demolition mess to the on-site dumpsters. The stuff for recycling went into a different bin. Come Monday morning they would begin hanging the new sheetrock.

After slogging up a sweat for several hours, they broke for lunch at twelve-fifteen. He went over, sat down beside Troy so they could take their break together.

"What kind you got today?" Troy wanted to know as he opened the baggie and took out a tuna fish sandwich.

"Baloney and cheese."

"Used to love baloney until I had to eat it every single day. Most days, cheese was a luxury."

"Yeah, I know how that is."

"You do? But you were in the military."

"You ever chow down on an MRE? After eating a crapload of those you learn to block out the taste of any processed food and make the best of it, especially if you're hungry."

Ryder noticed Troy shoot a glance in Zach's direction. The two men had been avoiding each other all day. "Is Zach still giving you a hard time about asking out his sister?"

"Some. But I asked Bree to dinner on Sunday anyway. She must've mentioned it to him."

"Good for you."

"I'm a little nervous about it."

"The date? Hey, don't let Zach intimidate you."

"It isn't that."

"Then what? From what I hear you and Bree go back a ways, to grade school together. You already know each other. It isn't like a blind date where you sit there squirming in your seat to pull out a few excruciating details just to fill the void of conversation."

Troy laughed. "That's true. The thing is Bree's going to college to better herself, been going almost two years now. This May she'll graduate with an associate's degree in computers. She'll probably head off to Santa Cruz or Santa Clara to get a better job. Me? I'm just a guy who works with his hands, a man who loves woodworking, and this." He spread his arms wide to take in the scene around him. "I love to refurbish old buildings. This whole town, I figure there's a lot of that in its future."

"Like the museum? The old strip merchant storefronts along Main Street?"

"Exactly. You and I both know I'm not going anywhere else. Bree is."

"I see. So you're saying you don't think you're good enough to be with a woman like Bree?" Ryder thought of Julianne. He could relate to Troy's misgivings. Hadn't he thought the same thing about starting anything up with the schoolteacher? Why would a woman like Julianne be interested in being with a construction worker? "There are jobs in Santa Cruz and Santa Clara," Ryder pointed out.

"But I like it here. I've established myself with

Logan. I don't want to start over anywhere else."

"Then you should probably make that clear before you take it to the next step. It's funny you should mention the way you feel. Because—"

"You're attracted to Julianne Dickinson," Troy finished for him.

"No, I'm not," Ryder stated. But in the same breath of denial, he noted the disbelieving look on the younger man's face. "Hell, was it that obvious?"

"Not to anyone else, no, but when you were showing her the plans for the remodel, there was a whole lot of…chemistry between you two."

"I'm staying away from women in general."

Again, Troy saw the humor in Ryder's words. "You're kinda young to be swearing off women, if you don't mind me saying so."

"I got burned by one toxic female. I don't intend to make that mistake ever again."

"At least you didn't get accused of killing one."

This time Ryder chuckled. "Okay, you've got me there. But if I ever find this particular woman, I might be tempted to make sure she never does the same thing she did to me to anyone else."

"I don't know the details and you don't have to tell me. But the thing is I can't see Ms. Dickinson doing a number on anyone. She doesn't fit the manipulator or user mold. She comes across like a nice person. They wouldn't want her as principal if she wasn't."

Ryder lifted a shoulder. "I'm sure you're right about that. What do I know about school stuff anyway? Until last week I hadn't set foot inside a classroom since I was eighteen, never even went through the doors of a college or university and I show up here to rehab this place—"

"Looks like we have something in common then."

Ryder slapped Troy on the back. "You're saying I shouldn't let the fact that Julianne's educated keep me from asking her out? Is that it? Okay, I'll make a deal with you. You don't let what you do for a living stand in your way with Bree and I won't let it stand in the way of mine. How's that?"

"Sounds like a plan because the women we're interested in are hot."

"They are that. But in matters of the heart, when it comes down to attraction, I don't think how much schooling a person has means a damn thing or at least it shouldn't."

"So does that mean you're going to Julianne's party?"

"Yeah. I'll have to move my ass to get home, do the milking, finish some paperwork, and then cleanup. Now that we've had this heart to heart, I wouldn't miss it."

"I wish Bree could come. She's working tonight though."

"After it's done, stop by the bar as her shift is ending. Timing is everything. Take her a plate of food leftover from the party."

"That's a great idea. Who knew you were such a thoughtful, romantic guy, Ryder?"

"Yeah, I'm a real prince." He'd forgotten how it felt to look forward to an evening out. He needed to dust off his manners and his ability to impress a woman—because as he saw it, he had some time to make up for.

That evening, as soon as Ryder walked through the door at Promise Cove, the size of the crowd blew him away. He'd heard rumors all week about the entire town getting an invitation. But for the first time he understood what that entailed and how it played out for real. The house that had been so calm and serene the night before when he'd sat down to dinner was now a sea of faces, some familiar, some not. They filled the house with laughter and chatter. So many that he wondered who was left to mind the store or rather the stores. He knew that McCready's was still open because Troy had mentioned

Bree had to work her regular Saturday night shift. But other than that he couldn't bring to mind a single business that didn't have someone here in attendance. The mayor and owner of Murphy's was in a heated discussion with Ross Campbell, the proprietor of Coastal Pharmacy about who was the best hockey goalie, Patrick Roy or Tony Esposito.

Bypassing that dispute, he nodded in the direction of the veterinarian Bran Sullivan, who'd soon retire letting Keegan and Cord take his place. He walked by a group he recognized from the Fanning Marine Rescue Center. Pete Alden was trying to prevent Russell Dennis from hitting on their sunny blonde coworker, Abby Anderson.

He said hello to Janie Pointer, the owner of the Snip N Curl, who'd cut his hair last month. He exchanged small talk with his work buddies, Zach Dennison and Drake Boedecker, before running into the mystery writer, Ethan Cody.

"In my spare time I'm reading your latest book. I'm halfway into it and haven't yet decided who the bad guy is."

Ethan grinned. "That's what I like to hear. Let me know if I start getting predictable."

"Not in this one you don't. Is there really a treasure lost off the coast around here?"

"You bet. This place used to be a smuggler's den. There are all kinds of cargo ships that hit the rocks around the area and broke up. Who knows what treasure lies out there in the bay. Be sure to ask Nick about exploring the little island off the cove here."

"That sounds like fun. Wish I had more time to do that," Ryder said as he spotted Troy guarding the buffet. After excusing himself, Ryder headed toward the feast on the dining room table.

"Should've known I'd find you around the food."

"Try one of these pastry things," Troy offered, pointing to the sausage pinwheels. "Jordan calls them canapés. They're tiny but tasty. Did you get a beer?"

"Not yet," Ryder said, picking up a paper plate and filling it with an assortment of appetizers. He'd barely gotten the words out of his mouth when his host handed him a bottle of summer ale.

"How's it going?" Nick asked.

"Good. Nice turnout for the teacher."

"Isn't it though?"

"Ethan was just telling me about an island around here."

"It's known affectionately as Treasure Island, not much to it though, but it's a must-see for a newcomer or a boatload of tourists. You want to go out sometime, let us know. We added another dinghy so more than one guest can launch from the cove below the cliff. Both have motors. The skiffs will get you there and back without a problem."

Ryder noticed Troy looked like he was deep in thought. "What're you thinking?"

Troy scratched his chin. "That maybe Nick might need someone to ferry guests back and forth during the busy season."

"We've been thinking about bringing someone on to do just that. Many of our guests aren't experienced with boats, yet they want to visit the island they can see from their rooms. Add in the fact that Ethan made the shipwreck famous in his book and we've created interest. It'd be great if someone could take advantage of the opportunity and start a cottage industry. These days the bank has changed. I'm always looking to provide opportunity to the locals. You know anyone?"

"I might." Troy was thinking about Bree and what she could do after graduation. It might prevent her from moving off to the big city. "What would something like that pay?"

"Pay? They'd own their own excursion business. For the right person, the bank would front the money for startup."

"A business loan?" Troy said, intrigued by the idea.

"That's right. In addition to trips to Treasure Island and the shipwreck, they could add to their services by taking tourists on hikes around the area. During the summer months, we have dozens of guests asking who in town can take them sightseeing. We routinely have to turn them down. Jordan and I are just too busy to act as tour guides. But there's money to be made in the effort."

"So it would be full-time?"

"Definitely a full-time proposition, although the load would taper off somewhat during the winter months, like now. The right person, a go-getter, could make enough money during the busy season."

"Anyone have claims on one of those rafts tomorrow?" Troy wanted to know. "I'd like to take Bree over to the island."

"I'll write it down in the reservation book." Looking around the room, Nick asked both men, "Have you seen our guest of honor yet?"

Ryder had purposely not wanted to ask where she was. But Nick had no sooner gotten the words out of his mouth when Julianne walked into his range of view. Across the room, she was in a conversation with two other women he recognized as Hayden Cody and Keegan Bennett.

As if she knew he was thinking about her, Julianne looked right at him. The classy little black dress she had on didn't exactly bring to mind the word, "schoolteacher." In fact, the outfit had him realizing how long it had been since he'd had a woman. It was hard to believe the vision in front of him making her way through the throng had anything to do with teaching first grade. He imagined slipping the sexy fabric off her shoulders and nibbling his way up to the velvet choker she wore around her neck.

"Ryder, are you okay? Your face looks sorta funny," Julianne said once she reached him. She took his face in one hand, the one that wasn't holding a glass of white wine and turned it side to side. "Do you need water?"

Did he? He wasn't sure of anything at the moment. His mouth did feel dusty as a ball of lint. He finally untied his tongue so he could string a few words together. "You look amazing."

"Thanks. I feel amazing. Look at this gathering. I'm not sure I've ever had anyone throw me this kind of party with this kind of turnout." She grabbed his arm. "Landon agreed to sell me the house on Ocean Street. It should close in a couple weeks."

She ticked off a list of things that needed the most work. "You wouldn't believe how many people in this room have offered to help me fix it up." Leaning closer, she murmured, "I heard a rumor that Perry Altman's new partner is thinking about opening a winery here in town."

"I heard it was a brewery," Ryder added with a wink.

Troy chuckled. "You know what I'd like to open?"

"What?"

"I'd like to make my own line of surfboards, sell them out of a little shop along the waterfront."

Ryder took a sip of his beer. "I'd open a boatbuilding business."

Intrigued, Julianne offered up a suggestion. "You both should talk to Nick then. During the week he's the banker and he's looking for people with a vision, a dream. You know, to bring new life into the town."

"Wouldn't do me any good," Troy lamented. "I'm not exactly rolling in dough."

Ryder slapped him on the back. "You and me both."

"Well, I still think both of you should talk to Nick. The people in this room make me realize there's such an overwhelming generosity of spirit here." She turned to Troy, slipped her free arm through his. "And this big guy tops the list. He's one of those who offered to help remodel my house."

"It's nothing," Troy said, self-conscious. "I'm not as busy as most other people are."

"Your offering to help is most definitely something. It's very thoughtful and kind. And I appreciate it."

To get the focus off himself, Troy changed the subject. "I heard Logan rented out the keeper's cottage at the lighthouse."

"Another newcomer? Cool, I won't be the only one now," Julianne reasoned. "When do they get here? Maybe they have children."

The temptation of a little gossip was too much for Troy. "It's a woman. And I don't think she has kids. She's a former ballet dancer. I heard she knows Logan from his travels in Europe, Rome I think. Or maybe it was Madrid. Anyway, I heard she wants to open a dance studio."

"Here in town? What a fantastic idea," Julianne said. "Oh, I hope she does. We could hold the recitals in the auditorium at school."

Ryder searched out the faces in the crowd to get a glimpse of his boss. "Where is Logan tonight?"

"Doc Prescott put Kinsey on bed rest until the twins arrive. That's what Hayden and Keegan were just telling me when I asked the same question."

Looking out into the faces of the crowd, she spotted Brent next to the piano with his wife. She leaned into Ryder and breathed, "There's something I need to talk to our police chief about. Want to come with me? It's about the box Troy found."

"Sure."

They got the horde to part like the Red Sea so they could get through to the living room. "Hi Brent, River," Julianne said in greeting. "When you get the chance I'd like to talk to you about that item you picked up the other night."

Brent nodded and directed the three to a more secluded spot where they could hear each other talk. They took off for the kitchen, gathered around the island. It was Brent who said, "I got the tests back from the lab yesterday. The fabric tested positive for human blood."

Julianne had expected as much. But it was Ryder who asked, "Any idea who this box might've belonged to?

Any unsolved murders in the area?"

"None that got reported. Besides, I'm not convinced a murder occurred. Yet. I'd say the key to solving this thing though is finding out who owns the box."

Julianne mulled that over. "Originally I thought it might belong to a child. But now… What circumstances would allow a child to have that kind of evidence in his possession? I shudder to even consider a situation like that. What will you do, Brent?"

"Keep checking it out until I find answers. In the meantime, I did discover in old town records that Andrew Richmond, the name on the property deed, used to own a hobby store on Main Street, specializing in trains. His son, Layne, worked for him. Layne Richmond just happens to be the husband of Eleanor Jennings."

"Whoa, really? That would make him the father of Cooper, Caleb and Drea Richmond or rather Jennings now."

"That's right. The thing is he ran off with a schoolteacher by the name of Brooke Caldwell. She taught third grade here back when the school was active. I'd like to tell you I'll be able to return the contents of the box to you…"

"But you can't," Julianne finished. "It's okay. When we discussed putting it on display we never considered it might be essential to solving a mystery."

"This whole thing's been driving Brent crazy for three days," River admitted.

Ryder looked at Brent. "Are you certain Layne Richmond ever left town? Because the deed is a direct connection to him. Why would it be in the box otherwise?"

"That was the gossip around town at the time. Layne and Brooke fell in love, ran off together. I'm going through records to check both of their socials and driver's licenses now. I won't offer any theories until I see if their social security numbers have been used over the years."

"All I know is this," River said. "I deal in old bones,

remains, and one look at that piece of shirt told me that whoever had it on lost his life wearing it. That's my gut feeling. My team's run across enough buried bodies before with tattered, bloody clothing either draping the bones or found nearby. That's what comes to mind with this shirt. Add to that, why would someone save a saturated piece of cloth like that? Saving it because of a bloody nose makes absolutely no sense to me unless that person died of it."

"Didn't the Zodiac killer do something similar?" Ryder offered. "Keep a bloody piece of cloth from one of his victims?"

Brent nodded. "Maybe I should sit down with Knudsen after all and see if he'll offer up any details."

"Wouldn't it be worth a conversation with him for that alone?" Julianne speculated. "The bloody shirt has obviously been in that box for years. Or… Could Brooke have done something to him? Maybe the man refused to leave his wife and the girlfriend got fed up with waiting—"

"Guessing won't do us much good," Brent interrupted. "At least not until I get a few answers. Who knows, maybe he and Brooke took off for parts unknown and live happily to this day on some island getaway?"

"But you don't really believe that, do you?" Ryder asked.

Brent grinned. "Not a word. But I have to consider all angles. I can't prevent gossip from popping up and adding to the equation though."

At that, Julianne turned to River. "It must be fascinating to do what you do, to travel all over the world to do it. The places you must've seen digging up old artifacts."

"I could show you slides from around the globe but you'd be bored within five minutes. Besides, my traveling days are over. Since we're wrapping up this dig on the dunes, all I'm waiting for are the permits to come in so that we can start renovating the building across from the marine center."

"I'll be the first one to line up for a tour. My grandmother on my mother's side was Chumash. She'd tell me fascinating stories about her ancestors, the way they lived and worked. Is it okay to come by the site sometime before you shut it down?"

"You bet. Stop by anytime."

After Brent and River disappeared through the swinging door to rejoin the party, Ryder captured Julianne's hand, tugged her out the back door to the terrace. Under the twinkling glow of stars, they walked along the garden path among budding lavender and jasmine.

"I didn't know your grandmother was Chumash."

"Santa Ynez Band. She was a teacher, too."

"Even though your father divorced her daughter…?"

"Pop encouraged me to visit her. My mother found her boring but I thought my grandmother was a treasure. Come to think of it, I guess my mother found most everything around here not to her liking, including the man she married and the little girl she left behind."

"Do you have any idea where she went?"

"Gran got a postcard from her from Florida about five years back, needing money, of course. Do you mind if we talk about something else?"

"Sure. You haven't once said a word about our kiss last night."

She sent him a roll of her eyes. "I didn't know I was supposed to alert the media. Like you, I relish my privacy."

"That's what I like to hear." He captured her waist, spun her into his arms. A breath away from her lips, he muttered, "If only we had music."

"I hum a mean rendition of *Somewhere over the Rainbow*."

"Excellent selection," he said, nuzzling her jaw.

They swayed back and forth to a Hawaiian beat until their mouths met, putting an end to the humming. A surge of heat speared its way upward as they found another kind of rhythm.

Abruptly, she ended the kiss. "I have to think about you."

"Why?"

"Because right now I need to get back inside. It seems rude that we're necking at my own party."

"I get the hint. We'll postpone this till after."

"Then what? Meet up in the parking lot? It's been a long time... Deal."

"Uh, Julianne?"

"Yes."

"I might need a minute."

She looked down, aimed her stare below his belt. "Ah. You're right. I'd better take point."

He grinned.

On her way back, Jordan intercepted her in the kitchen, handed her a napkin. "You might want to freshen up your lipstick."

Julianne felt her cheeks go pink—as if she were back in sixth grade and caught by a grownup playing spin the bottle. "I...we...were just getting some...fresh air. Is there anything I can do to help?"

She heard Jordan stifle a chuckle.

"Not a thing. I have Keegan and River making another pass with hors d'oeuvres."

"I can't thank you enough for welcoming me to town like this," Julianne said while taking out her compact to reapply her lip gloss.

"Nonsense. I love any excuse to throw a party."

"Come on, with the B&B to run, two active toddlers, guests to deal with, I'm aware this is a *very* big deal, especially since Nick's time during the week is spent at the bank in addition to splitting time on the town council."

"Like I said before, now is our slow season. As soon as business picks up in March, Nick steps back into the role of innkeeper—part-time at the bank. That was the deal he made with Murphy."

Julianne watched as Jordan neatly loaded up one tray with bacon-wrapped chicken bites, then another with coconut shrimp. "I'll take that. My turn to do more than lock lips with Ryder."

When the man walked in through the back door, she grinned at him, gathered up one platter, handed it off before grabbing the other. "Let's go feed the masses."

Carting food gave them both the opportunity to chat with the rest of the partygoers. Despite the fact the get-together was in her honor, she knew Ryder needed to circulate, too. So they made the rounds.

Their ears pricked up when they realized the buzz had turned to the discovery of the box along with its contents—so much for their attempt at secrecy. Who needed the Internet when news traveled like wildfire in a small town?

Some of the more senior guests, like Wade Hawkins, the retired history professor and member of the town council, began to reminisce about Andrew and Layne Richmond. Wade scrunched up his face, pondered the past. "I remember Andrew. He used to stock his hobby shop with train sets and a treasure trove of baseball cards. Walk in there and Andrew could tell you anything you wanted to know about batting averages and the Southern Pacific Railroad."

"Unusual blend of interests," Ryder remarked.

"Indeed it was but that was Andrew. He passed what he knew down to his son. Eleanor never seemed happy with the man she married. That woman could pick Layne apart in public like a vulture on roadkill and leave him humiliated."

Mayor Murphy nodded. "Now those two were an unusual pairing. Talk about opposites attract. I remember when word got out that Eleanor wouldn't even let him take a shower in his own home—people were rooting for Layne to leave the witch."

"Get out," Brent said. "I never heard that story. Are

you saying this man couldn't shower inside his home? The home he paid for? How could he put up with behavior like that?"

Bran Sullivan shook his head. "I don't know. That's the simple answer. But for the most part he put up with Eleanor's craziness because of the kids. Oh, every now and again he'd talk about getting out to his dad or to me or whoever would listen…"

"But then there were the times she'd go bat-shit crazy on him or the kids in a public place. Those incidents, no one could hide," Murphy added. "Couple of times Eleanor stole things from the store. I saw her do it myself."

"So no one was really surprised when she committed suicide?" Julianne ventured.

"Or that her husband took off?" Ryder posed.

"I never believed a word of it," Wade said. "Layne loved those kids too much to leave. That's why he put up with her crap. Cooper, Drea, and Caleb were his pride and joy. Eleanor knew that and used it to her advantage every single chance she could—did her best to turn those kids against their own father."

"My God, so she used her own children to keep him churning out the income, bringing his paycheck home to her? How miserable the man must've been," Julianne concluded.

"There has to be a way to check to see if Layne actually left town with Brooke, even if it has been twenty years," Ryder offered.

"And there is—databases to check, a cold trail to follow. If they're alive, I'll find them," Brent promised.

After the guests left Julianne walked Ryder out to his pickup as she had the night before. Feeling a bit sad on the heels of learning the details about Layne's unhappy life with Eleanor, she had a hard time letting the subject go. "Do you think it was wrong of him to get involved with Brooke when he was still married?"

"Wrong? Sure. But the man was obviously unhappy

living with a woman who wouldn't even show him the most basic respect. What do you suppose the kids thought of him? You know, when they saw how their own mother treated their dad like a dog in his own home? Did you know Bran told me Layne spent three years sleeping on the couch? I don't condone cheating, but that alone goes a long way to show Eleanor certainly wasn't committed to making the marriage work."

"Myrtle Pettibone told me it was common knowledge that Eleanor had a habit of shoplifting from every store in town. Eleanor wouldn't let the kids have any friends over and she constantly complained that her husband never made enough money. That's why she had to steal."

"Yeah, she showed all the classic signs of a control freak. Right now, my sympathy is lining up with Layne."

"Mine too."

He drew air deep and the wind rushed into his lungs. "There's a flea market over in San Sebastian. I thought you might like to go with me, check the place out. You might find something for your house or your business there."

"Oh Ryder. What a great idea! That reminds me. While we're at it, why not check out Cleef Atkins' place? Logan says it's the farm where everything from the school's been stored all these years. It's located south of town which means it isn't out of the way at all. Why not stop in, see what he has left from that time-frame?"

"You mean the stuff's been stored there all these many years?"

"Yep. We could decide for ourselves if any of it is worth bringing back, which would save a good chunk of the budget."

"That *is* Logan's mindset."

"Then it's a date."

He took her hand, drew her in, and nibbled a line down to her chin and to her lips.

"Mmm, I'd forgotten making out could feel so good."

"Here, let me see what I can do to make it feel even

better."

After the party broke up, Ryder wasn't the only one with a woman on the brain.

Troy took his advice and headed for town. He was waiting for Bree outside McCready's when she walked out the back door carrying a trash bag headed for the dumpster.

"What are you doing here?" Bree asked before spotting what Troy held in his hands. "You brought me food? From Ms. Dickinson's party? Oh my God, Troy, that is the sweetest thing anyone has ever done for me."

Troy chuckled. "Somehow I doubt that."

"No, really. I'm starving. I was headed home to eat a carton of yogurt or fix a peanut butter and jelly sandwich. What have you got there?"

"Crusted chicken tenders, some mini meatballs, spinach sticks, a few empanadas, and for dessert, a plateful of strawberries and chocolate sauce."

"There's enough food here to feed four people. I'll never be able to eat all this."

"You couldn't come to the party so I brought the party to you. At least a small sampling of all the appetizers. Jordan did mind me packing it up for you. Although they did run out of the mini lasagna cups."

"Where should we eat this? Back at my place or sit on the dock and watch the waves come in."

"You've been cooped up all night in that stuffy bar. I'd say the pier."

Bree stuck her arm through Troy's. "Excellent choice. It's a beautiful night. Why don't we take a walk?"

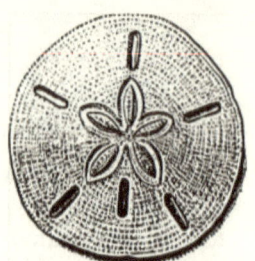

Chapter Eight

During the morning milking, Ryder began to let doubt seep in about the wisdom of asking Julianne to spend the day with him. Not because he didn't want to be with her. But as so often happened, when he thought of Bethany, it was like a layer of ice formed in his veins. It wasn't fair to Julianne that he wasn't ready to make a connection like that with another female. It didn't take much for his self-confidence to nose-dive, especially when it came to the opposite sex. He needed to ask himself some hard questions. Was he attracted to Julianne? Hell yes. What man breathing wouldn't be? But was he willing to risk his heart again? He thought about Layne Richmond.

"Layne was a great guy. He deserved better than Eleanor, that's for sure," Scott said out of the blue.

Startled, Ryder did his best not to show it. "You knew him?"

"Sure. I'd go into the shop to talk trains or trade baseball cards with him."

"See, that's what bothers me. How in the world do two people like Layne and Eleanor hook up and decide to stick it out and make each other miserable the entire time. I don't want that for myself."

"No one wants that."

"Didn't Layne have any idea she was so mean-spirited, let alone spoiled and self-indulgent, *before* he tied the knot?"

Scott cocked a brow at the question.

"I'm just repeating Ina Crawford's list of Eleanor's best-known personality traits. Ina talked my ear off last night."

"I suppose the why of it remains a question for the ages."

"I'm not in the mood for riddles."

"Okay. How's this? Layne used to be a teacher, a good one. He taught fifth grade. He was born to the role because he loved the classroom, connected with the kids. But too many years listening to Eleanor bitch made him give it up."

"Geez, did this guy ever stand up to her about anything? Let me guess. The crappy salary didn't sit well with Eleanor."

"That, plus the fact being a teacher wasn't as prestigious as touting that her husband was a business leader in the community, even if everyone knew it was Layne's father who actually owned the store."

"You knew Eleanor?"

Scott sighed. "Everyone knew the 'Pelican Pointe Princess' which is what we used to call her behind her back because of her snotty disposition. She had a habit of acting like she was royalty and better than everyone else."

Ryder found that funny. "I guess she forgot about her penchant for stealing."

"The five-finger discount wasn't her trademark."

"What was?"

"The shitty way she treated her husband. He deserved better."

"That's just sad, man. I would've walked. I don't know a man who wouldn't have. Why the hell didn't he leave? Who would put up with the constant verbal assault?"

"According to Layne, she'd threaten to hurt herself, threaten to hurt the kids, if he left. She had him played. He even mentioned to a friend that one night he packed his bags to leave. But Eleanor was having none of it. She actually woke the kids up at some ungodly hour, marched them downstairs like little soldiers, and told them that

Daddy was leaving and never coming back. The kids started to cry."

"Of course they did. She knew that. God, the woman was a major-league manipulator," Ryder decided. "That's a helluva pressure cooker to find yourself in on a daily basis and not be able to get out."

"The thing is Layne made even less money working for his father than he had teaching which led to even more fights."

"Ah. That probably just made her verbally abuse him all the more."

"The guy just couldn't seem to win with her, no matter what he did or how he tried to make her happy. As to why he stayed in that miserable living arrangement, Layne adored his children. He wanted to make absolutely certain they had a chance at success without the stigma of divorce."

"There are no guarantees in life, certainly not with kids. You want a guarantee buy a waffle iron," Ryder grumbled. "Two-parent homes are idyllic. Everyone's onboard with that. But some relationships can't be resurrected and shouldn't be. People make mistakes. They get with the wrong people. What are they supposed to do, stick it out? In my opinion, living in a verbally, physically abusive atmosphere hurts kids more because they end up thinking that's the way adults resolve their conflicts. Relationships like that are far more toxic to them than splitting custody."

"You speak from experience. Back then, I don't think you could get anyone in town to believe Layne and Eleanor were ever a good match."

"That's just sad. So why didn't she let Layne go? And why didn't he stand up for his kids? Don't give me that crap about the stigma of divorce. Those kinds of people usually assume kids like me are headed for prison because my parents split up. That's ridiculous thinking just because my parents chose not to share a home. From my perspective having to deal with a mother like Eleanor is what put the kids at risk in the first place. Not some archaic idea of living apart. And what about Eleanor's erratic behavior, her wild mood swings, and a lot of the other shit she pulled? Her antics had to stick with those kids for life. People should've taken that into account back then instead of tiptoeing around the problem."

"I'm with you there. That continual hostile environment between two adults couldn't have been good for the kids."

"Layne was obviously stuck. I actually feel for the guy. But why should the sane parent have to put up with a mean-spirited spouse because of some antiquated label? And why stick a label on the poor kids as failures before they have a chance at life, at proving anyone wrong? What about the kids who lose a parent to war? Is that okay to raise kids in a one-parent home? Or car accidents? What about cancer? Cancer takes its toll and leaves plenty of kids with only one parent. How about heart attacks? I lost my dad to one. After that, I just had my mom. She never remarried. Was she supposed to walk down the aisle just so she could say, 'okay, now Ryder has a father figure in his life.' Was I scarred because I grew up with only one parent? I don't think so. Some circumstances are simply beyond a father's or a mother's control. Yet kids from divorce are considered at risk. Why is that?"

"You're angry."

Ryder ran both hands through his hair, realized he was livid. "Damn right I am. It irritates me when I hear couples say they'll stick it out for the sake of the kids. I remember my parents fighting about everything. I've spent time as a soldier in a war zone and felt less static. But after the divorce the calm settled in. I might've had to shuttle between two homes but it was a damn sight better than listening to them hate on each other. Even at five years old I knew neither one was happy."

"That's why you're having second thoughts about Julianne?"

"Not at all. I need to get my head clear of Bethany first, that's all." The silence that generated had him looking up at Scott. "Okay, maybe there's still a degree of trust issues with me."

"You can't possibly believe Julianne is anything like Bethany?"

"No, but look at Layne Richmond. Did he know he was marrying a bitch upfront? I doubt it. Did she turn into one after the ceremony ended? Maybe. Was he a dickhead and that's what turned her into the wife from hell? All I'm saying is there's a chance Julianne might be hiding the fact she's a despicable human being, hiding her true self."

Scott gave him a hard look. "That's total bullshit and you know it."

"Yeah. I do. I'm crazy about Julianne. That's why I hope to God she isn't hiding an Eleanor Jennings persona behind that adorable face."

Next door at the B&B, an eager Julianne had no idea Ryder was having misgivings about them spending the day together. Had she known, she might have been tempted to call the whole thing off. Instead, she ate an egg and veggie omelet on the terrace, lingering over her third cup of coffee as if she had all the time in the world—no traffic to deal with or rush to reach her class.

That's why she took the opportunity to take a leisurely pass under the blossoming magnolias, picked a few drooping daisies that had not fared well in the coastal wind. This weekend had accomplished one thing. It put to rest any remaining doubt about the move. She couldn't wait to put down roots here.

As she headed upstairs to get ready for her date, she tried to figure out how long it had been since she'd gone out with anyone. As she put on her makeup, she counted the months. It had been last summer when Brian Kramer, a math teacher, had asked her to go to a local music festival held on the boardwalk. She couldn't remember why that had been their only date. Then it hit her. Brian had had an odd habit of droning on about movie facts, probably trying to impress her. It hadn't worked. Even his voice had grated on her. Then, there had been Ron something-or-other around Christmas. Ron had taken her to dinner. He'd been eerily quiet over his fish until they'd gotten back to the car where he'd developed a serious case of octopus hands. Ugh.

She heard her cell phone ding with a text message.

Pulling up in front now. Ready?

Yep. On my way down.

The minute he caught sight of her in a mint-green knit dress, his uncertainty faded.

After she clicked her seatbelt in place, he smiled and said. "Just so you know, I took your advice and contacted CID. I was surprised when they told me what happened to me occurs on a fairly regular basis to many soldiers. They added her fake name to a database they keep on people who run scams on service members. On the off-chance she uses a variation of that, they might get a hit."

"See, you have to cover all the angles. I'm thinking of doing something crazy."

"If it involves you wearing whip cream and a black teddy, I'm in."

Julianne threw back her head and laughed. "That could be arranged."

"Really? I'm there already. How crazy do you want to get?"

"I was thinking of poking my nose into who owns that box. While Brent does his thing, I'm thinking of starting with what we know."

"We know it has some connection to the Richmonds. Otherwise why would the deed be inside?"

"Good, we're on the same page there. I say we slide the bar over to the Jennings family. A Richmond married a Jennings. That alone gives us a point of reference. I say, when I close on the house, we go through it for anything that might indicate who owns the box. Are you game?"

"Or, here's a thought, we could just ask one of the kids or both."

She grinned. "Definitely the more direct approach. I like it. Jordan told me this morning Drea owns the florist shop. I could stop in, even though I don't think a girl owned that box. I could be wrong of course. But I could go in, browse, then ask her using your direct approach, get to know her, tell her something about me. Maybe she'd open up enough, see how it goes and then get her to tell me about her older brother, Cooper."

"Meanwhile, I could approach Caleb. I see the guy around town at least every other day making deliveries or working at the garden center in some capacity or another. We've always stuck to safe subjects like the weather and seedlings. It might be interesting to get his take on how he grew up."

"Then it's a plan."

"If that's your idea of crazy though, I'm a little disappointed."

"You were envisioning the whip cream and black teddy." She lifted her eyebrows up and down. "I've been known to work with both."

"Now you're just getting me hot and bothered. And while I'm driving no less."

She ran her finger down the side of his cheek up to his ear. "It's mean of me, huh?"

Ryder thought of Layne and all the crap Eleanor had dished out over the years. "If that's the meanest thing you ever do, I'd be shocked."

"I'll work on my darker side, how's that?"

"As longer as darker equates to hot and sweaty sex instead of mean or mentally unstable…"

"Oh, Ryder. You're thinking of Eleanor and Bethany now. Stop it. My dark side consists of a temper now and again just like everyone else. I'm not a menacing person, not even very mysterious. I'm just a regular person."

Trying not to take his eyes off the road, he found her hand, squeezed it in his. "That's me, too. Scott showed up this morning."

"Really? How'd that turn out?"

"I'm beginning to get a better handle on the guy."

"How so?"

"For one, he gave me insight into Layne." Ryder went into an account of their conversation. He noted the stricken look on her face. "What's wrong?"

"I'm having second thoughts about approaching Drea because I'm convinced Layne and Brooke never left town."

"Wow, where did that come from? Why would that pop into your head?"

"The most obvious reason of them all. Layne would never leave his kids behind with Eleanor. Everyone said so last night. I don't know why it didn't occur to me until now."

Ryder mulled that over. "I'm suddenly getting a sick feeling in my gut. If the couple didn't leave town, then where are they?"

"That's the number one question these days."

About that time, Ryder pulled into the lane leading to the Atkins farmhouse. Junk lined the rutted pavement—two rusted-out Chevys, a slew of old tractor tires, broken discarded furniture sat among knee-high weeds. It looked like a rural version of *Sanford and Son*.

"This is where our desks have been stored?"

"Looks like."

The man who greeted them looked as ancient as the barn itself. But there was a smile plastered across his worn face as if he was happy to have the company.

"You the folks that called about the stuff I salvaged from the school?"

"That's us," Ryder replied.

"I'm Cleef Atkins. Glad to meet you. Hear you're reopening the place up, 'bout time."

Julianne introduced herself. "We're interested in anything you have left that's in good enough condition that we might be able to reuse or repurpose."

"I got it all, desks, chalkboards, lockers, light fixtures, water fountains, you name it, I kept it. My son and I hauled it out of there ourselves. Nobody wanted the stuff till now, although I did sell the display case to a retail shop over in San Sebastian five years back or so."

Cleef slid open the barn door. "Been gathering dust all these years, that's why I'm in a position to make you a good deal on all of it."

Julianne looked around at the treasure trove of antiques amassed floor to ceiling. Sneezing in rapid succession while turning sideways to make it through the labyrinth of furniture, she called out, "Ryder, you need to see this."

He followed the trail she'd blazed through the jumble of junk upfront to get to the back and the reason they'd made the trip. There, in the massive vault of barn, the old desks were lined up and stacked on top of each other, hundreds of them.

Spotting the nest of desks, Julianne said, "Look at this, two different kinds. The one-piece units are for the upper grades, fifth and sixth. The single desks with chairs are used in kindergarten through fourth grade. Most are in good shape. The legs might need recoating but it beats blowing the budget on new. Nick and Logan will be delighted."

"The tops could be replaced with new wood or Formica."

She ran her fingers across the finish where the kids had gotten creative with carving their initials into the grain. "How old do you think some of these desks are? Looks like they reused items from the fifties. The teachers' desks are even older. But that's okay. There's nothing wrong with refinishing them."

"Some of this stuff has no doubt been around since I went to school," Cleef said aiming a grin at both of them.

"So the plan is to use what we have here?" Ryder asked.

"I think it's the best use of the money." She turned to Cleef to get ready to bargain. "What's your asking price?"

Cleef tossed out a figure.

"That's your idea of a good deal?" Julianne shook her head and threw out a much lower number.

The old farmer countered.

Ryder stood back and watched a master negotiate to hammer out the deal.

"Don't forget all this has been sitting here gathering dust all this time. If we walk away, what chance do you ever have of unloading the lot of it? And it's for the kids," Julianne reminded him before posing what she considered a fair price.

Cleef chewed on his lip before admitting, "Anyone ever tell you that you're a tough wrangler? You've got a deal."

Julianne responded by throwing her arms around the old man's shoulders with such force she almost knocked him back a step. "Yes, but they usually don't hold it against me. I want you to promise me you'll come to the open house. Mark your calendar."

Embarrassed by the display of affection, Cleef shuffled his feet, turned to Ryder. "You got yourself a spirited female here."

Ryder's lips curved up before he slapped a hand on the old man's back. "I don't know what kind of man doesn't appreciate a spirited woman." He took out his cellphone. "If it's a done deal then I'll make the call to Logan. Give him a cost estimate to refurbish what we have here."

While Ryder made his call, the three drifted back outside into the sunshine.

"Someone said that the Jennings family used to own a spread around here. Is that true?" Julianne asked, not wanting to admit she'd already looked up the information online in county tax records.

"Sure, I knew Euell Jennings for years, grew up together. These parts it'd be hard to find an old-timer like me who didn't. As a matter of fact, his ranch was a couple miles down the road from mine."

"Is it still there? The ranch, that is."

"House is, but not any of the other buildings. As I recall a couple moving here from Los Angeles bought the place, decided to demolish everything but that mansion. Growing up, his family and mine went to the same church. Torn that down too though, a shame. I miss that old church. Anyway, his kids and mine were classmates. Euell and I remained friends. That is, up until the day he died."

"You must have known Landon and Eleanor pretty well."

"Oh, I did indeed. Landon had a good disposition. Now Euell's daughter, Eleanor, was a whole other story."

"We've heard stories that she was a real piece of work."

"That's because she was. Rumors floated around that the girl was the one who took the rifle out to the barn that morning." Cleef leaned closer. "Killed her own father, girl was just mean enough to do it, too."

"You really believe that?"

"I know for a fact she was so out of control at the age of fifteen, Euell didn't know what else to do so he sent her away to one of those rehab places you hear about on TV. You ask me, didn't do a damned bit of good. She said all the right things to get out. Then when she got back to Pelican Pointe, she came back madder than a dozen hornets and twice as devious. She was only sixteen. Try to imagine what she was like by the time she latched on to Layne."

"She learned to play the system," Ryder acknowledged.

"By that time she'd perfected her act."

"You bet," Cleef agreed with them both, scratching his stubbly chin. "I always suspected she tricked Layne into marriage."

"How?"

"She just wanted to get hitched. Said all the right things but didn't mean a single word that came out of her mouth. That was Eleanor."

"She sounds like a real phony."

Once Ryder and Julianne got on their way, a silence hung in the air until Julianne said, "Should we tell Brent about what Cleef just told us?"

"Even if it's true, what good would it do? Eleanor's dead. How would we prove she was the one who shot her father and made it look like a suicide? There's no way."

"I don't know but I really think Brent needs to have all the facts at hand. How can he solve this thing unless he knows all the deets?"

Seeing the troubled look on her face, he took her chin. "Change in plans. The clock is ticking on your getaway weekend. You have to checkout at the B&B this afternoon, right?"

"You know I do."

"Then let's do something spontaneous and fun."

She looked over, saw his eyes glow with a devilish gleam. "Like what?"

"Are you up for an adventure?"

"I suppose. As long as it's legal and I'm back in class by tomorrow morning."

"Ever heard of Treasure Island?"

"Of course, Robert Louis Stevenson's classic."

"According to Nick, we have our own right here. How would you like to go there and laze away the afternoon?"

"We've plenty of time to explore the area," Ryder assured her as they trudged down the steep set of steps to get to the Cove below the cliffs. "Besides, while you were upstairs changing into jeans, Jordan said not to worry about getting in a hurry to check out. There's no rush."

"Jordan shouldn't have put together the picnic basket. That was too much. Everyone's been so great to me this weekend. I'm almost sad to go back to Santa Cruz."

"But you'll soon be here full-time, able to enjoy everything the place has to offer."

"Look at this," Julianne said when they reached the sandy beach below. It was everything she'd heard about and more. The stretch of pristine beach hidden away from the tops of the bluffs was a prime sample of what set the B&B apart from others along the coast. With the rock wall as a backdrop, sugary sand met up with lapping sea.

"According to Nick they keep the ketch tied up in the cave over there."

They spotted the motorized lifeboat and dragged it to the launch. He helped her in before climbing aboard, started the motor.

Within the first few minutes the choppy sea had her wishing she'd stayed on shore. The up and down motion made her wish she hadn't eaten breakfast hours earlier. They hadn't gotten far when Ryder picked up on the way she looked.

"You okay?" he asked, noting her grayish pallor.

"I'm a bit queasy."

"You should've said something. I didn't know you'd get seasick. It never occurred to me. I never would've suggested this."

"It's okay. I guess I got caught up in the adventure of the moment."

"We'll be there in a few minutes. Can you stand it for that long? Or do you want me to head back?"

"No, let's keep going. I want to see this place."

She didn't look okay, Ryder decided. But he could see the shoreline within sight so he continued on, all the while the little raft bounced over foamy whitecaps. Once they reached the shallow inlet, he tossed the mushroom anchor into the water to moor them as close to the little sliver of island as he could get.

Hopping out, he lifted her up out of the boat. Hugging her to his chest, he trekked through the waves and up the beach to the hilly terrain.

Her feet touched down on ground more rock than sand. Knee-high bunchgrass mixed with fragrant white sage, and eucalyptus peppered the tiny island landscape. Mosaics of bright poppies and blue storm mingled with perennial herbs. Budding California blackbrush fought for turf among hardy huckleberry. Looking around at the coastal shrub, she saw California quail nestled among the grassland.

"I'm not sure what I was expecting but this is downright primitive."

"Are you okay?" He took her by the shoulders, lifted her chin to peer into her eyes. "Your color's better. You aren't as pale as you were before. Weren't you ever a girl scout?"

"Yes, but I excelled more at meeting my cookie quotas rather than camping or sailing."

"Really? So you're not the outdoorsy type."

"I love the outdoors. I just never considered myself much of a wilderness freak or sailor. I'm more the lifeguard type who sits on the beach and blows my whistle when there's a problem."

He laughed. "So you don't surf?"

"Sure I do. I'm a California girl, a regular Sarah Gerhardt."

"Who?"

"Sarah's famous. She's the first woman to conquer Mavericks, the spot around Half Moon Bay, the Mount Everest of big waves with nasty breaks. Sarah used to teach, chemistry, I think. You don't surf?"

"Not yet, but I'm willing to have you teach me."

"It's a deal. Too bad we didn't bring a board."

Once they got settled near a stony wash, Ryder spread the blanket next to a circle of stones. The fire pit would come in handy for overnight stays. Too bad they were only there for the afternoon.

Surrounded by the lapping water, Julianne dug into the picnic basket, brought out a bottle of Shiraz. "Can you believe all this stuff Jordan packed?" She set out leftovers from last night's party—cheese, crackers, cucumber salad, bite-size quiche, cold chicken and pesto.

Stretching her legs out, her hands out in back, she tilted her face up to the sun.

Watching her, something inside him clicked.

He dropped beside her, raked his fingers through her hair and tugged it to get her to roll into him. It didn't take much for her to respond. Their interest in food vanished replaced by attraction, need, heat.

Ryder forgot about the unforgiving ground and urged her to crawl on top.

She inched her way to his body, hovered over his face. Their lips met, hunger ramping up. His hands roamed down her back, gripped her butt.

From the sandbank, they heard voices, laughter. Both realized about the same time they weren't alone.

In a split second, she banked her passion, rushed back into the present. She rolled to the side. "I recognize that voice."

A flicker of annoyance flashed over Ryder's face. He flopped on his belly, scooted so he could pop his head up around a patch of wild buckwheat to get a look at the spot where they'd left the boat.

"It's Troy and he's with Bree. Looks like we have company."

"Damn, that is *so* not right."

Troy and Bree had spent the morning sending text messages back and forth which had Bree agreeing to come early enough so they could row over to Treasure Island before they ate supper. But Troy had a surprise in store.

He'd spent his Sunday prepping the apartment for Bree's visit, doing all the necessary chores he'd neglected during the week—dishes and clothes tended to pile up. He took out the trash, dusted, and changed the sheets on the bed. He piled up all the dirty laundry, tossed it into a basket and took it to the main house for washing.

He'd done all that before Bree drove up in her Chevy Cavalier.

As soon as she got out, he'd met her at the bottom of the steps leading to the studio.

"Was Zach really upset about you coming here today?"

"Nah. He just doesn't like the idea of me dating. Period. Especially since Dad died. It seems he's appointed himself my substitute father."

"Has he always been this possessive?"

"Not at all. That seemed to come with the stand-in father thing once he got back home from Colorado. We've discussed his overprotective attitude before. What did you fix me for dinner?"

"I hope you aren't disappointed but I put together a picnic basket. I thought it'd be a surprise for when we get to the island. But I do have to lug the thing to the boat."

"Why would I be disappointed? A picnic on the island sounds so romantic!" She threw her arms around his neck to prove it.

"Jordan suggested I cut the crust off the bread. It makes the sandwiches look more like finger food, so I did."

"Why Troy, that's so fancy. If I remember correctly, you like the outdoors, like to surf? Could we finagle a surfboard in the boat?"

"Already have a short board picked out. We'll have to take turns though. And I know you like the water."

"Hey, remember our senior trip? We went down to San Diego and spent all that time surfing at Swami's."

"Good swells there. But what I recall most is you in a bikini. I particularly liked that red one you wore that set off your hair."

"How do you remember that? I got sunburned that trip, was so burned it hurt no matter how much aloe vera I slathered on. In fact, we both looked like lobsters—you with your pale skin and me with mine. That's what I remember."

"What do you plan on doing when you graduate in May?" Troy asked.

"That's a tough question. I might have to head to Santa Cruz or even San Jose to find work."

"What would you think about opening up your own excursion business?"

"What excursion business? How? I make tips, Troy? I don't have money to invest in—"

He cut her off. "Nick might need someone to ferry guests back and forth to visit the island during the B&B's busy season, take people out to that old shipwreck Ethan wrote about in his book, too."

"You're serious about this."

"Yeah, and so is Nick. He called it a cottage industry. You'd need a larger touring boat and a base but it could be a moneymaker."

"Wow, I'd have to think about it. I've taken business courses and all but I never once considered owning my own. So when do I get to see your apartment?"

"Later when we get back. I want to get going while we still have the light."

They'd toted the basket down to the Cove like the kids they'd once been. They had no way of knowing anyone else had already converged on their romantic island getaway.

The island was too small to go undetected for long. So Ryder decided to confront the issue head on. He made his way down the slope to shore. But Troy had already spotted the other dinghy bobbing in the water. Neither man could say they were overjoyed to see the other and spend their afternoon together.

"What are you doing here?" Ryder asked.

"Same thing you are," Troy returned. "This was my plan."

As disappointed as Troy felt, Bree was clearly in the other camp. At the thought of a get-together, her cheerful nature kicked in. She chatted away like a magpie. "What luck that you and Troy had the same idea. Great minds think alike. You must be here with Julianne. Perfect. We can combine our picnic baskets. It'll be like potluck."

"We're just up the hill there," Ryder directed Bree, who took off in a jog.

But Troy lagged behind and murmured, "You ripped off my idea. Admit it. You knew I planned to bring Bree here today and you beat me here."

Ryder blew out a guilty breath. "I guess I did. I forgot you called dibs. My fault. In my defense though, I wanted to show Julianne a nice afternoon before her weekend ended and she had to head back to Santa Cruz."

Troy adjusted his ball cap down over his curly hair, glanced up ahead where the two women were already chatting away and busy going through the food he'd brought. "It's too late now. We might as well make the best of it. But this is definitely not the afternoon I had planned out."

"Yeah, me either," Ryder uttered, following Troy up the embankment.

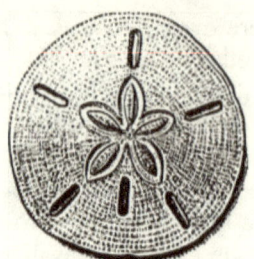

Chapter Nine

On Monday, Ryder worked under the sound of a steady rain as it pounded the new roof. The old tar and pitch composition had been the first thing to go last month. Since then they'd revamped it with a thin film coating and solar panels added for energy efficiency.

"This is the first good rain we've had since we started. A good test of workmanship," Logan told Ryder.

"How are we doing so far?"

"Stellar."

"How's Kinsey?"

Logan let out a huge sigh. "Who knew impending fatherhood would make me as nervous as an old hen scared witless that it's about to face the chopping block."

"That bad?"

"Worse, in less than two weeks I'll be the father to, not one, but two babies."

"Double the panic."

"And then some."

Paul Bonner came up to them, followed by Drake Boedecker. "Someone better get over there. Zach and Troy are about to go at each other's throats."

Ryder glanced over at the two men standing nose to nose inside the administration area. "You have enough to deal with," Ryder said to Logan. "As foreman, I'll handle this."

When he reached Troy and Zach, Ryder barked out, "What the hell is going on over here? This is not the time or the place for crap like this. You sign up to give a hundred percent to a job you do it as a professional, not act like two junior high brawlers. You two want to fight? Do it somewhere else other than this worksite. This is gonna end right here, right now, today, or I'll know the reason why. Do you both understand me?"

"Hey, ask Troy why Bree came home all excited last night about some stupid idea this jerk put in her head, some ridiculous notion that she could start an excursion business after she graduates community college in May. Of all the stupid…"

"It's not stupid," Troy stated. "It's a viable business option."

Ryder's mouth gaped open. "*This* is what you two are bickering about? You guys are unbelievable. For your information, Zach, I was there Saturday night when Nick told Troy the B&B could use that kind of commercial enterprise around here. Don't blame Troy for simply suggesting it to your sister."

"Really?" Zach said, dropping the attitude. "I just assumed he was bullshitting her to get her in the sack."

"You'll have to ask him about the why—on your own time. Let's back up a minute though. Zach, what exactly do you find wrong with Troy dating your sister?"

"Go on, tell him," Troy demanded in challenge. "Tell him you don't want *anyone* taking Bree out. Not me, not even if I had a million bucks in the bank would it matter. You don't want anyone going near your sister. Tell him."

"Is that true?"

Zach dropped his stare. "Yeah, I guess it is. Look, ever since our mom died, it's been up to me to see to it Bree was taken care of. Then when our dad passed away…I don't know…I guess…I don't want to think of her like that…with anyone."

Ryder relaxed his stance. "Okay. So what you're basically saying is that you have no real basis for the obstinate attitude you've had toward Troy? Is that about right?"

"Yeah, I guess."

"Does that mean you'll stop getting upset every time I talk to Bree?" Troy wanted to know.

"I'll try."

"Good," Ryder said. "Have we cleared the air then? Now, could we cut this bullshit between you two and get some work done around here?"

Later, the crew gathered at the back of the school near the shipping and receiving area to eat lunch and watch the rain come down.

"I wouldn't mind owning a business of my own," Paul said. "If I had the money I'd open up a bicycle shop. I like to fix them up and resell them."

"No bikes for me," Troy said and repeated his dream about making his own surfboards. "Wally Pierce collects the old wooden ones. He has them hanging up all over his garage. They're really cool."

"I don't even know how to surf," Ryder admitted. "But I still think I'd like to try and build a boat, make it sleek and fast, one of the wooden kind from long ago."

Zach turned to the man he'd been at odds with since the job began. "First chance we get we should show you how to surf," he suggested. "You can't truly call yourself a Californian until you've been up on a board at least once no matter what your driver's license says."

"Growing up here, learning to surf was like learning to walk," Troy agreed. "That's why I showed him a few moves yesterday. He didn't fall off…much."

But instead of ribbing Ryder, Zach latched on to what the boss had said. "Why would you tackle such a career like boatbuilding? Is there any money in that these days?"

Ryder stared off into the downpour. "The summer before my dad died, I was about nine. He took me to a camp for fathers and sons where the owners taught us how to construct boats, not big ones, but those miniature skiffs you see sailing on the little ponds or lakes. Then my dad died. After that my grandfather, on my mother's side, picked up the slack. Gramps was as an architect and loved building things in his spare time. It was one of the first times I remember really connecting to the man. Anyway, he saw to it that we went back over the years. And I enjoyed those days creating something with my hands. It's what I was meant to do."

"Why didn't you?" Troy asked.

"I went into the military instead."

Zach sat hunched with his hands dangling on his knees, considering that. "Did you know there used to be an old shop sandwiched between the fancy restaurant and the marine rescue center across the street from here that built sailboats?"

"That must've been way before my time," Troy cracked. "I don't remember it. The place was always empty."

"It was there," Zach insisted. "A Swede by the name of Gunnar Borgerstrom owned it. You used to be able to smell the fresh wood they used and put through the electric saws. My dad worked for him before the town dried up and the place closed its doors."

"So you have some idea how to build a boat?" Ryder asked, curious about the man who'd been a thorn in his side in some fashion since the entire project began.

"Not exactly. But I used to watch my dad work on the hulls. I think it'd be a pretty cool way to earn a living, if you ask me."

"That makes two of us," Ryder said, swallowing a bite of leftover pasta. "I wouldn't mind seeing the inside of that old storefront. If Nick really is open to making loans to new businesses, I wonder…"

But Zach's prickly nature surfaced. "Do you honestly think a man like Nick Harris would lend money to a couple of construction workers for a pipe dream?"

"I don't see why not. All he can do is tell us no."

"But making surfboards might be more practical, especially around here," Troy advised. But after thinking about it for a few minutes, he added, "If you do this, I want to be a part of it. I've been saving every penny I can scrape together."

"Then maybe we could combine the shops. Split it up into two ventures. We'd put out a line of surfboards long before we could ever make our first boat," Ryder pointed out.

"Not if we got our boat buyer up front. Although making surfboards might keep us afloat during the time we're in the design phase. Is this really feasible?" Zach wondered.

"It doesn't hurt to explore the possibilities," Ryder said, packing up his lunch. "But for now, it's time to head back to work."

The bad weather made for a long day without much of a break for her students. Because it had been Julianne's turn to supervise recess, which didn't take place outside due to the downpour, she'd spent her time maintaining order in the gym.

Now, as she sought to correct one of her more active pupils, a headache formed at both temples.

"Miles, remember to raise your hand each time you want to speak, okay?" Julianne reminded the fidgety six-year-old.

"Why?"

That one-word question had her believing the children were just as ready to call it a day as she was.

"So that I'll know you have something to say and I'll know to call on you so you can say it. Think about it. If everyone talked all at once without raising their hand, then I'd have trouble hearing them all at the same time, now wouldn't I? Do you understand?"

Miles bobbed his little head, but immediately shot out of his chair. "I have to go to the bathroom."

"Go ahead for now, but next time, remember to raise your hand." Her temples throbbed even more than the dull ache she'd had earlier. Even her eyelids were starting to hurt. It had been one of those Mondays that seemed never-ending.

When Rita Coffee, a third-grade teacher and potential recruit, tapped on her classroom door, Julianne went to answer it.

"You don't look good at all. Is my interview still on for three-thirty?"

Julianne rubbed at her forehead. "I'm sorry, Rita. I forgot all about it. I hate to do this to you but could we postpone this for a couple days. I'm not feeling well at all."

"Sure. You let me know because I'm so excited about starting at a new school."

When the blessed final bell rang at three o'clock, all Julianne wanted was to make it to her car and get home. Because of the rain, it took her longer to make a drive that usually took no more than ten minutes at the most. By the time she got home, her dress and shoes were soaking wet. She changed out of her clothes and into a pair of comfy PJs. She barely made it into the kitchen to put on a pot of tea before having to sit down. Cold, she carried her cup and saucer into the bedroom and crawled in between the sheets.

But by that evening, her fever started to shoot up along with a bout of chills and nausea. She supposed this was the downside to coming in daily contact with children. Knowing it couldn't be the flu because she'd had a flu shot, she fell asleep without identifying what horrible disease she'd contracted or which one of her thirty students had been the germ carrier.

After several of his text messages went unanswered, Ryder took the initiative and hunted down the street number for Julianne via Murphy. After learning she'd been sick, he decided he needed to do something.

It was six-forty-five by the time he pulled his F-150 up to the curb in front of a bungalow as cute as a button and about as small. The lawn was almost nonexistent but the flower beds were draped in deep colors of plum and gold. He'd done his share of landscaping back in Philly and knew from experience she'd made the most of her courtyard on a tight budget. She'd do a whole lot more with the house she planned to buy.

The windows were the old-fashioned crank kind and the front door was mostly glass.

He rang the bell and waited.

When the door flew back, he stood there staring at Julianne. Her hair was tousled. She wore cream-colored pajamas with bright pink and yellow flowers. The cropped top showed a smidgen of bare midriff. The bottoms were snug around her slim waist. But it was her eyes that showed the first indication she didn't feel well. They looked puffy, red, and glazed.

"Ryder, what are you doing here?" she croaked out. "I'm sick."

"So I heard, but I decided to see for myself." He held up the bag of provisions he'd picked up from Perry Altman's fancy restaurant called The Pointe. "My mother always said chicken soup is good for what ails a person, no matter if it's the flu or a cold or what. Chicken noodle soup puts you on the road to recovery."

"But I could be contagious."

"I never get sick. Don't I get to come in?"

"Oh. Sure." She swung the door wide so he could enter.

She noted Perry's logo on the bag. "You bought me soup from The Pointe?"

"I did. Perry says to get well soon. Troy pointed out it's the best soup in town and Zach backed him up. It might be the first time in two months those two have agreed on anything."

Smoothing her hair back, she made room at her coffee table for the sack of food by rearranging her box of tissues and nasal spray. "I feel like such a grub."

"You're uncomfortable that I'm here."

"I wouldn't say that, just embarrassed that I look so awful."

He took her chin. "You look like you don't feel good. Big difference. You couldn't look awful if you tried."

"I'd kiss you for that if I didn't think I'd give you this crud I have."

"Downside to coming in contact with rug rats five days a week." He took her by both arms, placed his lips on her forehead. "You feel like you still have a fever."

She sighed. "Low-grade now. I've felt so rotten I haven't even looked at the paperwork for my house that Nick emailed me."

"Don't worry about that now. I know how excited you were but that house isn't going anywhere. A couple of days delay won't make a difference in your grand scheme."

She sniffed and grabbed for a Kleenex, blew her nose. "I'm sorry."

He started unpacking the bag, brought out some extras besides the soup.

"Is that chocolate mousse from The Pointe I've heard so much about? Ryder, you shouldn't have."

He laughed at her reaction to getting chocolate. "My mom swears that it fixes anything."

"I'm beginning to feel a real affection for your mother."

"My mom's a gem. When you get to feeling better why don't you schedule a field trip for your class, bring them out to Taggert Farms. We have teachers making arrangements for class trips all the time. Better still, bring the kids after April First when the fruit stand is up and running."

"Actually that sounds like a good idea. They'd get to see a real working farm up close."

"Now that that's settled, let's eat and then pop in a movie."

"What movie did you bring?"

"Something I think you'll like. My own personal favorite. I hope you like monsters." He located her DVD player and slid in the disc.

Julianne recognized what he'd brought as soon as it began to play. "How in the world did you know *Aliens* is one of my all-time favorites?"

"Who in their right mind doesn't like sci-fi thrillers featuring an ugly, giant, menacing space alien? And this one is tops in my book."

For the next two plus hours, they sat glued to the screen watching as Ellen Ripley took charge on planet LV-426. By the time the credits rolled, they'd drained the containers of soup and scarfed down the remnants of the pudding.

"Being sick I've had time to think about our next step." When she saw him cringe at the words "next step" she sighed. "Relax. I'm not talking about the next step in our relationship, not that we have one. No, I mean I think we should try to figure out the names of the people in those class photographs I saw."

"Isn't that Brent's job?"

"It is. And I plan to talk to him on my next trip to Pelican Pointe. But in the meantime, I thought I might get in touch with the former principal, a guy by the name of Henry Nash."

Ryder frowned and shook his head. "I talked to Brent this morning when he wandered over to the site to see how much work we've done so far. Even though I prodded him, he wouldn't give me specifics. But he did give me the impression he's making progress on the case by talking to several of the former staff members still in the area."

"I should've known Brent would be one step ahead of me. It's just as well. I'm no cop and with everything else on my plate, not much time to devote to solving mysteries."

"It's normal to be curious, especially since you're the one who discovered the bloody fabric. You look better," Ryder decided as he stared at the way she stretched out on the opposite end of the couch.

"I feel better thanks to you."

"What are friends for?"

"I promise I'll return the favor when you come down with this crap."

"I never get sick," he echoed.

"Uh-oh, famous last words."

Two days later, the virus had worked its way through Ryder's system enough to knock him on his ass and cause him to miss a day of work. Every bone and joint in his body hurt. Even his eyelids had trouble closing without causing him pain.

It sure as hell was no way to spend a Saturday.

He pulled the blanket from the bed, threw it around his shoulders for warmth. Coughing and hacking, he hobbled into the kitchen to get water, convinced this must have been what Valley Forge felt like in the winter of 1777. It was impossible to get warm. Even jacking up the thermostat hadn't produced enough heat. He couldn't remember the last time he'd eaten. And frankly at this point, he didn't have the strength to fix anything other than to reach for a loaf of stale bread.

About that time, he heard a car pull up outside. He hoped to God it wasn't another problem to deal with. He'd already had a disagreement with a vendor who was late on a delivery. On top of that he'd authorized overtime for several employees, and approved shipments that had to get where they were going by Monday. The bad thing about living so close to your job was that sometimes you couldn't get away from its demands.

Redirecting his momentum, he shuffled to the window to look out. His eyes hurt so much he thought he was seeing things when Julianne got out of her minibus. He watched as she removed a crock pot from the passenger side and hauled it up to the porch.

Dragging his feet to the door, he turned the knob.

She stood on his stoop beaming back at him sunny as a spring day. At the sight of her, he felt suddenly grubby, sporting a day's worth of stubble. He wasn't too sick to notice her snug pair of jeans and a form-fitting sweater. Her dark brown eyes glistened with amusement. Her smile radiated out like a thousand-watt bulb.

"What…are you doing here?" he wheezed out.

"Returning the favor. I thought you said you never got sick."

"No need to rub it in. You must've had some super bug that attached itself to me and doesn't want to let go. How did you know?"

"I talked to Nick this morning when I closed on the house. He mentioned you were noticeably absent at the site yesterday when he stopped by the school. I asked him for Troy's number. Troy pretty much painted a picture that you were at death's door. So…I brought…wait for it…chicken soup. Sorry it isn't Perry's famous recipe. But you don't look like you're in any shape to exert a picky attitude. Mine's homemade *plus* you get plenty of leftovers that'll last for a couple of days."

"Bless you. I'm starving. But aren't you afraid of re-catching this terminal flu or whatever the hell it is?"

"Now, now, let's not exaggerate. I got over it in a couple of days. You will, too. Where should I put this?" She held up the slow cooker.

"Kitchen. That way."

"Go ahead and sit down. I'll fix you a tray. Bring it to you after I've made you some tea with lemon and honey."

He disliked hot tea but it seemed rude to mention it now. He dropped his body down into the recliner and didn't think he could budge unless an earthquake jolted him out of it.

He heard the cabinet doors opening and closing, realized she was hunting for bowls.

When she came back into the living room, she carried a tray he didn't even know he had. "First, let's get a little broth in you and then we'll see if you can handle the noodles."

He let her spoon-feed him the liquid, alternating between sips of the tea. "This is the best tea I've ever tasted."

"That's because I spiked it with bourbon."

"Ah. No wonder. Good move."

She laid a hand on his forehead. "You're burning up with fever. Have you taken aspirin?"

"I'm pretty sure I took some kind of something yesterday."

She sighed, went down the hall in search of the bathroom and the medicine cabinet.

She came back clutching a glass of water and a bottle of ibuprofen. After she watched him swallow the meds, her eyes landed on the fireplace and the stack of firewood beside it. The chill in the air had her tossing a few logs on the grate before using kindling to get the flame going.

Digging in her handbag, she pulled out the DVD she'd brought, held it up. "This time I picked the flick." She slid it into the player, got settled on the ancient couch.

His eyes zeroed in on the box. "*Raiders of the Lost Ark*. A classic. I had an Indiana Jones lunchbox, used it to conk Bobby Harding on the head after he tried to take off on my bike."

"How old were you?"

"A very worldly six."

He looked tired she noted. And sure enough, halfway through the movie, Ryder dozed off.

She got up, went in search of blankets and tucked him into his chair.

She cleaned up her mess in the kitchen, saved the leftovers into a container for the fridge, and tidied up the living room. The fire needed tending, so she added more logs and turned off the lights. Still not a hundred percent herself, a little tired after the chores, she curled up into a ball on the sofa.

A sound jolted her awake. Sitting up, she blinked at the time on her watch. Four-fifteen. She looked over at the lump in the La-Z-Boy® that was Ryder still sacked out.

Creaking floorboards, in what she considered the middle of the night, put her on alert. In unfamiliar surroundings, she tossed back the cover. Fully clothed, she stood up and zeroed in on the source of the noise.

All caution evaporated.

Gritting her teeth to keep from yelling at the sight of Scott, she lowered her voice. "It's four in the morning. Mind telling me what you're doing skulking around here?"

"I saw your bus in the driveway. I wanted to see if the two of you…you know…hooked up."

She put her hands on her hips. "You're spying on people now? You're using your ghostly powers to go covert? That's…that's…intrusive. That's…so wrong."

"Hey, there isn't a lot of opportunity for me to have fun. This is it."

"Well, cut it out. Get out of here. Now!"

"I can see I've caught you at a bad time." Scott eyed Ryder in the armchair and added, "This would've been so much more interesting if you two had been…you know…sharing the same space."

"He's sick. No, on second thought you are." She looked around for something to throw at him and swiped up a sports magazine off the coffee table. It sailed through the air just as Scott managed to vanish and the booklet thudded against the wall.

Ryder bolted upright at the sound. "What? What's wrong?"

"Go back to sleep," she said to him, stepping over to test his forehead with the palm of her hand. It wasn't as hot as it had been before but he was still feverish and his eyes still looked dull and glassy.

Before she could take her hand back he held on to it. "You stayed."

"We both fell asleep during the movie." She didn't see the harm in the little white lie. "You never made it past the snake pit scene."

"Damn. I love that part. Did I hear voices just now?"

"You were dreaming. Now go back to sleep," she repeated.

He yanked her down into the chair with him. "Only if you stay right here with me, curled up against me for another few hours. It'll make me feel better."

"There isn't room for the both of us."

"Sure there is." He scooted over so they could scrunch together and had her snuggled up against his chest in one smooth move. In less than two minutes, he was snoring softly again.

Looking into his face, she was very much afraid she was already falling for the guy. Closing her eyes to the beat of his heart, she drifted into dreams.

Several hours later when the light peeked through the curtains, she moved to get up but Ryder caught her around the waist.

"Don't go," he said sleepily.

"I'm just getting up to put on coffee. How're you feeling?"

"Better, thanks to you. Do you have plans for today?"

"I'd hoped to take a run by the house, other than that…"

"Then spend the day with me, here. The weather's gray and dreary out. We could hunker down here, watch the movie you brought, listen to music, or just lounge around if we want. Taggert had this old record collection. I promise you it's worth a listen."

"What about the milking?"

"Silas has that chore till tomorrow morning."

"How do you like your eggs?"

"Scrambled with a little cheese."

They got to their feet together, made their way into the kitchen. Ryder dumped coffee into a filter, pushed the button on an ancient Mr. Coffee while Julianne dug into the refrigerator for breakfast fixings.

She got out a skillet, tossed in strips of bacon. While it began to sizzle, she whipped up the eggs.

"Did you get the impression Nick was serious about loaning money to people with a business idea?" Ryder asked.

"Absolutely. Thinking about one?"

Over the meal, he told her about how he'd always wanted to build boats and why.

"Ah, the influence from the architect grandfather. Makes sense."

"It does?"

"You obviously have fond memories of spending that time with him. It was special and something the two of you could do together. Where was the camp?"

"Beautiful Maine. My first year there was spent with my dad. Good times. Then after he was gone, every summer after that…from eleven to fifteen…I'd get out of the city with my Gramps, go up there and spend June to mid-August on the water. We got to create and design our own watercraft. It was a world away from Philly. I'd like to take you there sometime."

"And I'd love to see it. Your eyes light up when you talk about that time in your life. Did you know that?"

Together, they began to clear the dishes. When she noted the look of embarrassment on his face she wanted to know, "I'm curious. Why didn't you keep going back to the camp after fifteen?"

"My grandfather was diagnosed with cancer. He passed away a couple months later. Money was tight so I went to work installing cabinets on a construction crew."

"And just like that, your childhood pretty much came to an end."

"No self-respecting fifteen-year-old considers himself a child."

She picked up his hand, squeezed his fingers. "But you have fond memories before that."

"That one summer, I learned a lot from my dad, then later, my grandfather. No one can take that away from me."

She decided to get that wistful look off his face. "Let's go through that treasure trove of albums."

As it turned out, Taggert's collection offered up a wide variety of music. It seems the farmer's taste ran the gamut from Louis Armstrong to Frank Sinatra to Beethoven to Gerry Rafferty. Perusing the selections, they took turns reading aloud the liner notes and the track listings.

"Ed Sullivan presents *Annie Get Your Gun*."

"Here's one, *The Best of Nat King Cole*."

Julianne slid out an LP from its paper sleeve and gently placed it on the turntable, pointed the needle to the groove. "How about this instead?"

"Billie Holiday. There's one here for Bonnie Raitt from 1971, different time maybe, but the man obviously loved his blues."

They swayed to *As Time Goes By* and then, when the track changed to *Moonglow*, they made another pass around the room. As the saxophone riff introduced *Baker Street*, Julianne closed her eyes to the refrain.

Ryder took the opportunity to breathe in her hair, nibble on her neck and run his hands down her back. He boosted her up, dipped his head down, angled his mouth over hers. The press of lips ramped up, heated. Teasing tongues wanted more while hands roamed to slide clothes off to the side.

He thumbed a nipple through her shirt. Her fingers were moving down to his zipper when someone pounded on the door.

"Ryder! Ryder! I know you're sick, but you got to come quick. You gotta see this."

"What now?" Ryder said through gritted teeth. "Is there a hidden force at play here to explain why we keep getting interrupted?"

Julianne looked down at the bulge in his pants. "You can't open the door like that, at least not until you…"

He spared a glance downward at his sweat pants sticking out. Doing his best to stall for time, he yelled through the door, "What's wrong, Silas? What has you in such a frenzy today?"

"Someone let the cows loose. They're out on the highway. It's just me here today. I need help getting them rounded up."

"Let me get my boots on and I'll be right there." He grabbed Julianne, covered her mouth in a sultry kiss. "Sorry, but it looks like I'm on the clock. This may take a while."

"But Ryder, you're sick."

"Not anymore."

While Ryder chased down and rounded up a bunch of cows on the road to town, Troy and Bree spent their day exploring Treasure Island. This time, they had the pebbly beach and craggy ground all to themselves.

"We should really take some time to dive the shipwreck."

"I've only snorkeled in shallow water, never dived before."

"Hmm, that pretty much sums it up for me, too. Maybe we should take lessons together," Troy suggested. "Russ

Dennis dives. We should go see him about it. Maybe he could point us to a good instructor."

"You're really thinking I can do this?"

"I know you can. And it would be good for the area."

"I've never had anyone believe in me like you do, Troy. You make me want to succeed at whatever I try."

"We all want to get ahead. In fact, I'm talking to Logan about buying one of the houses he bought in his grandparent's old neighborhood. You know the one, that row of little Spanish bungalows on Athena Circle, behind the old newspaper office. They're tiny but so is the cul-de-sac they're on. Logan bought three of them. They need a lot of work but I'm willing to fix it up. Just look at what Julianne's taking on with that beat-up old cottage over on Ocean Street. I figure if I help her I'll learn how to do my own."

"You're amazing."

"I'm glad you think so because I think you're the most beautiful woman on the planet." He picked up the strands of her red hair as the breeze tossed it around her face. "All this ginger color makes you stunning."

She leaned into him, pressed her lips to his. "It's nice having the island to ourselves. We should make a fire."

"I think we already have."

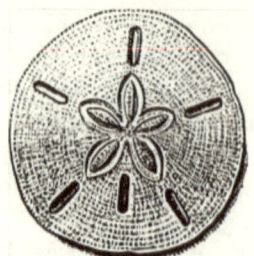

Chapter Ten

The first Saturday in March Julianne showed up at the gingerbread cottage along with her dad to a waiting crowd of townspeople.

Her jaw dropped at the sight. The group headed by Ryder and Troy stood on the lawn. She looked into the faces of Nick, Brent, Murphy, and a man she recognized as Wally Pierce from the service station.

"What are you guys doing here?"

"Ready to remodel a house," Ryder stated with a grin. "Logan spared Troy and me for the day. Give the word where you want us to start first and we'll kick this weekend project through the roof."

"All of you are…incredibly generous with your time. Look, Pop and I were prepared to do the work ourselves."

"No need for that," Nick assured her. "Logan would've been here too but Kinsey is about ready to pop."

"Anything we can do for them?"

"If there is, I'm sure Logan will let us know."

As Julianne led the way up the steps, she was all but bouncing on her toes. She stuck her key into the lock and turned to the group.

"I really need to thank Nick and Logan, even though he isn't here, for making this all possible, for bringing me to this point. But right now we have a house to renovate."

To make the most of the workforce, they split up into three teams. Julianne, Ryder, and Brent started in the kitchen, ripping up the flooring. Troy used his people to bust up the fixtures and cabinets in the bathroom, and then rip out an adjacent closet wall to make the space larger. Nick's team spread out to the living area and the bedrooms. Using commercial sanders, they buffed out the hardwood floors.

At their first break, Julianne turned to Brent. "I've been meaning to ask you about the case. Have you found who that shirt belonged to?"

"My standard response is to say I can't comment on an ongoing investigation."

She rolled her eyes. "Yeah, yeah, yeah. Can you at least tell me if Henry Nash was of any help IDing anyone in those photographs?"

"Stubborn, that's Julianne Dickinson," Brent muttered to Ryder. "Henry was as helpful as his memory allowed. He has Alzheimer's. I'm in the process of going through the list of students that I got from old records."

Julianne couldn't help prodding, meddling. "That box belonged to a member of the Jennings family, didn't it?"

"How'd you come to that conclusion?"

"Easy. The deed gave it away."

"I hate to burst your bubble but the box doesn't belong to them. None of the Jennings kids recognized anything inside except for their grandfather's deed and a couple of the class pictures. The photos were of classmates taken while Cooper and Drea were enrolled there. That was it. No big mystery."

She shrugged and traded glances with Ryder. "Okay, so much for me grilling the florist on my own."

"Julianne, do *not* do that," Brent insisted. "Stay out of this."

"It was just a stupid plan that I never had time to put in motion anyway. But are you certain none of them claimed the box? Did you talk to each one? You don't find that strange?"

Brent cocked his head, gave her a withering stare. "Yes, I talked to each one. Visited Caleb at the garden center, Drea at the florist shop, and emailed Cooper wherever he's living now. I think he mentioned something about Oregon, or it might've been Orinda. I forget which."

"But no one else in those pictures has a father who went missing," Ryder insisted. "How did they explain the deed in the box? None of them laid claim to the toys?"

"No. They had no idea how the deed ended up in there. But the store closed several years back after Andrew passed away. Who knows how long the deed had been lost? It's a moot point anyway since the county collects the taxes on the store property and the three kids go in together every year to pay it."

The notion she'd been building of solving the case, evaporated. "Well, that's disappointing."

To keep the conversation going, she told Brent about what Cleef Atkins had said accusing Eleanor of doing away with her own father. "If you had the original medical examiner's report on Euell Jennings' death it might shed some light on what happened that day."

Before Brent could answer, Ryder asked him, "Did you know Eleanor? Do you think she was capable of something that sinister?"

"I didn't know her. But I'm learning a lot about the woman's state of mind back in the days *before* Layne took off with Brooke. You won't find a person around town who will do much vouching for Eleanor. Not a single one. As to whether or not she could have shot her father, I honestly have no idea. But I suppose it's worth looking into."

"Julianne doesn't think Layne ever left town," Ryder explained.

Brent turned to stare at her. "Why not give up teaching for real. Come work for law enforcement. The pay's just as lousy as teaching but the mayor says I can add on a deputy in about six months."

Julianne huffed out a laugh, tilted her head in response. "Sarcasm won't work with me. But it is a nice way of telling me to butt out."

It was Ryder who piped up, "Actually, that's his way of paying you a compliment because he agrees with you."

She glanced at Ryder then Brent. "Really?"

"What I'm curious about though is why you made the jump," Brent wanted to know.

"Because everyone is of the same mindset. The consensus is Layne would never have left those kids behind in Eleanor's care. She was too unpredictable, too unstable, too mean, whatever 'too' you want to apply to the situation. Layne felt very uncomfortable at the idea of walking away from them. I doubt seriously he would have."

Brent nodded. "After talking to half the town and those that were still around back then, Layne's reluctance to leave seems to be the prevailing reason he didn't. Layne didn't trust Eleanor to take care of his kids. Period."

"So if Brooke and Layne didn't run away together, that could only mean one thing."

"Don't go leaping," Brent urged them both. "I've submitted the piece of shirt for DNA testing and if I have to I'll ask for swabs from Layne's kids."

"To see if there's a connection blood to blood?"

"Yeah."

"Isn't there a Native American ceremony that covers this sort of thing?"

"You mean moving into a new house? Sure."

"Hmm, interesting, that would be cool, too. I'd like one of those here. But no, I was thinking more along the lines of a ceremony for clarity, something that would tell us what happened to Layne and Brooke."

"Oh for God's sake," Brent huffed out. "Why don't you say what you mean? You want to procure the services of my father or brother and their psychic abilities?"

"Well, they have done it before. And your father is known for that, Ethan not so much. He keeps that side hidden from everyone else other than his close circle. Even if we just got a few of those people to come together for a…"

"Séance?"

"That isn't where I was going with this at all. I was referring to an enlightening ceremony." Just to needle him, she added, "But we could definitely add séance into the mix. The more people, the merrier."

"It's fairly ridiculous. I prefer old-fashioned police work, if you don't mind."

"The séance thing was your leap, not mine. The more energy we generate there has to be power in that. We might learn something we didn't know. Besides, you're Native. I know for a fact you've used your father or brother before on some of your more desperate cases. Why not now on a case this cold?"

Ryder realized the two squabbled like brother and sister. "She has a point."

"You'll go talk to both of them no matter what I say, won't you?"

"No, not if it's something that upsets you this much." When she saw Brent take a calming breath she had hope.

"I'll think about it. Right now, that's the best I can do."

"Then I guess we're on hold until you get back to me."

"Why don't you stick to what you know best? Getting teachers lined up for next year. I'll do what I do best."

"Fine," she muttered under her breath.

For the remainder of the morning the three of them worked in companionable silence. But their conversation caused a cloud to hang over what should have been a festive gathering. Her fault, she decided.

The idea that the bloodstained cloth might belong to Layne meant someone, presumably Eleanor, had killed him. Or were they rushing to blame the evil wife without proof of anything? Could Brooke have killed Layne in a fit of rage because he had refused to leave with her and then fled to parts unknown?

Those questions lingered while they worked. Around noon they hauled out the mess they'd made—old laminate, rotting wood—then started knocking down the old pine cabinets. Once that was done, they dragged everything out, filled up the dumpster again at the curb.

By three o'clock they were exhausted and starving.

"I'm buying everyone dinner," Julianne announced.

"Not me," Nick said. "I gotta get home and relieve Jordan from having two toddlers all day."

"Same here," Brent said. "River's planning spaghetti."

Julianne looked at Troy, but he shook his head. "Live music at McCready's tonight for me and I'm spending the evening with Bree, even though she has to finish her shift. I have to get home and clean up." He wiggled his eyebrows up and down. "Gotta look my best."

"I can't stay either. We're expected at Carla's mother's tonight for chile relleno," Murphy called out.

"What about you, Ryder? Want to join Pops and me for dinner?"

"Count me in. But I need a shower first."

"Oh no you don't. We all smell. Which means I'm ordering takeout from the Diner. I already know Pop wants a burger with everything. So what's your pleasure?"

"I'll take their Saturday special, the steak sandwich with everything."

"Got it. Be back in a flash." She took her dad's truck and cruised past the pier and the dig site, spotted River trying to corral her three-year-old.

On impulse, Julianne pulled to the side of the curb and waved. River jogged over but continued to keep an eagle eye on Luke since the toddler was running around on the beach like a little wild man.

"Your hubby's back at the house packing up for the day."

"I know. He sent me a text. I'm letting Luke burn off excess energy. Did you get a lot done? I'd have joined in the fun, but trust me, with Luke underfoot it would've been a challenge."

"It's okay. We had plenty of hands on deck. We got off to a great start. I felt like one of those shows on DIY where everyone pitches in to renovate my house. I can't believe how generous the town's been."

"This is a good little place to live."

"What about you? Is the dig over?"

River glanced back at the area they'd recently expanded. They'd originally started among the dunes directly under the lighthouse but over the last few months, after having trouble extracting the canoe, they'd slowly moved southward and closer to the pier. Keeping the tide out was still a problem. By utilizing sandbags, they were able to keep the work zone as dry as possible.

"I was prepared to shut down the site but last week my crew spotted several more artifacts at a depth of eight feet—namely, hunting tools and a harpoon. As the rep for the tribe, Brent gave us another three months of dig time. Getting an extension wasn't easy even if I am married to the guy in charge."

"That means more goodies for the museum."

"You bet it does. I'm stoked. And Brent's been getting really lucky this week."

Julianne howled with laughter. "That must be why he worked like two men. I guess it's okay to admit now that I was afraid you might be standoffish since everyone in town seems to think Brent and I were an item. We weren't, by the way. You seemed so...friendly at the party I thought I should say something."

"My turn for honesty then. Brent and I had words about you moving here, a misunderstanding. He told me months ago that nothing happened between you two. And even if it had, it was well before we got together. Your being here doesn't bother me at all. So relax."

"That's a load off my mind. Brent and I are just friends. But no matter how many times I deny it, someone always comes up to me assuming we had a torrid affair at one time."

"I hear ya. It's the mentality of the small town. Don't worry about it or me."

"How does the tribe feel about you taking charge of the proposed cultural center?"

"Because I'm Pueblo and not a Chumash descendant? Good question. It was a struggle at first. But Brent carries a lot of weight with the elders. Not to toot my own horn or anything, but I'm the most qualified person around for the job. I'm absolutely committed to making sure the antiquities are handled properly. The Codys know now and have been very supportive." All the while they talked River kept watch on her son who sat on the sand playing with his trucks. "I'm so glad the town's reopening the school. As you can see, we have a vested interest. I'm glad it's you they selected for the job."

"That means a lot to me. I hope all the parents feel that way. A lot of people think I'm making a big jump from first-grade teacher to principal."

"Sometimes we have to leap to get anywhere."

She told River about her idea to consult with Marcus and Ethan, to employ the men's abilities in a mystic way that might give up what happened to the missing couple. "You want to talk about taking a leap, that's a major hop, skip and a jump."

River grabbed her arm. "But it's not! That's a terrific idea! I've seen ceremonies like that performed all over the world."

"Surprisingly, your hubby didn't think so."

"Of course not, let me guess. That would be veering off the normal track cops usually take. But this is a cold case. Why not shake things up a little?"

"Or a lot. If you ask me, and no one did, a cold case needs all the help it can get from any source."

"Exactly. So when is this taking place?"

"I don't know yet. Next weekend maybe. I hadn't really planned it out that far ahead mainly because Brent is not onboard with it yet."

"If you need help, let me know. By the way, how's it going with the hunky construction worker?"

Lines formed on Julianne's forehead. "Ryder? We're in the early stages of…something."

"Relationships are thorny, aren't they?"

"I don't have many to compare to but I'd have to agree. Are all single guys in their thirties stuck in a holding pattern? When it comes to trusting women, Ryder's wedged in the past. He prefers to remember the ugly someone who hurt him."

"If they've been burned, it's difficult to get them past it. Brent certainly fell into that category. It's like the legend of the two snow-white, wolf lovers who mated for life, Myko and Zeeka."

"I guess I don't know that story."

"Ah. Allow me… Like any alpha male, Myko strutted back and forth in front of Zeeka with his head held high, trying to get her attention. But Zeeka was no pushover. She made him work for the privilege of being with her. After several hours of watching him showing off, Zeeka finally let him get close to her. Even though their attraction was smoldering, Zeeka still made him work for it. But soon, both wolves became cold and hungry and went off to find food together. The hunt took them through thorny bushes and rough terrain until they finally found fresh food, an elk. Being the alpha male, along with trying to show off a bit, he tried to take down the animal alone, by himself. Big mistake."

River took a breath and went on, "All the while Zeeka sat back, ever patient, and waited to see what would happen next. It became clear Myko couldn't handle the beast by himself, he needed help. No matter how much he tried he couldn't do it alone. It would take both of them to attack and bring it down so they could eat.

"Zeeka went to Myko, explained that if he would put his pride aside and let her work as his equal, they could do it together. So together the two wolves stalked and circled. And that night, they ate a feast of elk."

"I love legends," Julianne said with a smile. "If only life was more like the inspirational folktales handed down through the ages."

"It can be. Brent and I are living proof, it can be. You just have to hang in there."

Once the others packed up and headed for home, Ryder found himself left alone with Julianne's father—a towering man who leaned toward a quiet nature rather than joining in the earlier conversations. After busting up flooring and cabinets together, Ryder decided to break the awkward silence between them.

"So how long have you been at this?"

"Been a carpenter since I was fifteen," John answered. "Worked alongside my father growing up, couldn't get enough of his workshop. How about you?"

"I started working construction during the summer months in high school. It paid well enough but at the time I wanted to see someplace else other than Philly so I joined the army."

"No desire to go to college?"

"None whatsoever. I always did okay in school but hated the structure. The idea of spending four more years going to class made me cringe. I like working with my hands."

"School's all I heard from Julianne. From the time she was five she'd pretend to be the teacher, in charge of everyone. She used to drive me crazy begging me to listen to her plans for all the other kids in the neighborhood. I used to have to remind her, you can't always make people do what you want them to do. I know part of it was the fact she wanted her mother. But Ruthie was gone."

"Hey, my parents didn't stay together either. Sometimes matchups just do not work out, no matter how much those online dating services tout their success in commercials."

"I laugh my ass off at those. My girl finally got past not having her mother around, I guess, as much as any child can that is. Ruthie never bargained for motherhood. She told me that right up front. Julianne doesn't know this but, when she was a baby, her mother would refuse to get up with her at night whenever the baby cried. That was always my job. So I learned to put in fifteen hours on the job and get up with an infant at night. Later, it was so much more I had to learn on the job. Like how to braid hair. Or how to cook a decent meal without setting the kitchen on fire. Or helping her with homework. I think that's one of the reasons she likes teaching so much. She's a big influence on the kids."

"She'll make an even bigger impact as principal."

"You think so? I don't know. Maybe. But I'm afraid she'll miss the interaction with the kids. I don't want to discourage her though."

"Miss the one-on-one concept? I hadn't thought of that." Ryder could see Julianne as the stern little dark-haired girl growing up, the precocious child who expected everyone to fall in line.

It made him realize the two of them were very different—she educated—him barely getting out of high school. She couldn't get enough of a classroom, while he avoided one at all costs. Could two people so completely opposite really make a go of things? He was no longer so sure.

By the time Julianne strolled in with the take-out, she spotted her father and Ryder with their tape measures in hand going over every inch of the house, making notations as they went.

"Food's here. We already measured every room, twice," she pointed out.

"Never hurts to make sure," the men said in unison.

"Why does that not surprise me? Okay, after the backbreaking first day, let's hear your take on the job." When both men looked perplexed, she added, "Both of you must have an opinion."

"Your goal is end of May? You'll be cutting it close but I believe it's doable," Ryder said.

"Even if no other help shows up, I think we can get the worst of it out of the way and you can move in after the term's done."

"Okay, good, now let's eat."

They took the food outside and ate sitting on the porch steps. But Julianne sensed a change in Ryder. He seemed pensive, distant. As the trio watched the sun dip into the water, she wondered if he'd had a disagreement with her dad about something while she'd been gone. But when Ryder finally spoke it put her more at ease.

"That's a pretty sight. Just think how many sunsets over the ocean you'll be able to sit here and take in every evening after work."

"I know. It's one reason I wanted this close to the water. I mentioned to River about going to Marcus and Ethan to shake things up with this Layne and Brooke thing. She liked the idea."

"But Brent didn't," Ryder reminded her.

"I know but shouldn't we do something?"

"That's Brent's job, isn't it?"

After he'd swallowed his last bite, John got up to leave. Turning to his daughter, he said, "If you're riding with me, I need to get home, get some sleep in time to do this all over again tomorrow."

"I'll bring her home," Ryder heard himself offer.

"Are you sure?" she asked. "Santa Cruz is so far out of the way."

"I don't mind."

"Okay, Pop, I'll see you tomorrow."

After her dad left, she led Ryder back inside and grabbed the paint samples she'd picked up at Ferguson's Hardware. She went around to each room beginning with the kitchen. "I need another eye in here before I settle on the right shade. Since the backsplash is a subtle blue-green, tell me if you think this white is too blah."

"A bolder blend might work better in such a small space."

"Okay, what about this? It's called Misty Mimosa."

"Still too bland, not enough pop. Try the Copacabana Marina."

"Oh, much better. Good choice." She jotted down the color code on her notepad, moved on to the living room. "Keeping with a beach house feel, I'm thinking a soft Hampton-style blue in here. It's called Seashore Teal and it reminds me of sea foam without being too dark bluesy."

"I like it."

They tried out the color wheel in each of the rooms, decided on shade variants from Bermuda Lagoon to Caribbean Spray, for each space.

"Have you thought anymore about the street fair? Because around here it's a big deal. The town voted to hold a special one last fall just to donate all the proceeds toward the school project. It was my first foray into Pelican Pointe's dynamics. It was pretty impressive."

Her mouth dropped open. "And no one bothered to mention this to me until now? I feel like a total idiot. I was planning on putting what I made toward remodeling my house, namely splurging on the cabinets and the new plumbing fixtures."

"As far as I know, Nick and Murphy aren't planning to strong-arm anyone into handing over their profits next month. They held an auction the first of the year, made a tidy sum when Logan donated one of his art pieces to a collector back East. And if we're running really lean come summer, they'll have a huge community sale at the church as backup."

"But that's not the point. I'd love to contribute. I had no idea the townspeople had gone to such great lengths to get this off the ground. I mean, I knew about the fundraisers, primarily the individual donations from Nick and Logan. But I never once thought to turn over what I made at the fair. Which makes me feel…like a miser."

"Don't do that."

When the live music kicked in across the street coming from McCready's, Ryder tilted his head to listen. "It might be a good time to test the waters."

"A little late for that since I already sunk my life savings into this house," she reasoned. She spread her arms out wide. "The neighbors here don't seem to mind. If it's noisy I'll just have to learn to live with it. Besides, if it gets too much, the town cop is right down the street. And he and River have a child to put to bed every night."

"Then let's go experience some of the local flavor for ourselves, get us a beer, celebrate your new digs."

"Now you're talking."

They walked across the street to the bar—more like a combination Irish pub and pool hall. They squeezed into the standing room only crowd at the counter until Ryder heard his name over the din. He turned, caught sight of Troy who motioned them over to a tiny table.

"Word has it Kinsey went into labor," Troy yelled over the roar of guitar strings from the new band, Ninth Dog, a group of twenty-somethings who'd started playing grunge.

"Logan will be relieved," Ryder barked out.

Julianne hooted. "I'm sure Kinsey's a lot more relieved than he is."

Bree came over to take their order. "Hey, how's it going? You gotta shout it out otherwise I can't hear ya over the band's kicking beat."

Eyeing Troy's soda, Ryder shouted, "Just bring us three summer ales."

"You got it."

Julianne's eyes wandered to the smidgen of a dance floor. She grabbed Ryder's hand. "You owe me a dance."

She saw the wall instantly go up again, heard the bristle in his tone. "I can't dance to that."

Her heart sank. But she refused to let him see that. She turned to Troy. "What about you?"

"Not me either."

She shot a look at the group of women gathered between the pool tables. "Well, this is certainly a fun outing. I think I'll go see if anyone wants to play eight-ball."

Ryder watched as she joined a group he recognized as Drea Jennings, Abby Bonner and Donna Oden.

"What's up with you two?" Troy asked.

"Beats the hell out of me."

"Oh come on, she asked you to dance and you acted all snotty to her."

"She asked you, too. I noticed you turned her down."

"Are you nuts? I'm not dancing with your girl and getting you pissed off at me."

Ryder chewed on that. Was Julianne his girl? Just because he wanted to get her in the sack that didn't make her his girl. They just weren't a good match. It was better knowing that going in than later.

The women's laughter had Troy turning his head to watch the game in progress. "Why aren't you over there rooting her on against Donna?"

"Because I have news for you, Julianne Dickinson is doing just fine without me."

Chapter Eleven

Sunday morning when Julianne returned to the house with her dad, she learned the town had two new citizens. Overnight, Kinsey and Logan had become parents to a boy they'd dubbed Liam and a girl they'd named Leah.

But babies coming into the world didn't mean Julianne could go into slacker mode. The way she figured it she only had seventy-five plus days to stay on schedule, less if the only time she could devote to remodeling was Saturdays and Sundays. If she meant to move in by Memorial Day, which she did, her goal was to spend every weekend in Pelican Pointe making headway on each room, one by one. The place didn't have to be finished by the end of May, but it did have to be livable. That's why the kitchen along with the plumbing took priority over everything else.

For the rest of the day, they pulled out the old porcelain tile in the house—the bath tub along with the toilet. They dragged it all to the waste receptacle at the curb.

"I hope you know you're taking on an awful lot," John told his daughter as he wiped the sweat from his brow. "Why is it you always expect so much of yourself? I've never understood it. You always think you can pull off the impossible."

"That's because I take after my old man," she deadpanned. "He's done the impossible on a regular basis for as long as I've known him."

"You know that boy likes you."

"Boy? Oh. You mean Ryder."

"He likes you otherwise no one in their right mind would volunteer to put in the work he did yesterday in his spare time. I like him."

"Good for you. But he seems to have had a change of heart in a short amount of time. He barely said a word to me on the trip to Santa Cruz last night. If that wasn't bad enough, when we got back to my house, I got a peck on the cheek at the door. He couldn't get in his truck fast enough. I felt like I had the plague and he was afraid of catching it."

"That's odd. He was fine at the house yesterday. Although he did seem odd after you got back with the food."

About that time John pointed to the corner of the block. When Julianne followed his trail of vision, she spotted Caleb and Drea Jennings walking their way.

"That's two of Layne's three kids."

"The guy who used to live here, the one who went missing?"

"Yep. Wonder what they want."

"I guess we're about to find out," John mumbled.

Julianne noted that warm smile of Drea's must be why she was so good at retail.

"We stopped by to officially welcome our new addition to the Pelican Pointe family."

"Thank you for that."

"When you get closer to moving in we'd like to landscape both the front lawn and the backyard for you."

"You're kidding? Really? Why would you do that? I...I...don't know what to say. Thank you. I'm...blown away by your kindness... Everyone's been so amazing. In fact, I'd love to have you all over for an open house as soon as I get settled."

"We think opening the school back up again is a wonderful first step to attracting young families to the area," Caleb finally said. "It's exactly the one thing this town needs, an influx of new blood."

"That's such a noble sentiment."

But she wondered if she should mention to these two who stood in what was now her front yard what she had planned. The kids who'd lost so much—their mother, their father. Would they have any interest in seeking out a psychic, a ceremony that might shed light on what happened to their father? After seeing the sparkle in Caleb's eyes, the smile on Drea's face, Julianne didn't have the heart to bring up a painful period from their past. At least not until she had more answers. All she could do was keep to her promise.

The house needed TLC. And she intended to see it get there.

All day Ryder had been MIA which was fine by Julianne. She had a house to renovate and plenty of other things on her plate. She didn't need a sulky man giving her a hard time.

But around five o'clock River showed up with Brent in tow. In Julianne's mind, Brent was just another impossible broody male to deal with today.

"We wanted to invite you to that get-together with Marcus and Ethan—the one that you thought was a good idea," River explained.

"I'd rather not."

Brent couldn't believe his ears. "Why? You've been nothing but a pain in my ass since you found that damn shirt. Now that you have my attention, you're taking a pass? Why?"

"In case you haven't noticed, I'm a little busy at the moment," she snapped back. "I have better things to do than stick my nose where it doesn't belong, especially when it isn't appreciated."

"Since when?"

"Since I realized it pissed you off. I was only trying to suggest that a mystical approach might be just the ticket to produce at least one new clue in a twenty-year-old cold case."

"And I've tried to explain that I'm doing just fine on my own without any input from a psychic," Brent argued.

"Then why bother?"

"Because… It's not a bad idea."

"What! All this grumbling and you're giving in." She shot a look at River. "You prodded him into this, didn't you?"

River raised a hand for peace. "Does it matter how we arrived here? The point is Marcus and Ethan might add some insight. You were the one who thought of it. Look, the meeting isn't until Tuesday night. If you're able to come, we'd love to have you."

"Fine. Where?"

"Ethan's place over on Landings Bay. Their house is bigger and will accommodate more people."

"Okay, I'll see you then."

After they left, she still wasn't convinced she'd go.

John had been listening from the other room and came out into the hallway to add his two cents. "Getting involved in a decades-old mystery is coming at a bad time for you."

"You're telling me."

"But what's really eating at you is that Ryder didn't show up today. Admit it."

"That's just it, Pop. I have no idea what I did to scare him off."

"Go ask him."

"No way. He's the one who acted like an ass. He ought to be the one to make things right."

Ryder spent his Sunday in a foul mood, bitching at other people. He yelled at Marty about leaving his tools out. He wrote up one of the field hands for being late without listening to the reason. He took advantage of his bad disposition to fire off a scathing email to his private investigator for lack of results.

When his cell phone rang, he picked it up, found he was disappointed to see it wasn't Julianne's number on the display. Instead, he saw a Philly area code.

"Hi Mom."

"Does my wayward son ever think to call his mother?"

"Sorry, I've been busy."

"Too busy to tell me you're alive and well? It takes five minutes to let me know, twenty seconds to compose a text. Ryder Shane McLachlan, do I have to come out West and check on you? Because I will."

Chastised, he caught her up with his work schedule and the goings-on in small town versus the big city. But he didn't mention anything about Julianne.

"Hmm, interesting that I'm not hearing anything about a female in your life? That's disappointing. I'd like grandchildren before I'm too old to enjoy them."

He sidestepped the familiar bait and went on for another twenty minutes about his boatbuilding idea.

"You let me know and I'm happy to invest."

"I'm not taking your life savings, Mom. How's work?"

"You think you're so good at changing the subject. Work is fine."

"And the hunky ER doctor…?"

"Is taking me to dinner later."

Even his mother had a better social life than he did. After another ten minutes, they said their goodbyes. After hanging up, Ryder realized he was either homesick or feeling sorry for himself. Either way, he needed an attitude adjustment. He thought he knew where to find one. After all, how long did he intend to let someone like Bethany rule over his future?

"You did act like an ass."

Ryder heard the voice, angled around to react. For a reply, Scott got his middle finger.

"My, my, you *are* in a pissy mood. It's times like this I see why women think we're not in touch with our feelings."

"What do you know about it? You've never had to deal with her. Julianne could make a man want to join a monastery."

Ryder saw Scott look around at their surroundings. "I can see that. You're alone, been alone for two years. Seems to me, you've created your very own cloister. All you need is to shave your head and put on a robe and you'd have the character down pat."

"Fuck you."

"No thanks. No matter what you think, it's in our DNA as human beings to seek out relationships. A hermit-like existence isn't good for anyone."

"With Julianne I want… I want…"

"A future?"

"I don't know. The idea of moving forward with a schoolteacher scares me."

"Why don't you give it a chance? See what happens. Maybe you aren't cut out to be with one another."

Ryder pulled his pickup to the curb at the gingerbread house about the time John was packing up his tools to hit the road.

"She's in there." John pointed a thumb over his left shoulder. "Been in a bad mood all day."

For some reason it pleased Ryder to hear it.

"Head on out, I'll bring her home."

"That sounds nice and all, but you'd better ask her before you make solid plans."

Ryder headed in the house, went through each room until he found her in the tiny laundry room off the kitchen. She was bent over in a pair of tight jeans, inspecting the plumbing.

"Pop, we could knock out this wall into the garage and it would open up the area quite a bit, give us room to put a sink in here. I've always wanted one of those. What do you think?"

"I like what I see."

At the words, she straightened up, bumped her head on the overhead shelf. "Ryder. What are you doing here?"

"Apologizing for being an ass."

"I don't even know what I did to piss you off."

"Nothing really. You and I, we're different." He ticked off his list, beginning with what he considered the number one problem—the gap in education. "I started dwelling on that and it freaked me out."

"You are an ass. My first and only love up to this point was Danny Panguino, a mechanic. He fixed cars for a living, Ryder. We met in high school. From day one, Danny let me know he had no intentions of ever setting foot inside a college. It wasn't for him. I didn't give a rat's ass. I loved Danny with all my heart. We planned to marry, would have, too, if a drunk driver hadn't taken care of his future. From the age of sixteen to twenty-three I never cared whether or not he had some piece of paper tucked away in his closet that said how smart he was. That would be incredibly petty of me anyway since my own father never graduated high school."

"I had no idea what Danny did for a living."

"That's because instead of talking to me about how you felt, you clammed up. Last night, you barely said two words to me before dumping me on my doorstep. You couldn't run back to your truck fast enough."

"You're right. I'm sorry. Could we start over?"

"I don't know. Can we? Will you communicate a little better or will you close off and keep things to yourself?"

Scott's words about feelings echoed back at him and made him grin. "I'll do my best."

"Okay then."

"Take a walk with me. It's a nice night and there's something I'd like to show you."

After locking up the house and watching her dad drive off, she asked. "Where are we going?"

"Some place I think shows potential, like this house."

They headed toward the pier under a glittery night sky. When they were standing in front of an empty shell of a store, Ryder took her hand. "I'm not a mechanic although I do like working with my hands." He inched up to the dirty windows. Peering inside, he said, "According to Zach, this used to be where they built sailboats. It's hard to believe it was once a viable business. I'd like to bring it back to its former glory."

"And I'd like to see you do it."

"What do you say I treat you to the Sunday night special at the Diner—Max's meatloaf and mashed potatoes."

"I'd be nuts to say no to an offer like that."

Tuesday night as planned, she and Ryder gathered in Ethan Cody's living room. But so far the psychic summit hadn't exactly gone the way Julianne thought it would. The debate between brothers, Ethan and Brent, was often heated, not to mention centered toward a stubborn attitude, primarily Brent's.

"I'd think you would appreciate the support and recognize help when it's offered. Anything at all that would give up something of value to point you in the right direction." Ethan roamed the room before coming to a stop in front of his brother. "What I don't understand is why such a hard-headed approach on this case? It isn't like Layne Richmond went missing on your watch."

"Is that what you think? No offense to you, Dad, or to you, Ethan, but I do have investigative skills."

"None taken," Marcus Cody said as he took a glass of tea from his wife, Lindeen.

"Speak for yourself," Ethan stated.

Not afraid to enter the fray, Julianne spoke up. "I thought we'd gotten past all this?"

"Talk to him," Ethan said, pointing a finger at the town cop. "He's acting like this is the first time we've ever come together on a case."

Turning to Brent, Julianne stared at the stubborn look on his face. "We all know you've called on your family before now. Getting together like this provides a way for us to jump start new ideas. So I'd just like to point out that we shouldn't forget about the other victim in all this, Brooke Caldwell. Maybe there's something in her past we haven't considered. I don't hear as much about her. Although, I'm convinced wherever Layne is that's where we'll find Brooke too."

"That's just it, no one's forgetting about anybody, not if I have anything to do about it," Brent stated.

"I don't know what the big deal is. It isn't like police departments haven't turned to psychics before as an investigative tool," Ryder pointed out.

But Ethan sensed something else was at play. "If Dad and I take a look at this, what is it you're afraid we'll see? You've used us before. Why the brick wall now?"

"I'm not afraid of anything." But the police chief looked around the room at the faces staring back at him. His gaze landed on his wife.

"You might as well tell them," River urged with a shrug. She tossed a no-nonsense look Ethan's way, then at Marcus. "Sometimes you both forget that Brent has his own gift. He senses things, too. And it's usually from up close and personal."

Ethan considered that, stopped his pacing around the room and dropped down into a chair. "Okay, you're right. What is it you see then?"

"Before I share that, I'd like to point out that two of Layne's kids still live here and are a major part of the community. For the first time since hanging up my county badge and taking this job, I'm concerned about collateral damage."

"Wait, does that mean you think Eleanor did something to her husband and to Brooke?" When he took a long time to answer, Julianne plopped down on the sofa beside Ryder. "Well, crap. You do believe it."

"I didn't say that. But emailing Cooper, talking to Caleb and Drea, I got a sense that they'd suffered incredible pain, deep, deep sorrow that goes back years, along with regret that goes to the heart of innocence lost."

"Powerful medicine," Marcus said with a nod of his head.

"These young adults, Layne's children are obviously still reeling from the psychological effects of whatever happened in their childhoods." Brent looked at Julianne. "Whatever they endured, happened in that house, the same house where we showed up and pulled out rotten flooring. That's why I suggest a cleansing ceremony as soon as you move in. Get rid of the dark and the evil aura around the place."

"Good idea, but you're sort of scaring me, Brent."

"There's no need to be afraid now."

"So what you're saying, if I'm getting this, is that finding out what happened to Layne and Brooke might possibly take his kids deeper into that dark and evil abyss?" Ryder wondered.

"Yeah, and it won't be pretty."

"I feel like such a jerk," Julianne said. "I came here hoping to see Marcus or Ethan or both in action. Not only do I learn Brent is like his brother and his dad, but I discover something about myself. I'm thinking more about me than the consequences to Layne's children."

"Same here. I never once considered the kids. Does this mean you're done with the investigation?"

"Hell no, the search is just ramping up," Brent said. "What I ultimately learn won't factor into the equation about the kids. Nor will the fact that no one ever cared enough to look before now."

Later after Julianne and Ryder had gone, Marcus, Ethan, and Brent left the women inside and wandered out into the backyard for privacy so they could talk.

"That was a good front you put up in there for everyone. Mind telling me what that was all about?" Ethan asked.

"Let's just say, if I follow my instincts, you could have your next bestseller without too much of an effort."

"What are you saying?"

"I wasn't kidding when I used the words dark and evil to describe Eleanor. I just have to be able to prove it."

As Ryder and Julianne walked out to their cars, she turned to him and admitted, "I hate to be a wuss, but that might've been the scariest conversation I can remember ever having."

"I'm with you there. Not even seeing Scott is freaking me out as much as the talk about an 'evil presence' inside your house."

"Tell me about it. I'm done playing amateur detective. I'm not cut out for this investigative thing."

"There's something going on with Brent. He definitely knows more than he's sharing."

"Yeah, I got that, too. Do you remember what I said about turning the house inside out to see if I could find any clues?"

"Sure."

"Pop and I did that Sunday, turned up nada. There are no hidden panels in any of the closets, nothing in the heating ducts, no loose boards in the attic."

"Maybe *the clue*, whatever it is, isn't in the house at all."

Her eyes darted to the dark street, the shadows on the lawn, even the flower beds and bushes. "You mean outside in the yard?" She thought about that, lifted one shoulder. "I wouldn't even know what to look for. That's why I refuse to act crazy and dig up my grass."

"A wise decision, I'm sure."

"But what I am doing is calling Marcus as soon as I get back to Santa Cruz and scheduling that cleansing ceremony as soon as possible. I sure as hell am not waiting until moving day."

Chapter Twelve

For the rest of that month, Julianne ran herself ragged seven days a week, spending her usual five in the classroom while weekends were dedicated to the house alongside her dad.

In one weekend, from seven in the morning until six that night, father and daughter replaced the bath tub, the toilet and the sinks. They put in all new tile in the shower and bathroom area. The next Saturday and Sunday they installed modern, light-colored oak cabinets in the kitchen, put in slate countertops, replaced and hammered out more rotten wood and drywall in the laundry room, opening the space up a good four feet.

Ryder showed up whenever he could spare a precious moment but for the most part, the sweaty task fell to Julianne and her dad.

After Brent's suggestion, she'd enlisted Marcus Cody to do a thorough purification ceremony of the premises, both inside and out. She didn't care whether anyone found it strange, crazy, or nuts. Watching the elder go through his ritual made her feel better about the house and its less-than-happy-history.

She divided her time between rehabbing the place and prepping for the Pelican Pointe Street Fair. Scheduled for the third week of March, it lasted three days, Friday through Sunday. Her busy days made it tough to get her booth ready. But she wasn't about to let an opportunity pass without the chance to make extra money. She'd also be able to get rid of some of her inventory at the same time.

As the event got closer, out-of-towners jammed the sidewalks, the beaches and the waterfront. Vendors descended in RVs and campers along with the carnival workers pulling their portable booths. Tents began popping up along Main Street. Parking became a problem. People flocked to the beaches, the pier, and the shops. For a week the little town of less than three thousand burst with the sights and sounds of a spring fair in the making and the chaos that came with it.

She'd seen for herself that Brent had a crime wave on his hands. Complaints poured in from locals—the usual bitching about cars illegally parking in front of houses escalated to fights breaking out among the carny workers. There was talk about turning one of the old storefronts on Main Street into a police station.

Even a newcomer like Julianne recognized a challenging three days ahead.

In order to set up on time, she had to get an early start. With the help of her dad they started loading up all the items she thought might sell into the Turtle at five-thirty. They pulled into Pelican Pointe a little after seven o' clock. She went in search of Murphy to get her tent assignment and found the grocer inside his store manning checkout.

"Who do I see about donating my profits toward the school renovation?"

The surprise on Murphy's face said it all. "Who spilled the beans?"

"Let's just say, the subject kept cropping up over the last few weeks."

"It isn't necessary. Feel free to keep what you make."

"No, I want to do it. Don't argue with me about this, Murphy. It's what I want."

"Any trouble getting today off?"

"I lucked out. Today is a county-wide administrative holiday. Now tell me where to set up and I'll get out of your hair?"

Her booth turned out to be a good location, right across from the store. One piece at a time, she and her dad hefted the furniture into the tent—pretty chairs and tables, dressers and chests—all things she'd refurbished and polished to a gleam. There was the sideboard she'd put back together. The old cabinet she'd rescued from the trash bin.

Once they got everything unloaded and set in place, she breathed in the smell of fresh coffee. "Pop, I don't know about you but I could use a shot of caffeine."

"You read my mind. You making the run or am I?"

"I'll do it. You get off your feet."

John shook his head. "Girl, I'm not even winded."

"Sit down anyway. I have a feeling it'll be a long day."

She followed the smell of warm dough and cinnamon coming from the food court, set up practically next door. A high-traffic area, she decided, as she made her way to the common area between the bank and the market. The park, such as it was, already swarmed with activity. People waited in line to order from the menu of breakfast items someone had scrawled on a chalkboard along with a list of flavored coffees.

"You have a very good location."

Julianne turned at the voice and saw it belonged to Drea Jennings. "Well, hello. That's what I was thinking. A lot of foot traffic near the food court is always a plus. This is like a circus atmosphere. I didn't expect to see so many people."

"I know. For the next three days it's absolute gridlock. The throngs are getting bigger and bigger each year."

"By the way, Jordan loved the arrangement of tulips you made for her. I'm glad you suggested the pink. I'm staying out at Promise Cove again this weekend and I need to stop by and pick out something else for her. The woman adores flowers, has an amazing green thumb. And I know she's giving me a discounted rate for the weekend so..."

"Hey, I'd be terrible at what I do if I didn't keep track of what my customers prefer."

"That must be a story in itself."

"Oh it is. For instance, I know for a fact every time Bran Sullivan goes fishing, he always comes back into town and orders his wife, Joy, yellow roses. So you come by and see me when you get ready to order Jordan's next thank-you and I'll fix up something special for her."

"I will. So you sell a lot of flowers during this event?"

"A ton, not just in bunches either, but herbs and specialty plants, so many we have to restock the garden center afterward."

About that time, Ryder and Zach walked up, followed by Troy and Bree.

"You're out and about early," Julianne said to the four of them. "Making the rounds already?"

"It's tough to work when the place is bursting at the seams," Zach grumbled. "You can't even get from one end of town to the other without detouring to Ocean Street, let alone find a decent place to park."

"You walked over here," Ryder pointed out. "You walk to work every single day."

"Zach just likes to bitch," his sister said to Ryder. "Zach needs a girlfriend. If he'd get out of the house once in a while and do something other than work, he'd be a lot happier."

"Bite me," Zach returned in the way of familiar sibling conflict. "Could I at least get some coffee in me before you air all the family secrets on Main Street?"

Bree laughed at her big brother. "Come on. Admit you haven't dated since you got back from Colorado."

"Excuse me if my priorities are keeping food on the table and my wayward kid sister in college."

Bree ignored his grousing and leaned in so only he could hear. "What about the cute florist?" she suggested eyeing Drea Jennings, the brunette. Aiming an elbow at her brother's rib, she added, "There's a dance tomorrow night, maybe you should ask her to go."

"Cut it out, Bree," Zach demanded with one lethal glare. He looked back, hoping Drea hadn't been listening. When he realized she was still in conversation with Julianne, he dropped his head to whisper, "Stay the hell out of my business. Do not embarrass me like that again."

"Okay, okay. No need to come unglued." Bree neatly changed the subject. "McCready's will be packed from noon on. I'll be on my feet for almost ten hours straight." She turned to Julianne. "But the tips I bring in should pay for that white lace dress you have on display, the one on the mannequin. Please don't tell me you want two hundred dollars for it or something equally beyond my budget."

To Julianne the Battenberg lace and bolero sleeves made it look more suitable for a wedding, but who was she to question a potential customer so she kept her opinions to herself. "You want to buy the 1950s cocktail dress?"

"If the price is right, I do. Did you make it? It's so sophisticated-looking, so Nicole Kidman-ish."

Julianne fought an inner battle to divulge that she'd come across the outfit in a pile of old clothes dumped on the curb after one of her neighbors moved out. It had been her rotten luck that the ecru gown had been two sizes too large. But even as she'd lamented about the fact she'd never wear the vintage frock herself, she'd assessed its resell value. "No, I didn't make it, but I guarantee I'll give you a great deal on it."

After the group finally got their coffee, Ryder walked her back to the booth just as the marching band echoed out over the streets.

"Pretty soon, you'll be inundated with people and I won't be able to do this." He stopped, turned her into his arms. With all the people milling past them, the kiss was hardly more than a slight press of lips. But it was one of those classic gestures that said, "I don't care who knows we're together."

"Want to do something after all this madness tonight?" she asked.

"That's what I wanted to tell you. Troy and I are picking up a few extra bucks this weekend pulling security detail for Brent. He's swamped. For the next two nights we'll be keeping an eye on the vendor booths."

"But Ryder, you're practically working round the clock as it is. When will you sleep?"

"I'll take turns with Troy grabbing some shuteye. Look, Julianne, I know you wanted to spend time together this weekend but I need the money."

The light finally dawned. "You're using it to hunt for Bethany, aren't you?"

"I tried one investigator, now I'm trying another."

"Ryder, don't waste your money like this. Go to Brent. Let him help you track her down."

"It's a little damned difficult to admit I was nothing but a pawn in her scam, admit I was so stupid to Brent." When he saw the disappointment on her face, he quickly added, "I'll consider it, okay? How's that sound?"

"I wish you'd save your precious cash without throwing it down the drain again when Brent could pull out every resource."

"Why do you have to be so smart?"

Her lips curved. "Because I'm Miss Dickinson and I say so. You know, I've been thinking. Once I get to town, I'd love to pull together a concert night at the pier. Make it a regular weekly thing. I'm not sure about the logistics of such a gathering but, hearing that marching band this morning, started me thinking. There has to be a number of musicians in town that would love to showcase their talents or their bands and need a venue to perform. It's a win-win."

Ryder stood back, amazed. "This town will really benefit from having you as part of their community."

"I'd say that applies to you as well."

"Where are you staying this weekend? Are you making the drive back and forth to Santa Cruz?"

"Nope. Dad is, but I'm at the B&B. He works at the house all day tomorrow and Sunday while I watch the booth. I took the last room Nick and Jordan had available. It isn't the luxury suite and I have to share a bathroom but nothing beats the accommodations or the food at Promise Cove."

"I'd drive you out there this afternoon if I didn't have to go on the clock."

"It's okay. Will we ever get time for just us, Ryder?"

"You bet. We get this weekend behind us and we'll have a real, honest to goodness date."

"Promise?"

"Promise."

Stepping back inside the tent, she handed a steaming Styrofoam cup off to her dad.

"Why don't you go take a peek at the floats," John suggested as he took the caffeine.

"Nah, I want to be here for my first sale. I already have a buyer for the lacey ivory dress."

"You mean the wedding gown?"

"A versatile evening dress that can be used for exchanging vows or dinner out," she corrected with a wink. She found a piece of paper, a black marker, and began to write the word "hold" on a sign to drape over the outfit she now considered Bree's.

For the next several hours she and her dad waited on a steady stream of customers. She gave Jordan a great price on the little side table with the curved legs. Emma Colter bought the cabinet to help organize her sewing room. Janie Pointer just had to have the wing chair recovered in a robust plaid for the man in her life—and Flynn McCready's birthday.

"We're doing better than I expected," Julianne announced after Abby Anderson left with the sketch of two playful dolphins that had been reframed using leftover wood from an old window. "Or should I say the school? I'm so caught up in meeting everyone new that I don't even care that we don't get to keep the profits. The important thing is that Pelican Pointe has a future."

For the first time since his daughter had made the decision to move here, John decided she'd picked the right town. "So do you," he said wrapping her up in a bear hug.

At work, Ryder took his coffee and checked the sheet assignment. He headed into the gym and what used to be the boys' dressing area. He could tell it had belonged to a bunch of guys by the sections of the blue walls that still remained. For several hours he worked alongside Troy at ripping out drywall. Together they knocked down the one barrier separating the two anterooms.

The school had never had air conditioning, didn't really need it this close to the ocean. But it did have a network of air ducts that ran throughout the building. He was almost done for the day when he drew back the single jack and with one swing brought down a cascading mountain of debris. He heard metal ping on the concrete, saw something russet-colored ricochet and hit the bottom of the wall.

"What the hell?" Troy noted. "What is that?"

"Looks like an old metal strong box."

"Another box?"

Ryder stepped over, picked it up. "This one's kinda beat up."

"Wow, this entire place is full of junk stuffed into hidey holes. The day you were out sick Zach found an old cigar box."

Ryder turned to stare at Troy. "What was in it?"

"Same kind of trinkets as the first one."

"Why didn't you say something?

"I didn't think it was worth mentioning."

"What did Zach do with the one he found?"

"I don't know exactly. I think he took it home."

"Go get him. Tell him to bring the box back here."

"Okay, but why? It's just a box full of odds and ends that belonged to a kid."

"Do it," Ryder directed. Taking out his cell phone, he punched the speed dial.

When her cell phone dinged, Julianne was in the middle of helping Bree slip the dress over her shirt and jeans to get an idea of the size.

"Julianne, can you get your dad to watch the booth for you for a little while? You need to get over to the school. Now."

"Okay. Sure. Ryder, what's wrong?"

"I'll explain when you get here."

"Be there in a sec."

"What's the matter?" John asked. "You look absolutely stricken."

"I'm not sure but Ryder sounded like there was a major problem. Pop, watch the booth for me, will you? Bree, take the dress with you, pay me first chance you get. If it doesn't fit, you can take it to Emma Colter and get it tailored."

When Bree started to protest, Julianne waved her off and shot out of the tent, heading down Main toward Cape May.

By the time she walked into the gym, Zach had gone back home and retrieved the small cardboard box he'd found and kept.

"What's going on?" Julianne wanted to know, picking up on the tension in the room.

Ryder told her about the two boxes. "They may not be related to the first one Troy found but I thought you needed to be here when we opened up the other two."

"I had no idea the one I found was significant," Zach admitted.

"Did you take anything out of it?" Ryder asked.

"For God's sake I'm no thief."

"Zach, no one is accusing you. Drop the attitude. We just need to know what was inside when you found it and where exactly it was hidden when you came across it," Ryder stated.

"It fell out of the air duct in the east wing." Zach flipped open the simple lid. "See, nothing of value—a few shiny coins that were minted in the nineties, a couple of music cassettes, namely R.E.M. and Guns N' Roses, and some stained piece of ugly fabric—just junk a kid might collect, nothing more."

Julianne eyed the ragged scrap of shirt, knowing it matched the first one. She picked up one of the quarters, noted the 1992 date. "Each box is like a mini time capsule. What about the other one, the one you found just now?"

Ryder worked the latch up, opened the beat-up metal case. He rifled through the stuff. "Look at this, a few drawings done in crayons, more baseball cards. This is a 1991 Upper Deck Michael Jordan baseball card. You're right. This is the simple possessions of a kid, a boy, I'd say."

"Is the card valuable?"

"Not really, five bucks maybe at the most."

He rummaged through the rest. "A rabbit's foot, some cash." After counting out the rumpled dollar bills, he proclaimed, "A whopping nine dollars." But at the bottom, something caught his eye. A stained piece of fabric under everything else. Ryder's mouth went dry. "Julianne."

She stared at another matching sample of the same material. "Oh my God. It's as if someone planted these all around the school. It's as if they very much wanted them to be found."

"It just took us twenty years to do it. But why?"

"The first one was obvious. The bloody shirt. And now…"

"What bloody shirt?" Troy and Zach repeated at the same time.

It was Julianne who took them through the rest. "If we try to connect the dots, it's obvious to me that some child felt the need to hide his possessions like this, away from the prying eyes of adults. He had a secret he wanted to share but didn't know how."

"Maybe someone who didn't have a place to put his stuff," Troy ventured. "Maybe the kid was homeless. I know how that feels."

Ryder thought about that. "Or someone who wanted to get it out of the house. For safekeeping. Which one of us makes the call to Brent?"

"You do it," Julianne suggested. "I need to take a walk."

"Go ahead. Why don't you head across the street and get everyone a bottle of soda from McCready's. After we're done here, I'll treat you to a beer."

"Sounds like a plan. Be right back."

But Ryder followed her out the door. "Are you okay?" he called out.

"No."

He had to run to catch up with her. "I know this whole thing is weird but—"

She whirled around to face him. "Weird? Personally, I don't care what the Jennings kids told Brent. Finding these boxes has to be related to Layne and Brooke. It has to. Let's say for argument's sake though that it's something else. Whatever conclusion you come to one thing is clear. Whoever that child was hid away the awful bloody clothes. They did it because he or she was troubled and haunted about something horrific."

Drea's bright, eager face popped into her head. The florist hadn't seemed to be harboring a dark secret this morning while she'd ordered coffee. That aside, Julianne's fury didn't lessen. "Need I remind you that even Brent used the words evil and dark to describe this whole thing? There's a reason for that. He senses something that he isn't willing to share."

"I don't disagree with you. But without some sort of proof what good does it do to speculate?"

She tried to tamp down her rage at the idea that a child had been dragged into a sordid situation involving death, perhaps even murder.

"At this point, someone needs to do more than speculate."

After the fair ended for the day, Julianne knocked on Brent's front door. When he answered, the words rushed out. "I'm not here to debate about a spooky séance or the psychic vision thing so relax."

"Good to know," Brent said flashing his grin.

"Don't try to use that smile on me, Brent Cody. It won't work. Since I'm more like an honorary sister to you than a female, that charming face of yours is of no concern to me."

"I'm pretty sure you're both. Come on in."

"No, I didn't come here to intrude on your Friday night with your family. So if it's all the same to you, I'll just stand out here and say what I came to say."

He stepped out onto the porch, motioned for her to take a seat on the steps. "Do you plan to tell me why you're so mad and yelling at me?"

"I'll tell you why. When an adult drags a child into something dark and evil—your words not mine—it pisses me off. Now, more pieces of the bloodstained shirt turns up, which just proves it wasn't a fluke. So don't try to placate me."

"You're so worked up, I'm not gonna try to do anything at the moment."

"Good because that would just piss me off, too."

He snorted out a laugh. "Why Julianne Dickinson I don't believe I've heard you utter a curse word before now, let alone two times in one night. What would my mother say?"

"She'd probably want to wash my mouth out. Look, I have nothing against the Jennings family, nothing at all. I even spent a Saturday night not that long ago shooting pool with Drea and she seems like a nice person. But when Layne's kids told you that box didn't belong to any of them, I don't think they were telling you the truth. All three are hiding something."

"I know that."

"You do?" She suddenly ran out of steam and dropped her butt down on the steps.

"Julianne?"

"What?"

"I've been in law enforcement since I joined the army at eighteen. I have a pretty good second sense when I think someone's deceitful. But I won't discuss…"

"An ongoing investigation," Julianne finished. "I get it. What do you think happened the night Layne and Brooke vanished then?"

"Didn't I just say…?" He blew out a sigh. "Oh hell. These days it's very difficult, if not impossible to disappear without leaving a digital footprint." At the look of confusion, he added, "Technology-wise you use a credit card, an ATM, a social security card—it's easy enough to track. Back in the nineties when Brooke and Layne went missing it might've been somewhat easier. For what it's worth, I already mentioned that I don't think the two ever left Pelican Pointe…so…what I'm about to tell you is not for public consumption, understand?"

"Of course."

"Brooke was from Scotts Valley."

"That's just a few minutes north of Santa Cruz."

"That's right. So after a couple of days of not hearing from her, it was no big deal for her family to drive over to Pelican Pointe to check up on her, make sure she was okay. When her parents arrived at her house—the one over on Pacific Street—they discovered her car still parked in the driveway. It was Brooke's father who called in a missing persons report right then and there. The thing is

Layne's car was found a few miles south of town, parked on land that used to belong to Eleanor's family."

"Ah. That makes no sense. Why would Layne do that? Wouldn't you need a mode of transportation to run away with your lover and start a new life together? Isn't that essential for escape?"

"Exactly. So if they didn't take Brooke's car or Layne's, what wheels did they use to head out of town? How did they get to a train or bus station? Hell, how did they get to the nearest airport? A taxi? There's no service from here. You can rent a limo or a car at the Santa Cruz Airport but back when this happened they didn't provide service to pick you up in Pelican Pointe. I checked."

"What about tracing the 1984 class ring? Because Gerald Colter told Ricky Oden who told his wife that he was pretty sure Layne went to UC Santa Barbara."

"Cut it out. I'm not willing to discuss specifics with you."

She huffed out a breath. "I'm sorry, Brent."

"Why?"

"Because now I see that the new police chief has a handle on this whole thing. More than I thought he did."

"I understand why you're upset. After all, you're the one who discovered the evidence that kicked off this entire investigation. You have a stake in it."

"Does it matter that Eleanor's dead and can't be prosecuted if it turns out to be her?"

"My attempt at learning what really happened to those two that night won't factor in that Eleanor's gone. If I find out it was Eleanor who did something, it closes the case. But I'm more determined now than ever to uncover where they went. If, after all this time, I find out the couple is living a quiet life in Fiji, or somewhere equally tropical, then I'll wish them well and put them on my Christmas card list."

She bumped his shoulder. "I should be mad at you for making Ryder work the entire weekend. By any chance did he talk to you about anything…significant?"

"Julianne?"

"What?"

"In all the years I've known you, I never realized you were such a nosy busybody."

"Oh, be quiet or I'll tell River about your disgusting habit."

"I'm sure she knows all about it." But he cocked one eyebrow as if he'd just thought of something. "You wouldn't?"

"Oh yes, I would. I'll tell your wife how you're addicted to chocolate ice cream, especially triple chocolate fudge with double chocolate syrup. I've seen you gorge on the stuff until you make yourself sick."

"You're a cruel woman, Miss Dickinson."

"And don't you forget it."

Once she left the Cody house, she bypassed the food court, even though it was still grilling burgers. The line was too long to wait so she made a stop at the Hilltop Diner to order take-out—greasy cheeseburgers with everything on the side and fries to go. She added vanilla milkshakes and dessert—a triple fudge tunnel cake—Mona, the waitress, dubbed it as her father's own version of death by chocolate. She figured Ryder and Troy could both use the sugar rush.

She tracked Ryder down at the corner of Crescent Street by the booths near Ferguson's Hardware.

"What have you got there?" he asked.

She held up the bag and dangled it in the air. "Food. Can you take a break?"

"Sure, as long as we keep it close. What are you doing here, Julianne?"

"I just had a long talk with Brent."

"That's odd, so did I…earlier when he came to the school."

"That's good to hear."

"I took your advice. After giving him a photo of the woman I knew as Bethany, he says he'll do what he can to find her using something called face recognition software. If she has a driver's license anywhere in the US, she should pop up. First, he'll start with licenses issued within the last couple years. It may take time but for the first time in a long time…I'm hopeful."

"It's a start."

"What about you? Why did you go see Brent?"

"You know why. I was upset about so many boxes turning up. I vented because I didn't think Brent was doing enough. Turns out, he has it handled. For the second time, he made me feel like an idiot but at least he listened to what I had to say."

She munched on a fry before assembling her lettuce and tomato on top of her burger. She took a generous, juicy bite. Looking up at the evening sky, the stars winked back at her. "I met a lot of new people today. I started out this morning at five-thirty. I'm exhausted."

"I stayed up last night until one o'clock putting a business plan together."

"When do you plan on meeting with Nick?"

"Whenever I think I'm ready. It's a little intimidating to take a dream to the bank and ask for a loan."

"But you know Nick. He handled my mortgage like it belonged to him. Professional, thorough, he even explained everything to me in detail."

In the dark, Ryder saw her eyes sparkle. He drew her close, muffled her words with the press of his lips. "I want you."

"Same here. I'm tired of waiting, Ryder. We need some alone time."

"We could pray for rain."

"How would that help?"

"You could close up the tent."

"Ah. I'd just like it if we could go to the dance tomorrow night together."

"I'll see what I can do."

Around two a.m. drowsiness hit Ryder.

The streets were deserted. The diehards had closed up McCready's an hour earlier. Even the carnival workers had called it a night.

Bored, he sat down on the bench at the pier to listen to the lapping water hit the shore. He found the sound only made him want to curl up in his bed even more. To fight his weariness, he took out his Thermos, poured a cup of coffee.

He looked up about the time a man appeared right out of the water. He decided he must be seeing things until the figure got closer. He narrowed his eyes, prepared to leap to his feet to defend the wharf against an invading army of one. But then he recognized the walk, the face, and relaxed his stance.

"You're like the Gill-Man from the black lagoon."

Scott raised his arms, wiggled his fingers. "See, no fish hands."

"Might as well sit down, although I'm not sure that Troy won't freak out when he spots me talking to myself."

"How do you know Troy doesn't see me?"

"Does he?"

"Why don't you ask him?"

"It's a little embarrassing to ask a guy if he's seeing a ghost walking around town."

"It was a good move asking Brent for help."

"That was Julianne's idea."

"Another good move."

"You know, I was told you could help me find Bethany. So far you haven't taken out a map and been my guidepost to her front door."

"Helping you is why I'm here. Have you ever wondered why Zach acts so belligerent lately? Like today.

Why he gets upset at the least little thing? It isn't like him."

"Could've fooled me. Since I've been here I only know Zach's prickly side. It seems to me he carries around a lot of resentment about something. That chip on his shoulder is about as big as Yellowstone."

"Ask him about it."

"You mean the fact he doesn't want anyone dating his sister? Troy's putting that to the test."

"No, it's more than that."

"Did you see him this morning in line for coffee? He almost bit his sister's head off and it was all in good fun. Then later, at the school…"

"Zach's troubled."

"Let me guess. Drug habit he picked up working construction in Colorado?"

"No."

"He's torn about his sexuality?"

"Not that either."

"Then what? I get tired of your guessing games especially at two in the morning."

"Back in Colorado Springs he got picked up for stealing equipment and fencing the goods."

"Zach got arrested?" Ryder shook his head. "Logan finds out he's liable to can him on the spot."

"He wasn't guilty, you idiot. He was wrongly accused, spent a week in jail before the cops finally wised up and were able to straighten out the mess, get down to the truth, and find the real culprits responsible. The charges were dropped. Like you said though the chip on his shoulder is an indication he hasn't put the incident behind him. No one stood up for him when it counted. Since then, he puts distance between himself and just about everyone."

"What about Bree?"

"Bree doesn't know. He never called her."

"How's anyone supposed to stand up for him if he won't let anyone past that thick armor of his? He keeps pushing people away."

"Don't give up on the boatbuilding idea. It'll be good for the town, good for you, and good for Zach. Include Troy, because no one works harder than Troy. Stop being such a wuss and go see Nick, talk to him about the viability of such an enterprise."

Ryder turned to his right to respond, but Scott was already gone.

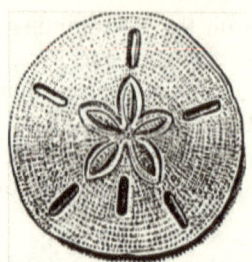

Chapter Thirteen

Ryder was able to grab a couple hours sleep before doing the milking. After taking a shower he sat in the executive offices in front of a computer screen and opened a software program to cut payroll checks. From there he entered all the supply orders online, checked the delivery schedules for the upcoming week and authorized payments to vendors.

By the time he grabbed his tools and walked in to start his Saturday shift at the school, it was fifteen minutes after eight.

Along with the other crew members, Ryder helped to finish the demolition in both locker rooms, all the while fearful they would uncover another mysterious box. They didn't, and were relieved when the wall came down without them having to place another call to Brent.

At the first break Ryder noticed Zach hanging back from the rest of the men. He was surprised when the guy said, "The other day over lunch, were we just bullshitting each other about the boatbuilding thing?"

"I wasn't. I'd love to do it. Why?"

"Because I might know someone who'd trust us enough to build one."

"You're kidding? Here in town?

"No. There's a guy by the name of Jacob Hettinger who races boats. I happen to know he's looking to add to his fleet. We could do it, Ryder."

"Is he a flake? Can we rely on him to pay?"

Zach chuckled. "His daddy has major bucks, comes from old lumber-mill money in Portland. Plus, he owns a construction company that puts up buildings all over the Pacific Northwest and as far south as Colorado and New Mexico. Believe me the guy is good for the money."

"What type boat does he want? We'd have to work on the design, sailboat, speedboat, or one for sport fishing? Me? I prefer to build a sailboat but we shouldn't pigeon-hole ourselves by specializing."

For the next thirty minutes they went over an abbreviated business strategy. Ryder realized he'd need to make a few corrections to his proposal.

After they clocked out for the day, they took a walk to check out Borgerstrom's old place together. This time, it might be more than just a longshot.

"We need to find Troy, form a solid plan between the three of us on what exactly we do with that old space before we bring it to Nick. And Zach?"

"What?"

"I need to ask a favor."

People browsing and milling about kept Julianne hopping most of the day but it was the ones with cash in their pockets that made the time blow by in a flash. Her inventory dwindled to four side chairs, a few odd tables and one high-back settee. She'd re-covered the Warrington-style bench in a bright red-and-cream-striped fabric. She'd known when she chose the pattern it would take a special buyer to fall in love with the color scheme.

So when the Harley-riding Russ Dennis expressed interest in the little loveseat, no one was more surprised than she.

"This will make an excellent accessory in my bedroom," Russ confessed. "I need something at the end of the bed so my favorite girl has a place to curl up."

Julianne sighed. Even the tattooed Russ seemed to be getting more action these days than she did. Just sad, she decided. She and Ryder definitely needed to take care of that problem. And soon. Maybe tonight was the night. But then she remembered he'd be walking guard-duty instead of spending time with her.

"Did I just see Russ carting away a girly settee?" Lilly Pierce asked from the doorway of the tent.

"You did. A piece he assures me goes with his bedroom ensemble."

Lilly chortled out a laugh. "Who would've thought? I hope you plan on going to the dance tonight."

"I'll be there."

"Wally and I are ecstatic you'll be the principal next fall when the school opens. I hear you bought the old Richmond house."

"That's odd. You're the first person to call it that."

"Why? That's what Wally calls it. People seem to forget that it was Layne's house in the first place. According to Wally it was after Layne married Eleanor she painted it that dreadful pink and purple."

"But the deed at closing said the property belonged to Landon Jennings."

"That's *after* Eleanor committed suicide. The way Wally explained it to me she transferred ownership to her brother before taking her own life. And before that, since California is a community property state, she went to court to get some kind of judgment to own the house outright after Layne walked out. Wally has a problem with that though. He says all this talk lately about Layne's walking away is ridiculous. Layne would never have left those kids."

"That seems to be the prevailing sentiment. It's heartbreaking what Eleanor did in front of her children that night."

"All I know is what Wally's told me about it. She must've been seriously whacked to end her life the way she did, to make a big production out of it right in front of her babies. What kind of mother does that?"

"Like you said, seriously whacked."

"I'm looking forward to the live music. You know, the town council added it to give parents a night out. The good thing is we don't need a sitter. It's a family event where the kids are welcome right along with the adults."

"That's what I love about this town. It's a community that comes together when it counts."

Her father had already headed back to Santa Cruz and Julianne was closing up for the day when she looked up to see Nicole Cannon standing in the tent.

"I'm never surprised to see you surrounded by a bunch of second-hand junk," the sandy-haired woman said.

"Then why did you drive fifty minutes to get here?" Julianne shot back.

"I wanted to see firsthand what you'd gotten yourself into. I drove by the school before asking someone to point me to your tent. That place is a mess. There's no way it will open on time."

That comment along with Nicole's behavior had Julianne leaping to defend her school. "*That mess* when it opens will be the finest, state of the art school in Santa Cruz County."

"I doubt that."

"I don't care if you believe it or not. And what I've gotten myself into is a terrific town and a fantastic opportunity. It's a shame you can't stand the thought of me having either one."

"My mother and I knew you'd eventually sink to this."

"Sink to what? To principal? To having my own school? Where I come from that's called advancement but since you're still stuck substituting I can see where you'd be so jealous it's eating you alive."

"Jealous? Of a woman who didn't even have a mother around? Don't be absurd."

Only when Keegan Bennett walked in did the hostile banter come to a sudden halt and Nicole turned to leave.

"What was that all about?" Keegan asked. "I didn't mean to interrupt."

"It's nothing. Childhood bitterness."

"Hmm, pettiness is what I heard. Anyway, I came because I want that oak table with the beachy blue and white ceramic inlay."

"I love this piece so much I thought about keeping it for the new house."

"Too late. I want it to replace my end table in the living room. You put the tile top in there, didn't you? How on earth did you manage that? I'd love it if I had a creative side like this."

"Me? You do the tough job rescuing animals. I just fiddle with fixing things up. Let me help you tote this over to the house."

Since she passed right in front of Hidden Moon Bay Books on her way back, Julianne made a stop she'd been meaning to make to check out the bookstore. This was her perfect chance.

As she walked in the door, the beautiful blonde behind the counter balanced a stack of paperbacks in her arms. "Hi Julianne!"

"Hi Hayden."

"How'd you do today? We were swamped. Ethan had a book signing early this morning and we sold out of all his books."

"Congrats. Turns out, I sold more stuff today than I did yesterday. Are you and Ethan coming to the dance?"

"Wouldn't miss it? We're leaving Nate at home though and getting a sitter to have us a little alone time. How about you?"

"I'll be there but by myself."

"That's no fun. Don't tell me Ryder's working."

"All right, I won't tell you," she said with a laugh.

"I'm sorry. What can I do for you today? Are you looking for anything in particular?"

"I know it's a longshot but… By any chance do you have any books on building boats?"

"That's a tough one. If I have anything at all, it would be in the how-to section. Let's take a look."

Julianne followed the store owner into another room where all the shelves were jammed to capacity. "Your inventory is amazing." Her eyes immediately went to a hardcover on flea markets. "I've been looking everywhere for this, tried to find it online but it's out of print. I walk in the door and find it among your stock."

As Hayden perused the shelves, she talked as she searched up and down the aisles. "Did I mention the other night when you were over that my sister has decided to relocate here?"

"To Pelican Pointe? Really? From back east, right?"

"From St. Louis. Sydney's an ER nurse. She's fed up with living in the city. She's been trying to get up the nerve to make a new start. Ever since my wedding she's wanted to make the move here but her on-again off-again boyfriend always talked her out of it. Now, she's finally had enough of both."

"Good for her. When will she get here?"

"As soon as she sells her condo." About that time, Hayden spied what she'd been looking for. "How about this? It's a manual, like a textbook. Will that work?"

"Perfect."

"Really? Do you want it gift-wrapped?"

"You do that?"

"All the time."

"Then wrap it up. I'm taking the flea market book too."

Julianne had one more stop to make before heading out to the B&B. She dashed through the door of Drea's Flowers. The place wasn't as large as it looked from the outside because all kinds of greenery and blossoms took up the display space.

"Hey there, Julianne. What can I do for you?"

"I'm hoping to persuade you to put something together extra nice for Jordan. She and Nick have been so nice to me."

"No problem. Yesterday I received some gorgeous, rare blue orchids especially for the fair. They're tall and elegant and would make an impression on anyone. I'll give you a great price on them."

"Sold. Could I take them with me today? I'd like to give them to her while I'm here this time."

"Absolutely. I'll just be a minute."

"You obviously love your job," Julianne said, keeping up the conversation even though Drea had disappeared into the back.

"Oh, I do. I've always loved everything about flowers. Even as a little girl the best place on earth for me was the garden center, second to being around my dad, that is. He worked for his father, my grandfather, at the train store, the only hobby shop in town. It used to be across the street."

At the mention of her father, Julianne's heart went out to Drea.

But the woman went on, "All three of us would go in there to hang out to spend time with both of them. That is…" Her voice trailed off. "When my mother would allow it."

"Your mother didn't like the idea of you visiting your own father? That's so…odd. Why?"

"My mother was ill." Drea tapped the side of her head. "Up here. I don't remember all that much about her. And what I do recall was…not good. Caleb was just a baby but I know Cooper loved that store. He'd sneak in there after school and spend hours and hours until she'd come to drag him out of there, Saturdays too. He'd get in trouble for it. Poor thing. My mother wasn't very kind to her oldest for some reason."

"How sad."

"It was. But then she took her own life and it was like we'd been saved. I know that sounds horrible, perhaps even callous, but my mother wasn't a very nice person."

"I'm sorry."

"Hey, life isn't perfect." When Drea finished arranging the buds in a clear vase, she said, "Here you go. Will that be cash or charge?"

"Charge," Julianne said as she handed off her MasterCard. Sensing this was the perfect opening to find out a little about the florist, she blurted out, "Do you ever wonder what happened to your dad?"

Drea ran the plastic through the reader, appearing unfazed by the question. "I used to. But years go by and you realize that no matter how much you wonder, I'm not sure we'll ever really know. It was heartbreaking for us when our dad left though."

"So you think that's what happened? He left town?" But Julianne could see the words were difficult for Drea to handle. "I'm sorry. You don't have to answer that."

Drea handed her back her credit card. "I went through all this with Brent. I hope he comes up with the answers."

Julianne left it at that and made her way back to the B&B. On the drive, she tried to judge whether or not the florist had come across as honest. But then she realized Drea had been six years old at the time, no older than the children in her class. Eleanor's suicide and the way it happened had to weigh heavily on Drea's young mind. Julianne shook her head. Simply put, some women weren't mother material.

After getting back, she almost chunked the whole night. What was the point of getting dressed up to go to a dance without a date? It was only after Nick and Jordan played the guilt card that she went upstairs to her room and changed clothes.

She put on her sexiest outfit that showed off her skin tone and dark hair—a short Aztec-patterned skirt, a blue silk top, and a bright red cuffed blazer. She added a layer of beaded chains around her neck, a clunky bracelet to match and three-inch feathered earrings that swung from her ears.

Slipping her feet into a pair of dark blue, four-inch, sling-back heels, she posed in front of the mirror. She beamed in approval. If she did say so herself, she looked ready to party.

Downstairs she was shocked to see Ryder standing in the foyer. He was decked out in a jacket, a button-down shirt tucked into a pair of crisp blue jeans. "What are you doing here?"

"I wanted to surprise you. Turns out Zach wanted to earn some extra cash. He took over guard duty for me tonight."

"Remind me to find a way to thank Zach."

It was all that dark hair cascading down her shoulders that had Ryder taking her by the hand, twirling her around. "Wow, you look fantastic. I should issue an advance warning. Wearing that outfit, don't expect me to keep my hands off you."

She leaned in and whispered, "I'm counting on it."

Jordan came out of the kitchen, carrying the vase full of flowers. She was also in the process of giving last minute instructions to Emma Colter, the woman pulling babysitting detail for them tonight.

Julianne waited for her opening. "Before we go, there's something I'd like to talk to both of you about." She watched Nick trail Jordan who finally took a breath and stopped to arrange the bouquet in a prominent position on the table in the entryway.

"What's that?" Nick said absently as he looked around for his keys. "We all really need to get moving. We're running late as it is."

"This won't take long I promise." With that, Julianne went into a spiel about her ideas for the summer once she got to town—concerts on the pier using local talent and movie night in the common area. "But what I really noticed right off was that the area in question isn't really a park at all. It doesn't even have a name. That space between Murphy's Market and the bank is just wasted space. With a little work it could be an honest-to-goodness park. And if that happened, it would need a name. What I'd really like to do is propose to the town council that it be named for Scott. Make it Phillips Park or whatever you two think would be appropriate."

Julianne immediately recognized her mistake when she saw Jordan stutter to a stop and her eyes grow watery. Even the flowers she'd thought would lessen the blow didn't do the trick. A heavy silence followed. Even Nick seemed upset that she'd brought it up and blinked back at her with a sad expression on his face.

"Oh my God, what a wonderful idea!" Jordan exclaimed in a burst of emotion, wiping the tears away from her cheeks.

"Really?"

"It's perfect. How wonderful that you thought of something like that for Scott, for Hutton. Why didn't we?" she said, turning to her husband.

Nick nodded in agreement. "I'll see to it first thing Monday that you're slated to address the council at the very next meeting. You'll want to make sure and stay for the vote."

Once they reached the truck, Ryder turned her into his arms. "That was a good thing you did back there."

"For one long, drawn-out minute, I wasn't so sure."

"I've been waiting to do this all day." He covered her mouth, had the blood pumping in an instant, drawing out the need.

The only thing that had them moving again was when Nick and Jordan flew out the door behind them.

"I'd suggest blowing this whole dance thing off but too many people are expecting us to show up."

Ryder opened the door to the passenger side, helped her maneuver into the seat in the short skirt. "I'm not sure I've ever been to a dance in the park before. How does this work?"

"From what I understand, the food booths line one side of the park on the bank side, the dancing on the other next to Murphy's Market. I don't know. Maybe people drift out into the street to dance."

Once they got to town, Julianne turned in the seat and said, "It's silly I know, but I'd like to put a name to my little bungalow."

"Why's that silly? Logan refers to that place on the hill as Sea Glass Cottage."

"He does? It was Scott who actually inspired the idea. He had me thinking about all the famous ghosts. Casper. Canterville. Grey Lady. Remember the house in that movie, *The Ghost and Mrs. Muir*? They called that one, Gull Cottage."

"You've obviously put some thought into this, so toss me some ideas."

She pitched out a few, but none hit a homerun. "I'm still thinking it through."

Ryder found a parking place the pickup would fit into on Ocean Street. They passed the wharf, heard the water slapping against the wooden pillars below.

Before they ever reached the park, they heard the music. The band Blue Skies had already tuned up and tested the sound by playing a lively tune that reverberated in between the buildings. The guitar refrain from Dwight Yoakum's, *Guitars, Cadillacs* had couples pairing up, stepping and strutting in time to the beat.

As they approached the entrance to the common area, Julianne pictured the future, the concrete sign with Scott's name carved on it, maybe a few more benches, even a swing or two, and a larger grassy area where the kids could play.

Just as they had thought, the crowd overflowed onto the street. The dance floor was a bump and grind where space allowed. Among the masses she recognized Troy and Bree—wondered how the waitress had talked McCready into letting her have the night off. Ethan and Hayden were dancing with the baby sandwiched in-between them. Julianne decided their babysitter must've backed out. She spotted River and Brent two-stepping in each other's arms. Even Logan and Kinsey had wanted a night out and brought their two-week-old twins nestled inside a double stroller.

Julianne couldn't resist leaning in and taking a peek at the newborn faces, the little fists, the soft pink and baby blue outfits.

"You both did a good job there," she told the new parents.

"We did, didn't we?" Kinsey said in agreement.

"They're beautiful, kind of like their mom and dad. You look fantastic, Kinsey."

"Now that little white lie just makes me like you all the more," the new mom admitted. "But don't stop. I love hearing it."

"They got the beautiful genes from her," Logan said, planting a kiss on his wife's mouth. "So how many teacher slots have we left to fill?"

"Two. River gave me a lead on two out-of-town candidates in Santa Fe willing to relocate. I'm doing a phone interview next week with both. I'll let you know how it goes."

"Sorry to break up this talking shop, but I've been chomping at the bit to dance with my date. Come on," Ryder said. Taking Julianne's hand in his, he led her out to the makeshift dance floor, a stretch of framed plywood, painted and arranged over the grass. They moved and swayed while the fiddle led them into *Wild and Blue*. Keeping time to the beat, they rocked into Ricky Oden's version of *Seven Year Ache* before sailing into *Guitar Town*. The throng weaved, twirled, until the band slowed down the tempo with *A Thousand Miles from Nowhere*.

They made another pass around the floor while the rendition of *Cigarettes and Chocolate Milk* played in the background. The song had Ryder leaning in, whispering, "Have we been here long enough yet? Can we get out of here now?"

"And go where? Last time we tried your place, we were interrupted by a cow emergency. I'm not taking that chance again. We can't go back to my room at the B&B. Emma Colter's there babysitting. I won't traipse through the living room and sneak you into my room. I'd feel uncomfortable with her right downstairs."

"Then what do you suggest?"

She poked a finger into his ribs, murmured, "The only place I know where we'll have total privacy is my house."

"Back in Santa Cruz? That'll work."

"Can you last until we get there?"

He nibbled her ear. "Can you? I'm willing to try." The consent in her eyes had him wasting no time moving through the swarm of people. "Then let's get out of here."

Like a man on a mission, he drew her along the streets, down Main, up Beach toward the pier. On the rush back to the car, Julianne breathed air deep. "I smell rain."

"Wishful thinking. I smell grilled burgers."

She laughed and it echoed out into the night. They didn't say another word until they climbed into the truck. The drive seemed to take forever. But when Ryder finally came to a stop in front of the house, he admitted, "My palms are actually sweating."

"Why?"

"I haven't been with a woman in two years. You had to know that after…that woman…I refuse to say her name tonight and ruin this moment. But you had to know I'd sworn off women."

She looked at him long and hard, sleeked her hand along his arm. "I don't think a certain part of your anatomy ever got that memo."

"Not with you around." They locked fingers. "Julianne?"

"What?"

"I can't wait to be inside you."

"Then why are we just sitting here."

He trailed after her to the front door, waited while she stuck the key into the lock. If he didn't get his hands on her soon he thought he might explode. So he reached out, fingered her hair, brushed several strands to the side. He ran his tongue along her neck. She tasted like sweet orange blossoms.

She spun around, used both hands to angle his head down to her mouth.

Weeks of waiting, the tender kiss became fierce, needy. They stumbled over the threshold, bumped into the wall wrapped in each other, lips fused.

He barely kicked the door closed before running his hands inside her blazer, yanked it down her arms and off. In one fluid motion, he went after her silky top. Like a magnet, the sexy bra she wore drew his fingers to the red lace. Underneath, he saw her nipples go taut at the foreplay.

Kicking out of her shoes, she reached around to undo the skirt in the back, slithered out of the mini fabric. She got him rolling out of his jacket, couldn't work the buttons on his shirt fast enough.

Eyeing the black and red army tattoo, she ran her nails over it and along his arm. "Let me see if I can find a way to thank you properly for your service."

He snagged her around the waist, boosted her up and off her feet.

"Which way?"

"Down the hall."

Mouths fed off each other. Teeth scraped against skin like hungry vampires savoring the soft sweet flesh just before a bite. Tongues tagged and played a game of hide-and-seek.

As soon as they reached the bed, he dropped her on the mattress, skimmed his hands up her thighs and ripped down her panties.

"Red. I really like red."

"Good to know," she drawled, kicking out of them. She ran her hands across his chest as he dispatched her bra. She rose up again, guided his rough fingers to her breasts. Her head fell back as pleasure slammed into her. She arched her body, urged him to lick his way around curves, find his way to each nipple.

His fingers roamed to stroke, to wet, to slick. While sensations triggered every nerve from head to toe, she purred out encouragement, one slow chord at a time. "Ryder. You. Do. That. Oh. Oh. So. Well." The last chorus drew out into more than one syllable.

It was that music to his ears that had him doubling down. His goal was to taste and lick the skin along her lean belly, travel down to satiny thighs.

Another rush of pleasure took hold, dug in. It twirled in circles of gilded light and shimmered in rippled explosions. She wanted more and lifted her hips, realized he was still wearing his pants.

He dealt with the shoes while her fingers found the snap of his jeans, worked it open. She tugged downward on the boxers, wrestled them over his hips and pleaded, "Now, Ryder! Now!"

He sunk into her body, watched her soulful eyes shimmer in heat as the join became complete. Hands spread, their fingers locked, their breath warm and close.

As he moved to cover her mouth, she threw her legs around his waist. Her nails scored along his back, felt each muscle bunch as he drove them toward the peak, the whirlpool, that riptide that drew them under and then over.

Body to body, she raked her fingers through his hair.

Sweaty and spent, breathing hard, Ryder grunted, "I'll move in a sec."

"S'okay."

"No, I must be squashing you. You're so tiny."

She puffed out a laugh, bumped his chest with hers. "Right this minute, no complaints about where you are."

He found that funny and rolled to his back. "I'm pretty happy about it, too." With a free arm, he wrapped it around her shoulders and brought her into him. "We should've thought to bring food. That way we wouldn't have to get out of bed."

"Ah. We forgot to eat."

"I was too focused on this, on you."

"Same here. We could get up, explore what's in the kitchen. I don't have much as I've been busy going back and forth between two places and haven't had a lot of time to shop. I'm out of my routine."

Ryder didn't want to let her go, hated to move from this spot, but after his stomach rumbled once too often, he sat up.

"I think I have cereal or maybe some eggs," she said. "I wouldn't want you to starve."

"That'll work."

She went to the closet, found a robe. Not the frumpy, functional one she wore in winter to bundle up against the chill but the short silky one that showed off her form.

As he stuck one leg into his jeans, Ryder noticed. His head whipped up. "Who knew the teacher was so fond of red?"

"I like color."

"I like that you like color."

He followed that laugh again as it rang out, down the hallway and into the kitchen.

"There's not much here," Ryder said as he perused the refrigerator. He opened the carton of milk, did the sniff test. "Milk's okay."

She retrieved a box of Frosted Mini-Wheats out of the cabinet and two bowls, two spoons.

They sat down at the table and dug in.

Just before taking her first bite, she looked over at his bare chest. "You know it's a long way back to Pelican Pointe."

"I was thinking the same thing. Look how long it took us to get here."

"Exactly. It's even farther back to the farm. You could call Troy, see if he'd do the morning milking for you. That way…"

"This time of night, it's best to send him a text."

Troy and Bree had just left the dance in his GMC Canyon pickup and were headed out to his apartment when Ryder's text came in.

"Who's that?" Bree wanted to know.

"Ryder. Looks like he finally experienced 'touchdown' with Julianne. He wants me to take over his milking chores in the morning."

Bree snickered in delight at the idea of Ryder and Julianne spending the night together. "You won't say no, will you?"

"I'd have to get up at the crack of dawn. And I have my own plans for tonight." Troy lifted her hand, brought it to his lips.

"It's all for love. I'll help you."

"But… I wanted you to spend the night with me tonight."

From the passenger side of the truck, she turned in her seat, tilted her head and ran a finger along his cheek. "Now how would I help you milk cows if I didn't stay with you tonight and wake up when you wake up?"

Troy's eyes flicked from the road and lit up. "Really?"

"Yes, really. I'm pretty sure if you play your cards right, you'll experience the same sort of 'touchdown' for yourself as Ryder is right about now."

The likelihood of that had him stepping on the gas. "I can't believe Flynn gave you the night off."

"Oh, I can. I bugged him about it for weeks."

"Zach and I may not see eye to eye but we do agree on one thing. I don't like you working at the bar."

Her back went up. "I'm not listening to this with you too. I have to deal with Zach enough as it is. I'm earning a living doing the only job in town I can get at the moment. Please don't ruin tonight by giving me a hard time about my job."

"I'm sorry. It's just that I want you to know I'll do everything I can to make this excursion business a reality."

"I know that. But until I graduate, it's just a pipe dream and I still have to go into McCready's whenever he needs me. It pays the bills. So you concentrate on your thing and I'll work on mine. Deal?"

"Okay. Okay. I don't want this ruining our night."

Bree scooted closer, whispered in his ear, "I splurged on new lingerie."

That had Troy increasing his speed again.

She laid a hand on his arm. "It's okay. We have all night."

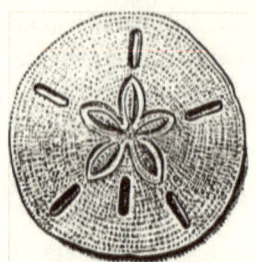

Chapter Fourteen

Julianne opened one eye to the unmistakable sound of dripping water. But it didn't sound like the pipes had burst. Could it be rain pounding the roof?

Before the other eye shuttered open, she felt the hard part of Ryder's anatomy nestled against her leg that she'd enjoyed twice last night.

She tried to move to the edge so she could extricate herself from the sheets without waking him. But as soon as she inched over to the side of the bed, he latched on in a death grip and started nuzzling her neck.

"Where ya goin'?"

"Pee."

"Ah." He raised his head to listen. "What's that sound?"

"Rain. Which only makes me want to pee more."

He rolled to his back, allowing her the freedom to dart to the bathroom. "Are you saying we got our wish?"

As she beat a path down the hallway, over her shoulder she hollered out, "The rain gods must've been listening. The sky opened up and the rain's coming down out there in buckets. I have no idea for how long."

When she got back, she snatched her cell phone off the nightstand.

"What does all this rain mean for the fair?"

"According to the text message Murphy sent at seven o'clock, that's forty-five minutes ago, the storm put an early end to the festivities. Wind damage to some of the vendor tents. Even the carnival is packing up and calling it quits, heading to the next town."

"Should we go check on your stuff?"

"I didn't have many items left," she said as she slid in between the covers. "And if the tent collapsed, what's still there is probably already soaked from the downpour."

The phone on the nightstand rang and she flipped back over to answer it. "Hello. Oh hi, Pop. You know what? Let's both take the rainy day off and be slugs. No, there's no reason… Pop, why won't you stay put? You deserve a day to kick back. Instead of picking up what's left, indulge yourself, catch a preseason baseball game on the tube from sunny Florida. Okay. Great. See you then."

"Nicely done."

"He's been working too hard. Like someone else I know."

"But maybe we should go load up your things."

Wrapping her arms around his chest, she snuggled into his body, ran a hand down his midsection. "If you really think my father will stay where he is, you don't know John Dickinson. He's probably already heading over there now despite what I say. Besides, do you really want to move from this spot?"

He kissed the top of her hair, nibbled down her jaw to her neck. "No."

"Then I say we make the most of today."

He rolled, reversed their positions. "Just so you know I'm more than okay right here."

"And just so *you* know, I'm stronger than I look. I'll keep you where I can take advantage of you. Don't exert yourself. Save your strength. Because you're going to need it."

"Same goes."

When they finally crawled out of bed, they had to get creative to scrounge up something for breakfast.

Julianne made use of her last three eggs and the last drop of milk to scramble up an omelet.

Because Ryder had scouted her kitchen the night before, he made himself to home and started coffee.

Over their first cup, the phone rang again.

While listening to the caller on the other end, she mouthed the words, "It's Jordan wanting to know if I'm alive."

"I'm sorry," Julianne finally said aloud into the receiver. "I didn't mean to make you worry. I should've found you at the dance and explained that I had decided to spend Saturday night back home in Santa Cruz. I appreciate the concern. No, no, really, I'm fine. Thanks for caring enough to make sure that I wasn't in a ditch between here and there."

When she hung up, she turned to Ryder. "I don't think I fooled her for a second."

He chuckled into his mug of caffeine. "Probably not. Are you worried about your rep because you're the school principal?"

"Not really. I haven't even started the job yet. And…well…my private life is my own."

Pleased to hear that, he said, "Have you ever thought about opening up a resale shop in town in one of those empty buildings along Main?"

"But I love being around the kids."

He shook his head. "I'm not saying give it up. Rent one of those old empty spaces, stock it with your inventory, pay someone to run it during the nine months you're principal. With jobs so scarce it shouldn't be that hard to find a willing employee."

She sat back, sipped her brew. "That's not a bad idea. It might be a way to add to my second income, which I might point out, will be sorely missed if being principal takes up most of my time. What about you? I'm not trying to needle you but when do you plan to take your idea to Nick?"

"Monday. That reminds me I need to make a few changes to my business plan. You know, I'll need to get back to the farm for the evening milking."

"We could work on the proposal for Nick here."

"I don't have my laptop."

"We'll make notes the old-fashioned way. Let's do the dishes and get started that way you can transfer everything to your computer file, print out the hard copy before morning."

It continued to rain throughout the morning as they put on music and absorbed themselves with all the right buzzwords to impress a banker about Ryder's acumen, as well as Zach's and Troy's.

In between putting together the game plan for the boatbuilding venture, she tossed every wilted vegetable she had on hand—potatoes, carrots, celery, spring beans—into a soup pot to simmer for lunch.

"Whatever it is you're cooking, it smells delicious."

"Nothing like having soup on a rainy day."

He leaned against the doorframe and watched her mince garlic, strip fresh rosemary and chop basil to dump into the pot.

"Where did you learn to cook?"

"Between Pop and Danny's mother those two taught me all I needed to know about putting together a meal on a tight budget."

"Tell me about Danny."

"You want to hear about Danny? Now? Today?"

"You don't say much about him. While I've gone on, ad nauseam about 'what's her face' to the point that I'm sick of hearing myself talk."

She continued to dice up leeks as she talked. "Danny was a gentle soul. That's not to say he didn't show his temper when the situation warranted one because he did. And he could be stubborn to the point that I wanted to knock some sense into his head. That's what put him on the road where he was killed. You see, we used to love going to junk yards, exploring old second-hand shops for just about everything we had on hand. He'd pick up old car parts he could use in his garage while I'd find some old table or chair I couldn't live without. But that day I had to study for exams. I was working on my Master's at the time. I begged him not to go. Call it a second sense or a premonition or whatever but I wanted him to stay and fix a leaky faucet in our apartment. But he went running out the door anyway to pick up some stupid special carburetor for a Mustang he'd been refurbishing for a friend." The knife in her hand stilled as she bit her lip, fought back tears. "Danny didn't make it back."

Ryder came up behind her, wrapped her up, and kneaded her breasts through her shirt. He grated his teeth along the underside of her ear. "You know what I've always liked to do on a rainy day?"

She relaxed against him and breathed out, "What?"

"I like to take a leisurely bath, especially if I don't have to do it alone."

She turned into him, buried her face in his chest.

He scooped her up, carried her to the bathroom, dropped her on her feet to turn on the tap to let the water run. She began to pour in bubble bath. To get the perfect balance of froth and fragrance, she dabbled with two different bottles before getting it just right.

They took turns undressing each other. As eager as they'd been the night before, this was an unhurried, seductive intimacy born of a lazy afternoon. It was a time to share secrets, discover mysteries.

His eyes took in her slender waist, the curve of hips and breasts until he reached for her to feast on her mouth.

Ryder stepped into the steamy foam first, took her hand to help her over the rim. The smell of coconut and vanilla had them easing down into the velvety bubbles together. Their bodies hummed with want as she settled against him, surrendering to the moment.

His hands roved along her slick skin, nudged her legs apart. The brush of his tongue along her neck brought delightful quivers. His lips skimming flesh created quakes that went on and on. He turned her in his arms to join, to mate. She straddled him, locked her legs around his waist, her hands around his head. Sinking together, the water rose and swished back and forth as they floated through their own swells. Then it was all lust, a rush, a race to reach the torrent. Greed flooded them. The finish came in a burst, a tsunami of tremors and triumph.

He labored to catch his breath, rested his forehead on hers. "I can't get enough of you."

"For someone who hasn't done that in a while, you don't seem out of practice," a breathless Julianne noted. "This was a grand idea."

"I was inspired." He ran a hand down her cheek. "You have to check out of the B&B and I have to get back to the farm. I hate to say this, but it's about time we left our little nest."

"I know."

During the downpour, Troy and Zach helped take down the vendor tents. But it was Troy who spotted John Dickinson loading the leftover odds and ends of furniture belonging to Julianne into the back of his truck.

"Need some help?" Troy asked.

"Thanks, I wouldn't turn down an extra pair of hands," John said.

"Where's Julianne and Ryder?"

"Taking a day off I reckon."

Troy caught the gleam in the man's eyes and knew Ryder and Julianne weren't fooling anybody, least of all John. With no wish to plod further into that minefield, Troy changed the subject. "Are you taking this stuff back to Santa Cruz?"

"Don't see why I should. I thought I'd just store it at the new house in the garage. What do you think?"

"That's a good idea. Practical."

They were hauling it out of the pickup when Julianne and Ryder pulled to the curb.

"Pop, I knew you'd do this. I told you to take a day off. Why don't you ever listen?"

"I'd already made the drive to town to extend the flooring from the kitchen into the laundry room. I decided I might as well remove the stuff in the tent."

She threw her arms around his neck, kissed his cheek. "How did I get so lucky in the father department?"

John blushed as he always did when his daughter heaped on praise. "You'd better check out the floor inside and see if it meets with your approval."

"Pop, with you doing the work, I already know it's perfect. Now head home and get some rest before you have to go back out tomorrow." She aimed a finger in his direction. "Do not argue with me about this."

"And how will you get back home?"

"My van's still parked at the B&B. I still have to go get my stuff and check out."

John didn't push for details. "Then I'll head back."

"Pop."

"What?"

"Be careful driving back."

When John had gone, Ryder turned to Troy. "Thanks for covering for me at the farm. I owe you."

"Just get that business proposal done and we'll call it even. I'm no good at stuff like that."

"Julianne offered to help. I think we hashed it out to where we won't embarrass ourselves in front of Nick."

Out of earshot of Julianne, Troy lowered his voice. "If you worked on the business plan something tells me you didn't have the kind of night I thought you had."

Ryder gave him the one-finger salute. "This is your IQ."

Troy guffawed with laughter.

"What's so funny," Julianne wondered when she came up to them. But without waiting for a response, she added, "I have an idea. Why don't we call Zach and Bree and get their take on what we put together, get their input before tomorrow? In the meantime I'll go back to Promise Cove and get my stuff."

Ryder nodded. "We could all meet at the farm."

"Sounds like a plan."

While Ryder did the milking and caught up on work in the admin offices, Julianne started a batch of cornbread and cheesy macaroni. Comfort food on a rainy day seemed a good complement to talking business. To offset the starch, she tossed together a salad, sliced apples and made veggie omelets.

"Need help? Bree asked.

"Nope, I've got it. Ryder doesn't have a lot, so I put together a meal with what he had on hand."

"Leave it to a guy. It looks good anyway. My omelets never look like they do in magazines. That's why I usually serve eggs up scrambled.""

Ryder came in the back door and after washing up, he reached over to plant a kiss on Julianne's forehead. When Zach handed him a beer from the six-pack he'd brought, he twisted off the cap, leaned back on the counter. "Smells good in here."

Once the cornbread came out of the oven, the five of them gathered around the table, eager for the food.

"Looked over the proposal, looks fine to me," Troy muttered in between bites. "What about you Zach?"

"I like the way you laid out the responsibilities of each of us."

"Nick may ask how you know this Jacob Hettinger. Are you willing to tell him?" Ryder asked.

"Other than the fact the multimillionaire owes me a huge favor? Not a problem."

"What about a name for the business?" Bree asked.

"No point in doing that until we take the first step," Ryder said in between scooping up macaroni.

"Yeah, we should make sure we get the go-ahead before getting too excited about all this."

"I still don't see how the bank will loan us money," Zach said cutting into his eggs.

Bree sent a glare in the direction of her brother. "Do you think you could can the negativity for five minutes? Just once try a little positive thinking instead of that dour, sour face."

Zach nodded and buttered his cornbread. "Sure, I can try. We'll see if it does any good."

Chapter Fifteen

Monday morning Ryder, Zach and Troy stationed themselves outside the First Bank of Pelican Pointe before it opened. They'd told Logan about their plan and the boss had given them the time off along with a much-appreciated thumbs-up.

When Ryder spotted Nick's car pulling in, he readied for the meeting they'd both dreaded and prepped for.

"Hey guys, good to see you." But then Nick noticed that all three men were sporting matching white shirts. The only difference in their attire was the varying fade of their jeans and a different shade of brown work boots.

"I hope you'll feel that way when you hear our crazy idea," Ryder stated.

"What's up?"

Zach and Troy let Ryder do the talking. "Remember at the party for Julianne when you encouraged locals to apply for business loans. The three of us are here to do that. Zach and Troy grew up here. I'm the outsider but one who decided to make this place home, put down roots and see them grow." He went on to explain about building boats.

"Okay, let's go into my office."

Before they all sat down, Ryder handed Nick the proposal.

Ryder watched Nick look it over, flip through the pages—a little too quickly to suit Ryder. After a short five minutes of perusing what had taken him days to put together, Ryder feared that was the end of that. That's why Nick's speech took him by surprise.

"When I took over this job, the bank was in deep trouble. Not only had the previous president, Milton Carr, pretty much run it into the ground by showing favoritism to certain depositors in town, he mismanaged funds to do it. He wouldn't extend loans to anyone with potential. In fact, he discouraged taking applications. Even after Carr resigned, for six long weeks, we had the feds crawling up our ass. It was an embarrassment to the hardworking people who make up this town—the ones who had a dream, who busted their tails to keep it from turning into a ghost town.

"Having the feds here was awkward and a humiliating experience. Something I never want to see happen again in my lifetime for obvious reasons. Not only did Carr bring shame to the town, but he refused to keep up with technology. The bank lagged behind in how it did business every day. I tell you all this because after skimming your proposal, my initial reaction is positive. So relax. But I wouldn't be serving the depositors if I didn't ask a series of pertinent questions."

"Okay, shoot," Ryder said, his dread beginning to ease up.

"First, do you three actually know each other well enough, get along well enough, trust each other enough, to go into business together, share bills, headaches, lean times. Because it's almost like a three-way marriage which is tough enough with two headstrong people let alone three. Each of you has to be willing to accept each other's imperfections, as well as recognize your individual strengths and build on them."

Ryder nodded. "We've only really gotten to know each other over the last three months. I admit there might be some things we still need to iron out. But we all share the same work ethic and the same approach to putting out a quality product."

"I echo that," Troy said.

"Okay then. I need to know what unique talent each of you brings to the partnership?"

Zach took this one. "Ryder prepared the business plan. As you well know from his work at the farm, he has the know-how to use the computer and the software to keep the books, pay the bills electronically, that sort of thing. And Troy and I can certainly learn. If we have to, we'll take a course to get up to speed in the tech arena so it all doesn't fall on Ryder's shoulders down the road. Add to that, we all three have above-average carpentry skills. Ask Logan and he'll tell you the same. We plan to all three share in the physical labor. All three of us plan to work on the boat design. To do that we'll probably have to take a class to get more familiar with the software program they use for drawing up models."

"And if it's a requirement to getting the loan, we'll seek out an advisor, someone who has experience in the industry. There's a guy up in the Pacific Northwest who mentors the younger generation," Ryder added. "We're more than willing to pay him as a consultant."

Satisfied with their answers, Nick said, "I don't know anything about boatbuilding, but I guarantee I know a few high-rollers who'd love nothing more than to own a watercraft, one custom made, especially for them."

"Really?" Troy said.

"Los Angeles. My old stomping ground where there's a lot of money, egos and people who'll pay for the privilege of made-to-order…anything."

"Does that mean…we get the loan?" Troy asked.

"Come back and see me in forty-eight hours. I want you three to do a bit of soul-searching among yourselves during that time. I need to know you're committed and willing to not kill each other at the first crisis that comes up. And believe me, I guarantee a crisis of some sort. There always is."

"You and Jordan deal with a crisis at the inn?" Zach asked in disbelief. "But I've been told you make it all look so easy."

Nick grinned. "We both try. That's where a professional approach comes in handy along with a willingness to roll. Almost weekly there's something that goes south or not as planned or not scheduled. Of course, we have kids, which is another potential for disaster altogether."

Nick leaned over the desk, linked his fingers. "The point to the forty-eight hours is a cooling off period. If, after you've had time to find out things you don't like about each other, things you won't be able to overcome, like personality traits that just piss you off about the other. If, after all that, you decide to back out, then we'll revisit the plan or chunk it altogether. How does that sound?"

Ryder looked at Zach, then at Troy. The three men exchanged long stares before Ryder finally said, "If those are the terms, we'll take it."

"See you in two days," Troy said with confidence.

As soon as they got outside on the sidewalk, Zach admitted, "That wasn't as bad as I thought it would be. Mind telling me what exactly a three-way marriage is though? Come to think of it that might be a good enough reason to tie the knot."

Ryder laughed. "I was wondering that myself. Maybe we should consider this partnership more like forming a band of blood brothers. I always wanted one."

"Never had a brother before," Zach said. "Might be interesting."

"Me either," Troy repeated. "If we take Nick's advice how exactly do we find out if we can't stand each other until we're up against the wall?"

"That's easy," said Ryder. "Lock ourselves in a house for two days and see if we kill each other."

"But we have to head back to work."

"Figuratively, not literally," Ryder stated. "I propose we go home tonight and make a list. In one column we put every single thing we don't like about each other. Don't leave anything out. Write out the stuff that drives us crazy. Be brutally honest. Then, in the other column we jot down what we like. We meet tomorrow at work and go over the list. Bang out any problems."

"I can do that," Troy said.

"Come clean about it all?" Zach mused. "Sure. I just hope we're still speaking to each other afterward."

That afternoon Julianne couldn't wait to find out how it had gone at the bank. Under dark overcast skies, she left school and turned the car toward Pelican Pointe. Even though she could've just called him for the update, she wanted an excuse to see him, to catch a little alone time with him. She told herself if it hadn't gone well with Nick, then he'd need cheering up.

Traffic was heavy even for Monday drive time. Halfway there, she started to fret that there had to be a reason she hadn't heard from him. He hadn't called. But then she'd been in class all day. He hadn't bothered leaving her a text though. How long did it take a person to key in a text?

Indecisive about making the trip, she talked herself into using the book about boats as an excuse, which was just plain obvious. Any reasonable sort could figure out you didn't drive all the way from Santa Cruz to give someone a book.

It didn't matter. The whole thing was rather tricky because if Nick said no to the venture, Ryder couldn't put the know-how in the manual to good use anyway.

By the time she pulled into the farm it was five-thirty and she'd worked herself into a serious doubt-fest. She didn't see Ryder's truck anywhere so she got out of the minibus to wait on the porch. She grabbed the book Hayden had wrapped in pretty blue foil and headed to the house.

Thunder rumbled overhead so close it shook the ground. Glancing up at the clouds it looked as though the dark billowing masses were moving way too fast for them to hang around for long.

She didn't feel like waiting on the porch so she decided to wander around the property. Leaving the book on the welcome mat in front of the door, she wasn't sure which way to go. She'd seen the barn but she'd never checked out the rows of vegetables and the grove of fruit trees. If she intended to bring her students out here on a field trip, she needed to familiarize herself with the layout.

Before the rain hit, she crossed to the growing area, marveled at the height of the plants and waved to a couple workers who were diligently tending the crops. She'd have to remember to ask Ryder how they were able to grow such hardy kale.

She'd reached the orchard when she spotted Ryder's truck hauling down the lane at a fast clip headed toward the house. She tried to wave him down but he blew by leaving a trail of dust.

Ryder saw the minibus before he came to a stop near the porch. He got out, caught sight of the pretty package by the door, wondered about it and then looked around for Julianne. She was nowhere in sight.

About that time the sky burst open and the rain poured down. Instead of darting into the house or the barn, which would have made more sense, he took off in search of Julianne.

He found her standing under a tall cherry tree for shelter, shivering. Blossoms had dropped off the branches and littered the ground around her feet.

"What are you doing here?" he shouted over a crack of thunder.

"I didn't hear from you all day. I wanted to find out how it went at the bank."

"I'd planned to call."

"Why didn't you?"

"I got busy. The meeting with Nick put me two hours behind schedule." He narrowed his eyes at the fact she was soaking wet but seemed angry about something. "Why are you pissed at me?"

He stood there, waited for her to answer as they glared at each other from five feet away.

A voice rang out that belonged to neither one of them. "Run. Get out of the orchard. Move. Now!"

They took off, darting and weaving about the time lightning slashed out of the sky and connected with the top of the tree where she'd been standing only seconds before. The bolt of white light split the timber in half. Sparks flew causing branches to crack and crash to the ground.

Ryder snatched her hand, led her away from the copse of trees. They tromped through mud to make a mad dash to the house.

By the time they reached the porch, their clothes were drenched. Her long hair dripped water. Raindrops beaded her brow and ran down her cheeks.

Even in the damp cold, he found those brown eyes, exotic and sexy, warming his blood, drawing him in, bit by bit. In her trembling, he loved the fact that she clung to him with fists gripping his shirt.

"I… I heard a voice. It was…it belonged…to Scott. I'm sure of it. He warned us right before the lightning hit, right before…"

"I know. I heard it, too." He planted a kiss on her forehead, tightened his hold. "You're still shaking."

"So are you."

"I guess I am."

They stood on the stoop, him grooming the wet mass of hair off her face, unwilling to let her go. He thumbed the raindrops that had pearled on her skin. Their lips met. She tasted as sweet as the cherry blossoms smelled.

"Why were you mad at me out there?"

"I wasn't, not really. I wasn't sure how you'd take me showing up here, unannounced."

"Don't ever worry about that. I can't think of a better way to end my workday. But right this minute I have cows to milk. Go inside and get out of those wet clothes. Put on one of my shirts and a pair of my sweatpants. I'll be back in half an hour."

With that, he kissed her forehead and she watched him race back out into the storm.

After changing out of her wet things and into a pair of baggy sweats and T-shirt, Julianne wrung out her clothes and draped them on the rod in the bathroom to dry. She heard the phone ring somewhere in the house and listened to an answering machine click on to record a message. A female voice she didn't recognize got her moving down the hallway and into the living room.

"Ryder, this is your mother. I'm giving you a heads up. That woman you used to live with, that Bethany Davis called my house today looking for you. I didn't know if you wanted me to tell her anything, so I didn't. Call me back though and I'll give you the play by play."

The front door opened and Ryder walked in soaked to the skin. "It's still coming down. This is some March weather we're having."

"Let's get you into some dry clothes and then you have to listen to your messages."

Over thick slabs of fried ham and potatoes, Ryder mulled over his mother's call. "It couldn't be that easy, could it? Bethany contacts me? How is that even possible? I mean, I'm sure it's money she's after."

"Maybe she misses you."

"Yeah. Right. She misses the take from selling off everything I owned. But it might be my only chance at getting my grandfather's sketches back."

"Your mother still doesn't know they're gone?"

"No. Look, every time I work up the courage to tell her, I can't bring myself to follow through. I'm humiliated enough without letting my mom know how I got played."

"Then what will you do?"

"I don't know. Right now I need to get to work on my Troy and Zach list so I'll have it ready for tomorrow."

"What list?"

He took her through how the meeting with Nick had gone and then explained about their self-imposed homework assignment.

"You're planning to put in writing what you don't like about the other?"

"Bad idea?"

"It's one way to clear the air or create more friction between all of you." She got up, went into the other room to retrieve the book. "I brought you something."

He looked her up and down. "I'll say. Oh, you mean my present. It's not even my birthday."

"Open it."

Ripping off the paper, he blinked at the book, flipped through the pages. "Julianne, this is a classic, an out of print hardcover written by an actual boatbuilder. It takes you through a step by step process. I tried to locate a copy of this several years back. Good thing I didn't find it otherwise it would've ended up in the stuff Bethany cleaned out. Thank you. Will you stay while I work on my list? Maybe spend the night?"

She draped her arms around his neck, ran her fingers through his still-wet hair, and then scraped her teeth along the lobe of his ear. "And miss out on a sweaty bout of sex on a rainy night? No way am I passing that up."

The next morning before daylight, Julianne woke to a dark room. When she realized she was alone, she crawled out of the covers, made her way into the bathroom. She gathered up her still-slightly damp clothes from the day before and got dressed. Following the smell of coffee she found Ryder at the stove scrambling eggs.

He looked over at her mussed-up appearance and said, "You look beautiful."

"Sure I do. I'm wearing the same clothes I had on from yesterday and my hair looks..."

"Like you were thoroughly made love to last night," Ryder finished.

"While that's probably true I have to get moving to make it to class."

"Sit. Eat." He waved the steaming pan in front of her before divvying the bounty between two plates.

She sat, dug into the eggs. "What do you intend to do about Bethany?"

"First, I go to Brent. Hopefully talk him into letting me run a sting, lure her out here. Maybe once she's arrested she'll tell me what she did with my stuff."

Julianne frowned. "I honestly don't like the idea of that. Is there any way I could talk you out of it?"

"Why would you want to?"

"Hello? Because in order for your idea to work, this woman has to come here. Personally, I don't think she'll do it. She'll more than likely try to persuade you into coming to... Wherever she is. And I like that idea even less."

"How do you get this kind of insight into a woman you don't even know and have never met? That's exactly what she'll do." He thought about it for a few minutes then it dawned on him. "You don't trust me?"

"I don't trust *her*. Big, big difference."

"I'd very much prefer you not do that. Baiting this woman is not the answer," Brent explained to Ryder, or tried to.

One thing the new police chief did not like about his current position was that the job meant people had started showing up at his door at all hours of the day and night. In his mind that would have to change. He needed an office somewhere other than the same house he shared with his wife and child. He'd prefer it be located on Main rather than across the street along Ocean. After all, having it on Main put some distance, albeit not much, between him and his job. Several streets over might not seem too far away to most but to Brent it was miles.

Add to his dilemma, a man like Ryder, who wanted to see an ex arrested, and Brent had a situation to resolve.

"Let me handle this, Ryder. I know you want her to pay for what she did. And she will. But you need to let me do it my way."

"That isn't fair.

"Life usually isn't. Finding someone, solving a crime, isn't like you see on television. That isn't real life. Sometimes it takes patience and trusting people like me to do my job."

"Just tell me what you found out."

Brent watched as Ryder paced back and forth in the living room. "Okay, but you will not go after her. Do you understand?" When he got him to nod, he went on, "The woman you knew as Bethany Davis was a scam artist who ran cons on at least twenty servicemen that we know of. She wasn't particular about which branch of the service she aimed for either. Throughout the years, her husbands were equally represented by stints in the Air Force, Navy, Army, even the Coast Guard. She turned thirty last year and has eight marriages under her belt."

Ryder scrubbed both hands over his face. He'd known it, but hearing it confirmed was, once again, a blow to his ego. "So I wasn't the only one?"

"Not by a longshot. The name she's using now is Melinda Sykes but her birth name is Crystal Dawn Lazarrio."

"How do you know that?"

"I got a hit on her. After she left Philly, she applied for, and received, a West Virginia driver's license using the name Marisa Simms. But the address she used ended up a vacant house. My guess is she didn't stay in the area long enough to set up housekeeping before she moved on. Since fleecing you, Crystal's been a busy girl. She's run three other cons."

"Jesus."

"Do yourself a favor. I want you to forget about luring her here. Women like this smell a setup from ten miles away. She won't fall for it."

"That's the same thing Julianne said to me."

"Smart woman. Listen to her. Forget the bitch who stole your stuff and move on."

"But I need my grandfather's drawings back. Bethany, or rather Crystal, or whatever the hell she's calling herself these days, is the key."

"Do you honestly believe she still has those or anything of yours still in her possession?"

"Probably not."

"Then let the authorities, myself included, be the ones who draw her in. Now get out of here and go to work. My advice, do not spend another minute thinking about getting your ego busted up. We've all been there."

Once Ryder stormed out, River came into the living room, rubbed her hand over Brent's back. "You're all knotted up. With this, and the thing with Layne and Brooke, all the fights you had to break up during the street fair, this job is getting to you."

"I don't mind people knocking on my door to borrow my lawn mower, but if I don't put a stop to the idea they can just show up anytime they want at all hours without notice or calling, I may give this up."

"No one's using that old Springer place. The realtor's former office would be perfect for a police station. With a little remodeling in the back you could add a holding cell."

He picked her up, planted a kiss on her lips. "And that, Mrs. Cody, is why I love you. I'm so desperate I'll go see Murphy about it now."

On the short drive to work, Ryder considered Brent's words. Could he give up the pursuit of Bethany/Crystal so easily and let it go? He wasn't sure he could do it. Spotting Troy unloading his tools from his truck, Ryder waved him over.

"Where should we do this list thing?"

"We still have thirty minutes before work. I say we go around back to the loading dock as soon as Zach gets here."

A few minutes later the three men gathered on the back dock.

"Who goes first?" Troy asked, nervous.

Ryder rubbed his palms on his jeans and said, "I'll go. My lists are fairly short."

He turned to Troy. "I'll start with you. It upsets me how you don't value your own worth. You don't think you're good enough for Bree. You are."

He immediately pivoted to look at Zach. "And don't look at me like that. If he makes Bree happy what more could you want for your sister? There are worse guys out there she could date. Troy here is a good guy. You know it's true. You've seen how hard he works just like you do."

Before either man could say anything, Ryder barreled on. "And that's what I like about both of you. You're hard workers. You'll commit to a job and won't look for ways to shirk a responsibility. That goes a long way in my book."

Ryder looked Zach in the eye. "What I don't like about you is that major chip on your shoulder you carry around. It's a real problem. Ask yourself why you do it? My guess is you'd like to see a little more emotional support from the people close to you. But how can anyone give you what you need when you refuse to let them? We've all tried to be your friends here but you do your damnedest to push us away at every opportunity."

"Are you done?" Zach demanded. "Because I don't like how bossy you are."

"But Logan made him foreman when the project started," Troy reminded him. "With all Ryder's construction expertise Logan thought he was the best man for the job."

"I don't care. He's always pointing out how to do this better or that better," Zach insisted.

"How many construction sites have you worked on?" Troy asked, his voice rising.

"It's okay," Ryder said to Troy. "Let's hear it all, Zach. This is a clear-the-air venue. Get it out now or forever keep your trap shut."

Expecting the worst, Ryder stood there waiting for Zach to take a swing at him. Instead, he watched as Zach dropped down on a wooden crate that held laminate and put his head in his hands.

"God, I'm so angry."

"About what?" Troy said.

"I got arrested in Colorado Springs on a job for stealing." He quickly lifted a gaze at Troy. "I didn't do it, so I know what it's like when everybody looks at you as though you've committed a crime. Turns out, a few of my construction buddies set me up to make it look like I'd pilfered supplies and equipment. The owner, Jacob Hettinger, bought into the whole thing and pressed charges."

"That's why he owes you a favor?"

"Yeah. But not before I spent almost a week in jail. Those so-called 'friends' of mine thought they'd set up the stupid guy from out-of-town because he's a chump and wouldn't be able to figure out what was going on."

"How'd you get out of the mess?" Ryder wanted to know.

"Sheer luck. Before I rolled into town there were other major thefts at sites going back five years. It turned out the cops had been keeping track of the players, waiting to bust them. But I was furious that these guys I thought were my pals would turn on me like they did. They never saw me as a friend at all. From the get-go I was nothing more than their convenient scapegoat."

"I got framed for murder. How's that for world-class chump?" Troy uttered.

"Yeah, I guess that trumps stealing." Zach waited a beat. "I don't have a problem with you and Bree."

"That's good because I think I might want to marry her." At the frown on Zach's face, Troy added, "One day, not like, June or anything."

Brent's earlier words came back to Ryder. "You two aren't the only ones who have ever been conned."

"But you wouldn't so easily get set up like that," Zach shot back.

"Wanna bet?" Ryder decided then and there if he was going into business with these men he needed to come clean about what happened with Bethany, all of it. "We've all crossed paths with people we wish we hadn't. As Brent reminded me this morning, we've all had incidents that put a major ding in our egos. Bethany was my personal disaster, a major regret in my life I can't change."

"I'm sorry," Zach finally said. "Not about Bethany but about coming across as an asshole. I'm really not like that. Ask anyone that's known me here in town, they'll tell you I'm a pretty decent guy."

"So is this it?" Troy wanted to know. "Because I couldn't really come up with anything I don't like about the two of you. I mean, except for the fact Zach's been pissed off about me spending time with Bree. That was the main thing on my mind. But now that that's out of the way..."

Ryder started laughing and shook his head. "I'm sweating bullets about getting a business loan and this guy's thinking about his love life."

"Do you think we'll get it?" Troy wondered.

"Hey, even if we don't I'm convinced there's plenty of work around town to keep us all three busy with renovations."

"What do we call our business?" Zach asked hopeful.

Ryder looked at his watch. "A discussion for another time. Right now, we're on the clock."

Chapter Sixteen

A week later, Julianne sat on one of the pews inside the auditorium at the Community Church waiting her turn to address the town council.

The sanctuary was jam-packed. Apparently, word had spread about the vote tonight. Everyone wanted to be a part of it. From young to old, she recognized many faces in the crowd, especially those she'd met during the street fair. They seemed excited which had her a little nervous to speak before such a large assembly.

When Mayor Murphy called her name, she rose and walked to the podium. "Although I haven't moved here yet, I feel as though I'm already a part of your community. I almost feel like I belong here already. What I'd like to propose is simple. I think the town should turn the tract of land between Murphy's Market and the bank into a park and that it be officially dedicated and renamed for one of your longtime residents, Scott Phillips. Everyone knows the soldier who grew up here and lost his life in Iraq. I recommend the name be Phillips Park."

Applause broke out. Julianne cleared her throat and leaned into the microphone again. "And if you do agree, then I'd like to further suggest we add more benches, make some improvements to remove weeds and trash along the back so that the children have more room to play and to picnic, maybe add a swing set or slide."

More clapping had her waiting for it to die down before going on. "I'd also like to suggest that once we dedicate the park, come summer, we begin holding movie nights there during the week throughout the months of June, July and August, movies that the entire family will enjoy."

Another roar went up and again Julianne waited for calm. Since she seemed to be on a roll, she quickly added, "Further, I think it would be a good idea if we used the wharf to hold concerts on Friday or Saturday nights. It would offer a venue for any local musicians who want to try out and perform there. We could call it something like, 'a night of music over the bay.'"

The room erupted in more applause. Hoots and hollers rang out as everyone got to their feet to show their support. Even the entire council stood up and started applauding her ideas. That's why she was shocked to hear a dissenting voice drone from the back.

"Big plans but who pays for all this?" Joe Ferguson grumbled. "I'm not doing it."

Julianne turned to address the hardware store owner. "I made a spreadsheet before I suggested this. Knowing how tight city budgets are these days, I calculated the cost, Mr. Ferguson." If we have donated labor and hold a few bake sales along the way, it won't cost the taxpayers anything."

From his seat at the council table, Nick glared at Joe. "Your attitude is one reason we won't trouble you further. Since we've had this discussion with you over other improvements many times before, we'll leave you the hell alone from now on. We'll take our business over to San Sebastian and order the benches from someone there."

"Now wait a minute," Joe returned. "That isn't fair."

"Sit down, Joe. You're out of order anyway," Murphy said, banging his gavel. "Your objection is duly noted. Since it's already been resolved, we're moving on. Anyone else?"

From the back, another voice rang out. This time it was Milton Carr. "Who says the park should be named for Scott? My daughter Sissy's dead, too. Why not name it for her?"

Even Julianne knew about Sissy Carr's history with the town. Stolen money didn't prevent a father from grieving for his daughter. She didn't want to upset the older man but felt the need to defend her proposal. "Scott is a fallen hero, a shining example to the community. That's my reasoning for putting forth the idea," Julianne explained. "But if you'd like to dedicate something to your daughter, we could certainly plant a tree there in her honor, or you could pay for one of the benches and add a nameplate to it in her memory."

"That's an excellent suggestion," Wade Hawkins tossed out from the stage, not waiting for any further discussion. "I say we bring this to a vote."

"I second that," Nick said in fast agreement.

From there, each idea passed without further rancor. In addition, the council voted for a resolution to pay for the benches and any playground equipment would be paid for by donations or fundraisers. Murphy called for volunteers to clean up the property and scheduled another meeting to choose a date for the park dedication.

With business concluded, once everyone started to leave, Ryder leaned in with an amused twinkle in his eyes and whispered in her ear. "Have you ever thought about a career in politics?"

She snickered. "I play politics every day at school. That's good enough for me."

After the meeting broke up, Julianne and Ryder met up with Troy and Bree and Zach at the Diner. As they slid into the largest booth in the corner, the jukebox cranked out the old Beatles song, *All My Loving*. While the five waited for Mona to take their orders, they pitched names for the boat enterprise. Which Nick had agreed held opportunity as a moneymaker.

"Smuggler's Boats."

Ryder shook his head. "Sounds too much like a drug-trafficking operation. Wrong connotation."

"How about a combo of your initials? ZRT, RZT, TRZ," Bree suggested.

"Nah, I don't like that. Too gimmicky," Troy asserted.

"Blue Water Boats."

"That isn't bad, but… Too bland."

"You know, River has a fantastic old canoe ready for display when she opens the museum. Maybe you could somehow build off that," Julianne proposed.

"Like how?" Zach asked.

"The Chumash had what was known as The Brotherhood of the Tomol. Ryder mentioned that you thought of yourselves like three blood brothers. Maybe you could use some form of that."

About that time Mona ambled over with a new look, sporting short, spiky, bluish hair. "Hey, Troy, how's it going?"

"I'm good. How about you? Last I heard you were headed back to Texas."

"Maybe this summer. What can I get you guys? It's Tuesday so you already know the special is Max's chicken-fried steak."

Zach decided on that and Troy went along with it.

"Make it three," Ryder stated. "But make mine with fries instead of mashed potatoes."

Julianne and Bree decided to split a basket of chicken tenders. When Mona left to put in their order, Bree turned to Troy. "At least you can still be friends with her."

"I wouldn't call it friends exactly," Troy returned. "She still isn't comfortable around me. How can someone who claims to know me think I had anything at all to do with what happen to Gina Purvis?"

There was an awkward silence until Bree intervened. "Sorry. Bad vibes and bad memories. But it's hard to avoid this place when it's the only eatery around."

"It's okay," Troy said.

"If Nick gives me the loan after graduation to ferry people back and forth to the island and to the shipwreck, maybe I'll be your first customer. You can build me a boat."

"It takes about three months to build one," Troy told her with a kiss on the lips. "Starting out, the dinghy will work. But for the trip farther out to the shipwreck, you'll need one of those sixteen-footers to ferry them there. You'll need certifications to dive. I checked."

"You're graduating?" Julianne asked looking over at Bree. "When? That's a big deal."

"It's just community college," Bree said with a shrug.

"I don't care. It's still a big deal. You need a graduation party."

Bree's eyes grew wide. "Really? That would be fantastic. But you know I'll still be pushing drinks at McCready's until I decide what to do. It isn't even a sure-thing about the loan. I haven't even approached Nick yet."

"Doesn't matter. I'm still throwing you a party."

"Where?"

"Depends on how many people you invite. I'll figure something out," Julianne promised, wondering how many people her little house would hold. "In the meantime make a list of who you'd like to see there. When's commencement? You'll need a cheering section."

"That's a great idea," Troy agreed. "We'll all show up and when they call your name, we'll whoop and holler like they did tonight at the meeting."

"You'll embarrass me."

"That's the point. We'll do our best," Zach teased.

"What with Zach's friend, Hettinger, and Nick's getting the word out for us, we might actually have a few customers right up front," Ryder reasoned. "When not building and designing, we'll focus on refurbishing older boats, putting in new hulls and decks to help our cash flow."

"Maybe pick up emergency work from the fishermen in the area," Troy added. "Keegan and Cord have that research vessel they take out all the time. It could use an upgrade."

"Good call. As long as they don't come to us needing engine repair and understand we're strictly doing metalwork and carpentry," Zach reminded.

"Exactly. Now if we could only settle on a name."

"I like the brothers' angle." Bree threw in.

"Yeah, but we're not really brothers or Chumash," Ryder concluded. "Besides, Blood Brothers Boatyard is kind of a mouthful."

"Simple then. What about Tradewinds Boatyard," Julianne concluded.

Ryder's eyes went wide. "Not bad. I like it. Guys?"

Zach nodded. "It's a keeper. How about you, Troy?"

"Tradewinds Boatyard it is."

About that time a young woman walked through the door, a beautiful exotic creature that all but had Zach coming up out of his seat.

"Who is that?"

Troy elbowed Bree in the ribs, nodded his head in the direction where the woman had taken a seat at the counter, waiting to pick up her to-go order. "*That* is Logan's new tenant. He calls her Izzy. She helps out Kinsey with the babies sometimes."

"Izzy," Zach repeated as if in a trance. "You mean like a nanny?"

"Never said she was the nanny. Since Kinsey doesn't have any family, she needed help with the twins. All I know is that Isabella showed up here about the same time the Doc put Kinsey on bed rest. She's from Italy, I think."

"Then she won't stay. A woman like that won't stay around here for long."

Bree slapped at her brother's arm. "What a thing to say! How would you know? What exactly does that mean for the rest of us? What are we? Excess waste hanging around waiting for a better place to go?"

"You know what I mean."

"No, I don't," Bree snapped back. "This town isn't the dump you make it out to be. And you're getting ready to start a business here with these guys? Invest in a future? Sometimes I wonder about you, Zach."

Troy snickered out a laugh. "So much for hooking Zach up with the florist, I don't think he's interested in Drea." He snapped his fingers in front of Zach's face. "Hey, you want to meet Izzy?"

"You could arrange that?"

"Maybe. But what will you do for me?"

Like brothers, the two men quibbled about it first, railed on each other next, then got down to striking the deal. Troy would set up a meeting with the enchanting Izzy and Zach would forever let him pick the music when they worked next to each other.

After they finished the meal, Zach, Troy and Bree took their squabble and went their separate ways.

On the walk back to Julianne's minibus she'd left parked at the church, Ryder tugged her along on the sidewalk as if in a hurry to get somewhere.

Once they reached the van, he pushed her up against it, fused his mouth to hers, kissing her breathless. "You're here in town already. Come home with me. Or I'll go home with you. I don't care which. Either way I want to spend the night with you."

"Same here," she whooshed out. "But your place is a lot closer."

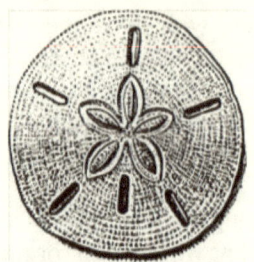

Chapter Seventeen

March kept its lion tendencies intact as it roared into April. The same kind of intense storms hung around to wreak havoc on Julianne's plans to take her class to Taggert Farms. Twice she'd been forced to cancel the field trip. She refused to set out in bad weather with her charges after what had happened in the orchard. That's why she didn't mind bumping it to later. The previous month, she'd sent out permission slips to parents. She'd even talked a few of them into volunteering to come along. Turns out, the kids were excited about tromping around a real farm while the adults could meander through the fruit stand.

So when the elements finally gave way to spring like conditions, Julianne lined up the driver again, did the scheduling and prepared for an adventure with thirty kids in tow.

With skies that looked as though an artist had dabbed his brush into cobalt blue and put it to canvas, they started the long drive into the countryside.

From the minute her rambunctious, inquisitive class piled off the yellow school bus en masse, she had a difficult time maintaining order and getting them to stay in line. Spending ninety long minutes cooped up inside a vehicle, the kids itched to bust out and go every which way at once.

While it certainly wasn't the first field trip she'd taken with students, it was the first time she had so much ground to cover. In addition to the cows, there were newborn calves to hold, seeds to put in the soil, solar-powered watering systems to learn about, along with water conservation. For many, it was the first opportunity to see where food started out, how it was packaged and how it ended up at their local market.

She wished Ryder wasn't stuck at the job site. But she had to give it to Silas. The man knew the ins and outs of the farm, knew how to capture the imagination of children and keep their attention for more than five minutes.

While touring through the vegetable patch—grown specifically for "you-pick your own"—Julianne's curious troop handpicked their own berries, tugged carrots up out of the dirt, and plucked cherry tomatoes off the vine. She could see there was a joy on their little faces in the simple harvesting, the filling up their own baskets with what they'd chosen themselves to take home.

The group peppered her with questions. On any given day she'd come to expect queries out of the mouths of babes that could range from the silly to the profound.

"Can we grow stuff when we get back to school?"

"What about growing Twizzlers? They're vines."

"Um, um, can I take a chicken home with me?"

Ryder found her there surrounded by a slew of kids who all seemed to want to talk at once. They vied for her attention like tiny adoring fans. He wondered how she kept her sanity in such chaos. It was a testament to her patience and temperament.

"How's it going?" he asked when she finally noticed him watching her.

"Ryder. It's almost time to get these minions rounded up and back on the bus."

"I know but I wanted to see the teacher, tell her what I'd like to do to her…later."

She sent him a wide smile, made sure the kids weren't within earshot. "Coming to Santa Cruz?"

"After I get done with my work, count on it."

She ordered the stainless steel appliances for the kitchen and laundry room the same day she fitted the new mantel over the fireplace and put down polyurethane coating on the hardwood floors.

The days were speeding toward the end of school and her self-imposed deadline. It seemed she couldn't work fast enough to get it all done. Sometimes, like today, it scared her that she still had so much to do. But then she'd look over at Ryder and the look he gave her seemed to embolden her to believe she could do it.

Every spare minute Ryder helped her complete some chore that needed doing she hadn't considered. He'd installed new windows in each bedroom, the bathroom and kitchen. He'd even designed a new railing for the upstairs landing.

While they spread a second coat of Seashore Teal on the living room walls, they discussed the last time either one of them had seen Scott.

She didn't bring up the magazine incident because she was pretty sure that Scott's absence meant only one thing. He was angry with her. "Last time for me was during the street fair. I'd walked down to the bookstore, was headed back to the car when I saw him moving toward the lighthouse. I remember thinking that I hope he doesn't scare Logan's new renter. Although I do wonder why he's been avoiding me, I realize he only sticks to Pelican Pointe, never shows up in Santa Cruz. And since I spend most of my time there... What about you?"

"A couple of nights ago I heard him walking around the farmhouse, creeping around in the middle of the night like the restless soul he is. Strange that he hasn't been back in the house in weeks though."

"Maybe that's proof I upset him in some way."

"Why?"

"Okay, I threw a magazine at him the night you were so sick."

"Ah. Somehow he doesn't look like the type that would let a magazine keep him out of a house. Did you ever think up a name for this place?"

"You'll think it's silly."

"Lay it on me."

"I could keep calling it the gingerbread cottage but that just doesn't work for me. Gingerbread brings to mind gumdrops and Christmas and… I want a different kind of house altogether. I feel as though I'm building my own sandcastles here in a new place so… Sandcastle Cottage?"

"Not bad. I'll make a plaque for it, put it on the front of the house to make it official."

"That would be perfect."

"Brent's decided on a site for the new police station, using the office where Springer Realty used to be. He wants the sign taken down and the work to begin as soon as possible."

The look of concern on his face told her something else was bothering him. "Why does that trouble you?"

"There's so much work here, I wonder if I'm making a huge mistake on a business venture right now that could be slow-going for all of us."

"Ryder, is it something you've always wanted to do? If it is then go for it, don't let fear prevent you from doing what you want."

"Just because I want it doesn't mean it's the right thing to do. A commercial loan now might be a foolhardy jump. Once we get the money the boatyard will still have to undergo its own rehab. So close to the water that building is in pretty sad shape with rot. And we'll have to buy equipment, saws of our own, mahogany, teak, and all kinds of wood, whatever the customer wants. All three of us will more than likely still have to take on jobs whenever we can get them in order to sock away money to pay the loan back during the lean times. What if…?"

She put her fingers to his lips to stop him from going on. "I've no doubt you'll make it work. In fact, you all three will."

"You believe in me, in the business?"

"You know I do."

"Logan's hard at work on the dolphin sculpture that's slated to go in front of the school."

"The pod with babies. With his own babies, where does he find the time?"

"Same place we all do. We put in the hours, catch sleep when we can, and hope like hell we meet the deadline. Nick and Logan authorized payment to Cleef for all the salvaged materials. We'll have the shipment of desks and old lockers delivered to a designated workshop. We'll need a separate space, other than the school, to sand and repair the old stuff, rehab the wood and metal in order to have it all ready when the work is done at the site."

"Refinishing those old lockers will be a chore. You'll need volunteers. Just talking about everything that has to be completed over the next few months makes me exhausted and a whole lot intimidated."

They were packing up to go home for the night when Landon and Shelby showed up.

"We know you haven't had time to paint the outside yet because you've been concentrating on the inside. That's one of the reasons we'd like to do it for you."

"I couldn't let you do that, Mr. Jennings. I planned to get to it once I get moved in."

"Landon," he reminded her in his easy manner. "Call me Landon. It's what we want to do for you. We all talked about it and Caleb and Drea want to get rid of that pink color." From his pocket, Landon pulled out at least twenty paint cards, sample exterior shades for her to choose from. "You look these over. Make your choice and we'll do the rest."

She tried to protest again but it went nowhere. Tears welled up in her eyes. "Why? Why are you being so nice to me?"

"Because my family and I have a stake in seeing you settled here. We want it to happen almost as much as you do." He twisted up his mouth. "Okay, maybe I dragged my feet at the beginning, but now that I know how much this means to the kids, I want it done with. Part of that is giving the place an entirely new look. Leave it to us. You pick the color scheme and we'll make it happen."

Because she wanted to get it right, Julianne spent three grueling days trying to come up with the perfect color. She avoided kitschy purples and Pepto-Bismol pinks for obvious reasons. She didn't want Landon and his crew going to the trouble of painting only to slap the familiar florid shades of yesteryear on there.

At home, she researched pictures of the type of Cape Cod look she wanted to achieve. Finally, she settled on a soft pale yellow for the house itself, a snowy cream trim for the porch, the lattice work and the scalloped edges along the second story. But it needed a splash, a bold statement, something that said to the town she was unafraid of making a new start. For that, she picked an inviting shade of lavender for the shutters and the front door.

"It's not purple," she insisted when she glanced over at the surprise on Ryder's face.

"Hey, bottom line is, it's your investment, your money, and your house. You paint it the color you want. Forget about what anyone else wants and don't let them strong-arm you into using something you find ugly."

"But what do you think about my choices? Soft yellow with cream and lavender trim."

"I think Sandcastle Cottage looks like a million bucks."

She sighed. "Me too."

Julianne and Ryder weren't the only ones making plans for the future.

Troy and Bree spread out on the bed inside his studio apartment shuffling through paperwork. The two were up late going over every document they thought they'd need for a business loan.

As they sorted through bank statements and Bree's W-2 forms, she blew out a frustrated sigh. "This is hopeless. No one will ever give me a loan based on this. I don't make enough, Troy. That's the simple truth."

"Don't give up now, Bree. Promise me you won't. We have a future together. This is the place." He looked around the tiny studio. "Maybe not right here, but I've signed the papers on the house. Soon I'll be able to start the rehab. We'll make it all work. You'll see. If I have to, I'll ask Logan and Ryder for advice on how best to get the tour business up and going."

She rolled into him, ran her fingers through his curly blond hair. "I love you, Troy."

He kissed her mouth. "I love you, too. That's why we're going to make this a reality."

Chapter Eighteen

Moving day for Julianne came the last Saturday in May. With Memorial Day on Monday, she had a tough time getting the truck even though she'd reserved it two months in advance.

"Why do those places always make it so difficult on people stressed out from moving to begin with?" she wondered aloud to her dad as she pulled the eighteen-foot truck up to the curb in front of her house.

"Part of the pain that comes with moving means putting up with all the things that don't go as planned."

"I'd say waiting an hour for the truck definitely falls into that category. I hope the four college students I hired to help load didn't give up and leave me in the lurch."

"They'll be here. Good thing it isn't a long-haul move."

"Long enough," Julianne grumbled. "Nick assured me that all I need is someone on this end to load. He said that when I get to Pelican Pointe, there will be plenty of hands at the cottage. I hope he knows what he's talking about."

"Stop worrying," John said for the tenth time that morning. "Ryder would be here if he wasn't on a tight schedule getting your school ready."

"It isn't exactly my school. But yeah, I'd say his job is the more important one. They're on a time crunch and the clock is ticking. I can't believe next week is already June. I get the sense from Ryder they're all feeling the deadline."

"What happens if they miss it?"

"I don't even want to consider that possibility. Since we didn't meet the pre-enrollment limit, it looks like we'll open as a private school for now."

"Are you disappointed?"

"Nope. As long as those kids get a state-of-the-art education, I'm happy."

As soon as she pulled the rental truck up to what she now thought of as Sandcastle Cottage, it wasn't the new color scheme that caught her eye but Ryder. He stood beside the front door holding a drill, positioning the plaque in place. Her heart clutched at the sight of him.

It didn't go unnoticed by her father.

"You're falling for him?"

"Yes, I'd like to deny it but I won't."

Taken with the man, she totally missed the group of people standing off to the side. Nick had kept his word. He'd lined up six guys with strong backs to move her in and see to it she was settled.

"Let's get you into your new place."

Even with going up and down stairs, it took less than two hours for the men to get everything she owned out of the van and into the house. The consensus from them all was that the little cottage was a masterpiece of craftsmanship and creativity that looked nothing like its former abandoned self.

Another hour had them splitting the work to get the bed set up. They made sure to hook up the TV so she'd have sound and picture.

The hardworking guys refused payment but settled for sandwiches and beer instead.

After everyone left, Ryder busied himself with getting her desk organized and Wi-Fi set up so it worked. When he was done with connecting the wires, he discovered she wasn't anywhere in the house and went looking for her.

He found her across the street sitting on the beach with her toes buried in the sand. Instead of unpacking, he couldn't believe she was wasting time stacking a bunch of rocks on top of each other in an intricate, odd formation.

But with her hair glittering raven black in the waning light, she looked like a gypsy who'd decided to make camp for the night.

"What are you doing?"

"I'm building a cairn with these pretty stones."

"A what?"

"A cairn," she repeated. "It's to mark my new beginning here, my new path, a new chapter in my life."

He grinned, shook his head. "You are something, you know that?"

Her lips curved up. "I hope so. Otherwise I wouldn't be able to hold your interest for more than five minutes."

"I guarantee you'll always manage to hold my interest."

"I'm told *always* is a very long time. I can't believe I'm really moved in."

"Technically," Ryder corrected. "You're moved in but not unpacked."

"I still have Sunday and Monday to get everything set up. You're staying tonight, aren't you?"

"I was hoping you'd ask."

Once they got back to the house, she put clean, crisp sheets on the bed, puffed up pillows, even cut flowers to put by the bed.

They told themselves they were saving water by taking a long, hot shower together. The scent of vanilla and lavender hung in the air as anticipation built. Toweling off they drifted to the bedroom where the soulful voice of Moya Brennan echoed out of the speakers—the ones Ryder had insisted on hooking up.

The couple sunk down to the mattress. Still damp from the shower, they'd staved off need. But now their bodies still slick and steaming, they melded together in a blast of heat. He wasn't sure who ravaged whom, only that whenever he touched her it felt like he could never get enough. He fed his desperation by savaging her mouth, then dragging her across the sheets. Their eyes locked, sharp crystal to velvet dark, as he plunged inside.

For Julianne, fireworks came early. Rockets exploded. Glorious bursts of red, white, and blue had her gasping out his name. Up and over, they fought through jagged wind. The wild tide beat against the rocks—that ultimate mountain high in sight. Finally the switch snapped, leaving them languid and loose.

She ran her hands up his muscled back. "Can you believe we're actually sleeping here tonight? It's official. I'm a Pelican Pointe resident. No more making those trips back and forth to Santa Cruz."

"Not only here but taking advantage of my expert skills." He rolled to his back, taking her with him.

"Your expert skills are the main attraction."

"You don't worry what people will think if I spend the night?"

"Should I be? Are people that judgmental here? You've been here longer."

"No, no. They don't come across like that. But you never know."

After he fell asleep, she crawled out of bed with a case of nervous energy. Instead of feeling exhausted, the first night in a strange place made it difficult for her to come down off the high from moving. She took a tour through the house, going from room to room and ended up downstairs. When that did nothing to help calm her down enough to sleep, she grabbed a sweater to head outside. Once her bare feet hit the wood she realized how chilly it was and ran back inside to get a blanket. Wrapping it around her shoulders she went back out, took a seat on the hard steps.

While waiting for him to show up, she decided she'd have to order a swing for the porch. It would be perfect for times like these when she wanted to enjoy the quiet time of night.

About that time she finally caught sight of him. She'd known he was here, somewhere.

"Do I get points for not coming in and intruding on your space this time? Or would you like to throw something at me again?"

"I'm sorry," she said aloud, staring at Scott standing on the lawn, just as she'd seen him that very first time, with his hands in the pockets of those khaki shorts. "I thought you were mad at me because of the magazine thing. In my defense I wasn't fully awake. But you had no right to come in like that, expecting to see... Whatever might've been going on between Ryder and me at the time."

"I crossed a line. I apologize. I shouldn't have done it. This is a good town... Suggesting the park... That was a...nice surprise. What made you think of it?"

"The town needed a park. What better name than yours?"

Scott turned to look back at the house. "You like it here?"

"I love it. Everyone did a beautiful job on the inside. And just look at the gorgeous color scheme out here. It's the prettiest house on the block now, although I'm sure I'm biased. May I ask you something?"

"Sure."

"Ryder mentioned his concern earlier. Will people talk about us, him staying here with me?"

"People always talk."

"Okay, that prepares me for the gossip. I'll just have to withstand it. Ryder's not going anywhere—that I know of anyway."

"The cleansing ceremony did the trick then?"

"It did. There's no residual bad karma that I can tell." That's when it occurred to her. "Is that why you've stayed out here in the yard? You can't come into the house?"

"Observant, aren't you?"

"So the protection ritual works on you, too? I didn't realize. It wasn't intentional."

"I know that. It's your new beginning though."

"Did Layne and Brooke get a new beginning?"

"Why do you want to know so badly? Maybe it's better if you let it go."

"I can't do that anymore than Ryder can let go of his obsession with Bethany. There's something about those boxes we found that don't make sense. First, why would a child go to such bother to let go of their personal possessions. Some of those baseball cards were quite valuable. Layne and his father owned a baseball card store, which is the major reason I keep coming back full circle to the Jennings children. Caleb was too young to attend school. Drea would have no interest in collecting sports cards. That leaves Cooper, the oldest."

"You want to find him?"

"I want to do more than that. I want to talk to him. But Brent has pretty much quashed my interfering. So much that I don't want to make an issue of it."

"Then follow your instincts."

"Is that your way of telling me I'm on the right track with Cooper?"

"Eleanor had a warped sense of entitlement."

"What I can't figure out is why hide those little boxes all over the school?"

"Maybe it's the only place he felt sure they'd be found."

"If that's the case, we really let someone down then, didn't we?"

Chapter Nineteen

The next day Ethan picked up his tool belt to help his brother Brent knock out a wall inside the house that used to belong to Kent Springer Realty.

The new police station was taking shape slowly. Lilly Pierce had already started work on the wooden sign for the building. With help from Troy it would be a simple blue and white design with the words: "City of Pelican Pointe Police Department" etched on it. Above that, a series of lines signifying waves.

"You couldn't find anyone else to help you do the work this early?"

"Every available man is getting the school ready. We're already at the end of May with ninety days left to go. I believe Logan and Ryder are feeling the heat more than anyone else."

Brent looked around at the new digs. "I want this place up and running within a week so people will stop dropping by my house without so much as a phone call. River's about to get fed up and move out. Last night was the final straw."

"Don't tell me some drunk showed up?"

"Yes and no. All hell broke loose over at McCready's. It seems Archer Gates stumbled into the wrong bathroom, was standing there peeing when Joy Sullivan walked into the ladies' room. Flynn drags him out of there, out of the bar, across the street and up my steps at midnight.

Archer's blind drunk so Flynn asks me to drive him home."

Ethan snorted with a shake of his head. "Prissie's boy? Archer always did like his whiskey."

"*That boy* is forty-two-years old with a major drinking problem. He could use an intervention."

"What did you tell Archer?"

"That I planned to tell his mama he was out drinking again just as soon as I got him home. That seemed to sober him enough to get in my truck."

"You know the old joke. You're the police chief in a small town when you hold the most powerful threat of all over a grown man's head. You're gonna tell his mama on him."

Brent laughed so hard he almost dropped his drill. "So very true."

"Do you miss Santa Cruz?"

"Not a bit. Surprisingly, I like it here. And most days, when people aren't banging on our door, so does River."

"If you honestly think that getting an official police station will prevent folks from knocking on your door in the middle of the night, you're delusional. When I was in that house, it happened to me all the damn time. The only way to prevent it from happening less frequently is to buy another house."

"But I don't want to move."

"Then Mr. Chief of Police you'll have to think up something else."

While Ryder spent his Sunday morning at the farm doing chores, Julianne hung pictures on the wall, unwrapped knickknacks and finished her unpacking. When she grew tired of putting away dishes and setting the kitchen right, she drove the van over to Murphy's Market and loaded up on groceries to the tune of a hundred dollars' worth of food.

After putting away meat, bread, and canned goods, she stepped outside to the backyard. The flagstone patio her dad had installed made the backyard a real showplace. Her little ice cream set looked great out here but Bree's party would surely mean that down the road she'd need to add more chairs out here for more guests.

The bank of flowers Landon and Shelby had added— tall birds of paradise dotted with gold and pink hibiscus— lined the edge of the stone. Even though it was a start, she'd want to build on the landscaping once she could afford the cost. Maybe next fall.

Watching the leaves of the summer maple sway in the breeze, she saw Scott come walking through the jungle of plants behind the property that was the garden center.

"Promise me something, will you?" she asked Scott.

"What?"

"Don't ever stop doing that."

"Walking into your backyard?"

"Yep. No matter what happens, make sure you always come by this house for a chat."

"Are you sure?"

"Absolutely. I love it here. Who knew I'd ever own a house where my yard is haunted? What do you do for Halloween?"

"Ha. Ha. Very funny."

"Just saying. If you could rattle a few chains…"

"That's a stereotype. Do you see any chains?"

"No, but it's never too early to get your 'Marley' on."

Later, she put a pot roast in the oven for dinner, peeled potatoes and carrots to go in the pan. She called her dad and invited him to supper on Monday.

When Ryder walked through the front door, smelling like farm and man, she greeted him with nothing on but a smile.

His mouth dropped open. "You know, I almost brought Marty home for dinner tonight."

She tilted her head with a coy smile. "Hmm, from now on, it might be better to call first."

"I see that," he said, wrapping her up in his arms. "I need a shower. I smell like cows."

"I was hoping you'd say that. Any objections to taking care of that detail before dinner?"

His mouth had gone dry at the sight of her. "I'm having trouble thinking at the moment."

"Good," she said, taking his hand and leading him up the stairs. "For what I have in mind we don't have to say another word."

That night as they took a walk on the beach, Ryder spotted an older model blue Nissan van with peeling paint, parked near the pier.

"That's strange. That vehicle wasn't here earlier."

"I don't remember seeing it when we set out on our walk either, which means it hasn't been here that long." As if reading his thoughts, Julianne squeezed his hand. "You're on edge. I doubt Bethany would be driving a car like that one."

Ryder approached the driver's side, realized an unshaven man sat slumped behind the wheel. On closer inspection, he saw a woman in the passenger seat in the same pose. In the backseat, he could make out a couple of small heads buckled in child car seats. There were boxes packed in the back along with visible toys and household furnishings. Ryder relaxed his demeanor. It was obvious a family of four had found a place to sleep for the night. He tried to backtrack out of the driver's line of vision but the guy came fully awake.

The look of sheer terror on the man's face indicated to Ryder the stranger thought he'd done something wrong and feared trouble. Instead of leaving it at that and walking away, Ryder decided to take an approach Scott might approve. "Are you guys okay?"

The man rolled down the window. "I didn't realize we were breaking any laws by parking here. We just needed a place to sleep without getting hassled."

"Are you visiting the area?"

"Just passin' through, mister. I lost my job six months back, couple months ago we lost our apartment, been on the move ever since." The man extended a hand. "The name's Gavin Kendall." He bobbed his head toward his now-awake passenger. "And this is my wife, Maggie."

Ryder shook the man's hand, noting the guy couldn't have been more than twenty-five, the wife, a couple years younger. "You don't have a place to live?"

Kendall shook his head. "We don't."

"Where were you headed?"

"We usually just stay on the move. Sometimes we hang out at the library if the town has one. You guys don't."

"What type of work do you do?"

"Are you kidding? I'll do any job you got."

From a few feet away Julianne had been eyeing the sleeping boy and girl in the backseat. She'd guess they were preschool age, maybe three and four years old. All at once an idea hit her. Stepping up to Ryder's side, she introduced herself to the parents. "I'll be the new principal at the school in the fall. Ryder, there's always plenty of work to do out on the farm, don't you think?"

"More than. Would you be willing to do farm work?"

"I'll scrub toilets if that's what it takes to feed my wife and kids."

"Great. But I need to get an okay from one of the bosses before I make any offers. Knowing Cord and Nick, I don't think there'll be a problem."

Ryder turned to Julianne. "There's a little cottage just sitting empty on the place. It's where the original caretakers used to live. They could stay there for a while."

She took out her cell phone. "Any objections to my calling Nick now?"

"This late?"

"I don't see letting these kids spend another night trying to sleep while buckled into their car seats, do you?"

"Good point."

As the Nissan van followed them out to the farm, Ryder wanted to know what Nick had said.

"That if the couple has kids we shouldn't waste time getting them out of the car and into a place with a real roof over their heads. So I figure we all take a chance on the adults, hope they don't steal you blind at the first opportunity they get."

Taking his eyes off the road for a second, Ryder spared a glance at her. "The teacher who emits sunshine wherever she goes has doubts about the family behind us?"

"Why does everyone think a teacher is Miss Perfect? I'm not. In my profession I see deceit all the time. I'm surrounded by it. Kids who tell me the hamster chewed up their homework. Little round cherub faces that stand in front of me and swear they left their reader at the vet's office where they had to take their dog after it got hit by a car. I've been lied to by parents. Little Joanie would never pull out another little girl's hair. Little Johnny would never shake down other boys in the bathroom."

He busted out laughing. "You lead a hard life, Ms. Dickinson."

"Don't I know it," she commiserated. "So just because Gavin Kendall says he'll work at the farm, doesn't mean I trust him to do it."

"Don't worry, Sam and Silas run a pretty tight ship, they'll keep an eye out for any red flags."

While Ryder and Julianne wondered whether or not they could trust the Kendalls, Gavin and Maggie were wondering the same thing about the couple in the car up ahead.

Driving off into the middle of the night behind a strange truck, the pair, whose luck had been awful lately, had a hard time believing someone could befriend them by letting them sleep in an actual house.

"Maybe it's a trick. What if they're leading us out into the countryside in the dark to slit our throats and take everything we own?" Maggie said, alarm rising in her voice.

"The woman claimed to be a principal. She looked trustworthy enough."

"Looks can be deceiving."

"True. I tell you what, if we get out here and there's no farm, I'll step on the gas and high-tail it out of there. How's that sound?"

Maggie blew out a nervous breath. "Okay. But that could be too late. Just in case, I'm digging out the craft scissors I carry in my handbag for emergencies."

"I hate to tell you but those won't do much damage. I have my pocket knife though."

"That's something, I guess."

When Gavin spotted the Taggert Farms sign, his jaw dropped. "Isn't that the kind of milk we used to buy for the kids?"

"It sure is. Do you really think these people are on the level?"

"We can only hope. God knows, it's about time our luck changed."

Getting the Kendall family settled into the caretaker's cottage—a box of a house painted bright cheery red with white trim—turned out to be a treat for Julianne and Ryder. Watching Maggie and Gavin with their kids, the care they took to get them out of their seats and then bundle the boy and girl up to their shoulders— went a long way to dissipate the skittishness. Maybe it worked on two fronts. Both sides seemed to relax with each other.

"This is a real farm," Gavin said to Ryder. "You weren't scamming us."

Ryder chuckled realizing the young father had been just as nervous as he'd been. "Nope, it's quite an operation."

"Why the house is as cute as a button," Maggie noted with the still-sleeping little girl hugged up to her chest.

Ryder led the way up to the porch, opened the door, flicked on the light. "The electricity's on, but no one's lived here since a friend of mine found his own apartment. Because of that I can't guarantee how many layers of dust there is on everything."

"That's okay. We can get it clean," Maggie said eagerly.

"There are only two bedrooms but it has a large, fully functional kitchen at the back and a working fireplace in the living room," Ryder went on. "You'll find sheets in the linen closet. Blankets should already be on the beds."

"Are you sure our staying here is okay with the owner?" Gavin wanted to know. "This isn't what we expected."

"Positive," Julianne assured him. "We called him and he didn't hesitate. As Ryder told you already the place has been sitting here gathering dust. Now let's go into the kitchen and see if there's anything on hand to eat for breakfast."

As soon as the light came on, Maggie let out a gasp behind her. "Oh, this is precious. Look at the size of this kitchen, Gavin. It's truly beautiful."

"I... We don't know what to say."

"Except thank you," Maggie said her voice beginning to tremble.

Julianne went to the fridge, which was empty except for a bottle of ketchup and a jar of mustard. She opened the door to the pantry, frowned. "There's cereal but no milk, canned goods but not much else. Tomorrow's Memorial Day and Murphy's Market will be closed. Ryder and I will bring you over some supplies from his place to get you going until Tuesday morning. Right now, settle in and get a good night's sleep. Be sure to come back into town for the fireworks tomorrow night. The kids will get a kick out of them."

She'd no sooner got the words out of her mouth when Maggie broke down in sobs and rested her head on her daughter's. "Thank you. Thank you so much. We'll work to stay here. Both of us will."

Gavin reached out for his wife's hand despite the little boy snugged in his arms. "For... How long? How long do we get to stay?"

"Do you know anything about milking cows?"

"Not a thing. But that don't mean I can't learn. I normally work as a machinist, done some construction work, too. I'm good with my hands."

"Okay. Then you'll start work on Tuesday."

"I'll start tomorrow if it's all the same to you," Gavin insisted.

"Will filling out an application on Tuesday pose a problem for either one of you?"

"No, not a bit."

"Okay, then get a good night's sleep. There's enough work on a farm to keep you both here until you get ready to move on."

"Mister, whatever job you got, we'll do it."

Ryder slapped Gavin on the back. "Get your kids to bed and we'll talk tomorrow."

Once back in the truck, Julianne sat in the passenger seat, met Ryder's eyes. "Is it just me or did that feel good? Really good."

"If anyone had told me six months ago I'd be helping out a homeless family I wouldn't have believed them. I was pretty self-absorbed with my own troubles. I'm beginning to realize how Scott feels about this town and why Nick and Jordan encourage people to settle here."

Caught up in a pleased state of excitement, she rolled on, "Do you realize those children might be my future students? I hope the cynical side of me doesn't rear its ugly head again because Gavin and Maggie seem like nice people."

"With a ton of rotten luck. Let's go get them the food we promised."

The next morning, Julianne decided on the spur-of-the-moment to hold a barbecue on the front lawn. She used two sawhorses with a sheet of plywood leftover from the renovation to set up for her outside table, covered it with a bright blue sheet. She made phone calls to friends letting them know her plans and told them to pass it on.

"I can't think of a better way to thank everyone for all the hard work they've done to get me here," she told anyone who thought she'd lost too many brain cells for having such an event on short notice.

"The only problem we might have is running out of food. I didn't really put too much planning into this."

When Perry Altman got wind of her worries, he had hamburger meat delivered to her doorstep along with his own special batch of coleslaw with a note that read: *This should feed another fifty people.*

By noon word had spread. By two people began to drift into the yard. Not a massive crowd because most had already made their own plans with family and friends. But the small group who did show up included kids running around and old-timers who set up posts to play horseshoes.

The venue provided a chance to get to know her neighbors. It also gave people like River's archaeological crew—Julian Gustave and Laura Angleton and Sandra McFarland, away from home and stuck living out of an RV—a place to hang out for the day.

Julianne used the opportunity to introduce the Kendall family around and make them feel at home.

Ryder and her dad took turns manning the grill while she prepped simple food like deviled eggs and potato salad, opened bags of chips and dips.

Soon her little cottage became a hub with rock music drumming in the background. She had to drag out another table from the garage to set next to the porch to hold desserts after Ethel Jenkins, Prissie Gates, and Ina Crawford brought an array of cookies and pies that wouldn't fit next to the side dishes.

"What a great idea," Bree vaunted as she munched on the feast of food alongside Troy. "Zach will be along soon. He's loading up another grill just in case you need it."

"Ryder will appreciate that. I'm thinking of making this a tradition."

"The Memorial Day barbecue? Fantastic. It's brilliant you're keeping them out of the house and making this an outside event."

Julianne giggled. "Picnics are usually held outside."

"Oh. Right. I'm planning to wear the lace dress I bought from you on Saturday to my graduation party— didn't even need a single alteration from Emma Colter. How's that for a having a good eye? I can't believe you put together two parties in one week."

"The one on Saturday is planned while this one was more like impromptu at the last minute. Ryder thought I was crazy among a few others. I'm afraid it'll soon get out that I'm a bit...spontaneous with my ideas."

"Nothing wrong with that at all."

"It's just that I get these notions...and wham! I'm off and running then I have to deal with the weight of my actions."

"Yes, but your ideas have so far stirred us on to rename that wasted space and make it an actual park, have a movie night there, of all things, and a concert on the old pier. All good things that, up to now, no one else had ever thought of doing," Bree pointed out.

Troy looked at Julianne, echoed that sentiment. "You've inspired me to buy my own place. Ryder's inspired me to go into business. If not for you two, I wouldn't see that for myself, at least not for years down the road. Now I'm on this fast-track timetable."

"Nonsense," Julianne uttered. But then she focused on what Troy had said. "You're buying a house?" She saw his immediate glance at Bree. "Where?"

He told her about the bungalow on Athena Circle. "It needs a lot of work though."

"More than this one?"

"About the same as this one."

"Count me in when you get ready to renovate. Look at how everyone pitched in for me. Look at the results." She turned in a circle, spread her arms out wide. "I'd planned to be moved in, of course, but nothing prepared me to have all the help getting settled. I want to return the favor, pay it forward."

About that time Troy spotted Izzy biking down the lane coming from the lighthouse. He stuck his hand in the air in a wave and watched as the striking woman slowed to a stop. Pushing away from the porch, he turned to Bree. "Where's that brother of yours?"

"Over there, he's setting up the second grill."

"I'll be right back." Troy went over, grabbed Zach's arm. "Izzy's here. Try not to embarrass me."

Zach followed Troy's gaze, smoothed down his wayward mass of hair. "But I smell like charcoal and smoke right now."

"Trust me, it's a definite improvement over your usual sweaty scent at work," Troy whispered. On approach where Izzy had parked her bicycle, he dragged Zach along with him.

"You decided to show up. It's about time you met some of your neighbors. This is Zach Dennison. Zach, this is Isabella Rialto. But her friends call her Izzy."

Zach saw a pair of sultry green eyes looking back at him, a full mouth. Both came together in a striking face with her olive complexion. He wanted to reach out and touch all that silky golden brown hair. Instead, he stuck out his hand. "Are you just here for the summer, *Isabella*?" He met her eyes, watched the captivating woman retreat into herself.

"I like your little village. I appreciate you inviting me today but I can't stay. Sorry."

Even though she'd taken his hand in a brief touch of skin, Zach noticed she hadn't answered the question. So he asked it again. "How long will you be staying with us?"

"A while. I'll see you around, Troy. Nice meeting you, *Zachary*."

At the use of his full name, Zach rocked back on his heels and watched as Isabella and her long, lean legs climbed back on her bike and pedaled away. Although fascinated, he wasn't stupid. "I thought you said she was Italian. She doesn't even have an accent...of any kind. And you never mentioned that she was so snobby."

"She's never been that way to me," Troy said with a shrug. "She did seem standoffish today. Maybe she was in a hurry."

"Snooty," Zach grumbled as he headed back to help Ryder grill the burgers.

Julianne and Bree weren't the only ones watching the exchange from the other side of the yard. Every person there interested in the woman occupying the keeper's cottage, dived into conjecture mode about the woman's past.

At the same time Izzy took off down Ocean Street, Julianne listened to gums flapping amid speculation.

"She's too short to be a former ballet dancer. I'll tell you that," Ethel said, pointing a bony finger at Emma Colter. "Those dancers are usually tall and skinny. She couldn't be more than five-foot-six."

"Doesn't look like a nanny either. Doesn't live with Logan and Kinsey, that's for sure," Ina Crawford threw in.

"The girl looks more Spanish than Italian, if you ask me. I didn't hear a foreign accent in there anywhere. Did you? Got to be a reason she keeps to herself like she does," Prissie ventured.

Julianne hated to stand by and be a party to so much gossip about another newcomer. She couldn't help but wonder if these same women who were so eager to talk about Izzy did the same about her. She'd bet that none of the busybodies knew what it was like to start over in a new place. Because of that, she resolved to seek out Izzy and befriend her.

At the end of the day, most everyone had headed home including her dad. Left alone, Julianne and Ryder sat on the porch looking southwest while fireworks cannon-boomed across the street over Smuggler's Bay. Spectacular fireballs shot up and cascaded downward like shooting stars falling to earth.

She could make out the oohs and aahs of children and adults alike. The entire neighborhood seemed to be watching the sky light up. For some reason her thoughts went to Izzy. She hoped the young woman had a thick skin against the whispers and gossip.

"I think Bree and Troy are moving in together first chance they get," Julianne finally said aloud.

"What makes you say that?"

"For one, Troy's buying a house. Second, Bree has that look on her face that says 'I'm in love and I don't care who knows it.'"

"It bothers you."

"It's none of my business." She turned to look at him in the shadowy darkness. "Were you ever in love?"

"In lust maybe when I was around Troy's age but it was never the real thing. Even before Bethany I was too cautious to give my heart to anyone. Then when I did trust I got burned. I'm still paying for my stupidity."

It hurt a little to hear him so callous. But she couldn't do anything to change his past. If this thing between them was a simple matter of satisfying a hunger, how long would she be willing to settle for that? How long before all the gossip in town reached her front door?

If Ryder couldn't declare his love for her outright, did she want him to leave and never darken her door again?

She'd wait and see before making that kind of decision. She let out a huge puff of breath, resigned herself to keeping what they had... Whatever it was, as playful as possible. After all, Ryder had been the first real relationship she'd had since Danny. She'd be damned if she'd let anyone taint what they felt together for as long as it lasted.

Soon the long day caught up with them. The steamy summer night had them yearning for bed. When Ryder yawned, she tugged on his hand and pulled him into the house, and ultimately into her bed.

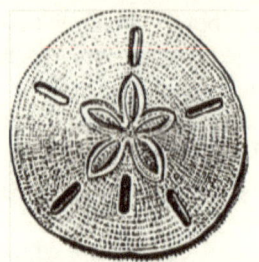

Chapter Twenty

Troy stared at his fire-capped goddess from across the room. He watched her excitement bubble to the surface as she put on her cap and gown. Someone offstage cued the music—the pomp and circumstance, a prelude to accepting her degree. His eyes watered and he looked around to make sure no one saw his state of mind. Everyone close to Bree was here. That made him just as happy as if he had a *real* family. He'd often heard the saying that family didn't have to be blood. Today, more than ever, he felt like that was true.

A graduation ceremony was a big deal to Julianne. That's why she'd brought her Nikon with the zoom lens to capture the moment when Bree walked across the stage to accept her degree. Just as Julianne already knew, no one in the audience particularly cared that it was "just" community college. It was a big step, a start and meant Bree could build on the experience as well as the credits anytime she wanted.

Since applying for the loan together, Troy and Zach seemed to have decided harmony might be better for Bree than conflict, especially today. The two men had been getting along so well Ryder noted the change as he took his seat in the auditorium.

"It's like a before and after. Peace between them on the job site, other than the usual good-natured ribbing, even a few tranquil trips to the beach spent surfing. It's almost as though alien pods took over their brains."

"And are you learning? To surf?" Julianne wanted to know.

"Enough to want to buy a board of my own and take you out on the waves one of these days."

She reached over, ran a few strands of his thick, black hair through her fingers. "I'd like that."

Back in Pelican Pointe, with Jordan's culinary help and guidance, Julianne managed to pull off a small miracle with very little planning in order to give Bree an event to remember.

Bree's well-wishers packed the rooms to overflowing. They brought gifts and dropped off envelopes.

Julianne noted Bree looked radiant in the vintage lace dress. "With your gorgeous red hair you look just like Nicole Kidman in *Practical Magic*."

"Today, I feel like her, too. Can you believe how many showed up?" Bree said, her voice dripping with delight. "So many people and every single one of them brought me a card. And guess what I found inside the cards?"

Julianne breathed out a laugh at the woman's excitement. "Oh, I don't know? A few bucks maybe."

Bree grabbed her in a hug. "Cash and checks. I'm saving the money for when Troy and I move in together and get our own place."

Julianne frowned and shook her head. "Moving pretty fast there, huh?"

"Not really. We've known each other since grade school. He's always been one of the sweetest guys I know. There was a time we lost touch but now…"

"But you're young. You shouldn't rush things. You know that cash is for you, right? Which means you should use it anyway *you* choose." She turned around and spotted Troy in the middle of her little speech. "Hi Troy."

He wrapped his arms around Bree. "Don't worry. I'll see to it she uses it on herself."

"Right now, every twenty-dollar bill and check is going into my savings account first thing Monday morning."

Jordan walked in with an empty tray, picked clean by the partygoers.

"And the food…" Bree said wrapping her arms around Jordan. "Is to die for. Thank you both for giving me such an awesome day."

"You're welcome. Now get out of the kitchen and go mingle with your guests. Both of you," Jordan ordered Troy.

When the couple disappeared into the other room, Jordan got busy with more appetizers. "Just so you know the park dedication is next week. Even though we've had the wooden sign done for a week now, we waited for you to move to town before scheduling the event. Troy did the design and engraving. Everyone's been great about pitching in to get the area cleaned up. The Plant Habitat donated the trees and the landscaping."

"I walked over and took a peek earlier. It's beginning to look like a real park now, a completely different use of the space instead of a vacant lot."

Nick came in, overheard the last part. "Thanks to you."

"I simply made a suggestion."

"A good one," Nick offered. "The town council had to stay after Ferguson to make sure he came through with the benches. But after several calls he finally delivered them Thursday. Murphy and I bolted them into the concrete yesterday."

"See, you guys are the ones who make things happen around here."

"Personally, I'll be glad when Joe's son, Tucker, moves here and takes over running the everyday hardware store operation so I don't have to deal with the old man. I've never really liked Joe at all."

"I don't know anyone in town who does. When will that be?" Jordan asked. "What if Tucker is like his father?"

"August. I heard Joe and his wife are heading to Florida, retiring there. So I'm hoping to get off on the right foot with Tucker. It can't be any worse with the son than it's been with the father."

Julianne took the cheese sticks out of the oven, refilled the platter. "Thanks for giving Ryder the loan. It means a lot to him."

"I believe in this town. Ryder, Zach and Troy want a chance at making it grow. I think they deserve a shot at their dreams. Otherwise I never would've agreed to the loan. It's a good investment for the bank. The boatbuilding idea has the potential to make money. Plus any time I can rent out one of those old storefronts, I'm going to jump on that."

Ryder came in about that time, making the tiny kitchen seem crowded. "Come on, guys. You can't keep hanging out in here. People are beginning to wonder where you went." He took the platter out of Julianne's hand. "Let me have the food. I'll circulate. Guests are beginning to get curious about Layne and Brooke. Brent was about to bring everyone up to speed."

By the time they got back to the living room, Brent was in the middle of what seemed like a Q&A. Like her party at Promise Cove, Julianne saw genuine interest on the faces of the guests. They all seemed truly vested in learning what had happened to the couple.

The town cop held court while the throng closed in around him.

"In my mind, there's nothing more deadly than playing with someone's emotions or their emotional state," Brent said flatly. "In my line of work, I've seen it happen a hundred times."

"But what happened to them?" Noreen prodded. "Where are they? If the couple supposedly ran off which was the scuttlebutt at the time, then why didn't they resurface at some point after Eleanor died?"

"So what do you think, Brent? Are you any closer to knowing?" Joy Sullivan asked. "I'm one of the women who helped put together the Richmond wedding. I look back on those early years of Layne's marriage to Eleanor and realize you could cut the tension with a knife. Those little kids weren't stupid either. They knew what was going on?"

"What was going on?" Donna Oden wanted to know.

Another woman, Julianne didn't recognize, added her two cents. "Brooke shouldn't have been running around with a married man."

That statement took the buzz in a whole other direction. Sniping at each other broke out as more people leapt to Layne's defense.

Listening to people take sides, Julianne decided the entire situation had to be depressing for everyone involved.

Which is one reason after the crowd thinned out that Julianne sought out Troy. She found him on the patio. "I want you to know I wasn't trying to discourage Bree from moving in with you."

"I figured that out."

"Good. Because I think you're one of the sweetest people in this town. You see, I've moved pretty fast before when I was young. At seventeen I fell in love with a boy."

"You?"

She nodded. "At first, my father didn't like it very much. But when he eventually saw that I truly loved Danny, he did everything he could to make sure we were happy. It's a good thing too because, as it turns out, we didn't have that much time together. Danny was killed by a drunk driver. We never got married because I was going to school. We got busy with other things. The reason I'm telling you this is because sometimes as we get older, we forget what it's like to be young. When I was talking to Bree it was one of those times."

"But you *are* young."

She laughed, touched his cheek. "Not like you are. The light I see in your eyes when you look at Bree reminds me there was a time I felt the same way about a boy. I forgot about that feeling, Troy."

"What about Ryder?"

"That's why I said what I did to Bree. Don't rush things. I didn't think I'd ever find anyone I felt this way about again. Turns out… I did."

"Ah, I get it."

"As long as you remember that sometimes love happens at seventeen, or twenty-one, or thirty and beyond. No one should let a number get in the way of a single minute of happiness. Don't let life bog you down. If you feel that way about Bree, be sure you let her know it. It's never a bad time to let her know it."

"I have."

She smiled. "Good. Then you don't need me giving you any more sage wisdom about your love life."

Back inside Julianne joined Ryder in picking up dirty plates as the two nudged Brent back into the discussion about Layne and Brooke.

"Obviously the town refuses to forget them."

Ryder agreed. "Coming from the big city like I do, people go missing all the time. But here in Pelican Pointe it had to be an unusual occurrence. What bothers me is, after getting to know some of the players, I'd say the residents around town were freaked out about this disappearance more than the authorities were."

Finishing his beer, Brent tossed the empty into the recycle bin. "I'm afraid you're right. That's why I'm determined to get to the bottom of it now." He turned to look at Ryder. "El Cerrito PD picked up a Melinda Sykes four days ago for having a phony driver's license."

"Why didn't you say something? El Cerrito? Where is that? Near San Francisco, right?"

"Who's Melinda Sykes?" Julianne asked. But studying Ryder's face, she got her answer. "Ah. Bethany."

"I'm going up there."

"It won't do you any good," Brent said. "They charged her with a misdemeanor because there was no loss of money involved and released her within twenty-four hours. She's due in court next month for a hearing. If she doesn't show, they'll issue a warrant and pick her up then."

But it was a frustrated Ryder who later took Julianne on a walk on the beach. Under the pearly glow of a half-moon, he linked his fingers with hers.

"Brent's doing his best to pressure me into dropping this thing, forgetting about it. Don't be mad at me but..."

"But you can't drop it. I understand you have to see this play out. Why don't we do this? Now that we know she's living in the Bay Area, let's do our homework and get a list of the military installations in the area. You already know she targets service personnel."

"Seems like a reasonable place to start."

"Good. Contact your private investigator."

"I've tried that route."

"I know. But this time give him the name and address she gave the cops when they picked her up with the phony driver's license. Maybe that way the PI could make the rounds with her picture, do a little advance recon before we get there. If he does get lucky enough to find her, I'll go with you when you confront her."

"You'd do that?"

"I'm crazy like that. Now might be a good time to be honest with you. I've done something I'm afraid has the potential to make our police chief furious when he finds out."

"You?" Ryder breathed in the night air and turned her into his arms, tilted her chin up. "What did you do, jaywalk across Main Street?"

Julianne ignored the dig. "I've been looking for Cooper Jennings, doing my research online about him. I've also been trying to look up the 1984 graduating class at UC Santa Barbara. But that's like looking for a needle in a haystack. Hopeless. The ring wasn't engraved."

He narrowed his eyes. "Why?"

"Because I think Cooper Jennings is the key to Layne and Brooke's disappearance. He makes his living as a photographer, travels quite a bit, that's why it's been hard to pin him down."

"But he was a child when this happened. What could a nine-year-old know about such things?"

She repeated the conversation she'd had with Scott. "I won't know exactly what Cooper knows until I locate him and ask him myself. Let's agree you want to find Bethany and I'm motivated to see what Cooper has to say. I tracked down his last known address. It's in Sausalito."

"Not Oregon?"

"And not Orinda either. So at some point, let's agree to take a trip to the Bay Area together. There's a huge salvage yard up there that sells stuff they've stripped out of schools. If anyone asks that's why we're going—to check out any material we can upcycle for the school."

"When? When do we make the trip?"

"Whenever you can manage time off from the farm and the job site. I've got the summer so it won't be a problem for me. If all you can get off is a Sunday then we'll make it a day trip. But obviously I'm hoping we can spend a weekend up there and get some answers."

They looked out across Smuggler's Bay, listened to the waves hit the sand.

"How many people do you think have stood right in this same spot where we are tonight and thought about murder?"

"Solving one or contemplating one?"

"Hmm, good question. We wouldn't be thinking about confronting Cooper Jennings if someone hadn't done the contemplating and then followed through with it. That's what we think happened, right?"

"Unfortunately, yes."

"Are you okay living in the house, spending a night there alone?"

Her heart felt like it wanted to drop out of her chest. But she hid it well. "Surprisingly, I don't feel the house has any lingering bad vibes."

She wanted to get to the root of why he'd asked the question. "Is that a nice, polite way of telling me you aren't staying tonight?"

"Of course, I'm staying. I just don't want people to start gossiping about the new principal because of me before she ever starts the job."

She let out a huge sigh. "If I'm not allowed to go about living my life here then it isn't the place I thought it was."

Chapter Twenty-One

Dedicating Phillips Park turned out to be an emotional day for the Harris family. Nick and Jordan showed up with their children in tow and tried to put on a happy face for the kids. But anyone with eyes could see they were both struggling with their memories of the man who'd brought them together.

Julianne and Ryder stood back admiring Troy's work. At the entrance, the simple wooden sign with the words, Phillips Park, hung between two stone pillars, metal lanterns on top of each. It became evident soon enough there were a lot of new things to explore. Landon and Caleb had planted dogwood and elm, cypress and birch and put down beds filled with golden larkspur and white river daisies.

To entertain the toddlers, Cord and Keegan brought a petting zoo—a few rabbits, kittens and puppies from the veterinary clinic. It worked wonders to keep the younger ones happy. For the older kids Murphy orchestrated a treasure hunt with clues that ended in a series of prizes— toys, music CDs, costume jewelry, ball caps, stuffed animals—no one went home empty-handed to commemorate the day.

Babies napped in strollers. Adults sprawled on blankets to doze in the sun.

The long day culminated with the town's first movie night—the feature-length film chosen, *Harry Potter and the Philosopher's Stone.* With Ryder's help, Julianne had spent the previous week getting the word out. The effort had paid off. Glancing around what was now Phillips Park, the movie idea had garnered the attention of adults, young and old, and kids alike. The place was packed.

Under a starry sky, people gathered to watch the orphan boy, once again, discover that he's really a wizard. No matter how many times you watched it and knew the ending, the magical storyline resonated.

They brought blankets to sit on or their own lawn chairs, picnic baskets and takeout from the Diner. Murphy had donated the popcorn. Perry Altman the ability to pop it. And the local soft drink distributor out of San Sebastian had donated the use of a fountain to dispense soda. They used the side of the bank for their giant movie screen and a donated projector from Jill and Ross Campbell.

While they waited for darkness to start the film, the prevailing buzz ran hot to cold. First, it was about Perry's new partner, a hot, young graduate student from the Bay Area and whether or not the two men had plans for opening a winery in town. Or was it a brewery?

It was a mystery for sure and no one was talking.

Spotting Isabella Rialto in the crowd sitting with Logan and Kinsey and their babies, Julianne realized there were all different kinds of puzzles. There were enough rumors floating around about the lovely Izzy to fill the entire park. For some reason, Julianne got the sense that the same tongues at play with one newcomer applied to her as well. It wasn't so much what they said to her face but how they acted whenever they were around her, especially if Ryder was nearby.

When Ryder came up behind her, kissed her ear, she settled against him, noting the display of affection garnered a few stares in the process. She shrugged off the gawking snoops, chalked it up to nothing more than curiosity.

"I want you to know you're the best thing that's happened to me in a very long time," Ryder whispered.

"That's the sweetest thing you've said to me. Want to prove it later?"

As the skies darkened, the projector began to flicker and the film credits rolled.

"Maybe we could sneak out and I could show you."

"My thoughts exactly."

The town council had scheduled Pelican Pointe's version of "music over the bay" for the third weekend in June. It wasn't the local favorite Blue Skies or Ninth Dog that raced onto the scene as a headliner but a couple of talented sibling teens, named Sonnet and Sonoma Rafferty.

Somehow word had gotten out that the person to see about headlining a show this summer was Julianne. The two girls had shown up on Julianne's doorstep the day after Memorial Day to show her what they could do with a fiddle.

After tuning up, it turned out the twelve- and thirteen-year-old sisters could do quite a bit. They didn't have to get completely through *Cajun Fiddle* before Julianne was convinced these two were her "stars" for the very first event.

"What else can you play?"

"We play country and a few Irish jigs our dad taught us."

"Who is your dad?"

"He owns the T-Shirt Shop. Over there, across the street," said Sonoma. "Malachi Rafferty. We work there sometimes while he goes over to Santa Cruz on weekends to play in a club."

"So he's a musician as well?"

Sonnet nodded. "Sure. But during the week he sells T-shirts and other stuff to the tourists."

"When we have them, that is," Sonoma added. "We did really good in March during the street fair this year."

"Well," Julianne corrected automatically. "You did well during the street fair. Is your dad at the store right now?"

"Yes, why?"

"Because it looks like I've found my headliners for the first show and need to nail down his permission."

Single father Malachi Rafferty stood behind the counter of his cramped T-Shirt Shop where he spent every day from nine to five. In the four years he'd owned the place, he hadn't bothered naming it anything other than T-Shirt Shop. It seemed unnecessary to get cutesy with the name. He sold souvenir shirts in various colors with the words "Smuggler's Bay Pelican Pointe" silk-screened on the front or back. His business targeted the tourists who passed through town wanting to pick up a memento from the beach to take back home with them. Along with tacky things like shot glasses, ash trays, sea shells, and the like, he crammed as many beach essentials next to the counter as he could. Suntan oil, flip-flops, and swimsuits made for pricey impulse buys from people who hadn't remembered to pack what they needed. Since his wife, Melody, had died three years earlier, he'd gotten complaints that the swimwear on display was outdated and looked it. But to Malachi that was their problem, not his. He never reordered a new line until the old stuff sold.

When they'd learned Melody had cancer, they'd decided to chunk their life back in Los Angeles to look for a new place to start over. They'd taken a trip through Pelican Pointe and fell for its proximity to the ocean. The town's affordability had been a draw too. With starting up a new business, their money might last longer. But that notion hadn't worked out during the unforeseen downturn in the economy. They hadn't figured on it taking this long for the town to make a comeback. By the time it had, Melody had lost her battle with lymphoma.

When the door opened and a woman walked in, followed by his daughters, Malachi sensed trouble. Mainly because he was on his own where his two teenage girls were concerned. Even though Sonoma was the oldest, Sonnet was just as willing to rebel. Lately anytime either one got out of his sight, they came up with ways to torment him or get into trouble. He never knew what they were planning, or what to expect from day to day.

"Mr. Rafferty, I'm Julianne Dickinson. I'm your new neighbor from across the street. You know, the house at the end of the block I recently redid."

"You did a great job, really improved it from the eyesore it used to be."

"Good to hear you approve. Tell me, were you aware your daughters auditioned for me not fifteen minutes ago for the local talent concert I mentioned to the town council several weeks back?"

Malachi shot his daughters a stern look. "I told them not to bother you. That it would be a waste of time since folks around here are more into Blue Skies than anything else. Apparently, they didn't listen."

"Normally I would encourage children to heed their parents but in this case, I'm afraid boldness had a definite upside. Did you teach them how to play?"

"I used to give lessons back in Los Angeles." He also used to play in a well-known, successful rock band but he didn't intend to go down that road again by bringing it up. He hoped his precocious daughters had been just as tight-lipped.

"Then you must be as musically inclined as your daughters?"

"I play guitar now and then, usually over in Santa Cruz on Friday and Saturday nights to bring in some extra cash."

Julianne smiled at him. "Excellent. I'd like to see you and your daughters headline the show."

"What about Blue Skies? They're usually the band of choice around here."

"I'm sure they are. But as of today, no one in the band has approached me with any interest in playing at the pier. They've had several weeks to contact me since the council voted to put on the summer concert event at the wharf. We have an entire summer to fill the slots up, so I'm sure when Blue Skies has an opening and they're ready, they'll let me know. In the meantime, I'm sure several local musicians will want to get in on the act, which is the reason I suggested this in the first place to provide a venue for talent in the area. Since Sonnet and Sonoma took the initiative, I'm recommending you and your daughters to appear together onstage and kick things off for us. They're quite good. Let's hope you're half as good as they are."

"I don't know what to say."

"I hope you say yes because you have less than two weeks to come up with a playlist."

When concert day arrived, the town turned out front and center. Again, they hauled out their lawn chairs to sit up on the wharf or stretched blankets over the ground much like they had with movie night. Even fishermen made their way into port, dropping anchor to take in the performance from the decks of their boats.

A steady stream of tourists started drifting from the shops despite a heavy marine layer hanging over the water most of the day. Right up to show time Julianne was certain that the fog would ruin the whole thing. But then, thirty minutes before Malachi Rafferty and his daughters took the stage, the clouds miraculously parted and revealed a perfect summer solstice sky.

Julianne fought the temptation to glance around looking for Scott—it was the only thing that added up. There wasn't time for such foolish thinking on her part though. She sought out Malachi to make sure he was ready and found him braiding Sonoma's hair.

"Is everything okay over here?" Julianne asked.

"I'm nervous," Sonnet admitted. "But Dad says there's nothing to it. Just go out there and play like we were standing in our own living room."

"That sounds like excellent advice. It's almost go time."

"How many people showed up?" Malachi wanted to know.

"The whole town."

"That's what I was afraid of. Okay girls, let's go out there and play our hearts out. Just get into the music and don't worry about the crowd."

The pier made for an intimate setting. Ryder and Troy had put together a stage, a platform two-feet high and twelve-feet square to give the performers an elevated advantage. With Malachi on guitar and Sonoma and Sonnet on violin, as soon as the trio began the first notes of *Boot Scootin' Boogie*, the audience roared its enthusiasm.

No one was more surprised than Julianne when Malachi began to sing out the lyrics. Her mouth dropped open as Ryder whispered to her, "Where did you say you found him? Why does his voice sound so familiar?"

"His daughters found me. They were right across the street. This guy owns the T-Shirt Shop. But wow, the question is why. His kids are prodigies and he has the voice of a rock star."

"Just shows you this town is full of surprises."

It was as if Malachi had used his voice and initial song to calm his daughters. Because after that one number, he let them have the floor. Sonnet and Sonoma didn't disappoint. When Malachi switched from guitar to mandolin, he led the girls from lively tunes into soulful classics and then back into toe-tapping Celtic ditties that had the crowd moving and on its feet.

Julianne noticed the pure pride on Malachi's face. The proud papa watched the throng get into the music.

She and Ryder never sat down. They swayed on their feet, arms locked around each other. That was pretty much what the other couples did as well—Nick and Jordan, Troy and Bree, Murphy and Carla, Ethan and Hayden, Cord and Keegan, Logan and Kinsey, Pete Alden and new wife, Betty.

A group of older women—Ina, Marabelle, Myrtle, and Prissie kept time sitting in their folding chairs.

Kids danced. But two teen boys, Jason Broderick and Connor Davis, seemed particularly fascinated with the main attraction—Sonoma and Sonnet.

Ninety minutes later when the Raffertys finally wound down, the enthusiastic multitude showed their appreciation. The town got to its feet, gave them a standing O while the boats in the harbor used their foghorns to signal a ringing endorsement.

A roar went up when the performers responded with an encore, a bouncy Irish jig that kept everyone moving for one final round.

Once it was all over, Julianne approached the trio. "You were marvelous, a true Pelican Pointe treasure. Thank you. I hope you'll do it again before summer's end."

"It's us who should be thanking you. That was a lot of fun. What do you say, girls? Should we repeat that performance midsummer?" Malachi asked his daughters.

Sonoma lifted one shoulder. "Sure. If you really want us but Sonnet will need to practice. She was dragging for half the set."

"I was not," Sonnet protested.

"Girls," Malachi said in his father voice, the euphoric mood sliding back into reality. "Say thank you and goodnight to Ms. Dickinson and let's get home."

The girls obeyed, but as they started walking down Ocean toward home, he heard them picking up the argument.

"How do you manage so many at one time in a classroom?"

Julianne smiled and told him the same thing she'd told Nick. "I referee. I keep them in line and then they miraculously go home to mom and dad."

After the concert Troy and Bree went looking for Nick. When they spotted his SUV parked on Crescent Street, they hustled over to where he was in the process of strapping his sleeping son into a car seat.

Bree noted that even though it wasn't even nine o'clock yet, Hutton rubbed at her eyes, looking as though it wouldn't take much for the little girl to drift off on the way back home. "Maybe this is a bad time."

"Don't be nervous," Troy assured her as he approached Nick. "I know you need to get home with the kids, so I won't keep you long," he began. "But I just wanted to tell you that I've found you a guide, someone who wants to take the tourists around the area. Bree wants to apply for a business loan."

Nick broke out in a grin. "That's fantastic. Why don't you come see me first thing Monday morning, Bree? We'll go over how this whole thing will work. Jordan and I have been waiting for someone like you."

"I don't make much," Bree admitted. "For the application. I went over my finances and they won't impress you very much."

Jordan came around to the other side of the car. "But you do."

That had Bree smiling. "I do?"

"Very much. If you're willing to take on fussy guests, we'll make a great team."

Bree reached out and gave Jordan a hug. "Not only am I good with people, but I'm getting certified this summer in diving and boating."

"Good first step," Nick said. "You'll put your business courses into practice all the while taking CPR and first aid for insurance purposes. We'll talk more on Monday morning."

"I'll be there."

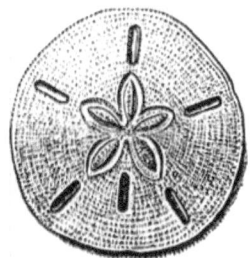

Chapter Twenty-Two

The minibus chugged along Main. The Turtle barely made it into the parking lot at Wally's service station before belching up plumes of smoke and dying in its tracks.

Julianne got out, walked into the station "Hi, Lilly. I need Wally to look at my VW bus. It died in the driveway."

"He's just finishing up Alma Whittaker's old Buick."

"I'll wait then."

A few minutes later, Wally popped into the little lobby area. "Okay, Lilly, you can let Alma know her car's ready. Hey Julianne, I noticed your bus. What's the problem?"

"Other than the fact it's older than I am you mean?" she cracked. "I think it's the carburetor thingy."

Wally cackled with laughter. "Let's go out and take a look."

Once they got to the van, Julianne watched him go to work. While he jiggled wires under the hood, she decided to do a little digging.

"Lilly tells me you knew Layne and Eleanor Richmond and Brooke Caldwell."

"Everyone in town knew Layne and his dad."

"Because of the train store?"

"That and their sense of community. I don't condone Layne stepping outside his marriage but Eleanor was a walking nightmare. We all knew he was miserable with

Eleanor. As to Brooke, the two of them just clicked. Both teachers, both with so much in common, how could two people not connect that way. I never believed they ran off, not for a minute."

"That's what Lilly said along with half the people I've talked to."

"I felt bad for Brooke's family, especially her kid brother."

"Brooke had a kid brother? Where does he live? Do you remember his name?"

"Yeah, I told all this to Brent already when he came by a few months back. I'm pretty sure Ryan Caldwell still lives over in Scotts Valley." Wally looked up at her face. "You're planning on contacting him, aren't you?"

"Guilty. Look, there's a reason I'm vested in finding out what happened to Layne and Brooke."

"Hey, I wish you would. I heard about all the boxes found over at the school. And there's something else you should know. Back in the day when Eleanor's father died, my dad was convinced that Eleanor had a hand in it."

"Why?"

"Because the day before Euell Jennings died, he came into the station to have his car fixed. Eleanor was with him. They had a huge fight right here in this parking lot over money. Eleanor wanted a thousand dollars for a trip to London or some equally exotic destination. Her friends were planning a shopping spree and she wanted in on it. Euell told her he didn't have that kind of cash on hand. She hit the man, smacked her own father right across the mouth."

Julianne's jaw dropped. That story had her repeating what Cleef had told her. "That's why it sounds like it was common knowledge."

"I guess it was. Why didn't the cops do more about it back then?"

"I don't know. Maybe Pelican Pointe fell into an abyss and no one really cared. What's wrong with my car?"

"I think it's probably vapor lock. I'll have to replace the fuel filter to make sure the fuel line is clear."

"How much to fix it?"

Wally tossed out a figure.

"Okay. Will I have it back before the weekend?"

"Sure. I'll put it up on the lift now and get started on it."

Later, Julianne used Google to hunt down Ryan Caldwell and get an address. That night, over a pot of spaghetti, she bugged Ryder to drive her over to Scotts Valley the next day.

"It's the only way to eliminate him as the owner of the boxes."

"If Brent knew we were butting in the way we are…"

"That's why he doesn't need to know."

"You don't think he'll find out?"

"Not if we keep our mouths shut," she said with a grin.

The next day they found Brooke's brother an amiable man who still remembered his sister with affection. "She always had a smile and the biggest dimples. That was one of the things I remember the most. We were ten years apart and sometimes she treated me more like a mother than a big sister because, ever the teacher, she used to read to me at night before going to bed."

Ryder told him why they were there and mentioned the boxes.

"Brent Cody already talked to me about that and I told him I didn't know anything about a hidden box. He also showed me a few class photos. I didn't recognize any of the kids' pictures because I didn't go to the same school where Brooke taught."

"What do you think happened to her?"

"I did my best to tell the sheriff's deputies at the time that she would never leave town without first saying goodbye to our mom and dad. But they didn't want to hear that. To them, I was just a kid back then. At the time she disappeared, Brooke was twenty-eight. She was also gorgeous with a big heart. But the authorities seemed dead set on writing her off as an inconsiderate woman who'd been having an affair with a coworker and took off with a 'devil may care' attitude without any intentions of ever looking back. The thing is Brooke wasn't like that. She might've wanted to get away from Layne's wife but at the time, I could see why. All these years later and the cops still do nothing. Do you realize my mother died without ever knowing what happened to her daughter? My dad's in a nursing home. To this day whenever I go to visit the man, he still asks me if I've heard from Brooke."

"It must be agonizing for you, for them."

"It is, plus it haunts me that I didn't do more. Every day I think of my sister, how sweet she was. She'd do anything for anyone. Her students loved her because she was such a great teacher."

"What did you think of the affair?"

Julianne saw Ryan's eyes go dark. "I didn't like it one bit and told her so. I did my best to get her to see that being with a married man was a mistake, that it would never go anywhere especially with Layne. Being with that man was dangerous for her. Brooke put herself in a bad situation."

"Why do you say that?"

"You obviously didn't know Eleanor. She threatened Brooke one day, showed up at the school and went nuts, yelling, screaming, pitching a fit. When Brooke told me, I worried about her after that. Then I got pissed off and went to see Layne, told him he needed to do something about his wife."

"But he didn't?"

"What could he really do about a nutcase? His wife was out of control. For someone who considered that she came from 'old money,' Eleanor acted more like a common thief to me. Brooke once told me that if Layne had fifty grand lying around in the bank, he could easily buy his way out of the marriage. That Eleanor was willing to give up custody of the kids for a price. Of course, she'd cleaned out Layne financially long before he and Brooke ever got together. She liked keeping him broke then complain that he had no money. So Layne buying his way out wasn't about to happen."

Julianne and Ryder exchanged looks.

"Are you saying Layne hinted to Brooke that his wife would've given him the kids for a cash deal?" Ryder asked.

"There was no hinting on Brooke's part, no misunderstanding on mine. I remember the conversation as if it were yesterday. I wondered what kind of mother would do that. If Layne and Brooke had ever figured out a way to get the dough, I'm certain Eleanor would've taken the money and run. I'm convinced Eleanor didn't give a whit about those kids, let alone her husband. I've no doubt of that."

"She did love money," Julianne pointed out.

Ryder agreed. "Yeah. More than anything else that woman coveted the almighty dollar."

"But to give up custody of your kids for money is a new low in my book."

"Eleanor seemed to strive for new lows."

On the way back to Pelican Pointe, a livid Julianne kept going over the conversation. "It struck me back there that the more I hear, the more I get the sense that Eleanor wasn't so much crazy as she was sociopathic. I once did a research paper for my psychology class. I think Eleanor shared a lot of the same traits that serial killers possess."

"Like what?"

She ticked off the highlights. "First, they get off on controlling people. Eleanor wouldn't let her husband take a shower or sleep in her bed. She wouldn't let the kids have any friends over to the house. Better to keep any outsiders from influencing them that way. Second, they have their own sense of superiority. Eleanor considered her family like royalty, herself from 'old money.' Third, they have no real sense of empathy for anyone else. Eleanor thought of her kids as possessions, her husband as someone there to do her bidding, to bring in the money as the pack mule, so to speak, and not a viable partner in the relationship like a normal couple."

"Stop. You're making me think of Bethany."

"Really? And you put up with that? Why, Ryder? Why would you let someone have that kind of power over you? You didn't have children with Bethany? What power did she wield?"

"The truth? I guess as a soldier I wanted to know there was someone back home waiting for me. It never occurred to me she was lying when she said she loved me."

"I'm really sorry she hurt you. Drop me at Wally's, will you? I need to pick up my van."

"Sure. You should know I overheard what you said to Troy the other day, about Danny, about me. After Bethany I wasn't sure I could ever let anyone in again. But I feel the same way about you."

Because she knew that was probably the closest she was ever going to hear Ryder utter a declaration of love, she said the only thing that came to mind. "I guess for people like us it takes a third party to convey our feelings."

After she hopped out of the car, Ryder stewed on her comment the rest of the day.

Damn it, hadn't he taken the initiative? Hadn't he been the one to tell her how he felt first? Even though he hadn't used the word *love*, she had to know what he'd meant. Was it up to him to point out that she hadn't used that word either with the third party? She'd never mentioned it to Troy specifically. So what was wrong with the third party catalyst angle?

He was pretty damn sure he didn't need any input from an outsider about how and when to tell the woman he loved how he felt about her.

The day was a short one and didn't do anything to offset his temper.

By the time he walked through the front door of her house, he'd built up a good head of steam. He found her in the laundry room folding clothes.

She glanced over from a stack of towels. "Ryder. Hi. Could you give me a hand with this?"

"What the hell did you mean when you said 'people like us' this morning? Who are people like us?"

Amused at his slow reaction, his obvious foul mood, she abandoned the pile, waded through the laundry scattered on the floor, to take his face in her hands. "I really wasn't looking for love but I found you. If I tell you how I feel, it will, no doubt, scare the bejeezus out of you and you'll take off so fast I won't be able to catch up."

Insulted, he protested. "I don't want to be anywhere else but right here with you. That is, unless you want me to leave."

"See, it's like you're waiting for what we have to expire. Plus, you don't seem at all comfortable telling me. Am I pushing you to? Nope. But it's obvious you don't want to love me. However, I think you do. You just find it difficult to say to me."

Hearing it so aptly nailed took the wrath right out of him. "I do love you. I…I've just never loved a woman as much as I do you."

She grinned and it showed off dimples. "I'm standing here ankle deep in dirty clothes and you choose *now* to tell me how you feel? Your timing may suck but—"

"What?"

"I love you, too."

Later after supper, she was on her laptop when she decided to check her email and found a message from a teacher she'd reached out to for help in searching the 1984 graduating class at UC Santa Barbara. Sure enough, Carol told her what she'd been doing wrong. There was a site specifically for classmates who were willing to sign up so they could keep in touch with one another. Julianne followed Carol's link and soon she'd reached a list of alumni.

Perusing the names, looking for one in particular, she went line by line. After all this time, it took no more than five minutes for her eyes to land on what she'd been searching for.

"Ryder, Ryder, get in here! I found Layne Richmond."

The browser still highlighted the web site and the information was still on the screen when Ryder walked into the living room.

"See, this shows Layne received his degree in education in 1984. The ring has to belong to him. That proves the boxes or rather the first box at least, has a connection to the Jennings family. So logically, why wouldn't the other boxes be linked too?"

"You've hit gold here. What do we do with this? Do you think Brent already knows?"

"Of course, he does. But if we ask Caleb or Drea or both about what the hell is going on it might be misconstrued as confrontational and look like fools while we do it. So we could sit on the info until we're able to ask Cooper Jennings what he knows about that night."

"I don't think I want to ask Caleb face to face why he lied about the boxes. Or Drea either. Do you? It's not our place."

"No, it isn't our place. So that only means we bide our time and wait to get to Cooper."

Chapter Twenty-Three

The rare July storm tossed around the boats in the harbor as if the sloops were nothing more than small bobbers at the end of a fishing line.

Ryder watched the torrent from his perch, the workshop he'd set up that was one-third his now that he'd signed the loan papers. The documents referred to the space as Tradewinds Boatyard. But it was still a mess of cobwebs and rat droppings. Not surprising since its primary inhabitants had been spiders and rodents for the past two decades.

Because most everyone with an interest in the school had high expectations for keeping on schedule he'd decided to spend this rainy Saturday morning in the dusty space where the old salvaged materials had landed. He looked around at all the stacked desks, lockers, at least twenty chalkboards, and several old water fountains.

Getting a jump on the repairing project, he'd left Julianne at the computer combing the Internet for info. She'd already printed out a list of military bases for their trip to San Francisco. As of yet, they hadn't settled on a definitive date, mainly because they were still putting together what they'd need to hunt down Bethany aka Crystal Dawn Lazzario.

Two days ago he'd heard from his investigator. Bethany had finally made a mistake. She'd tried to fence his grandfather's cartoons to a comic book collector in San

Francisco. Good thing he'd had the sense to have the gumshoe put out feelers to all the private art reps in the area who might be tempted to bite, just in case. No one had until now. The art dealer had delayed the transaction and called the private eye.

The rain drumming outside matched his mood. He weighed his options and decided they'd have to act soon. He didn't dare tell Brent what he'd found out otherwise the man would try to talk him out of confronting her.

As he worked, even during daylight hours the new place seemed a little spooky. Add in the overcast sky and he realized they'd have to do something about the poor lighting.

Maybe that was one reason when he spotted Scott hopping up onto the dock, it didn't freak him out. "I see you're working on my old desk there. See these initials carved into the wood? SDP & SD. Those letters stand for Scott David Phillips, and my first crush, pretty Selina Domingo. It was third grade. I was eight and madly in love."

"Holding onto your memories I see."

"No one can take those away."

"It's a plus if they're good ones."

"Try not to stay bitter about getting burned. There are never any guarantees when you begin a relationship. I've always thought marriage or cohabitation was difficult under the best of circumstances. Throw in a selfish, scheming individual into the mix, whether that person is male or female, and you have a recipe for disaster. Add in mental illness to conniving and narcissistic and you're looking at a deadly situation."

Ryder realized they'd moved on from talking about Bethany. "Layne and Eleanor."

"Julianne wants answers. Why don't you help her get them? I understand you're planning a road trip to confront Bethany. She's using a new name, Amelia Eggerton."

"The PI didn't mention that."

"That's the benefit of having me around. I also have an address." He started spouting out numbers and a street name.

Ryder looked around for a pen to jot down the info while Scott waited, impatient. "You want to know where she is, that's where you'll find her."

For the first time Ryder realized Scott was agitated. "Why now?"

"Because it's time. Right now, you might want to take a look inside that locker." Scott went over, stood by one in particular.

Ryder stared at him. "Don't tell me a rubber snake will pop out of that thing as soon as I open it up?"

"Just look inside."

Ryder did as he was told, bent down, stuck his hand into the twelve-by-fifteen-inch slot and noticed a container of some kind in the back—another wooden chest, this one small and plain.

"What is it with all these boxes? I'm almost afraid to open it." Despite what he'd said, he flipped up the top. "More baseball cards, more toys, more rocks. Wait. Here's a patch of shirt at the bottom. How many of these are there? Is this some kind of sick joke?"

"A child's way of handling a dark secret. You should get Julianne over here. Text her. Let her take a look."

"I should call Brent."

"Brent already has a DNA profile from the blood in the first box. The lab also picked up skin cells, or what's known as touch DNA. All he needs now is someone to compare it to."

Ryder was no idiot. "You're saying the answer is in San Francisco."

Scott nodded. "Do me a favor when you talk to Cooper, try to keep an open mind."

"Why so mysterious?"

"Because Cooper isn't doing well, hasn't really been doing well for years. He's in distress and he could use a friend. Two if you take Julianne. Go find Bethany first though. Deal with her. Leave now. This afternoon."

"You're kidding? But... Right this second?"

"You've been bugging me for months to help you find this woman. It's today or not at all. If you wait she'll get cold feet about selling the sketches and she'll be gone. It's a two hour trip into the Bay. What's the problem?"

"When you hold down two jobs, it's a little difficult to take off on a whim. That's why we haven't gone before now. I've been working my butt off."

"What about Gavin Kendall? How's he working out?"

"Fine. Great. He and his wife are hard workers."

"Then talk him into taking over for you at the farm. Tomorrow's Sunday so there's no work at the job site. Barter with Troy to cover for you if the trip stretches into Monday by offering him a night at Promise Cove. He's been batting his head against a stone wall trying to figure out something special to do for Bree's birthday in a couple months."

"I never noticed it before, but you're a romantic *and* a fixer."

Scott grinned. "If only I'd known I had a knack for it when I was alive."

Chapter Twenty-Four

Spending nearly three hours in the car, they went over scenarios about how it might go down with Bethany.

"According to the Internet the address Scott gave you, turns out to be an apartment complex twenty miles outside Camp Parks, a U.S. Army Combat Support Training Center. Thousands of soldiers end up there to get combat ready, sounds like it's a perfect place to pick up guys ready to be shipped out, right up your girl's alley."

From behind the wheel, Ryder agreed. "Large garrison with a variety of rank and file to choose from, officers to enlisted men. And she's not my girl."

"I don't think you should go up to the apartment door," Julianne cautioned.

"But we might have a long wait hanging around for her to come out. Don't get cold feet now. What's the alternative?"

"Confronting her in a public forum might work out better."

"How exactly do we do that?"

"Leave it to me. I need her phone number though. I don't suppose Scott was proactive and thought to include that with the other info."

He laughed. "No. Rude of him, huh?"

"Very. Okay, I'll improvise. Call your mother. See if she kept Bethany's message from before and the number that showed up on the readout. If so, there's a way to get her to bite."

"Really? How exactly will you improvise?"

"She loves scams, right? I'll run one on her. Everyone likes something for free. This trip may take a little longer than we thought though. Are you covered at work?"

"I'm good. What's the plan?"

"For Bethany, it'll be like a scavenger hunt. I've never followed instructions from a ghost before."

"That makes two of us. Should we feel incredibly silly about this?"

"Maybe. Did Scott actually say Brent had DNA?"

"Yeah. I'm almost as excited about talking to this Cooper guy as I am confronting Bethany."

"Hopefully we'll get to do both. As long as you remember to remain cool and collected when you approach her in public."

"Don't worry. I'm the epitome of cool."

"I'm sure you are. Not. Try not to get your hopes up though about ever seeing those drawings again, okay?"

"I know, I know. I've prepared myself for the fact that I may never get my hands on those cartoons ever again."

"As long as you know it's a longshot. Tell me, are you certain you didn't misunderstand Scott when he said Cooper was in distress."

"I know what he said. He was clear that Cooper was having major problems and could use a couple friends right about now."

Julianne's ruse was simple although it did cost them an extra day to set it up. After obtaining Bethany's phone number from Ryder's mom, Julianne persuaded a store clerk in one of the small, women's boutiques in the mall to let her use the shop's phone. In turn, Julianne placed a call to Bethany using the ploy that the woman had won a thousand-dollar shopping spree but she had to act within the next few hours to collect it.

Ryder stayed behind in his truck watching the apartment and waited for the shark to take the bait. It took half an hour for her to rush out the door with a man in tow and jump into a late model Pontiac, which Ryder followed.

Crystal / Bethany / Amelia, whatever the hell she was using today had dyed her hair a streaky blonde. That's the first thing Ryder noticed when he watched her go in through the mall entrance, hand in hand with the poor sap she'd targeted as her next mark. The second thing he noted was that she didn't look half as good as he remembered. Even from some distance away the scam artist looked rail-thin like she'd been using. He didn't know what exactly but by the spots on her face, he'd guess her drug of choice had been meth.

Walking at breakneck speed to get to the giveaway before the deadline, she took off in one direction. He had to move his ass to catch up with her. As she tried to get her bearings and determine which way to go to claim the prize, he inadvertently skidded past her. Standing face to face with the woman for the first time in two years had his temper uncoiling.

The man beside her sported the obligatory military-style look—cropped haircut, tattoos signifying unit, toned muscles—if he could do nothing else today, maybe Ryder could prevent another poor schmuck from following in his same footsteps.

Gazing over at the woman he'd known as Bethany, he heard his voice reach shrill status. "Why did you call my mother?"

Bethany tilted her head, her mouth gaped open, as realization hit her. "Ryder! What on earth! I don't understand."

"I want to know why you called my mother. Were you thinking she'd pay to get the cartoons back?"

She took a step in retreat. He could see her eyes darting around to check for exits. But it only took a matter of seconds before the lies spilled out.

"Despite what's happened between us I still care about you."

"Bullshit. What happened between us is the bitch I left living in my house while I shipped off to Afghanistan, stole everything I ever owned, lied to me about who and what she was and disappeared without leaving a forwarding address. Oh wait. That bitch was you."

"Who the hell are you?" Military Guy demanded.

Ryder held up a hand. "Stay out of this. This is between Bethany and me."

"Her name is Amelia. You obviously have the wrong person."

"And you obviously do not know when to back off. Where are my grandfather's sketches? Not two days ago you tried to fence them to a collector who called the private investigator I hired. This individual suspected the drawings didn't belong to you and alerted the PI. Those cartoons belong to me and I want them back."

"What's this about?" Military Guy wanted to know.

Ryder turned to the GI, narrowed his eyes. "Let me guess. You're in the service. Which branch?"

"Army. In the middle of training right now at Camp Parks."

"So let me see if I can play psychic today. You and your girlfriend here are out seeing the sights. The two of you are taking one last trip to see everything San Francisco has to offer before you're deployed overseas…somewhere. My guess is for a minimum of twelve months. With me, we went to Atlantic City. This woman you're with… She's calling herself Amelia Eggerton today, has a bad habit of stealing other people's identities and a whole lot more. When I knew her two years ago, she called herself Bethany Davis. That's the name she used when she sold my townhouse while I was pulling a tour serving my country. She cleaned out my bank accounts to the tune of thirty grand. Did she mention during the time you two have known each other that she was born Crystal Dawn Lazzario?" Ryder waited a beat, got a blank stare from

Military Guy. "No? I thought not. Did she tell you she's been married eight times? That number means you need two hands to count how many times this woman's tricked a military service man into matrimony. I wouldn't think that came up in the conversation either, huh?"

When Ryder saw Bethany start to edge away, he grabbed her by the arm.

"Now wait a minute," Military Guy said. "Get your hands off her. You can't do that."

"Really? After everything I just told you, you're defending this sorry piece of shit? Okay. Tell me this. How long have you known this truly, wonderful, amazing woman?"

"About six weeks."

"Six weeks and you completely trust her because she's proved during that time she's so devoted to you and loves you unconditionally. Am I right?"

"I don't have any family. Amelia's it."

"That might be touching if her name was actually Amelia. It isn't. Aren't you listening to me at all? 'Amelia' is about to end up in the slammer, serve jail time for fraud. Army CID is very interested in her past schemes. Now back off, because I plan on talking to this woman even if I have to go through you to do it. Are we clear?"

Military Guy lifted his hands up, finally took a step back. "As long as you don't want to punch her out or something and just talk…"

"Oh, I'd like to, but hitting a woman, even Bethany really isn't my style." Ryder guided her out of the high-traffic area. "Let's take a walk. Before I turn you over to the cops, I want to know what you did with my stuff."

"I don't know what you're talking about. After you left, your place was broken into, they ransacked the house, took everything. That wasn't my fault. I ran because I was sure you'd blame me."

"Stop it." Ryder shook her by the shoulders and then had to take several deep breaths to calm down. "If that's the way you want to play it, so be it. We'll let the cops sort this all out, right here, right now, today." Ryder started to punch in numbers on his cell phone.

"Wait. Okay. Okay. I listed the stuff on Craigslist for free and just told people to come get it. That way, I didn't have to pay for movers. Whatever was left over, I called a junk dealer in Haddon Heights. He took it all."

"Jersey?" He hadn't thought to drive across the Delaware River to check there. "Where are the sketches?"

"I was curious about what was in the leather tube so I snooped around, discovered the drawings inside, found them very…interesting."

"Translation. You found them valuable," Ryder corrected.

"I held onto them until I could find someone who appreciated their…uniqueness."

"Right this minute, where are they?" Ryder tightened the grip on her arm, glanced back at Military Guy. "Are they at his apartment? I swear to God if you don't tell me where they are, CID will crawl up your ass because I'll prosecute you for theft and whatever charges I can bring, I'll do it to the fullest extent… Choose jail time in Pennsylvania, West Virginia, or California. Your choice."

"Okay. Okay. They're back at his place."

"If you're lying to me…" Ryder saw Bethany send a seductive gaze to her mark. But he could see by the look on Military Guy's face his trust in the woman had begun to falter.

"Then let's go. I'm not letting you out of my sight until I have those cartoons back in my possession."

About that time, Julianne emerged from her post by the entrance to the boutique where she'd witnessed the entire scene unfold.

An anxious moment occurred when Bethany tried to convince an overzealous security guard to slap handcuffs on Ryder for harassing a helpless female shopper. But Ryder had wisely appealed to the man's common sense.

"Don't you understand? I want you to call the cops. Go ahead. I want this woman arrested."

The hapless guard eventually got fed up with the entire scene. "Both of you take your bullshit outside and get out of my mall."

All four did just that. While Military Guy got into his own vehicle, Ryder flipped Julianne the keys. "We're headed back to the apartment. You drive."

Ryder pushed Bethany into the truck still gripping her arm. "If anything happens to me while I'm inside, call the cops."

From that point forward, Julianne's heart hadn't taken a regular beat.

It seemed surreal when Ryder finally came out of the condo with the leather pouch. It was just as bizarre when he called the police and filed a complaint against Bethany for possession of stolen property—not for the sketches. While Ryder had been in the house, he'd spotted a diamond ring he recognized as belonging to his grandmother who'd passed it down to his mom. All this time and his mother had never uttered a word about the fact it had gone missing.

"I feel bad about not grabbing it too but I think I'm pushing it as it is."

They sat there in the car and watched as two uniforms pulled up to the curb to arrest Bethany and haul her ass to jail.

But the woman had so many aliases it took several hours for the authorities to sort out Ryder's story. During it all, Julianne had plopped into a chair in a dull, gray waiting area while he went over the details several times to a detective, who in turn, checked out his tale of woe with army CID *and* Philadelphia PD.

When he did finally appear, he looked exhausted. "What a mess," he said running both hands through his hair.

"Is it over? I was so afraid her friend was about to deck you back there."

"I was a little afraid of that myself," Ryder admitted.

"Do you feel any better at all?"

"Oh yeah, elated. But you know what?"

"What?"

"Sausalito is right across the Golden Gate Bridge. I say we're on a roll."

"But Ryder you look like you need a good night's sleep first."

"Nope, let's do this with Cooper before he does something that causes him to crash and burn."

Chapter Twenty-Five

Julianne couldn't argue with the view of the Golden Gate Bridge looking north toward Sausalito. She gaped like a tourist.

"We have to splurge and blow our budget to stay one more night in one of these inns with this spectacular view. We have to."

He laughed and picked up her hand. "If we have to then we will."

Using the map she'd downloaded before they left home, she instructed him to a secluded gated estate made of stone and red tile. Julianne had done her homework. She already knew Cooper resided in the guest house in the back.

"The gate may pose a problem."

"You wouldn't happen to have a phone number, would you?"

"Yes, but don't ask how I came by it. You aren't the only one who sprang for a sleuth." She punched in the digits on her cell and waited. When a voice answered she went into her pitch. "Is this Cooper Jennings?"

"Yes, who is this?"

"Okay, great. Don't hang up. Hear me out. My name is Julianne Dickinson and I'm here with a friend from Pelican Pointe."

"Is there something wrong with my family?"

"No, not at all, there's nothing wrong with Landon, Shelby, Drea or Caleb," she said emphasizing each name so he'd know she was for real. "As far as I know they were all fine when we left a few days ago. In fact, they painted my house." She rattled off the address on Ocean Street to prove who she was and the story behind his family painting her house. She talked fast, afraid that he would hang up on her.

"You're the schoolteacher who bought my childhood home?"

"That's right. I've moved in, I'm happy there. My friend and I have come a long way to talk to you about all those boxes we found when we remodeled the school." That one line brought dead silence to the other end of the line. "I'm out here at the gate. I know it's bold of me to ask but…"

"I don't know what you're talking about. Please leave me the hell alone."

"That won't work anymore, Cooper." Running out of ideas, she bluffed. "It won't work because Brent Cody, the police chief you talked to via email, has DNA from the bloody pieces of shirt left in the boxes."

"Go away!"

"It's only a matter of time before Brent shows up here. Wouldn't you prefer to talk to us like a dress rehearsal before you get down to the gritty details with the cops?"

A long silence followed. "Are you still there?" she asked.

"Okay. Okay. I'll be out to get you."

"Nice fake out," Ryder whispered while they waited.

"It's called desperation."

Cooper Jennings appeared on the other side of the iron fence holding a remote. When the gate clicked open, they walked up to a man with shaggy chestnut hair around his ears and bright blue eyes. He looked a lot like his siblings.

Julianne held out her hand. "It's nice to meet you."

"How did you find me?"

"I won't lie. I looked up everything I could find about you on the Internet. You're quite the photographer. When that went nowhere I hired a private detective."

By this time they'd reached his little house. He let them inside the living room where there were trains set up all around the room, some in motion, running around track.

"Your grandfather and father adored trains, didn't they? The deed to the shop was right there in the first box we found."

"Why are you here?" Cooper stated bluntly.

"Someone told us you might need a friend right about now." Julianne nodded toward Ryder. "You have two, right here."

"What would you know about it anyway? This isn't Facebook. I'm doing just fine, thanks. I have plenty of friends."

Suddenly Julianne wondered how she could get this man to open up about what must've been a very painful time in his life. "So these friends know about what happened to your father that night?"

She watched as the grown man went white as a sheet and dropped into the nearest chair. "No one knows that."

"Isn't it about time they did?" Ryder pushed. "I came here to San Francisco to confront my past, a past that has nothing to do with you. We all have our demons that need put to rest."

"Sure you do," Cooper said with derision. "I guarantee you've never known a demon firsthand."

Ryder's eyes met Julianne's in a worried gaze. "The point is it felt damn good to get it behind me. I happen to think you'll feel the same if you just talk to someone about it."

Cooper puffed air into his cheeks, scrubbed both of his hands down his face, and blew out a huge sigh. Tears formed in his eyes. "I don't know where to start."

"Your mother seemed…very manipulative," Julianne prompted.

"She was, possibly the most manipulative woman I've ever known. Of course, I didn't admit that to anyone until just a few years ago on a psychiatrist's couch."

"We couldn't find anyone in town to deny that sentiment."

The photographer puffed out a muffled laugh. "Oh I'm sure that's true. No one knew what she was really capable of though, least of all her husband and children. That night, the night it happened, I was sound asleep. My dad had tucked me into bed not three hours before that. But my mother woke me up in the middle of the damn night. She was always waking us up at some ungodly hour for some stupid, ridiculous reason. Like the night my dad had packed his bags to leave after they'd had another horrible argument. But to keep him there, she ran upstairs, made us get out of bed, and then marched us downstairs like little soldiers. She told us Dad was leaving us and he was never coming back. I remember Drea and Caleb started to cry. What kind of mother uses her children like that? What kind of woman treats her kids like that?"

"An unstable one."

"I knew even then my mother wasn't right in the head. People around town threw out the word crazy—the neighbors, the kids at school. But I just recall thinking how mean she could be to everyone. At nine, I knew enough to know my dad wasn't leaving us but was trying to leave her. For some reason, I understood. Of course, I didn't want him to go. I felt guilty about that later."

Cooper shook his head. "I knew she didn't want to see him happy, let alone be happy with Miss Caldwell. That was the ultimate slap in the face. My mother never wanted anyone happy, least of all her own husband or her kids. All she knew was how to be miserable so she wanted everyone else to be that way, too."

Cooper took a deep breath before he could go on. "Look, I was her son but sometimes my mother could be mean just for the sake of it. I had to accept that about her. Of course, there were always those she fooled."

"Are you saying she fooled your dad?"

"He wanted something that wasn't reality. Maybe he couldn't accept how she really was. I've had too much time to think back to my childhood, remember her in action. I was able to go back in my mind and watch her through the years. She was happiest when she created drama. Lots of drama. I watched her lie to my father numerous times. She'd trick him into believing something that wasn't real. I think I resented him for that, for getting fooled. I kept waiting for him to wake up, to get us away from her. But he never did."

"Do you think medication would've helped her?" Julianne looked into the man's sad eyes and watched as he sucked in a trembling breath before going on.

"She wouldn't take it, refused in fact. I'm not sure why."

"What happened that night when she woke you up?"

"I wasn't sure at first what she wanted me to do. But then, she dragged me downstairs, waited like a crack addict in an agitated state for me to at least get my shoes tied. Then we trooped out the front door and down the steps. It took me a while to realize we were headed to the beach. But after we crossed the street, she led me over the rocks and under the pier. And that's when I saw the bodies. First, I spotted my father, lying on his back. He was white as a sheet, no color in his face at all. I had no idea how long he'd been like that. Then, a few feet away, I spotted another body, a female. It looked like Miss Caldwell. I'd never seen two people dead before. It's nothing like the movies. Her eyes were still open. But my father's eyes were closed. Funny what you remember. I'll never forget their ashen faces. They'd both lost too much blood to still be alive. That much I knew. It was too late to help either one of them. They were both gone."

"That's a horrible thing for a nine-year-old to see," Julianne said, reaching for his hand.

"How did a woman and a little boy get the bodies off the beach?" Ryder asked.

"I helped my mother load them into Drea's wagon. We had to make two trips."

Julianne exchanged a shocked look with Ryder. "Oh, Cooper. I'm so very sorry."

"No one saw you?" Ryder asked. "Julianne bought your former home. The proximity to the pier is so close it's hard to imagine how no one heard the shots."

"It was the middle of the night," Cooper said sharply. "Besides, luck always seemed to be on my mother's side, no matter how many things she stole, there were a lot more times she didn't get caught. This was no different. I kept waiting for someone to show up. But… No one came."

"How long did it take you to…you know…?"

"Put them in the ground? It took us the rest of the night. We didn't finish up until around five in the morning."

"Where? Where did you…bury them?"

Because Cooper had a hard time going on, she said the first logical thing that popped into her head. "It wasn't on the beach. There's an archaeological dig very near that spot, the team would've discovered them by now with everything they've unearthed. They've gone down as much as ten feet. But it had to be somewhere close by."

"We pulled the wagon back home and around the corner, used the soft dirt on top of the compost heap."

"You buried them at The Plant Habitat?"

Despite the sick look on his face, Cooper nodded.

The three sat there without saying anything else for what seemed like an eternity, the eerie silence hanging over them like a weighted dome.

Finally Julianne broke the tension. "There's something I still don't understand. I'm sorry to be so insensitive about this, Cooper, but… I have to ask. Why on earth would you think to put a piece of your father's shirt in a keepsake box, several boxes in fact? And how did a nine-year-old even think to do that?"

The grown man ran his fingers through his hair, hung his head. "Even at that young age I was ashamed of what I'd done, what I'd been asked to do by my own mother. I needed to take something away of his for myself, a reminder of what I'd done. It may sound crazy but…"

"No, no, it doesn't." Julianne said, patting his back like she sometimes did to console one of her students. "You were just a small boy doing what your mother asked of you, doing your best to handle a horrific event."

"I remember digging in between all the crying. Sometimes I was bawling so hard I couldn't see what I was doing. But when my mother went into the house and came back with a pair of scissors so she could cut off Ms. Caldwell's hair, all of a sudden I stopped. I don't know but something kicked in. I watched in horror as my mother went wild, kicking both bodies, cursing, pitching a fit. I knew then I wanted something of my dad's. I told my mother I needed to take a break. She starting digging and while she was distracted, I used those same scissors to cut a piece of his shirt. The material was sticky. The dirt had stuck to it. But I didn't care. Initially I cut out one large piece from the front and then later cut that into smaller pieces. I had these little boxes, one my dad had made especially for me. And after…after helping to bury him… I thought maybe one day Drea and Caleb might want their own box. So I squirreled away the pieces of his shirt in mine until I could find boxes for them. I ended up locating an old metal one in the garage for Caleb. Drea had a cigar box so I used that until I ended up with four. I guess in my mind, I thought one day my mother might actually do the right thing so I made another box up for her."

Julianne was beginning to understand. "But you didn't present them to the others?"

"No. I wasn't thinking right that night. It took me several days to realize I had a secret that Drea and Caleb could never know. But by this time, I didn't have the guts to throw those pieces of his shirt in the trash. I couldn't do it. I thought maybe I should bury them. But weeks later, I knew I couldn't do that either. I couldn't pick up a shovel and dig up the ground, not again, not for any reason. I wouldn't go near the garden center after that."

"Okay, so was it simply a fluke that you had all the baseball cards in there and the toys, the rocks, the shells?"

He shook his head. "No fluke. I had to finish what I thought was part of the ceremony for saying goodbye to my dad. He needed a funeral, some ritual to mark his passing. I knew that even as a kid. So I took each box, put something from each one of us in there because it seemed like the right thing to do. I thought it was important my dad have something from his kids. Caleb's matchbox cars went in there—he was barely four at the time—Drea's collection of seashells, and my cards and rocks. A couple days went by before I realized I couldn't go back anywhere near where the bodies lay buried. I obviously had to think up something else."

"So at some point you decided to get all the keepsake boxes out of the house and find a hiding place?"

"That's what I did. I loaded the boxes up in a tote, rode my bike to the school." Cooper started to sob. "I buried my own father, I loved my dad more than anyone in the world, but I buried him under a goddamn compost heap because my mother told me to do it."

"Your mother was ill."

"That's no excuse," Cooper shouted. "Mental illness only explains certain things about her. She wielded love like a sword, used it like a weapon. I wanted her to love me so I did what I could to please her. But nothing ever worked for the long haul. It was always a short-term result that came undone as soon as she needed more attention, more affirmation. I couldn't give it to her. No one could."

"That's incredibly insightful for a child."

"You think I came to all this understanding as a kid on my own? Think again. It took years of seeing a therapist as an adult. I had to do something about my guilt. Do you understand what I'm saying? I helped my mother bury my own father when I was nine years old and then lied about it for twenty years. I couldn't take the guilt. It was a shitty thing she did."

"No argument there. So how did you come by your father's college ring?"

"That night before I rolled his body in the hole, I slid the ring from his finger before my mother made me toss the dirt over him. It's the only jewelry he had on. He'd long ago stopped wearing his wedding ring. The ring was right there... I slipped it in my pocket and then later added it to the other stuff. I found a hiding place in the teacher's lounge for it behind the old part of the furnace."

"What was the deed doing in the box?"

"I don't remember anything about the deed being in there. To be honest, I don't remember all the actual contents. I've blocked out a lot of what I put in there."

"You took the boxes to school because you wanted them found. Is that right?" Ryder asked.

"Yes, I desperately wanted someone to find them. If I left all of them at the school there was a greater chance someone would stumble on at least one box and know what she'd done, what I'd done for her. The only problem was, by then, they'd closed it down. I thought for sure it might reopen any day. So I took my chances, hid them in places I was sure someone would look. I knew for damned sure no one would ever stumble upon them stuck under a bunch of daisies in the backyard. But if someone could find them in a public place, find them at the school they'd somehow *know* and do something."

"I'm sorry it took us so long."

"Yeah? I am too."

"What about the night she committed suicide?"

An odd look crossed Cooper's face. "You mean the night she told me the harbor was her only way out, her last chance for happiness? That night?"

"The harbor was her last chance? Really?"

"That's what she told us. The night she made her three kids sit there in a goddamn boat only to watch while she jumped into the ocean. We must've been there in the boat for the longest time hoping she'd come back. She didn't."

"That's when the fisherman found you."

"Yeah. Old man Sundersen was his name. He towed us into shore. And before you ask, I didn't go after my own mother when she took that leap into the water. I didn't want to. I wanted her gone. God help me, but a part of me was glad she was gone. I just wanted it to be over with."

"How long before you knew it wasn't over with?" Ryder asked.

"We figure Eleanor is still alive, Cooper. You might as well tell us the rest of it."

At the words, Julianne saw the grown man flinch. "How do you know that?"

Ryder stuck his hands in his pockets, wandered around the little room. "You mean what gave it away? Julianne and I talked about this quite a bit. There was never a death certificate. We checked. No coroner's inquest, no attempt by anyone to ever have Eleanor Jennings Richmond declared legally dead. We wondered why? After a period of time it seems people just forgot about the whole thing until one of the workers found the first box."

Cooper closed his eyes, rested his head in his hands. "I'm so sick and tired of all this. Do you know what it's like to have a murderer for a mother? She killed the father of her children. Do you have any idea what it's like to have a mother who made her oldest son an accomplice after the fact? That's what my counselor called it."

"No, I'm sorry I don't. I grew up without a mother. Occasionally misinformed people tried to convince me I was destined for failure because I came from a one-parent home. So no, I'm happy to say, I never had a mother like yours."

"She was a constant embarrassment."

"When did you know she was still alive?"

"I was a senior in high school when I got the first letter. At first I thought it was one of my friends pulling a prank, playing a practical joke on me. But then I began to think how could that be? The envelope was postmarked Dallas, Texas. It looked like the real deal. How could kids pull off that kind of detail?"

"Why did she write after nine years of silence?"

"Why else? She needed money?"

"From a senior in high school?"

"Believe me Eleanor wouldn't care if the dollar came from a kid."

"How much did you send her?"

"All I had saved up. Five hundred dollars."

"Why?" Ryder asked. But then he got it. "She was blackmailing you. 'Pay me, or I'll let everyone in town know what you did that night.' Am I right?"

"You're right."

"You had to realize at some point she was bluffing. She wouldn't have let the secret be known to anyone."

"I know that. But the guilt kept me paying. That, and the humiliation of it all."

"That's why you didn't tell anyone."

Cooper shook his head. "I couldn't. I just couldn't tell my uncle or rather the man that treated me like his son. I just couldn't bring myself to have that conversation. By the second letter, I'd graduated high school. I packed my bags and headed north to Seattle. I figured if she couldn't find me…the letters would stop."

"But they didn't."

"She contacted me whenever she needed money. She lives in Savannah, Georgia, or she did the last time I talked to her about a year ago."

"Your aunt and uncle have no idea whatsoever?"

"Not a clue."

"What about Caleb and Drea?"

"They don't know either. As far as I know, they slept right through it all that night. They've never questioned me about the night Dad left. Even after Landon and Shelby adopted us, I laid awake at night listening while Drea cried for her daddy. It tormented me. The only traumatic event for them was about four months later when Eleanor rowed us out in the middle of the harbor and jumped into the water. To this day, I can still hear those kids bawling their eyes out. 'Mama, mama, come back. Don't go. Mama, mama.'"

"You have to tell your story to Brent Cody, Cooper." When he stared at her with blank eyes, Julianne insisted, "You have to tell him and get it all behind you, once and for all. He's the police chief now. You were nine years old. None of this was your fault."

"But I knew what she'd done and never said a word. I knew where my father was buried all this time and said nothing. Look around you. Does it look like I'd fit in at The Plant Habitat? It was never for me. I left when I was eighteen and I won't go back. There's nothing there for me."

"Not even for your father's proper burial?" Ryder wanted to know.

"That's a low blow."

But Julianne took another route. "You're wrong, you know. There's a lot back there for you. Your grandfather's store is available. I understand from Drea you loved that place as a boy, loved spending time there. I'm looking around the room, Cooper. You have all your dad's old trains here and I'd be willing to bet you have even more in a storage facility somewhere. You could have a life back in Pelican Pointe if you wanted it. You could breathe life back into that store to honor your father, be part of the community where he played with his kids. You know your brother and sister would love nothing better than to have you back in their lives, close by."

"I'm well aware now that I've opened my mouth, I'll have to tell someone officially."

"Then throw some of your stuff in a bag and come back with us."

It took another hour to convince the photographer to get his things together. While Ryder helped him, Julianne put in a call to Brent. But she had to hold the phone away from her ear.

"If you'll let me get a word in, I'll explain," Julianne yelled back. "There's no point in shouting at me. It's done already. In fact, it's over. We're bringing Cooper back. He has a story to tell you. And a surprise or two along the way."

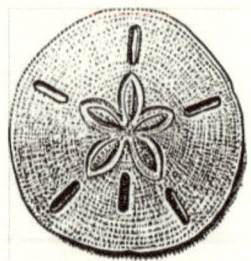

Chapter Twenty-Six

It was growing late when Brent sat inside his new office at the Pelican Pointe police station. He looked over the desk at an adult Cooper Jennings who'd gone over the heart-wrenching story of what happened when he was nine.

Four days ago Coop had taken him to the spot where he'd helped bury two people—his own father and Brooke Caldwell—at the direction of his mother. It had taken county forensics several hours of digging to go down far enough to locate the remains.

"I know it's been a tough couple days for you and it's still raw. But you did the right thing."

"After twenty years," Cooper charged. "She was mentally and physically abusive to my dad. I saw it myself. She treated him like crap. I guess that's why she thought it'd be funny to bury him under the compost heap."

"You were a kid," Brent said as a reminder.

"Doesn't matter. Tell that to my psyche, the one plagued by nightmares every night I don't seem to be able to shake. I've only come to realize this over the last decade, but my mother had no feelings for anyone but herself. She took off months after she killed two people and left a little boy to deal with what she'd done. Then she takes the easy way out by disappearing. Do I need to list how many ways she screwed me over?"

"Not tonight unless you really want to." When the man said nothing, Brent sat back in his chair. "If not, then there are a few painful facts we still need to get out of the way. For roughly ten years from the time you were nine to eighteen you believed right along with your brother and sister that your mother had jumped into the bay and committed suicide, correct?"

"That's right."

"The first contact she made telling you otherwise, you sent her money because she threatened to tell your secret." At the nod of Coop's head, Brent asked the other part. "The second time, how do you suppose she found out where you were living in Seattle?"

"She sent a letter to my old address and my roommate at the time forwarded it to me. I kept on the move hoping she would lose interest but since she refuses to work, she's always in need of money and where money's concerned, my mother is relentless. Money means more to her than anything else."

"Okay. How much do you normally send her?"

"Since my photography took off five years back, a couple thousand about four times a year."

"I used the last known address you had for her to track her down. She's still in Savannah, goes by the name of Loretta Eikenberry. I obtained a warrant for her arrest. Murder one. You'll be glad to know the Georgia Bureau of Investigation has already picked her up. She was shocked to say the least and offered no resistance. I'm headed there first thing in the morning to take her into custody, bring her back to Santa Cruz County." Brent met Cooper's frantic eyes. "Don't worry. She won't be coming back to Pelican Pointe. As soon as she steps off the plane she'll go directly to a jail cell at county lockup until trial. I promise you she won't make bail."

"How can you guarantee something like that? Women often get lighter sentences for murder."

"A couple reasons. For one, the fact she faked her own death. Judges frown on that. Second, she's been evading law enforcement for twenty years and blackmailing her own son. Judges take a pissy attitude toward mothers like that. Third, she committed a double homicide, took a father away from his children. As far as Brooke is concerned, Eleanor took a sister away from a brother and a daughter away from her parents. Add it all up and judges in this county usually fixate on those kinds of details. The district attorney will make sure the judge has all these facts. He'll file a motion to deny bail."

"But…"

Brent shook his head. "No buts. She won't get out so don't spend a lot of time worrying about that. With your testimony on the table, her attorney will more than likely talk her into taking a plea deal to avoid the death penalty anyway. We may not use it very much in this state, but it's a powerful tool to make sure she stays locked up for the rest of her life."

Brent took off his ball cap, ran a hand through his long, dark hair. "The thing is, Cooper, I'm sorry the authorities didn't raise more questions back in the day, didn't do a more thorough investigation into your father's disappearance and that of Brooke Caldwell. For what it's worth, I've talked to a great many people around town since this case surfaced. They all said the same thing. Your father would never have left you no matter how much he loved Brooke. He would never have left you with your mother. Not ever. Eleanor had him convinced she would hurt you kids and he couldn't risk that. No matter how much she was just blowing smoke up his ass, your father believed her threats."

"I already knew that. I lived in the same house, remember? Despite what adults think, kids aren't stupid."

"No, they aren't. There's one more thing you need to know. Medical examiner went over the autopsy results with me earlier on both sets of remains. It's your choice whether or not you want to hear them."

Cooper wiped his palms on his jeans. "Might as well get it over with."

"First, Brooke Caldwell died of a gunshot to the middle of the back. I'd hazard a guess that Eleanor more than likely shot your father first because the bullet went through his heart which meant he was facing Eleanor. Brooke saw it happen and more than likely tried to take off running to get away. But Eleanor aimed and fired, hitting her in the back."

"Jesus."

"On the other hand, your father would've probably died anyway within the year. His future, unfortunately for him, was entirely in Eleanor's hands, had been for a long time."

"Why do you say that?"

"The medical examiner found arsenic in his hair and bones. Long before your mother took out the .38 that night, she'd been slowly poisoning him over time. Coroner says it had been going on for about six months prior to his death."

"That's why he was so sick."

"He was sick?" Brent picked up his pen, jotted down that detail.

Cooper nodded. "Sick at his stomach, dizzy, night sweats, joint pain. There were days he had trouble getting out of bed, a hard time making it to work."

"Before that he'd been in relatively good health?"

"Absolutely. He'd ride bikes with us, take us to the beach. That sort of thing."

"If you hang around town for long you're probably gonna hear a few rumblings you hadn't heard before about your mother."

"They can't say anything I haven't already heard. People have been talking about her ever since I can remember."

"This is different. It goes back to when Eleanor was seventeen. Back then her father took a rifle and killed himself in the barn. I'll tell you straight out. There's speculation she's the one who killed him. I'm opening an inquest just to cover all the bases. Again, there was no real investigation done into it. I'm sorry for that, too. I mention it because your family hopes like hell you're coming back here for good, that you plan to stay. If you do, I don't want you hearing such things out of the blue one day when you least expect it without giving you an advance warning. They're just rumors."

"Yeah, but the thing is, God knows, my mother was crazy enough to do it," Cooper said, closing his eyes against the pain, the knowledge, the depth of what he came from. "Do Drea and Caleb know what I did? Do they know our mother's alive?"

"They do. I took care of that when I shut down the garden center so forensics could... Do their job. Cooper, your brother and sister both know what she was like. They lived in that house the same as you did, Caleb less so maybe because he was so young. But even a boy of four remembers the night she jumped into the bay. Clearly. Neither one of them blames you. Nor do your aunt and uncle. Having grown up with her, Landon knows fully well the way his sister was even as a kid."

"I'm sorry I lied to you about the boxes belonging to me. Try to understand. When I was a kid, I wanted someone to find the pieces of shirt without me having to actually wave them under someone's nose and say look what I did. I didn't know what else to do. By the time I hid those boxes throughout the school, the place had been abandoned. I just didn't think it would take twenty years for them to surface or that anyone would care when they did."

Brent grinned. "Those boxes hidden the way they were in the school drove Julianne nuts. I guess we both have her to thank for her persistence in running down the clues you left. I'm thinking of trying to persuade her to give up her job as principal and come to work for me."

For the first time since entering the room, Cooper gave him a wry smile. "I certainly didn't appreciate seeing Julianne standing outside my gate. But tonight, I feel like twenty tons have been lifted off my shoulders. Now I have to find a way to tell Landon I want to change my name back to Richmond."

"Cooper Richmond has a nice ring to it. If changing it is the first step you take to forgiving yourself, I think you should do it. Now get out of here. Your family's on the other side of that door waiting for you. They're in the other room, worried sick about you. Go home with them, Coop. And do me a favor. Stop beating yourself up for something you had no control over."

Julianne and Ryder sat with the family outside Brent's office. When Cooper emerged, they watched as his family surrounded the man they'd practically dragged back to town. She leaned into Ryder and whispered, "Look at that, I think we did the right thing."

"Yeah, now we just have to convince Brent."

Julianne got up, peered around the corner to see Brent settled behind his desk. "Are you speaking to us yet?" she asked. "You've been pretty busy up to now. This is the first chance we've had to talk to you."

Brent's head popped up. "I'm still busy... Thanks to you. And you," he added as soon as he caught sight of Ryder.

"I wanted to explain why we did what we did."

"Just so you know I had this handled. Three days ago I swabbed Caleb's cheeks, took his DNA to compare it to the pieces of shirt. Caleb's results came back as partially matching up. He was either the child or the parent of the person wearing that shirt in the box. Since I didn't think parent was an option, I went with the child."

"Brent..."

"Have you gotten used to how pushy she can be yet?" Brent said to Ryder.

"I just chalk it up to her schoolteacher persona."

"Hello? Excuse me, I'm standing right here," Julianne demanded.

"Then let me finish. With the familial DNA, not quite a match but close, the next logical conclusion meant it had to belong to Layne. But thanks to you persuading Coop to come back here, we were able to put the questions to him. I called Brooke's brother today and gave them the news. Ryan was devastated but at least now he knows what happened to his sister. I'm not mad. How can I be when you two were instrumental in this whole thing?"

"I found Bethany, or rather Dawn," Ryder blurted out.

"I know you did. Some detective called me because my name showed up in the database when they ran her name. Glad you can both put that behind you and move forward."

"Now can I say what I came in here to say?"

"Go ahead."

"It wasn't because we didn't have faith in your abilities that we went to talk to Cooper on our own."

"You could've fooled me."

"Oh, you go ahead and deal with him," Julianne said to Ryder, dropping into the chair Cooper had just vacated. "It's better come from you anyway."

Ryder stared at Brent. "I don't know if you believe in ghosts, but…"

"Scott told you to go find Cooper?"

"Ah. So you not only believe in the dark and evil aura you mentioned a couple months back, but you've seen Scott and believe in him as well?"

"A time or two," Brent admitted. "Need I remind you I'm Native? All manner of spiritwalkers exist, are common place among my people."

"Then try to understand. Scott was the one who told us we needed to act because Cooper was in distress."

"I see. Scott may have been right. After talking to him, Cooper, not Scott, I got the sense he was approaching his breaking point. After so many years of guilt, laced with a good dose of rage, Cooper is a very troubled man."

"Can you blame him?" Julianne rose again, paced in front of Brent's desk. "It's horrible enough that Eleanor committed a double homicide, robbing her own children of a father. But for a mother to involve her nine-year-old son in a cover-up is unconscionable. Having him help her dig the grave, she scarred that child for life. He may never rid himself of the things he saw that night along with the demons she put in his head."

Ryder thought that was apt. "I'd love to get a look at this woman. When do you pick her up?"

Brent swiveled in his chair, snagged a piece of paper off the fax machine. "This is what the GBI sent me about two hours ago. This is what she looked like at booking."

Julianne and Ryder huddled over the photos—a side shot and a front-on view—of a fifty-four-year old woman with dark hair and streaks of gray running through it. Her face lined with the beginnings of a few wrinkles at her mouth and crow's feet at the corners of her eyes.

"Not what I expected. She looks like a typical middle-aged woman."

"Yeah," Brent agreed. "It's a shame those sociopathic tendencies rarely show up in a photo."

Ryder waited another week for things to settle down. He stayed busy because work on the school had gone into overdrive and had to progress at breakneck speed in order to meet the deadline. Everyone was in a rush—Julianne to fill her last teaching slot—Logan to complete the dolphin sculpture he hadn't wanted to do in the first place.

The day the sculptor hauled his artistic endeavor in front of the school, a crowd gathered to watch six men unload the heavy statue and wrestle it into place on a circular piece of concrete. They would later bolt the bronze sculpture into its base. For now, when they untied the tarp it revealed a mother dolphin that stood seven-feet high from nose to slightly curved tail. She splashed up and out of the water, jumping into the air in whimsical play, surrounded by her two babies.

Ryder could have chosen that venue. But in the end he decided it was too public. For what he had in mind he needed ambiance. He'd never considered himself a romantic. That's why it would take planning on his part.

His opening came after dinner one evening. After going through what had become their ordinary routine—eating supper and then doing the dishes together—he'd thrown the towel on the counter and taken Julianne by the hand.

"Take a walk with me."

"It is a nice night for it."

Ryder laced his fingers with hers and tugged her down the front steps. In the August heat they crossed the street, leaving behind Sandcastle Cottage. A slight breeze stirred the air as they made their way past houses and greeted neighbors watching the sun go down from their front porches.

Once they reached the beach, the calm waters in the bay, made him realize this was a chance to show her what could be. With each step he took his nerves slid away.

He was so quiet tonight, so thoughtful, Julianne decided. She was sure something was bothering him. Maybe it was the pressure of beginning the business venture.

Hearing that first chop of waves, that first slap to land, she figured it was up to her to get his mind off something else. "You know, no matter how many times I ask I can't convince Cooper or either one of his siblings to set foot inside their childhood home."

"I've seen Coop around the pier. He won't even spare a glance at it."

"I think the younger ones are supporting their older brother's decision to avoid the house. I don't take it personal though. I understand Coop's up against bad memories here and that it'll take time. Drea's been sweet though, she sent us three dozen white roses, one dozen from each of them for being able to convince Cooper to come back. Since she put your name on the card, I guess that means half of those flowers are yours."

"That's generous of you. I want my half." He picked her up, swung her around before setting her feet back down again.

Julianne rolled out a belly laugh. "Drea even wrote me a note. Something about bringing the house joy and love to replace all the nasty words, the bad arguments that went on inside there while the kids were growing up."

With the sun going down over the harbor as the backdrop, Ryder unlocked the door to Tradewinds Boatyard.

Inside, Julianne spotted the trail of red rose petals first, then tracked the path leading from the door up to an old wooden crate. On top sat a bucket filled with ice and a bottle of champagne stuffed down in the cubes.

"Ryder."

"I hope we can celebrate." He pulled out a box from his jeans pocket and flipped up the lid, revealing a rose-cut vintage diamond solitaire. "I found it at an antique shop in San Sebastian. If you don't like it..."

"Oh, Ryder, it's beautiful. I love it! You shouldn't have spent the money."

He put a finger to her lips, silencing the protest. "That's the last thing I'm here to talk about is money. I was aiming for classic yet different. With the ring."

She threw her arms around his neck. "You succeeded. Slip it on. It's gorgeous. And this..." She eyed the romantic gesture a few feet away.

He slid the ring on her finger, tilted up her chin. "I haven't felt this kind of peace in so long. That's your doing. I've never felt this way about anyone. I want to be able to turn to you in the middle of the night and hear you say my name. I love it when you say my name when we're making love. I love you, Julianne. I want to know if you'll marry a boatbuilder, a carpenter, a risk-taker."

"Absolutely. Yes. Yes. I was hoping you'd get around to asking me one day."

He picked her up again, spun her around before dipping his head to brush his lips to hers. They clung to each other and the realization they'd both found home.

Epilogue

Four weeks later
First day of school
Pelican Pointe, California

Julianne stationed herself outside the main entrance.

In full swing, first day frenzy had children hurrying past her to class, as parents accompanied some of them inside to meet the teachers.

She knew their eagerness would change and lessen as the year wore on. But today, she did what she could to keep that electricity in the air, to meet and greet. She had a huge advantage. She already knew most of the names of the students and their parents who dropped them off. She knew she'd hired the cream of the crop and knew her staff would do the best job around.

She waved to Lilly and Wally making their way up the steps with brown-eyed Kyra in tow along with a wide-eyed Hutton walking between Nick and Jordan. Both girls proudly carried their tote bags. Julianne smiled knowing they'd be in good hands in Ms. Warner's kindergarten class.

Julianne bent down, closer to eye-level to talk to both girls. "Hi there. I love your dresses. Did you pick them out yourselves?"

Kyra bobbed her head up and down but tugged on her dad's hand. "We need to hurry. I don't want to be late."

Wally grinned. "You have an eager scholar here."

"I see that. A teacher needs more Kyras." Julianne turned to Hutton, noticed her hanging back, a bit wary at the bustle happening around her. But she thought she knew how to get around that. "Hutton, are you ready to learn how to write your name?"

"I already know how to do that," Hutton burst out, her voice tinged with pride.

Pleased that she'd gotten a response, Julianne straightened and took in the anxious parents. "Hutton will be fine. This is Ms. Warner's third year and she knows the ins and outs of making each of her students feel like they're special."

Jordan dabbed at her eyes. "It seems like yesterday my baby was in diapers."

"I remember changing a few of those and it wasn't that long ago," Nick echoed, scooping his son, Scott, up in his arms.

"Mom! Dad! Don't embarrass me like that," Hutton sang out. "I'm not a baby. You still have Scott at home with you. He's the baby. Now it's time for me to go to class like Kyra."

No, Hutton wasn't a baby, Julianne decided as she watched the three of them walk through the double doors. But with those big blue eyes and that smile on her face, Hutton did look an awful lot like her daddy.

After the first bell rang, Julianne dealt with her first emergency of the day—wet pants from a five-year-old who'd waited too long to concede the fact he needed to go. Good thing she kept several spare changes of clothes on hand, suitable for both boys and girls.

Recess was the-free-for-all she knew it to be that tested the new playground equipment—thankfully without any major mishaps. At noon, she supervised the pickup for the kindergarten class, which went better than expected. But it was lunch where hungry kids finally settled down long enough to eat. By this time they'd worked out their worries and uneasiness to enjoy what they'd brought from home or picked out from the list of school lunch offerings.

Julianne was helping to maintain order and usher the kids back to afternoon classes when she spotted a metal lunch box someone had left behind. She picked it up, stared at the dated image on the front depicting Luke Skywalker sitting in the swamp with his mentor, Yoda and R2-D2 along for the ride. *The Empire Strikes Back* logo stretched across the top. Her flea market sense kicked in knowing it was someone's cherished token from the past. She flipped the latch down and threw the lid back to look inside for the owner's name. She saw a hint of markings scrawled on the Thermos and picked it up to make out what it said. She bobbled the plastic container, almost dropped it when she read the name, Scott Phillips, handwritten in black, bold print across the side in Marks-A-Lot. But this couldn't belong to Hutton. Kindergarteners didn't stay for lunch. Not only that, but the little girl hadn't even been carrying a lunch box that morning.

That's when she noticed the folded note, written on a sheet of ruled, primary tablet paper in block letters that read:

Whether or not you choose to have children of your own, the town trusts you with theirs, trusts you with its future. The kids are the future. That's a fact. Teach them right, fill their lives with fairness instead of bitterness and anger. Make them thirst for knowledge. Don't let them take anything for granted. For life is precious and too short. Like other parents today, I'm trusting you with my child, my school, and my town so don't let me down.

Dear Reader:

If you enjoyed *Last Chance Harbor*, please take the time to leave a review.
A review shows others how you feel about my work.
By recommending it to your friends and family it helps spread the word.
If you have the time, please let me know via Facebook or my website.
I'd love to hear from you!

For a complete list of my other books visit my website.
www.vickiemckeehan.com

Want to connect with me to leave a comment?
Go to Facebook
www.facebook.com/VickieMcKeehan

Don't miss these other exciting titles by bestselling author

Vickie McKeehan

The Pelican Pointe Series
PROMISE COVE
HIDDEN MOON BAY
DANCING TIDES
LIGHTHOUSE REEF
STARLIGHT DUNES
LAST CHANCE HARBOR
SEA GLASS COTTAGE
LAVENDER BEACH
SANDCASTLES UNDER THE CHRISTMAS
MOON
BENEATH WINTER SAND
KEEPING CAPE SUMMER (2018)

The Evil Secrets Trilogy
JUST EVIL Book One
DEEPER EVIL Book Two
ENDING EVIL Book Three
EVIL SECRETS TRILOGY BOXED SET

The Skye Cree Novels
THE BONES OF OTHERS
THE BONES WILL TELL
THE BOX OF BONES
HIS GARDEN OF BONES
TRUTH IN THE BONES
SEA OF BONES (2018)

The Indigo Brothers Trilogy
INDIGO FIRE
INDIGO HEAT
INDIGO JUSTICE
INDIGO BROTHERS TRILOGY BOXED SET

Coyote Wells Mysteries
MYSTIC FALLS
SHADOW CANYON
SPIRIT LAKE (2018)

ABOUT THE AUTHOR

Vickie McKeehan's novels have consistently appeared on Amazon's Top 100 lists in Contemporary Romance, Romantic Suspense and Mystery / Thriller. She writes what she loves to read—heartwarming romance laced with suspense, heart-pounding thrillers, and riveting mysteries. Vickie loves to write about compelling and down-to-earth characters in settings that stay with her readers long after they've finished her books. She makes her home in Southern California.

Find Vickie online at
https://www.facebook.com/VickieMcKeehan
http://www.vickiemckeehan.com/
https://vickiemckeehan.wordpress.com